D1383011

THE WOMEN AT PINE CREEK

The WOMEN at PINE CREEK

a novel

BY ALLIS McKAY

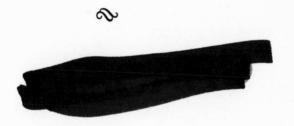

THE MACMILLAN COMPANY, NEW YORK

Second Printing 1966

The Macmillan Company, New York
Collier-Macmillan Canada Ltd., Toronto, Ontario

Library of Congress Catalog Card Number: 66-21980
Printed in the United States of America

PART ONE

1 NOTHING HAD really prepared them for the sight of mountains. There was a scalloped dark shape along the horizon that was not a bank of cloud and that did not go away, and as the train advanced upon it and it broke into separate peaks laced with snow, the sisters sat very close together, and gripped each other's fingers.

They were dressed in deep mourning, and their luggage was new. It bore the initials A. H. and M. H. Strapped to it were copies of *Munsey's Magazine* and *The Review of Reviews*, unopened, but the railroad timetable spread out on top was well-thumbed. For days the train had crawled through wheat fields and past water tanks, stopping at stations where the townsfolk stared at the passengers and the passengers stared back. Between meals in the diner, on a community stove at the end of the car, Althea perpetually brewed tea. (Mary was carsick, and had to take a soda-mint tablet with every cup.) The sisters slept in most of their clothes in the shelflike beds that Mr. Pullman had provided, and everyday they rehearsed their instructions: "We are to get off at Wenatchee. We are to give our baggage checks to the stationmaster at once. We are to take a hack to the office of Mr. Gillespie, who will have just received Arthur's latest letter. We are to book a room at a respectable hotel and ask Mr. Gillespie's advice about how to proceed."

As the telegraph poles flew past, Althea, who was the older and felt that she had all the responsibility, settled back with a little sigh. "Would you like to sit next to the window, Mary? I've had it for a long time."

"I don't care." Mary did not take her eyes off the rocky cliffs forming outside. "Are you tired, Althea? Perhaps you could nap a little. I'll keep track of the stations."

Althea shook her head. Her eye fell on the luggage, newly

initialed and bright. "Mary," she said diffidently, "I can't help being glad you . . . you came home. And I'm glad that—perhaps you don't wish me to speak of it—but I'm glad Judge Gordon gave you back your maiden name. I like to think of you as Mary Hollister."

My only slightly damaged name. You don't know what it was like, Althea. You don't know that the girls I went to school with didn't come to see me any more. And I couldn't let you know.

Aloud, Mary said, "I still wish Arthur hadn't been so dead set against our coming. He'll worry every minute."

Althea smiled a little. "Someone has always worried about people with Pillage blood. Some in every generation have to go forth, Mary. I feel that it was appointed. I have no qualms at all."

"We could have opened a bake shop in Oak Point," Mary murmured stubbornly. She could not truthfully say that she had had no qualms; she had them still. But from the time they had found Luther's bequest among her father's papers, it had seemed to burn in Althea's fingers.

I've always given Althea a bad time. We all have. We knew it but we couldn't help it. Her face when I eloped with Albert, and even worse, her face when I came back with bruises on my arms, and he came to get me and Papa met him with a horse whip. Althea, I'm sorry. How did I know he was no good? You're so stupid when you're eighteen. And she kept saying, Mary, why did you do it? And I couldn't say, I did it so I wouldn't be an old maid. Like you.

They crept slowly across a basin of red and gray rock. Mary looked at it nervously. "I hope Pine Creek Valley is not like this."

"I'm sure it's not." Althea's voice was serene. "Water flowing in the bottom of it, don't you remember? And steep sides, Mr. Gillespie said. Almost a canyon."

"I'll plant a garden," Mary promised. "I know it's a little late for peas and beans, but surely cabbage will still grow. I'm to do all the hardest work, you know, Althea. And Arthur made me promise just before we left that if there's clearing still to be done, we'll hire it. He said he would be glad to send more money."

"We'll manage on our own inheritance," Althea said proudly.

4

"The others were already generous when they let us take Luther's place for our share, and on top of that we each have our fifths of Papa's bank account for money to work it with. Arthur's a little bossy, but he's a dear boy. You're all good children, and you're all a credit to me. Perhaps Arthur and I are too near of an age—we always had spats when we were little. He's the only one of you that remembers Mama very well. I suppose I can't expect to measure up to Mama."

Tears came to Mary's eyes. "Althea dear," she said, "never talk that way. Never. You've been magnificent. It can't have been much fun for you, looking after us. You could have done so much better."

"Well, I could have done a lot worse." There was no malice in Althea's voice, but Mary was instantly aware that if you wanted to look at it that way, she had done a lot worse. Of course that was not what Althea had meant. *I must not be jumpy if Althea and I are to make a new life together. I must be calm, placid.*

"I've loved every minute of it," Althea went on warmly. "But you can understand, can't you, Mary, why I want to get out and do something new? Something of my own. Something of *ours*," she amended quickly.

"Yes, Althea," Mary peered out the window. "The trees are different. Oh, Althea, we're really in the West! I think we ought to get out Luther's bequest and read it over." Mary never tired of seeing the yellowed document, though its contents had shocked her a little the first time. Althea obediently took it out of the top of her suitcase and Mary began to read aloud.

" 'I, Luther Pillage, do devise and bequeath to Henry Hollister, for his kindness which made it possible to carry through this venture'—Althea, do you think we'll ever find out how Papa came to send him money?"

"He was a Pillage," Althea said as if that covered everything.

" '. . . the eighty acres of the northwest quarter and the southwest quarter of the southwest quarter of Section 20, Township 4 North, Range 2, in the County of Tillicum, State of Washington, newly admitted to the Union . . .' "

"Surely he didn't have to put that in," Althea commented as she always did.

"*I'd* have put it in if I lived in a brand new state. 'Being without issue . . .'" At this point Mary as usual began to blush. " 'Shall any circumstantial claim be made by any individual of either white or Indian blood to be my natural offspring, such claim shall be satisfied with ten dollars gold, to be paid by the same Henry Hollister, his heirs or assigns, out of income from the property herein described. . . .' Althea, I still think that's horrid." It was a word the sisters used often, and covered everything they could not, as gentlewomen, endorse. It was the superlative of a series: not nice, not at *all* nice, and horrid, which meant very unacceptable indeed.

Althea had made up her mind to take the frontier as she found it. "He was out there a long time alone," she said, "and men fall into temptation. I don't suppose it will ever happen, but if it did, Mary, I wouldn't cut them off with ten dollars. Would you?"

"No," Mary said. Then an entirely new thought came to her, and she raised startled eyes. "They'd be part Pillage," she said.

The Pillages had cleared land and built settlements from Salem, Massachusetts, to Salem, Oregon. There was a Pillage monument in an Indiana public square and a Pillage grave on the Santa Fe Trail. Few of them died rich. They were stubborn, impractical, and incurably optimistic, and they never learned their lesson. They broke their hearts in most of the corners of America, sinking wells that had no oil, founding firms that never got clients, running in elections that they monotonously lost. They had a terrible probity that handicapped them in their dealings with people. All too often, they did as they would be done by, with disastrous results in a business way.

The name of Pillage, like all unusual names, seemed quite natural to those who bore it. Mary had sometimes wondered about the brides—did it take them long to get used to it? There was a family joke that had come down from Amos Pillage, Luther's father, who, meeting in the California gold fields a man by the name of Burn, had suggested they form a partnership under the title of Burn and Pillage.

6

Henry Hollister's mother had been a Pillage. Henry never paid much heed to the fact, but his daughter Althea thought a good deal about it, especially after he told her she had the Pillage look. As she swept and scrubbed and washed and ironed and put things away in camphor bags and did all the work her mother had left behind, she felt that a good job, a workmanlike job, was what a Pillage would do, and she told her little brothers and sisters stories about Amos Pillage in the Gold Rush and Mary Pillage in Kentucky who had picked up her husband's musket and shot the Indian who had winged him with an arrow. But she also told them that the Indians, too, were God's children and that now that they had quietly gone to live on their reservations, we must join our good President Cleveland in being kind to them.

Mr. Gillespie turned out to be a comfortable leather-faced man in a wide-brimmed hat, which he took off as he seated the Hollister girls in his office. He also pushed the spittoon under the edge of the desk with his toe. The heat of early summer turned the little room into an oven, and Althea unfastened her sealskin cape.

"There's only one way to get there really," Mr. Gillespie said. "There's a road of a sort upriver, but I wouldn't advise your driving it, especially with hired horses. You'll have to take the steamboat. It leaves here at 4 A.M. and it reaches Pine Creek Landing late in the day. You have your household goods, of course? Pity you didn't arrange for some horses to be shipped, our horses are broke for riding but they don't drive well."

"I think we shall learn to ride," Althea said.

Mr. Gillespie looked gratified. "Bully for you, ma'am. You do realize . . . er . . . you know we don't have the sidesaddle here, I suppose? Thought I'd mention it. . . . Now, I've been up to look at your house and I'm afraid you're going to be disappointed. It's in bad shape. But there's water, a good stream of it coming from a spring, and in this country water is everything. The water rights go with the homestead and I don't believe you'll have any trouble. Although these fellows that stake out irrigation lines are apt to take water where they find it. So far, yours hasn't been disturbed."

"Will we have neighbors?" Mary said.

"Oh, my, yes. Must be four or five families in Pine Creek valley." The chart he unfolded was crisp and fresh, covered with blue lines. "Here's your plat. I just got it from the county office. Keep it by you, and if any squatters try to move in, know exactly where your boundaries are. This dang country's getting crowded. Used to be a man could look around and find eighty acres anywhere, to run his herd of cattle or plant his orchard. Now there's hardly a level mile that hasn't been claimed. You can't tell it from the plat here, but like I wrote to your brother, only about twenty acres of your eighty-acre place is level. The rest is hillside. That's the way things are around here."

"Is twenty acres enough?" Althea was crisp and business-like.

"Many a family makes out on less, ma'am. But of course the man of the family goes over and works in the wheat harvest, to help out, or has him a job when the sawmill is running." Mr. Gillespie shook out a red bandanna almost as large as a bedsheet and with some embarrassment wiped his dripping brow. "It's not an easy country, ma'am. It wouldn't be fair to you to say it was. Can either of you ladies teach school?"

"We don't have certificates," Mary said after a moment's thought.

"If you can pass some examinations here at Wenatchee, a certificate can be had. You might remember that. . . . Would you mind telling me what put it into your heads to come out here so far from your folks?" His voice was as courteous as possible, but it was tinged with the same unbelief that had been in Arthur's.

"We feel this place was given us by Providence, Mr. Gillespie." Althea's tone was vibrant. "At the time my father's estate was settled, this deed was found, and my sister and I were in need of a home. It all seemed so natural."

If Mr. Gillespie felt that Providence could have been a little more selective, he did not say so. "Your brother asked me to find out what I could about Luther Pillage. I'm afraid he was a high-stepping sort, ma'am. He was finally took with lead poisoning, as they say. That is, he lost out in some gun play down here at Dutch's Tavern. He's buried over there in the ground acrost the

8

river, and I think it would pleasure him was you ladies to visit his grave."

"We will," Althea said promptly. "Is there a place one can buy flowers?"

"Flowers? Law, ma'am, there's flowers aplenty in the spring, on the hills, but by now you'll find nary a blossom. Only them yellow roses, maybe, the women carry with them and plant wherever they go. I've seen yellow roses in dry gulches where they was nothing left of a ranch but a frame roof fallen in."

Mary moved restlessly. "You mean people try it and leave and . . . and never come back?"

"Dry farmers," Mr. Gillespie said succinctly. "Some dang fool is always trying to tamper with nature. But you'll never need to worry—you got water. . . . My buggy's down at the curb, if you like I should drive you around a little. We can see the town, and my daughter would be more than glad was I to bring you home to supper."

Carefully holding their skirts out of Mr. Gillespie's way on a high open seat, they looked warily at the unpaved streets and the plank sidewalks of Wenatchee. There was a theater among the markets and livery stables, its front starred with small white lights, and there was a bank. Althea noted this with relief, they would put their money in it. A breeze rose fitfully to stir the dust, which settled on the dashboard of the buggy and on their polished black shoes. Mr. Gillespie turned the horses off the main road toward the river, and they saw a dull breadth of silver-eddying water which swept furiously out of hills to the north and disappeared again among blue-black walls of rock. A thread of bridge soared across it, incredibly long, sickeningly high.

"Yonder's Luther's grave," Mr. Gillespie said with a wave of his hand at the rising benches of land across the valley.

"Do we . . . must we cross that bridge?" Althea slipped her hand into Mary's, who squeezed it hard. Mary thought of a more urgent question.

"Is that the river we take the steamer on?"

"Why, yes, Miss Hollister. That's the Columbia. Pine Creek flows into it up yonder."

9

Arthur dear,

Mr. Gillespie has been most helpful. He put us aboard the steamer this morning when it was barely daylight, with all our belongings. Oh, Arthur, it looked like so little when we were choosing what to bring, and now it bulks so large! The sewing machine and Mary's little rocking chair ride on top, and our pots and pans and flatirons. I am glad we did not try to bring the piano. I mentioned this to Mr. Gillespie, and he said with an expression on his face that I was not quite able to make out, that the principal musical instrument in these parts is the mouth organ. He insisted on our adding many cases of food, for he says there are few stores upriver and they are badly stocked. We will learn to order ahead, he says, and have things sent up by boat. Our belongings are on the forward deck of the steamer, ready to be put off.

Arthur, you would never believe this river. It is very wide but dwarfed by the great banks and surrounding hills. It is very smooth but not for one moment quiet, whirlpools and eddies coming constantly to the surface. The steamer gains against the current slowly, and they tell me that at the rapids we shall have to be winched through. I wonder what that means.

I am not afraid, Arthur. We are in God's hands. When I have looked too long at the water and it begins to distress me, I go inside the ladies' saloon, where I am writing you this letter. Mary stays outside and fixes her eyes upon the hills. She is very courageous. The engine throbs as if it would shake the boat apart, but I am sure it will not. Luther must have made this trip many times.

When Mary and I have made our fortune we shall see that a suitable monument replaces the little marker over Luther's grave.

There seemed to be few Indians on the streets of Wenatchee. But Mr. Gillespie says we shall see plenty of them at hop-picking time, when they travel downriver from their reservations to seek work. He says to "button down everything we have" when they are near. I think this is a most ungenerous attitude. Surely we can spare something for our red brothers with whom we share this land.

The sun is unflaggingly hot, and glares off the cliffs and the water. There is little greenery, but a color everywhere some-

thing like your old buff overcoat. Only on the sheltered side of
the hills are there scant forests . . .

Althea was interrupted by the entrance of a very large woman
in ruffles and flounces of flowered cotton. "Where you goin'?" she
asked sociably, sitting down on the bench that ran around the
wall, and fanning herself.

Althea hesitated. "To Pine Creek Landing."

"Travellin' through?"

"No," Althea said, "we're staying."

"That your sister out by the rail?"

"Yes."

"Thought you looked alike. Where's your menfolk?"

Althea had had no experience in rebuffing strangers. She answered with some reluctance, "My sister and I are alone. We are
taking up an abandoned homestead."

The woman withdrew her feet from her tight high-heeled shoes
and wiggled her toes. "Don't your feet kill you in this weather?
Well, dearie, you won't be alone long. Anybody can get a husband
in this country. I'm on my third. Dade was hit by a fallin' log,
and Joe took the dysentery. I got a real good looker now—you
may've noticed him down there on the deck. Black beard."

"I do not think," Althea said, surprised to find herself taking
part in this conversation, "that a beard becomes a man. My father
was clean-shaven. To the last."

The woman smiled. "Not many fellows got time to tussle with a
razor around here. That's all right, dearie. It pays to be choosy.
You girls got any money?"

"We have adequate funds," Althea said. "Do you mind if I
join my sister? This is remarkable scenery."

"Purty, ain't it? I get to ride the boat real often now. Joe was
never one for the river. He's just as soon piss in it as travel on
it. Give him a trail, he always said." Althea managed to get the
sliding door open and fled outside. "You might have to settle for a
mustache," she heard as a lurch of the steamer slammed the door
behind her.

"Mary, are you all right? I didn't mean to leave you out here alone so long."

Mary turned toward her a face pale with emotion. "Althea, you must stay and look awhile. It's so *tremendous*. See that tiny mark across the face of a hill? It's a road. It goes to that house above the beach there."

Rocky points came down to the water and fretted its current next to the shore, and beween them long sandbars baked in the sun. "Where it's green in the crack of a hill, there's water. And where there's water there's a house, and fields. And rows of trees," Mary marvelled. "You know how Mr. Gillespie told us the apple business is growing?"

"We must plant an orchard at once," Althea said.

"Pine Creek Landing!"

It was a sandbank like any other sandbank, cut by the outfall of a small stream that sparkled in the late-day sun. Upon the bank were piles of stones with logs protruding from them. The deck crew swung the boat in, leaped ashore, and fastened cables to the logs. The boat chafed uneasily against the sand while a gangplank went down. The Hollister girls looked on breathlessly as their household effects were carried off and dumped in the sand. Then Althea went first down the gangplank, her head held high, and Mary followed. A few loungers watched stolidly. The captain, briefed by Mr. Gillespie, stepped ashore and shook hands with them. "You let me know when you want anything," he said. "Stick a pole in the sand with a white flag on it."

The men cast off, the boat wheeled rapidly into the current, and began to crawl upriver. The loungers shuffled and milled, but no one spoke and no one came any closer. Althea caught the eye of a small man standing his ground beside a willow clump, and she went up to him valiantly. "Could you tell me where we can find a dray?"

A big voice, resembling that of a bullfrog, came reluctantly from the throat of the small man. "Be you for the old Pillage place?"

A little shock went through both women, though they did not glance at each other. The old Pillage place! It was actual. It was here. "Yes," Althea said.

"Heard you was comin'. I reckon I can take your gear up the road in my wagon. It ought to make about three loads."

"How long will it take?" Althea said uncertainly, as if she had any choice.

"What's left o' today, an' some o' tomorrow. One load tonight, and you can ride along of me on the wagon. It'll be six bits a load."

"And leave the rest here on the riverbank?"

"I reckon so," the small man said. "It don't never rain in June."

Althea looked at Mary. "What do you say, dear?" It was only to gain time, and Mary knew it.

"I think we must accept his offer, and thank this gentleman for his kindness," Mary said, for strangers made her feel shy and formal.

"Hey, you, Luke. Help me with this bedstid." The little man gestured toward a lanky chap, in overalls stiff with dirt, who walked over. The two took hold. Had they arranged it all beforehand, Mary wondered, or did the custom of the country provide for such emergencies? And how had they known there was someone coming? Of course—Mr. Gillespie had been here. She knew nothing then of the grapevine news of the mountains, which somehow operates over spaces untouched by road or path.

"One of us ought to stay with our belongings," Althea's voice was a shaky whisper.

"Oh, *no*," Mary said. "We must keep together, Althea. The furniture doesn't matter that much. Can we choose what goes in the load, do you think?"

Without answering, Althea took a deep breath and began to pick at the heap of luggage, drawing out the things she valued most. Silently she handed them to one or the other of the men, who accepted them and stowed them in the wagon, though the lanky fellow shook his head over the framed pictures. Pointing to a lamp with a hand-painted globe of rosy glass, which already had part of its packing stripped away, he cleared his throat and said kindly, "You'd best carry that in your lap, lady."

13

When they had done what they could, the Hollister sisters stood back and stared around them. Pine Creek, which cut the riverbank near where they stood, came from a valley bearing up westward. Its portal was narrow and two shouldering peaks of the same dun color they had looked at all day seemed barely to let the stream come through. Across the Columbia, which went its quiet, seething way, more hills marched in an endless carven pattern. They rose on all sides to a flawless pale blue sky, deeply rosy toward the west. Though it was only late afternoon, shadows almost as sharp as paper cutouts crept from the foot of each hill.

The small man followed their eyes. "Evenin' settin' in," he said. "By the time we git to yore place, it'll be nigh dark."

With the load stored to his satisfaction, he remembered something else. "Yore name Pillage? Mine's Plew, Bert Plew. This here that's givin' us a hand is Luke Walters. He's got a ranch downriver."

"I'm Althea Hollister," Althea said graciously. She had decided that under these circumstances the men of the mountains did not take off their hats to a woman, and felt she could overlook it. "My sister is Mary Hollister. We are second cousins of Luther Pillage. Did either of you know Luther?"

Luke Walters shook his head.

"Nope," Bert Plew said. "He was afore my time. Me and my wife live at the head o' Pine Creek. I'll just drop you an' your gear off at your place and I'll be down again in the mornin'."

The men of the mountains did not offer their hands to ladies who were climbing to a wagon seat, either. They waited in constrained silence, looking the other way, while Mary and Althea somewhat awkwardly mounted and settled themselves with the pink lamp globe in Althea's arms. The seat was broad and surprisingly comfortable, perched on the forward end of the wagon box on heavy steel springs. The two of them left plenty of room at the end for the driver, who presently got up in his place and picked up leather reins, so long that he used the last five feet of them as a mild, incessant, harmless whip that he played over the backs of the horses. The wagon pulled out of the sand with a reluctant crunch.

Bert Plew was not conversational, and Mary and Althea were

so absorbed in watching the road that they forgot to speak, even to each other. This would be their road. This dilapidated building would be their post office. The farther end of it held a store of a sort, with the screen door sagging. On the first shelf of the hill above the road was a schoolhouse, dimly glimpsed. It completed the village of Pine Creek.

The road went directly to the gap in the hills and through it. Immediately the creek bed broadened and a small valley appeared. "Fust house here is Yanling's," Bert Plew said. Several dogs barked and a woman appeared in the door of the little frame building, wrapping her arms in her apron. She watched them until they were past. I wonder how many people she sees in a day, Mary thought. I wonder how many *we* will see. Less than she does, because we live above Yanling's.

The road was a pair of dusty tracks, a certain width apart wherever they went—the width of wagon wheels. They kept alongside the stream for a little distance, then took to a low ledge on the hillside, from which they could look down on Yanling's fields of hay and clover. "Raises beef," Bert said. "Few Indian ponies, too."

"Mr. Plew," Althea asked him, "how does one buy a horse?"

"You take the horse," Bert said, not lifting his eyes from the road, "and the other party takes the money."

For some reason he's not pleased with us, Mary thought. Maybe it's not etiquette to talk about buying and selling so soon. They had gotten up in the middle of the night. The journey had become stranger and stranger—it was now like a shadow play in which she was incomprehensibly taking part.

But Althea was not easily discouraged. "Mr. Plew," she began again, "if you were going to buy a horse, whom would you see, and how would you know if it was a good one? And what would you expect to pay?"

"Well, now," Bert Plew said, suddenly becoming voluble, "the fact is Yanling and I both do a little horse tradin'. I'm not a-goin' to run him down, him or his stock, but if I was about to buy a horse for ridin' or plowin' the last thing I would get would be one o' them flea-bit, broken-winded, walleyed, half-starved nags o' Yanling's. He sells his hay, he don't feed it out to his critturs.

Leastways that must be why they come down out o' the range and bust down my fences."

"How shocking," Althea murmured. "We shall be needing horses to ride, both of us, and I will certainly ask you to show us some. A gentle . . ." she broke off suddenly. The road had descended and now went through the creek with a grinding and sucking under the wheels, emerging again as tracks on the other side.

"We forded that," Althea said, pleased. "I have always wanted to ford a stream."

"You'll ford this one every time ye come down to the pust office," Bert Plew said.

Mary stopped listening to them. *I am Mary Hollister. I am alive and real. This place is not a dream. It is a valley up which we are riding to our new home. These hills are like a fortress, that holds some beautiful and terrible secret.*

I don't think I would have minded too much, living with Arthur's family and helping Hetty with the children. Hetty has always been sweet to me, and she took my part when I ran away from Albert. But perhaps they didn't want me really. Althea says we must not be beholden to anyone.

After Yanling's came Muldoon's. The valley broadened, and Muldoon's lay on both sides of the road. Here at last was an orchard. The small trees wheeled in endless patterns on the gray soil. Rivulets of water flowed in tiny ditches from tree to tree, darkening the earth where they ran.

"Muldoon's takin' a gamble," Bert said. "Most o' his lumber money's tied up in this here layout. I don't plan to get in the apple game. Timber an' livestock is good enough for me."

"Does the valley keep on getting wider?" Althea asked.

"Directly above here it's wide enough for two ranches," Bert chuckled. "One of 'em's yourn."

He was thoroughly enjoying his part in the situation. He stole a look at the sisters, whoses faces remained impassive, though Mary's heart was thudding in her breast.

Beyond Muldoon's on the left was a meadow, and on the right the ground had gone back to sagebrush and mullein. It had visibly been cleared once, however, and the stones had been

16

carted off. It was surrounded by the remnants of a barbed-wire fence on sagging posts.

They scarcely dared to look. At the back and a little higher there was a house; it had some planting around it. Tall poplars fingered up to the sky among two or three cottonwoods.

He's not going to watch us have our first sight of it, Althea suddenly resolved. She said, "Do you mind stopping here for just a minute, while we walk up alone and look around?"

Bert grunted. He was not sorry to know that the thing had gotten through to them, stuck-up ladies as they were. He stopped the team and sat there while they made a job of getting down. As he saw them start up the side road he was more amused than touched. His compassion, which went out freely to animals and hard-luck farmers like himself, stopped short at women. Troublesome, demanding, helpless creatures, trapping a man only because of his unavoidable needs.

The side road went slightly upward, so that as they walked ahead the land gently but perceptibly rose. It ended abruptly at a gravelly hillside broken by a short, deep gulch. In front of this the foursquare house with a roof of split shakes stood dull and dark, the color of old rope. Every window was broken; the glass lay in sharp fragments on the ground.

Neither of them wanted to be the first to speak. They walked aimlessly a few steps back and forth, looking. *If I break down now,* Mary thought, *I'll be ashamed forever and ever.* She tried desperately to think of something, and after while she said, "From here to the road is all downhill. Those little ditches . . . the water will run . . ."

Althea came swiftly and kissed her. "Oh, Mary, darling Mary. You see it all, don't you? And I was just getting a little, a very little downhearted—Mary, dear, we mustn't linger here. Do you realize that it is up to us to help Sir Galahad unload that 'bed-stid'?"

Across from them the valley was thick with shadow. It was impossible to make out what lay against the other line of hills. "Let's look inside the house," Mary whispered. They walked to a window, hand in hand, and peered in. There were at least two rooms. Peeling newspapers hung from the rough plank walls.

Then they turned and retraced their steps. Althea, forcing her voice to be casual, said, "The first thing to do is to unpack the lamps and fill and light them. When the pink lamp it lighted, it will seem like home."

Hearing them come chattering and laughing down the road together, Bert Plew admitted to himself that they had spunk. It was now too dark to see plainly, and the women stumbled once or twice. But Bert Plew's horses were surefooted, and he let them take their own way up the slope and stop the wagon beside the door.

Half an hour later, their household gear lay stacked inside and out, Bert had driven off, their neat travelling clothes were gray with dust, and they were ready to collapse on the legless bed that had been temporarily made up in the middle of the front room. Mary wondered if she would sleep. It seemed as if she could see, through the thin walls of the house, the vast black featureless night outside. Leaving Althea sorting through a packing case in search of towels, she slipped out and closed the door.

Stars were beginning to prick out in the night sky. From side to side of the dark universe they were the only thing that looked familiar. A cool breath of wind came bringing the scent of pines and the sound of far-off water.

I won't stay. I won't stay here always. I'm still young and somehow, sometime, I'll get away. I'll do everything Althea wants and we'll make the best of this and I'll never, never let her down. But God will show me a way to get away. I'll leave here. Sometime. Somehow.

The next morning was crystalline and beautiful. Both sisters, exhausted, slept late and when Althea opened her eyes Mary was already stirring. By common consent they got up quickly and went to the door and opened it.

Tired and tense though they were, they cried out with joy. From the house to the road the slope was flooded with golden sun; every plant, every hummock cast a perfect small shadow. Across from them the other farm, whose owner's name Bert Plew had never got around to mentioning, began at the road and ran to its own steep foothill; it was mirror-wise to theirs, the house backed up against the upper slope. The dry air was exhilarating. They drew it into their lungs and laughed with delight and relief.

Then Althea began to sob. Mary could not believe it, Althea, the valiant, was crying in her arms. "It's . . . it's all right," Althea choked, "it's l-lovely. Oh Mary, I was so afraid."

Mary looked up at the fortress wall that towered at each side of the valley. She thought of the robbers' stronghold in Lorna Doone, for she was very romantic. One way in, one way out, with a secret passage besides. She too was afraid, and it would take more than daylight to help it. She hugged Althea and tenderly patted her arm.

"I don't know what ails me," Althea sniffed. "Mary, isn't this *wonderful?* We must clean up the house at once. That table will do to keep. It looks as though Luther might have built it himself. And that armchair in the kitchen is too far gone to use, but Mary, I think it's a Pillage piece. Aunt Hester had some of the same brocade on a sofa. Think of it, Mary, a Pillage chair! Luther must have taken it with him everywhere."

"There's a team stopping in the road down there," Mary said.

Althea hastily dried her eyes and looked. "Is that Bert Plew coming with another load? No, it's someone else. They're just stopping to stare. Mary, how very odd. One doesn't know what to expect, does one? We need some breakfast. We'll feel better after a cup of tea. Mary, dear, will you light the chafing dish, just as you do at home?" Then she stopped, and added in a small voice, "*This* is home."

Her compulsive talking went on while they cooked the eggs and bacon which (thanks to Mr. Gillespie) were available in a grocery basket. "Mary, did you see that *store?* We'll have to send away constantly . . . I want to live nicely, Mary, darling. We must keep up our standards. We can paper these walls, I'm sure, and dig a new—you know—in the back yard. But first we must make a place to keep chickens. I paid fifteen cents a dozen for these eggs."

Mary was glad to be silent. Now that she knew where they were, had seen, as it were, the shape of her captivity, she felt strongly drawn to find out what stuff it was made of; to learn where the spring water came from, to twist in her hands the shrub that gave that pungent smell. If the earth daunted her, that was all the more reason to look closely at it, to take its measure. When they had finished breakfast she said, "Before we go to work, shouldn't we walk outside and over to the hill?"

Althea looked at her. Then she nodded. "Perhaps we should. We may not have much time to dawdle later."

The mountainside began suddenly as if the ground had been bent sharply upwards. Here in the silence, all at once, the pretense that the land was clothed with greenery ended. The hill rose steep and studded with rocks, a few gnarled pine trees stabbing the hot sky. Silver-colored, prickly little plants lived each an erect and separate life in the gravel. From somewhere far off came the cry of an unknown bird.

"Let's climb it," Mary suggested recklessly.

Althea shook her head. "Some other day," she said.

2

DOLLY PLEW could restrain her curiosity no longer. She had heard Bert talk about the two "greenhorn" women till she was tired of the sound of it; their la-de-da way of speaking, their expensive clothes and furniture, their naive questions, the fact that they had a good piece of land there and would probably make a proper mess of it. He had sold them a riding horse (for Althea, impartially, had bought one from him and one from Yanling), and she had hoped the Hollister women would come to Plews' to make the purchase. But no; Bert, with the obtuseness of a man, had cut several ponies out of the herd and driven them down, and had come home without Rusty, a colt that she herself had helped to break and gentle. Bert admitted grudgingly that they had picked the right horse; they knew what they wanted.

Every time that Dolly Plew passed the old Pillage house she rubbered her eyes out, but she never could see much. She would stop there today and say hello to Rusty, and get a sight of "them." She saddled her own horse and before leaving, went out with a spade and dug a root from the tangle of thorns in the creek bottom, where Plew Canyon came down into the head of Pine Creek valley. This she wrapped in a piece of gunnysack and tied to the saddle.

In her sunbonnet, with her dull blue dress spread out on either side of the saddle, she did not mind the stifling heat of a July noon—in fact, she was unaware of it. Had she been going only to the post office, she would have have worn a pair of overalls, but this was a social occasion. She was a small, brown, hard-bitten woman with the habitual squint of eyes that have faced the sun, summer and winter. Lacing her worn black shoes, she thought wistfully of the many times she had asked Plew for the money to send for a pair of pretty slippers from the Catalog; but he had always said he did not have it. A country wife is obliged to regard the man she has married as the funeral service regards the Lord; the husband giveth, and the husband taketh away. He had taken away Rusty, which was all right she supposed. They raised the *cayuses* to sell, after all, and the money had gone for salt and sugar, coffee and flour, and other things they could not raise themselves.

The sound of Pine Creek kept her company as she rode. Pine Creek was formed in the bottoms near the Plew cabin, from two small streams that crept out of the hills, and it ran the year round, unlike the foamy washes that started up in the spring and quit when the snow was gone. Dolly loved few things, but she loved Pine Creek. It dappled for her over clean stones wherever she crossed it, and when the road swerved away from its bed, she could hear it chunking through a gully nearby.

When she came to the Pillage place—or the Hollister place, as she must try to think of it now—the stream ran down the bottom of the valley alongside the road, between Hollisters' and Conways'. Conway took water from it higher up by means of a flume along the hill. But of course the Hollisters had a spring of their own. She wondered if they knew how lucky they were. Her own folks had struggled through life on the fringes of an irrigation system that didn't always work, and when she had married Plew, they'd scarcely been able to give her a featherbed.

Well, that was a long time ago. Dolly turned up the Hollister side road. Rusty was nowhere in sight. Did they graze him, or did they give him hay? She had known the look of the old Pillage house since she and Bert had taken up their homestead, and she saw at once that it had been washed down with a bucket and brush, and new windows put in. There were curtains behind the panes, and a branch of serviceberry, its blooms dropping, stood in a jar on the front stoop.

So they liked flowers. That gave her something to go on. She took the bundle from her saddle and threw her headrein over a post. Full of misgivings, she rapped on the door. When it opened she said breathlessly, "I'm Dolly Plew. I brought you a piece of my yellow rose."

Mary looked down at the little brown figure and Mr. Gillespie's words raced through her mind. *Them yellow roses the women*

22

carry with them and plant wherever they go. I've seen yellow roses in dry gulches where they was nothing left of a ranch but a frame roof fallen in.

"Won't you come in," she said. "I'm Mary Hollister. And this is my sister, Althea." The other woman had materialized from somewhere at once, as if they were never far apart. Dolly saw in the background a fine-boned woman of perhaps forty, with hazel eyes that had a spark in them. She was nowhere near as old as Plew said. And the younger woman was not fat—she was fair and rosy, and had a pretty face. Plew had been prejudiced.

"How very nice of you to bring us something we can grow," the woman in the farther doorway said. "Will you have a cup of tea?" Her voice wasn't arrogant, it was self-assured and pleasant, and each word fell from her lips clear and separate.

Dolly said yes, though coffee was her tipple, or whiskey when she could get it. She perched on the edge of a chair and looked out the window for Rusty, and found courage to ask, "How do you like the horse? The one Plew sold you."

"We like him fine," Mary smiled, "but we don't think he likes us. When we get to be better riders, he might change his mind. We're just beginners, you know."

There now, Dolly thought, I wish Plew could hear her. "There's nothin' to riding, really," she said earnestly. "You just have to git used to it. You're up there all stiff and uncomfor'ble, and you don't *feel* what the horse is doing, but then by an' by you git so tired you got to relax, and then, if you just lay back an' let go, it begins to come to you."

"We must get you to show us," Mary said. "You're the first woman that has called on us. We're very glad you came."

"The first *woman?*"

"We have met a great many men," Althea said rather primly. "They seem to be always stopping by for drinks of water, or to fix their harness, or to know if there's gold up here in the gulch and would we be willing to have them prospect."

"They're very polite," Mary added hastily. "No one has been rude to us. On purpose anyhow. And they all seem to have business of some sort."

Dolly began to laugh. "They just want to look at you," she said.

"You're *ladies*. They wouldn't hurt a hair of your head. Unless it's the Miller Boys. And they wouldn't mean bad, but they might be drunk."

Mary flinched. Dolly was eager to reassure her. "You don't realize prob'ly, but a country has got to be opened up by men. They got to come in and live like hawgs, sometimes—or git along on what they can fish and hunt. It ain't easy to git a place started. This here place was started by a man. It never had no woman on it till now."

"We must think of them as being like Luther," Althea said soberly. "Lonely and far from home." She poured the tea from a pot that reminded Dolly of a lovely shell—white, with a little gold do-funny on top of it. Dolly's eyes were glued so fast to it that Althea asked, "Do you like Haviland?"

Dolly blinked. "I dunno. I never et any."

"This was part of my mother's set," Althea went on hastily. "There aren't very many pieces left. We've just baked by the way —may we offer you a loaf of bread? Mary, I'm sure it's cool enough to wrap. You might do some up in a tea towel for Mrs. Plew."

We could have opened a bake shop in Oak Point, Mary had said, and she meant it. Althea's bread, turned out through the years for the Hollister family, had reached a summit of golden, crisp perfection. Even the smell, preceding it from the shelf, was almost unbearably good. "Do you give this here to the fellas that come by?" Dolly demanded. "Why, you'll have 'em stopping in from as far away as Wenatchee."

Mary had been turning something over in her mind. "Mrs. Plew, I'd like to see what's up on top of these hills and where Pine Creek comes from. I'd like to see a sunset again—the head of the valley cuts it off from here. After I can ride better, would it be safe to go up into the hills? Alone, I mean."

"I'll take you," Dolly said eagerly. "You can go alone o' course, if you take a canteen and maybe a bite to eat, but then if your saddle turns or your horse steps in a pothole, where are you? I used to take my kids up the mountain when they was little. . . . They're married an' gone now, except Danny, an' he's courtin'. You let me know when you get the urge. . . . Could I see Rusty? He might be feelin' strange here."

24

"Rusty?"

"Our horse. The one you bought from Plew."

"Oh, of course. Althea calls him Pegasus. Just in fun, you know. She rides him, and I ride the horse we got from Yanling. They're both very nice, but we're not used to them. Come out to the lean-to—the horses are already in from grazing, because we planned to ride this afternoon. A man caught them up for us who stopped to ask directions. He was lost, at least that's what he said."

Dolly began to call out to Rusty before she reached the shed, and he stamped and whinnied. Inside, she put her arms around his neck and buried her face in his mane. Then with great simplicity, she caught up Althea's hand.

"Rusty, this here is a good lady. You treat her right. Don't you ever git sassy with her. Just be quiet, an' gentle, an' carry her good. She won't whip you none an' she won't leave you out in the rain an' snow. She's got a beautiful teapot an' she bakes good bread." She whirled on Althea. "You ever give him any?"

"Would he eat it?" Althea was a little confused.

"If he loves you, he'll eat a lump o' coal from your hand," Dolly said. "Goodbye, Rusty."

She rode off down the driveway, a little humble figure with the wrapped bread under her arm. They could not see her beyond the turn—perhaps she had ridden on down toward the post office. Or perhaps, Mary thought, she had merged back into a cleft hill or a hollow tree.

"The Miller Boys," Mary said at last. "Do you suppose they're the ones who go by here at night whooping and hollering?"

Althea was looking at the little trickle of water that cut its way down the slope and turned eastward along the road to join Pine Creek below the corner of their property. "It looks smaller than it did a week ago," Althea said with a trace of anxiety in her voice, for she knew where their treasure lay.

"Mr. Conway says it's enough to take care of this slope, and that's all we need to know. Luther had his pick, Althea, and he chose this." Mary had discovered that Luther's name acted as a sort of charm; it restored Althea's faith. Mr. Conway was the grizzled rancher across the road. He had helped them set up their cookstove, and got in a supply of dry wood. "I ain't saying I wouldn't of stole your water," he said forthrightly, "could I of figured how to make it run uphill again onto my field. But I got a good flume coming down out o' Pine Creek, and I'm satisfied." His wife, Mr. Conway had said vaguely, was "away." He had brought over a hatful of early apricots from his tree, and Althea had returned some of them in the form of a pie.

"I suppose we should get on with the washing," Mary said without enthusiasm. There was already a line of clean clothes fluttering from the corner of the house to a nearby tree, an unaccustomed sight in Pine Creek Valley. They had carried water from the spring box in buckets, heated it on the cookstove, and done out their petticoats and their household linens with the naphtha soap Althea set such store by.

"Right after the chicken coop and the privy, we've got to get a pipe to bring water into the house," Althea said. "Oh Mary, thank God for the money from Papa's bank account."

There had been no doubt in Althea's mind from the beginning that they were to go into the orchard business. Fruit from Wenatchee, shipped out in the last five years from trees planted at a hazard, had struck the public fancy "back East" and was bringing fabulous prices; plums, peaches, pears, above all the great ruby apples that this gray land produced and that this sunshine nourished. Even the frost, coming at the right time, reddened them and loosened them from the trees. "And we're here at the very beginning," Althea exulted. "Wouldn't you know, Mary, that if a new opportunity opened up in some part of the country, there'd be Pillages there to take part in it?" There was an orchard in Pine Creek valley already, the one that had been so disparaged by Bert Plew; and up and down the Columbia, outside the narrow slopes of Pine Creek valley, green was beginning to show against the sagebrush steppes wherever there was a canyon mouth or a hillside spring to irrigate it. Taking their horseback rides, which grew longer as they grew more confident, the Hollister girls sometimes passed the post office and the boat landing and ventured up or down the river, seeing log cabins, or shacks of raw lumber or tents with canvas-covered wagons standing by, but always new planting, the familiar checkerboard of frail, spindly-looking trees.

Nearly every time, coming or going, they stopped at the Muldoons'—the one orchard in Pine Creek valley. Muldoon and his wife were getting on in years. They had had a sawmill, and moved it from one timber location to another. "Mother wanted to settle somewhere," Muldoon looked affectionately at his gray-haired wife. All his mill money had gone into this deal, and as Bert Plew reminded everyone, he was taking a gamble.

"I think it's very sensible," Althea said in her downright way. "We're right behind you, Mr. Muldoon, as fast as we can make ready. 'There is a tide in the affairs of men,' you know. Even if we can't plant till spring, there's a lot to be done in the meantime. Tell us again how you prepared your land."

"Fust I had to get the rock off." Muldoon lowered himself heavily into his cowhide chair. "Your Luther Pillage already done that, and a good thing, too. It's a heartbreaking job. I don't know what he had in mind to grow, but in them days, it was mostly feed. Still is, for that matter. You sure you don't want to hedge by gettin' a few cattle? And you could breed out them stallions of yours to a couple o' good mares, and some time take back a colt in trade. A lot of people get a start that way."

"And let the apple boom go on without us? No, Mr. Muldoon, Mary and I have made up our minds. After you get the rock off, what comes next?"

"Fall plowing. The deeper the better. You can hire the plowing if you can find some rancher that'll come with his team. We all swap work more or less, or a lot of fellows can use some ready money. Can you girls spare it?"

Althea did not resent the question as she had from the woman on the boat. "I think so, Mr. Muldoon. And we need somebody to do a little bit of building and lay a pipe. How do you find a workman hereabouts?"

"There's no one hereabouts that ain't a workman, Miss Hollister. If you want an all-round handy man, you oughta get Bert Plew."

Althea shook her head. "Bert Plew disapproves of us. And the

27

storekeeper takes a poor view of us too, I'm afraid. But Mr. Conway has been very kind. Many people have been very kind."

"Conway's wife run off and left him," Mr. Muldoon said. "Just up and went one day."

"Some people say," Mrs. Muldoon spoke softly, "that this isn't a country for women. I don't know. I've been happy here. You find out what it is to get tired, so tired you think you'll never get rested. And when sickness comes, you don't know which way to turn. And no roof seems snug when the coyotes howl. But I like this country. It gives you back what you put into it."

"Then *you* don't disapprove of us?" Althea could be very winning.

"We admire your guts," Mr. Muldoon said sincerely.

Althea was to go to Wenatchee on the steamer and stay overnight. They had made several of these trips together, but this time Althea was going alone. The downriver boat arrived at the landing during the morning, and the upriver boat, which had left Wenatchee at daybreak, passed it on the way. So there was no return trip till the following morning, and the stay overnight was necessary. "You're sure you'll be all right?" Althea said for the dozenth time. "I can't understand your not wanting to come along."

I just want to stop talking a while, Althea. Talking and thinking. Nerving myself up. I might get out an old book and read and read. Or walk around the valley and try to borrow a new one. They say there are some books in the schoolhouse. I wonder how you get in? I don't want to think about being a Pillage for a while, or getting the place in shape, or facing the future.

"I won't feel good for a couple of days." She knew that Althea would know what she meant. A butterfly left the buckbrush clump outside and fluttered in the open door. "Oh, look, Althea, how lovely. . . . I might start to make up that material I brought along; it's been almost six months you know, and I'd like to leave off black sometimes."

"That yellow material is hardly suitable. You might wear gray, though, if you like. I'll be glad to bring you some. Really, Mary, one shouldn't be too prompt about giving up mourning. We should be *glad* to be showing our respect for dear Papa."

"I'd like to have it hanging in the closet to look at, anyhow, even if it's too soon to wear it," Mary said stubbornly. "And as for us both being away at the same time, we'd have to get somebody now to feed the chickens and gather the eggs, and I don't think we should ask the neighbors unless we need to. We shouldn't be beholden to anyone, you know."

Althea was to get some money out of the bank and consult with Mr. Gillespie about going into the fruit business. (This was pretty safe, for Mr. Gillespie had already given his opinion that it was the coming thing.) She was to find out where apple trees could be ordered for next spring, and what they would cost, and was to send a birthday present to Arthur's Hetty. This was how the sisters always thought of her, though they would have been surprised to hear their brother spoken of as Hetty's Arthur. And she was to bring home lemons, fresh pen points, camphor, and other little comforts.

They rode to the Landing together. Though Mary was in some pain, it was the only way to get Althea's horse home again. Sumac was turning red in the rocky gateway of the valley, and the vines that hung from a dilapidated arbor behind the store were loaded with purpling grapes. The days had become perceptibly shorter, and the Columbia River had fallen in its bed until its silver current, still rough with whirlpools and riffles, was sunk between great expanses of rounded, water-worn stones. Though the river still looked unfriendly and implacable, they now knew from experience that a trip upon it was safe enough.

The steamer came anytime between nine and noon, and passengers went down as early in the morning as they could get there and waited till it showed up. During low water, however, it made a slower trip, and in spite of several delays—Mary dropped the toast, and Althea found a rip in her best corset cover—they were in plenty of time to get the pole erect in the sand with a white cloth in the cleft of it. The boat appeared around the upper bend, and acknowledged the signal with a whistle toot.

"Have a good time, Althea!" They hugged.

29

"Dear Mary. Please take care of yourself. Don't save me any of the pound cake—I'll make another when I get back."

"I'll meet you tomorrow," Mary called, for Althea, ever prompt, was walking down the bank. Mary watched her on board, and waved as long as she could. Then she gathered up the rein of Althea's horse with her other hand and took off for home.

She tried to sit in a rocker and relax. There was, of course, no book not stale from many readings, but she and Althea subscribed to more than enough magazines; *The Delineator, Household Companion, The Country Journal,* Althea's favorite *Review of Reviews,* and *The Etude* which still came, reminding her sharply that she had no piano now. But it was her time of the month and she was restless. Always it brought this pointless urgency, this drive to get on with something, and always for a day or more she might be in sudden, erratic pain. She knew of many women who cleaned house at such times, turned out closets and attics, tackled big jobs of polishing or scrubbing. But in a house presided over by Althea, nothing ever needed such drastic treatment. She knew women too who were cross and difficult, women who sulked, women who cried. She had never felt that any of these things really helped.

She walked about the house and yard, and after the horses were cool she rubbed them down a little as Conway had taught her. Poor Mr. Conway. She wondered if his wife had given him any warning that she meant to leave, if there had been days and nights when he doubted and suffered. Nothing could happen to you here that couldn't happen anywhere, but here you were alone with it.

The skyline across the valley, long since learned by heart, showed its distinctive trees; The Man with a Hoe, The Mule, The Veiled Woman, as she and Althea had named them when they rested in the doorway after supper. On their own side, too, the hill had grown familiar, but they had never yet set foot on it. "Some other time," Althea always said.

But now Althea was gone, and it stood invitingly at the back of the yard.

I must be crazy. Today when I feel bad, and could make myself feel a lot worse. I'm supposed to be resting in there, reading in a magazine how the skirts are going to be up to the ankle this year.

Her feet took her into the kitchen, where she stood irresolute. Carry a canteen and something to eat, Dolly Plew had said. Still not sure she was going through with this foolishness, she found a bottle and filled it with water and cut a slice off the pound cake.

When she actually stood at the foot of the hill, however, she knew she was going up there. It was steep and ugly, but it was irresistible. And she would need at least one hand always free to hang on with. She threw the pound cake to the ants who threaded the hill with their tiny runways.

Climbing was very serious business. She put a foot up and it slid back, but not quite as far as she had raised it. Rocks underlay the hillside everywhere, even where it looked soft. Clawing and panting her way up, she did not look back until her face was scorching and her breath was coming in gasps.

Then she rested, and turned around. She was above the house roof, but not very far. Even at this height, things did not look the same, the angle of the house was different and the land seemed flattened out.

She started up again. For more than an hour, climbing and resting, she kept on; and at last the foot of the valley broke free, and she could see beyond Yanlings' the entrance through the gap, the great sweep of space and the foothills on the other side of the Columbia.

It was wonderful, wonderful. Tired to the bone, but still not in any pain, she sank down and lay on the ground like an animal, with just enough sense left to seek a patch of shade. It came from a pine tree hanging to the hillside by a great claw of roots, spilling its ancient needles downward. Along these she flung herself, and her body followed the humps and contours of the ground. *Oh, Mother Earth, how good you feel.*

Over there was the bowl at the head of the valley. She could not quite see the Plews' cabin. Pine Creek was maybe three miles long, they said, and now she possessed the whole three miles of it, just by looking. The Hollister place and the Conway place were small at her feet. Beyond Conway's hill rose other hills, shimmering in late summer haze. She rested a long time, filling her eyes with it. The ground was a bed; she nestled there.

When she got up, every muscle in her body was beginning to ache. She drank what was left in the water bottle and threw it away. Still she was greatly at peace. The descent would be hard, surely she would begin to feel pain. She drew herself up by dragging on a root, and with infinite slowness set one foot before the other.

Afternoon was drawing in when she slipped down off the last ramp. She made herself some supper and ate it, and in the absence of Althea's accustomed chatter sat quietly in the doorway for a while, watching the sunset light fade out. That night she slept like a child, without dream or sigh. The door was barred and the window frames locked, but that was against human error. The wilderness itself would not harm her. She had been "up there," and there was nothing to be afraid of.

Ben Lucas let his team stoop their massive heads to drink from the rill that flowed through the yard, while he walked up and rapped on the door. He did not know exactly what to expect. Stories about the two women were rife in the neighborhood, and whether they were favorable or not depended on who told them. He had brought both horses, as anyone who was going to pay for their work would naturally want to size them up.

Mary heard his knock. She was stiff as a board this morning, but she still felt wonderful. Since Althea was not there to see it, she had put on an old dress of dull pink that brought out the color in her face. She had fed the chickens and let them out, turned Rusty and Duke loose at the foot of the hill. (She must catch them up in plenty of time, for she would be meeting Althea at the boat that afternoon.)

She opened the door. A strange man stood there, but this was nothing unusual. He was younger than most, and deeply sunburned, but they were all sunburned. He had a cleft chin and steady eyes. "Muldoon tells me that you might have some plowing," he said.

"Why, yes. My sister is in Wenatchee, though, and I can't decide anything without her." As he continued to stand there, she said, "Would you like to come in and talk to me about it?"

I'm not chaperoned, but this is a business call. A lady may transact business in her own home.

"Thank you," Lucas said. He looked around appreciatively at the curtained windows, the clean floors, the braided rug under the table. "This is a sightly place you've got."

"We think it's nice," Mary said demurely. "Of course we've only just made a start. We're going to put in orchard. Are you an orchardist, Mr. . . ?"

"Lucas. Ben Lucas. Yes, I have a homestead upriver. It's planted to fruit—apples mostly. I put in a few pears and cherries too. There's still plenty to do around the place, but not like at first. You get a kind of a breather while the trees are growing. So I work out by the day."

"I can offer you a cup of coffee," Mary said, feeling very responsible in Althea's absence. She let down the firebox door of the range and thrust a couple of sticks in among the coals, and moved the teakettle to the middle of the stove, where it immediately set up a rumble.

"If it's not too much trouble, ma'am." All his sentences sounded oddly final, as if after this he would speak no more. He's bashful, Mary thought—but they all are.

She measured out the coffee, and put a cup and saucer on the oilcloth; then deciding to have some herself, she fetched another cup and saucer. It was up to her to make conversation, so she said, "My sister and I have ridden up and down the river. I wonder if we have seen your place."

"It's about two miles north of the Landing, directly on the road. When I begin to ship fruit, I'll have a steamboat landing of my own. The riverbank will allow for it, though it's a bit stony there."

"And where does that road go? We've never followed it for more than five or six miles."

"Toward Indian Spring, and some other towns. They're few and far between. I suppose, if you stay on it, it goes to the Canadian border."

"How wonderful," Mary said dreamily. "To think of crossing a border and being in a foreign land. Only it isn't very foreign, is it?"

"I guess not." Lucas accepted his cup of coffee gravely, and the little can of condensed milk with two holes punched in the top that served for cream; for Althea, though she "liked to have things nice," had found fresh cream impractical.

Mary uncovered the pound cake. "My sister told me to eat this up," she said mischievously. "Perhaps you'll help me?"

For a moment he looked startled, and then a slow smile thawed his features slightly. "I'll do my best, ma'am. A man gets mighty tired of his own cooking. Though that's not a hardship, properly speaking. I've been luckier than many—I haven't had a washout on my land, or too many grasshoppers, or gophers to speak of. The gophers will come when I plant alfalfa."

"And what is alfalfa?"

"It's a wonderful crop. You cut hay off it twice, sometimes three times a year. And hay is the one thing you can always sell in this country, without shipping it out."

"Luther was going to grow hay. At least we think so. You know, our cousin who took up the claim here." The name seemed to bring no recognition to Ben Lucas' face, so she told him about Luther Pillage and the bequest and Luther's remote grave across the Columbia River. For once she told it in her own way, unprompted by Althea. There was a brightening of tears in her eyes when she had finished. To cover her emotion, she cut him another piece of pound cake.

"That's what I mean," Ben Lucas said soberly. "It's a hard country and I'm lucky to be holding my own. Now that I understand how you came by the place, ma'am, may I ask if you've had any experience in farming? Any at all? Were you farm folk at home?"

"Why, no," Mary said. "We lived in a small town. But man is native to the land, don't you think? Surely he can learn to live with it—and surely woman can learn too. Althea and I are very willing. We're anxious to work and to succeed. It's just that some of it, like plowing, is beyond our physical strength. But we mean to plant our trees ourselves." She felt a certain rudeness in thus calling him back to the object of his visit, but Althea would want to know what he proposed to do and what it would cost.

Lucas took the hint at once. "Do you mind if I look around outside and get an idea what's to be done?"

Afraid she had been brusque, Mary said, "I'll come with you. I wish Althea were here; I can't agree to anything by myself. By the way we want pipes laid, to bring the springwater into the house, and several other things done. Althea will have to decide how much we can spend."

They went to look at the spring, a green half-circle not far back from the beginning of the short steep gulch, where oozing mossy banks were footed with clean gravel that welled and bubbled. The spring was to Mary a sort of miracle; some hidden water table, broken off here when the mountains were young, had delivered a stream to just this place, shaped it in just this way. For long ages, animals had lapped here, Indians had camped beside it. Luther had found it, and lost it again.

The old spring box was in fair repair. "But if you want a permanent job," Ben Lucas said, "the pipe intake ought to be set in concrete. . . . I'll get you some figures on it."

When they passed the lean-to he asked, "Your horses are out grazing?"

"I've got to catch them up, and meet Althea at the afternoon boat."

"I know your horses," Lucas said slowly, and a little reluctantly. "I know all the horses that are raised around here. I've wondered why didn't you get a matched work team, and not have to hire one? You could ride them too, you know."

"It would have been more sensible, wouldn't it? I guess we just didn't think of it." Mary moved her toe in the pale gray earth. "You wouldn't suppose this ground would grow anything, would you? Where we come from, good dirt is black. Black as midnight."

"This is volcanic ash," Ben said. "Those mountains between here and the coast—they used to blow off regularly. Rainier was a volcano, and Glacier peak, and Baker. Time and again they showered this land with dust. After it's weathered long enough, it makes real good soil—if you know what to put in it. I had a neighbor that pulled up and left because he couldn't raise corn."

Mary laughed. Nothing seemed baleful today, nothing was discouraging. The sun smote straight downward at noon time, and though most of the heat had gone out of it the birds still sought cover under leaves. Only the cold rasp of a cricket rose against

35

the silence. She lingered behind while Ben Lucas made a thorough tour of the slope to be plowed, and paced it off. Then he helped her catch up the horses. It was early, but they had had a good graze and were easily lured in with a little calling and coaxing. Mary bridled them and saddled them herself, refusing help—she would show this Lucas that women could do whatever did not require brute strength. He fidgeted uneasily, and finally, leading his own team out of the shade, he thanked her for the cake and coffee and left abruptly. Before she rode down to meet Althea she folded away the pink dress and got into her sober riding suit with the divided skirt. Althea would have packages, nursery price lists, the story of her adventures to tell. And she would bring some light gray material she had just happened to see, out of which Mary, if she wished, could make herself a new costume.

"Would you like to go to church next Sunday?" Mrs. Muldoon peered at Althea across her tiny parlor. "There's going to be a preacher coming down—he's got a church at Indian Spring but every so often he gets one of his elders to take the service, and he rides down here for a Sunday morning. We used to have church regular, the last storekeeper before this one was a Holy Roller, and he'd get us together and tell us we was all a valley of dry bones. I used to go, but it always bothered me some. But now we have regular preaching whenever the Reverend Johnson can get away. He's coming this Sunday. Mr. Muldoon has the keys to the schoolhouse, on account of being president of the school board, so we always know ahead of time and we tell everybody."

Althea gave her decisive nod. "We'd love to come. It'll be like home."

"Well, I don't know. The Reverend Johnson ain't much on education. He's a good, plain man. Mostly he keeps us singing hymns—he says it ain't him that makes it a church, it's us. Have you girls got a hymnbook?"

"We have two," Althea said proudly. "One was Papa's, and the

36

other came down to us from Samantha Pillage, and we didn't like to part with either one."

"Well, that'll be a real help. You brought a lot of things with you, didn't you? When we move, John Muldoon wants to throw away, and I want to keep. Was your home closed up? Back there, I mean. When your father died."

"We could have stayed on," Althea said frankly, for she felt close to Mrs. Muldoon. "But we are the only ones who might have wanted the house, and we would have had to scrimp dreadfully. Arthur took the house for part of his share—Arthur is so generous. But he counts on selling it. Hank didn't want it, and Kate didn't want it. My other brother and sister are both married and live in the fashionable part of town."

"It beats me why you don't get homesick. Coming from the East and all."

"Oh, we do," Althea said cheerfully. "But Mrs. Muldoon, we have a future here! I can hardly wait till spring, when we can plant our trees. Yours are five years old, aren't they? You'll get a crop next year."

"Muldoon can't hardly wait either," his wife said, smiling. "He's building a shed to pack the apples in, though I tell him it's bad luck to count your fruit before it's grown."

"I guess we're all doing that." Althea rose briskly. "I've got to get home. By the way, that was a good lad Mr. Muldoon sent us for the plowing. He's done a lot of handy little things. He says there ought to be dirt banked against the house before winter to keep the cold air from coming under the floors."

"I'd take Ben's advice if I were you." Mrs. Muldoon got up from her chair to walk the visitor to the door. "Ben Lucas knows a lot about getting along—he homesteaded his own place. Came here as soon as he was old enough to file a claim, and took up a real good piece of land, but he ain't had it easy. Ben's an Oregon boy, he was born and raised out here. I must get word to him about church, though I don't know if he'll come. There's a lot of people don't come. Yanlings, now, they keep to themselves, though it would do her good to get out and see people. She's in a family way. Sometimes I wonder if . . . "

37

Althea paused outside the door.

"I shouldn't say anything," Mrs. Muldoon went on, "for I don't really know. There's some people that come here because they've had trouble elsewhere and want to make a fresh start. If the law was looking for you, where would you go? Some place like this, where people mind their own business. And I ought to be minding mine. Come again, dear, whenever you're passing. I like to see you."

Althea braced herself against the breeze as she got on her horse and started off. After a few minutes' energetic riding, everything would be fine, her blood would rise and she would savor the clean, flowing air against her face. They must do all they could to be ready for winter; she felt that she was not afraid, only farsighted. They would bank up the house as Ben Lucas had suggested—perhaps he would be willing to come and do the work. She was well satisfied with the pipe he had put in, from the spring box to a sink in the house, burying it deep enough so that a freeze would not touch it. What a blessing that everything was downhill from the spring! "Gravity water," Ben had called it. Though he was not talkative, he had mentioned that on his place there was one upper bench with good soil that he could not irrigate because it was higher than his source of water in the nearby hills.

The spirit of adventure rode with Althea; there was so much to think about, so much to do. She had just come up from the Landing, and there she had seen boxes of apples actually put on board the steamer. The boxes still smelled of the yellow pine from which they were made. Through the cracks the paper wrappings were faintly pink with the luscious fruit inside.

She had set Mary to making a list of all they would need for the winter. Kerosene for the lamps. Canned goods in great quantity, even the flat-tasting canned milk, for until spring came they did not want the risk of keeping a cow. The horses were hardier—they would forage in the snow.

As Althea reached the turnoff road to their house she looked across, as always, to the place opposite, where poor Mr. Conway whose wife had run away kept his rather untidy house. There was someone moving about. Automatically her eyes were arrested and she stopped her horse. A woman was trudging around the yard. As Althea watched she drew a scarf over her head, hoisted a bundle to her back, and came down the footpath. That she was an Indian, Althea had by now had enough experience to know. Her face muffled in the scarf, she did not glance at Althea. Looking neither to right nor left, she entered the road and turned east, toward the village of Pine Creek. Down the valley she walked steadily at a slow, tireless pace.

There was something remote, submissive, matter-of-fact about her appearance. Althea, who was not worldly, nevertheless found herself able to read it. She went on up to the house and put Rusty away. Coming in, she hung her cloak on one of the stout hooks beside the door and prepared to get out of her riding skirt.

"Mary," she said, "I do not think we can accept any more help from Mr. Conway."

Mary looked up from her list. "What's the matter?"

Althea explained, choosing her words carefully. It would be embarrassing for Mr. Conway, she finished, if he knew they knew. But that was not the only reason, and both girls were aware of it.

"Althea," Mary murmured after a pause. "Do you remember what you said about Luther? That you wouldn't turn them off with ten dollars?"

"Yes, I did, didn't I? Oh Mary, it's so different when it *happens*. Right here."

"Was she pretty?"

"I couldn't see her face," Althea said coldly.

"Perhaps she's the daughter of a ruined chieftain who has sold her to the white man in desperation."

"Mary, don't be *silly*. Would you like to go to church at the schoolhouse next Sunday? Mrs. Muldoon invited us. I think I could do with a little uplifting talk."

"Why yes, I would. Ought we to ride to it, do you suppose? It might look funny, in our best clothes. But it's almost too far to walk in this weather. Ben Lucas thinks we ought to get a little one-horse sleigh by and by to drive around on the snow."

Althea was in a bad mood. "Ben Lucas is full of ideas, isn't he?

How does it happen *he* doesn't have a little sleigh to ride around in?"

"I suppose he's very poor," Mary said thoughtfully.

It was the first time they had seen the inside of the schoolhouse. School was in session now on weekdays, and there was a general smell of chalk dust and scratched varnish. The seats and desks were built in units, each desk supporting the seat ahead of it. Those in front were for small children, and the seats grew bigger toward the back. The first comers took the largest seats, and as the room filled up the late arrivals scrootched themselves into the foreground as best they could.

The Reverend Johnson had no seat and no pulpit. He stood before them easily and relaxed, his Bible in his hand.

In the morning sow thy seed, and in the evening withhold not thine hand; for thou knowest not what will prosper, either this or that, or whether they both shall be alike good.

The Hollister girls were gloved and hatted, and their black skirts barely cleared the ground. It had turned fairly warm for late October, and they had elected to walk so they could wear, as Althea put it, "something decent." There were few faces here that were familiar to them, for most of the church attendance was from up and down the Columbia. Pine Creek valley was poorly represented. The Yanlings were not there, and neither were the Plews. Nor Mr. Conway. Mary had all the names in the little valley straight now, and sometimes to help herself go to sleep she recited them; Yanling, Muldoon, Conway, Hollister, Miller, Plew. A sorry lot, in a manner of speaking. But they were all human beings, they all lived and dreamed and struggled and loved (would what Mr. Conway did be called loving?). She knew them all by sight, even the rowdy Miller Boys with their unkempt hair, and of the Muldoons and Dolly Plew she was genuinely fond. They might not see Dolly for weeks together, but one day her small brown hand would tap hesitantly on their door, and the Hollisters would drop everything and sit down with her, for talk was something precious in this arid land.

"Some of you have sowed your seed again and again," the Reverend Johnson said, "and as far as you know nothing has ever come up. You haven't withheld your hand in the evening, either. You've done your best—well, pretty near your best. Sometimes you wonder why you haven't got more to show for it."

We stick out like a sore thumb, Mary thought. *Not another woman in this room owns a pair of gloves, and as for some of those hats! . . . Well, they probably look all right to the Lord, Who doesn't keep up with the styles. . . . I wonder who it is that's coming in late.*

The latecomer was Ben Lucas. He was dressed, not in the overalls in which they had always seen him, but in a suit, decorously brushed. He entered quietly, took the nearest seat, and fixed respectful eyes upon the preacher. He had missed most of the sermon, which was not very long. "Now," the Reverend Johnson said, "we will sing."

This was what they had waited for. A pleased sigh went through the congregation. "Since our hymnals don't all agree, I won't give out numbers. Just find "Abide With Me," if you can."

Everybody knew it, with or without a book. To Mary's surprise, a fine high soprano soared up from one of the front seats. It came from a stout woman whose face was turned the other way. How vibrant it was, and the voices of several of the men supported it, rising note by note through the bass part. They not only knew the tune, they knew the chords. Oh lovely, lovely! Mary felt her throat tighten. Her father had been very fond of "Abide With Me."

They sang "Onward, Christian Soldiers" and "Come, Thou Almighty King" and "Rock of Ages" and "Sweet Beulah Land," and finally

> Glory, glory, hallelujah,
> Glory, glory, hallelujah,
> Glory, glory, hallelujah,
> My soul goes marching on.

The sound made the water pail vibrate in the cloakroom and rattled the shades at the open windows. It rolled out across the valley of the Columbia and lost itself among the frowning rocks and on the swirling surfaces of the river. It was made up of

41

bellows and pipings, the bright thread of a young girl's voice and the furry baritone of a deck hand who had been sleeping it off on the river bank after being dumped ashore for drunkenness.

They could sing, they could all sing. And singing, they were cleansed; they were halfway to heaven right then and there.

The Reverend Johnson stood at the door as they went out. Althea pressed his hand warmly. "This has been a very great pleasure," she said. "It is splendid of you to come. We'll be looking forward to your next visit."

He gave her a direct, humorous look from under heavily thatched eyebrows. "When you are in Indian Spring," he told her as if a trip of fifteen or twenty miles were nothing, "we would be very glad to have you attend our church. You are new in the neighborhood, are you not?"

It's our gloves, Mary thought, and our shoes. Anyone would know. While Althea was telling of their arrival and their plans—Althea loved a listener—Mary sought out the stout woman who had sat down in front. "You have a lovely voice," she said shyly. "I . . . it was nice to hear you sing." She ducked away quickly, for Mary never in her life had known what to say to an unexpected compliment, and she assumed that others were in like case. The woman looked after her smiling suddenly, flushing under the sunburn. I used to sing, Mary wanted to say, I used to sing and play the piano. But we have left all that behind. We have left the old house with the slate roof and the fanlight, and streets full of people doing their Saturday night shopping, and trolley cars, and porch swings. The feel of ivory keys beneath the fingers— "Hearts and Flowers" and "The Maiden's Prayer."

She found the gathering in the churchyard short, almost abrupt, compared to the pleasant lingering that she remembered at home; but all these people had chores to get back to. She and Althea had time for a word with the Muldoons, who must stay and lock up the schoolhouse after everyone had left. Ben Lucas walked over to them, his hat in his hand.

He spoke to Althea, though it was Mary who saw him coming. "I have a borrowed buggy here," he said in his deep voice with the odd note of finality. "I would be pleased if you would let me drive you home."

Althea looked surprised, but only for a moment. Mary, who knew her so well, could see the surprise quenched and a democratic graciousness taking its place. "Why, how nice of you! Though we had planned to walk. Mary, shall we ride with Mr. Lucas?" She called him Ben on weekdays, but this was different.

Mary liked the way he had said, "a borrowed buggy." He was stubborn and prideful, overscrupulous just because of his pride. She nodded and they moved away toward the hitching rack at the side of the yard.

Mrs. Muldoon looked after them. "Now there's something," she said in her sweet, cracked old voice. "Never did know Ben to go to that much trouble before."

Muldoon got out his keys, and hunted for the one that fitted the schoolhouse door. "I understand he's been working up there pretty regular. No harm to either party—Althea's bound to spend her money, and Ben can use it. Though the money don't pay for all they'll get, they need somebody to look out for them, God knows, and Ben will help us do it. And learn a thing or two."

"John Muldoon, I believe you sent Ben up there to do their plowing on purpose!"

Muldoon did not deny it. "Ben's a good boy," he said. "And lonesome. It's time he met some nice women."

3 THE DAYS were shorter now. The warmth had gone out of the air, making each afternoon more chill, more golden, bringing a blaze of yellow maple to the draw behind the house. Mary collected the tawny leaves as they fell, and pressed a few in the pages of an album. "No two are alike," she said. "Oh, Althea, I love fall."

"You're very young," Althea smiled indulgently. "After you've lived as long with the seasons as I have, you'll take them as they come."

"It's like great music," Mary went on obstinately. "Everything is tuning up together. 'The year is done. The year is done. We've had our flower and our seed and the streams are falling and the birds are flown and here is a great strong melody coming through.'" After this she felt rather foolish, and scrubbed down the floors and the doorstep with the now-abundant water that flowed out of a tap in the kitchen.

They had venison dinner with the Muldoons. The deer were coming down into the valley to feed, and a few times they saw a doe break out of the brush, stand startled, and disappear. The coyotes were creeping closer, too, and lacing the night with their hideous cries. Eagles came out of the cliffs and swooped to the last few marmots sunning themselves on the cooling rocks.

Dolly Plew announced that her boy Danny had finished courting a girl down-valley and would be married when he came home from the apple harvest at Wenatchee. Her account of the marvels he had seen there led Althea to say, "We really ought to see how the fruit is picked and packed, Mary. We need to spend a few days in Wenatchee, and buy some warm winter things."

"We can't leave the chickens," Mary reminded her.

"And we mustn't be under obligations to anyone. So I won't ask Ben Lucas to come and feed them, for it's too little to pay for, and too much to do for nothing. But Mary, I've been thinking. We could can them, like the Muldoons do their venison."

"Can them?"

"Why, yes. In jars, you know. Fix them like we would for eating, and put them in glass jars and put the jars in the wash boiler and cook them."

"Who would cut their heads off?" Mary came straight to the point.

"I would," Althea said grimly. "If Mary Pillage could shoot an Indian, I can cut a chicken's head off. I've often thought of it, I must say. I'm tired of their beeping and chittering."

Athea's getting nerves, Mary thought apprehensively. All this winter coming on, that gives me a glad strong feeling to be alive, makes her worry. And no wonder, we've got plenty to worry about. "I suppose we could if you say so, Althea. Mrs. Muldoon would tell us how."

"I remember Mama plucking chickens, when I was little," Althea brought out unexpectedly. "As soon as they're . . . as soon as the heads are off, you plunge them in boiling water. Then the feathers loosen quite easily."

"Where would we get the boiling water? We haven't got a kettle that big."

"Down at the store," Althea's determination was mounting, "there's a big iron pot. Enormous. For hog-scalding, they told me. We'll rent it from them."

"Oh, for heaven's sake," Mary said, "would you have tried to rent it in Oak Point? Just *borrow* it. People think we are too show-offy about money."

"All right then," Althea's voice was a little stiff, "we'll borrow it. How will we get it up here?"

"Bert Plew will bring it on one of his trips. And we can pay him, because he's in the business."

"I suppose you're right. We'll speak to Bert about it, then, and we'll build a fire under it in the yard."

"We'd have to have a lot of wood ready. I'll do that, Althea—I'm getting very good with the axe. I'll go out and practice—you've got Hetty's letter to answer."

If Mary thought the idea would blow over, she was mistaken. Althea watched the hens and penned off three or four of the best layers. "They won't do much in the winter anyhow," she said, and the rest were marked for sacrifice. When Mary threw their rations of food on the ground in the morning, on the thick white frost in the shadow of the house, Althea eyed it grudgingly.

It had rained several times; short, tentative, drenching rains that seemed to come straight down from tattered clouds hanging above the valley, and one night when they went to bed to the sound of rain they woke to find a thin film of snow on the ground. It melted quickly, but it gave them an ominous feeling. "We must can the chickens," Althea said. "Tomorrow."

That night they laid a fire under the iron cauldron, ready to light. There was extra wood beside the cookstove, too, for boiling the jars, which had been procured by the storekeeper after some argument, for the official canning season was past. He had never dealt with anyone who wanted as many arbitrary and new-fangled items as the Hollister girls.

They woke early, half expecting to see snow again, but the ground was clear, the day cold and overcast. The chopping block, diverted from its place by the woodpile, stood ceremonially in the middle of the yard.

"I'm best with the axe," Mary said suddenly. "Let me do it, Althea. You remember how I promised Arthur I would do all the hard chores? You've never let me, but this time you must. I'll . . . I'll make a big fuss if you don't."

"Well," Althea said, "it's almost as bad to hold the chicken. Perhaps we'll take turns. . . . We must get the pot boiling first."

Their fire crackled briskly, and when the steam began to rise from the cauldron they could, from sheer nervousness, wait no longer. Althea advanced upon a chicken chosen at random, picked it up by the legs, and bore it threshing and squawking to the block. "It won't hold still," she said breathlessly. Somehow she maneuvered it to the spot and Mary, pale and determined, waited through endless struggles till a safe and propitious moment. When she brought down the axe, she burst into tears.

"I heard the squawkin'," the tall man with matted hair said, "and I thought maybe sumthin' was wrong. Kin I help you?"

Mary, drying her eyes, and Althea, completely winded from her struggles, looked up in astonishment. There had been no one there a moment before. Now a stranger loomed over them and a horse stood quietly behind him with its bridle hanging. Mary was the first to recover herself.

"Are . . . aren't you a Miller?" she said with something less than complete civility.

"Yeah. One o' the Miller Boys." He spat far and accurately to the edge of the woodpile. "What's goin' on here?"

"We . . . we're just killing a few chickens," Mary said lamely. "We haven't had much experience. It's kind of difficult, isn't it?"

"We're going to can them," Althea offered, though she was not in the habit of explaining her business to passers-by.

"Well, now. Perhaps you'd like me to do the choppin' for you." He picked up their axe, which Althea had selected with the greatest care. "Ain't hung quite right, and needs sharpenin'. But it'll do." He indicated the nearest pen. "All o' them?"

Althea hesitated. "You're really too kind, Mr. . . . Mr. Miller. I think we could manage. But—"

"Might as well do it now I'm here," the Miller Boy said. "Grouse, now, you gotta have a good eye. If you chop into the meat they ain't nothin' left. But all you need to kill chickens is practice. Gotta have a rhythm to it. Look." He fetched a bird, swung it into place and delivered one neat blow. "Like that."

But they had not, regrettably, looked. If God had sent him, they had no desire to interfere. If he came from the opposite source, as a Miller Boy might, they could only hope the penalty would be within their ability to pay.

When the feathered bodies were in a neat heap beside the woodpile, they offered him the customary coffee, and Althea, who had just turned out a batch of doughnuts, pressed a sack of them upon him. "We're glad to make your acquaintance, Mr. Miller," she said in a voice that was still a little tense. "Everyone in the valley is so kind to us. I don't know what we would do without our good neighbors."

"Oh, pshaw," the Miller Boy said. "Ain't nothin'. Bert Plew says to us, you can't help but wonder how they're goin' to make out, coupla fool women, they do everything hind end to"—this had not been Bert's exact expression—"but they're in there tryin', and what the hell, it's a free country."

"I'm so glad you think so, Mr. Miller," Althea said, not batting an eyelash. "Though we didn't plan on help, there are times when we're very glad to get it. How many of you—that is—how many Miller Boys are there?"

" 'Lias and me—I'm Ezra—and Olly, but he's jest a little feller. Five foot ten. He's only fifteen, though, and by the time he's growed we figure he'll be as big as the rest of us."

"Fifteen!" Althea said, startled. "Why, I wonder . . . we have some of the books my brothers and I used to like . . ."

"He don't read very good, Olly don't. But he can handle a shootin' arn. Thanks just the same, miss. Olly goes to school, sometimes, but it don't seem like they can larn him much. . . . I hear as how you're goin' to grow an orchard here."

"That's what *we* think," Althea said, taking the very words out of Bert Plew's mouth. "Wish us luck, Mr. Miller. Our trees go in next spring, and then we'll see."

All day they soused the chickens in water and pulled off feathers and drew entrails and cut the bodies up. It was hard to keep the water hot enough, and the feathers came out reluctantly. There were pinfeathers that had to be plucked out and the bodies singed over the fire. A nauseating smell that they would never forget settled gradually over the whole proceeding. Their fingers were lacerated by sharp bones that came from unskilled carving, and wet feathers clung to their hair and clothes and drifted underfoot. The boiling got behind schedule, and it was past midnight when they took out the last jar. Ranged on the table, on pads of folded cloth, they were really very impressive.

"They look lovely, Althea," Mary said feebly.

"I'm so tired I can hardly hold my head up." Althea yawned wide and frankly. "I had a bad idea, Mary. I wish I'd never *heard* of chicken. And we've still got to clean up this mess, and return the kettle to the store."

"Nonsense," Mary said stoutly. "We'll be very glad to have them when meat is hard to come by next winter. How would we know what would work, Althea, if we never tried anything?"

It was part of the Pillage creed, kept solemnly alive in the Hollister household, that Pillages never held each other to blame. Consoling and comforting was the Pillage way, and not hitting anyone when he was down. Understanding why he had made his errors, or failing to understand, falling back on the sympathy that came so naturally from one adventurous, bumbling, fallible Pillage to another. "He already feels bad enough," Henry Hollister had always said to his children, "don't rub it in." He had not rubbed it in when Luther got stuck and needed money; he had simply sent the money. And because of it, his heirs were sitting here in this remote part of the world, free to get into trouble of their own.

The sisters let themselves have two precious days in town to buy winter clothes and send Christmas gifts. In the evening they went to see a motion picture called "Rescued From an Eagle's Nest." They would have liked to eat their supper in a restaurant, but they were guests in the house of Mr. Gillespie, and his daughter's feelings would have been hurt. She was a quiet, dark-haired girl who had left school and taken over the household when her mother died. Remembering how this felt, Althea was tender toward her, and kept the supper table gay. She told about canning the chickens, and Mr. Gillespie laughed till his stomach shook. He said, "You must come and cheer us up more often."

"I'm afraid we won't be out again this winter," Althea said. "The boats stop running during January and February, I'm told. We're planning on doing some dressmaking, and we must keep the horses ridden—a little, anyway. Perhaps it's just as well we have to go a mile for the mail."

The streets of Wenatchee were hard-frozen mud, and all the way upriver the clouds hung close to the steely water so that the tops of the hills were hidden. When they reached Pine Creek Landing, the rounded stones along the bank were goblinlike under a new fall of snow. Cold to the marrow, they walked up the valley, since there was no one to meet them with the horses. When they passed the schoolhouse, Mary said, "There'll be a program here at Christmas time, and a tree. We must do what we can."

For a heartbreaking moment Althea thought of Arthur's big house, the children in early morning Christmas raptures, the furred-and-coated aunts and uncles coming in, the hugging and kissing, the church bells, the mistletoe pinned crooked above the door.

"I've got some gold and silver paper from a candy box," she said a little too brightly. "We should offer them some little packets of raisins, don't you think, Mary, with bright ribbons around them, and I'll make some gingerbread men."

Ben Lucas' ranch had the shape of a piece of paper that has been rolled upward at one end. He had not arrived in time to get one of the very best pieces of land along the Columbia, but he had not done badly either. He had filed on a likely location, the day he was twenty-one, and before that for weeks he had scouted up and down the river, sizing up what was available.

Oregon—by which he meant the Willamette valley—was full. His Pa had come there as a child by covered wagon, and by now it was edge to edge with settled farms and towns. If a fellow wanted to strike out for himself, his Pa had said, there was plenty of acreage up to the north. Not along the coast, where mills were busy chewing up the timber and where the little seaports of Seattle and Port Madison were thriving. But inland, where the fur trade routes had run. There was a railroad now, his Pa had heard tell, which took you to Wenatchee from the coast. After that you were on your own.

Ben had loved the inland country at first sight. It was young and untried, like himself. He liked the great brown canyons and the defiant rock. He had left the train at Wenatchee, and taking no one's advice, had set out to see what he could find. When he had passed Badger Mountain and Bailey's Slide and the mouth of Pine Creek valley, he had come upon this level bench which had no man's mark upon it. There was already a settler to the immediate north, a scrawny little chap named Piggott, and he and Piggott had agreed how to divide the water from the canyon between them and had been to Wenatchee to have a record made of it. They had found a good lawyer, name of Gillespie, who had put it down in black and white.

Piggott had moved on, and now the ranch to the north was vacant. But the water rights still stood and Ben felt safe. It was true that the stream didn't come from high enough up to be led around the mountain to his upper benchland; however, this was not his fault or Piggott's fault, but Nature's.

He had planted his orchard the year after Muldoon's was planted, and like the Hollister girls and others, he had got counsel and help from Muldoon. The orchard was now four years old. He had made out since by working in the wheat harvest over at Waterville and cutting and stacking firewood for the steamboats, and doing odd jobs for people like the Hollisters. He had gotten his house built too, a prime requirement for "proving up" on the homestead. Instead of putting up a sketchy, minimum-sized frame or log cabin which would have satisfied the homestead law, he had copied his folks' house in Oregon; it was the one touch of homesickness he had permitted himself. There was a long raftered front room in which he cooked and ate at one end, while the other held nothing much yet but a bedspring and armchair. There was a bedroom roughed in along the back, and room for more if need be, and across the front he meant to have a porch. Women liked a porch. And he intended to marry a likely girl, when he was ready, and raise a family.

He himself was one of eight children, and he remembered his Ma best with a baby in her arms. When he went back to tell them about the land he had found, and his claim already filed on it, his Ma had stood with her arms tight around him for a long time, not speaking. Then she had said briskly, "We'll give you some gear. A man ought to be comfortable. You pick out a chair you like, Ben, and there's a spare bedspring, and plenty of dishes I don't need. I think I'll give you the sprigged set—I never use it." The sprigged set had come west in the covered wagon. Ben's eyebrows went up, but he knew better than to refuse. His father gave him a Bible and an almanac and a school history and a few well-thumbed adventure stories, and a new book that had come their way that his father was enthusiastic about. It was called *The*

Good Ship Earth, and it told all about the resources on the world's surface, the water and wood and minerals and coal and other expendable things, that man was using so prodigally. "I mighty near know it by heart," his father said. "You take it now and read it."

He had these things shipped to his place by steamboat, at considerable trouble, and had kept them under a tarpaulin while he was building his house.

As he walked up the riverbank and from there to the canyon mouth by way of the barbed-wire fence that marked his north boundary line, and finally up the hill to the upper bench where he could look down on the young orchard, he felt that he was pretty well ready for winter. The little trees looked fine. He had lost mighty few out of the whole planting. And on these, having bought from a nursery that guaranteed its stock, he had been able to go back to Wenatchee and collect a few dollars. His house and barn were banked with dirt; his wagon was still on wheels, but the snow-bobs were ready, repaired and greased. Once each year so far, he had been back to see his folks; and once each year, beside his crackling fire, he had read *The Good Ship Earth* and the old volume of history from beginning to end. While he was on his way to Oregon, if he went this winter, he would seriously consider buying another book.

The quiet joy that usually filled him when he looked at the orchard had lost its edge today. He could have gone down to Wenatchee or up to Indian Spring and gotten drunk, but Ben had been raised in a temperance family. As for gambling, he would as soon have gone down and tossed his hard-earned money into the Columbia as put it on the table in one of those card games. At least, that way, he would have understood where it went.

A hack came south along the road, not raising much dust because by now the rains had done their work. Seeing a man on the brow of the hill, the driver stopped the hack and made a courteous gesture of summoning him.

Ben started down at once. In this country, you never refused a man's hail. He could see as he came closer that the hack was a single-seater with a long back. The horses were well kept, but old. The off mare had a shifty eye.

The driver raised a hand in greeting. I'm looking for a man named Piggott, lives up thar acrost. Know where he is or when he'll be back?"

"Piggott moved out a couple of years ago," Ben said. "Didn't leave any address."

"Oh. Well . . . heard he had skill to find water underground. You know, with a forked stick. I need more irrigation for my ranch."

"We all do," Ben said with instant sympathy. "No, I'm sorry, Piggott pulled out. And I don't know any other dowsers hereabouts. You could likely find one in Wenatchee."

"It's a pretty fur piece to go." The man let his reins hang slack in his left hand. "Was he any good, do you know? Could he really find it?"

"I never knew Piggott was a dowser," Ben said thoughtfully. "But he had a lot of gifts. He could play the ocarina. He could mend canvas or leather as good as new."

They regarded each other, two lonely men in a lonely land.

"This yore place?" The stranger took in the sightly house, the tilled ground, in one long glance.

"Yeah. From the river up to above the first bench. It's not much to look at, this time of year, but it's coming along."

"It's real good to be on the river," the stranger said politely. "You can fetch your crop right to the boat, I reckon. I'm in Wolf Coulee, myself. We got a bad grade comin' down the hill there."

"Yes, I know. Log haulers use it too, don't they?"

"Not no more. Spicer's mill picked up and moved over to a new stand o' pine. Pine lumber's givin' out. Fust thing you know, we'll have to send our fruit to the market in gunnysacks. I favor bar'ls, myself. Like when I was a boy."

"It's the pine boxes the trade likes," Ben said instantly. "There's something nifty about a box. And they pack so easy."

The other man grunted. "Know anything about this moth that's broke out in the Wenatchee orchards?"

"Nothing but hearsay. I hope it never reaches us."

"It'll git here. Just like aphis, an' red spider, an' scale."

"How come you've got an orchard old enough for all that?"

The stranger brightened. "Luck. Just fool luck. When I bought my place I said, What good is all this fruit? Some old coot, a regular Johnny Appleseed, had been tryin' it out. I moughty near cut it down, to tell you the truth, an' put in wheat. And then the boom started, and whammo, apples was sky-high. Even haulin' down the grade, I kin make money."

"Do you think this mild weather's going to last?" Ben said, to make up for having been so opinionated about the boxes.

"Not more'n a few weeks. It's been too good far too long. I been watchin' the weather for thutty years, boy an' man, an' what I say is, when November an' December is decent, January's a stinker. . . . Well, so long." He lifted his hand again and shook the reins. The horses reluctantly pushed their shoulders into the harness and the hack moved off.

It was time to get supper. For supper he usually had mush or flapjacks, and for breakfast flapjacks or mush. For dinner at noon he ate salt pork and potatoes, or cheese or a bit of game, or, for a while, after one of his neighbors had butchered, pork chops cooked and put down in a crock of lard. There was garden sass in the summer—carrots and peas—and in the winter a box of dried apples or prunes stood under the cupboard. A lesser man might not have thrived on such fare, but Ben was hard and lean— his body gave him very little trouble.

It was his mind that was at loose ends. Sometimes the solitude bit into him like a toothed saw. He could go dawdle around at Muldoons' or the store, but a man shouldn't get to be a nuisance to his friends. And go to the Hollisters' he would not. He had gotten himself out on a limb there, with his confounded idea of taking them home from church. He had stepped out of his role as hired man, and how was he to step back in? How could he come around in the morning, after that, and say "Any work for me today?" If they sent for him, perhaps—but they had not sent for him. However much he might miss their friendly greetings, their pretty house and lavishly lighted lamps and good food, they did not miss *him*. They had a world into which he could not enter. And he did not want to enter it; he did not trust it. They were reckless, thoughtless, extravagant. They had no self-discipline. (This would have surprised Althea, who thought she had quite a

55

lot.) It was not only how they spent money, which was shocking in itself, but their whole outlook was frivolous. The way they rode around for miles and frittered away the days, eating picnic lunches in outlandish places. The heathen nicknames they gave things—"Pegasus" for a horse, "Castalia" for the spring.

He would go to Oregan, and he would go today. Muldoon would keep his other horse. He would go back to the only folks that really cared for him, no matter how casual they had been about letting him go. The casualness had not fooled him—it was because it had to be. His young brothers would whoop with delight when he showed up in the yard, and his Ma's face would be a sight to see. It would have to be a thrifty journey, for his money was very low. He would ride down the Columbia, and at Wenatchee he would cut across to the coast. It would be green there, settled country, something different; it would pleasure him. His spirits lifted a little, and he began throwing clothing into a canvas satchel.

Thus it was that when the big freeze came, two weeks later, Ben was already over the mountains and far down into the Green River country.

The cold stilled everything. The hillsides above Conway's and up and down the valley were carved in glittering white, through which meager stands of evergreens stood out darkly. There was no wind. Snow stood up straight in round caps on the fence posts and lay on the plowed slope below the house, exactly where it fell. There were tracks leading up the road toward the Millers' and the Plews', but they could seldom see any traffic. Bert went out with his wagon only when he had business, and the Miller Boys seemed to have hibernated along with the bears and the marmots. The Millers hardly bothered to go to the post office, and Althea said tartly that perhaps Olly wasn't the only one who couldn't read very good. As for the Hollister girls, they bundled themselves up and went for the mail everyday, forcing themselves to take the short, chilly trip for the exercise. There was always something in their pigeonhole above the battered desk, for they

56

took the Wenatchee paper, which came a day or sometimes two days late.

The rest of the time, they carried in wood and stoked their fire, breaking the ice from the sticks and piling them behind the stove to dry out before burning. Althea worked out a system of moving the dry wood from left to right, and bringing in more each day at noontime, when the sun had loosened up the woodpile. They washed and hung out clothes that froze on the line, worked the puzzles in the *Household Companion,* and sewed on a quilt for which Althea had been saving the pieces for many years. There were scraps of fabric from Mary's school dresses, from Papa's shirts, from the russian blouses Arthur and Hank had worn as little boys. (Kate, of course, had taken her quilt pieces with her when she married.) Sometimes on a plain section they put featherstitching of a different color. Not a word was said about their solitude, about the encircling white wilderness outside, either to each other or in their letters.

They banked the fire each night as best they could, but the pinewood burned out fast, and getting up in the cold house was the worst moment of all. To walk across the icy floor, to build a fresh fire quickly with newspaper and pitchy sticks, hoping it would catch and draw, to get under the covers again with teeth chattering, and wait until the worst chill was off and the teakettle began to sing, this was the hard, disheartening beginning of each day. "It got lots colder than this in Oak Point," Mary would say sensibly, remembering blizzards, and the river frozen over so they could skate, and Althea would say "Yes, of course." But everyday the thin boards of the old house seemed a little thinner, and everyday the temperature dropped a little.

There came a night when they could scarcely sleep for the cold. Mary woke when daylight had begun to filter into the room and lay shivering. She could see the bare outlines of the stove, black and sullen and empty. There was a restless movement from the cot on the other side.

"Althea, are you awake?"

"Yes, I'm awake." There was an edge of panic on Althea's voice. "Mary, what are we going to *do?*"

"We're going to take turns staying up and keeping up the

fire," Mary decided. "I'm going to build it *now*, and as soon as the room gets warm a little you go back to sleep if you can. Tonight you keep the fire up till midnight, and then call me."

"I don't like it," Althea said, for once caught off her guard.

"Nonsense, it isn't anything. We'll laugh about it next summer."

"Next summer," Althea said firmly, "we're going to make this into a better house."

"Now, Althea, the house is fine. We need to get acclimated, that's all." Mary summoned all her resolution and slid out of bed. Reaching for a robe, she wrapped it quickly around her, and crossed the room like a swimmer breasting an icy river. There was not much light, but she knew where everything was. Taking off the clattering lids, she put in the paper and kindling and a few small sticks and one big one, and a splash of kerosene from the jug beside the stove, and lit a match to it.

The fire, like a living thing, leaped up and began to roar in the firebox. Althea sighed and turned over. I'll stay up, Mary thought, it's really just as easy as all that hopping in and out. She hovered near the stove till her gooseflesh had abated, and then crossed over noiselessly to the front window, and put the curtain aside.

It was like the Fourth Day. The creation of the earth was finished and light gleamed in the firmament, but there was no beast or man. A dull blue dawn spread upward from the east, and its reflection crept along the valley, outlining ridges and draws. *The ends of the earth. The Pillages have come at last to the ends of the earth.*

Althea gave a small, ladylike snore. Mary put the curtain down and went to wash her face in the graniteware basin.

"It's about as cold as it's gonna get," the storekeeper said, and he was right. The thermometer hovered a while and then began to creep upward. It was still very cold when Althea, doing her stint for the first part of the night, was startled to hear a muffled pounding on the door. Mary was asleep and Althea was reading

58

a well-worn magazine by the light of the kerosene lamp. She opened the door and a man burst into the room.

It was Yanling. He said, "Can you women birth a baby?"

His words woke Mary instantly. Althea stared at the intruder. She was the oldest of a family of five, but she had never actually been present at her mother's deliveries. "I'll do what I can," she said. "Have you sent for the doctor?"

"Muldoon's riding to Indian Spring after him," Yanling gulped.

Mary sat bolt upright. "Oh, you didn't let Mr. Muldoon start for Indian Spring in this weather? He's too old and . . ." She checked herself. Muldoon had already started—there was nothing to be done. "Get Dolly Plew," she said from sheer instinct.

"Would you get her, miss? I got to get back to my wife. Mrs. Muldoon is with her. She's ahead of her time," he added miserably. "Way ahead of her time."

They had never dressed and saddled so fast. Althea shook down the fire and put water on it, lest it flare and start trouble. They put on every scrap of heavy clothing they had. Yanling did not wait, but flung himself down the road on his own horse. "I'll follow him," Althea said, "and you ride up after Dolly. You take the lantern—we don't know the road so well in that direction. I could ride down to Yanlings' in my sleep. Do be careful, Mary, and don't let Duke step in a chuckhole."

They had never returned Dolly's visits; as a matter of fact Dolly had never asked them to. She thinks Bert wouldn't be nice to us, Mary surmised. She and Althea had ridden toward the head of the valley more than once, but from delicacy they had not come too close to the small log cabin with its corrals and cattle shed. The road was quite strange to Mary and took all her attention. It skirted the Rock Patch where the cliff above had let loose, and crossed Pine Creek a couple of times. She felt the cold, but she did not think about it. Duke was wary and snorted occasionally. It crossed her mind that they had got their horses turned around. Althea's horse would willingly have found his way to the Plews', while Duke always had to be reined in when they passed Yanlings'. Well, he would be headed that way soon.

It took Dolly a few minutes to get up, and to peer out. "Land o' Goshen!" she said when Mary explained her errand. "Sure I'll come. I've helped many a mare to drop her foal. Come inside and get warm."

Mary could hear Bert snicker in the background. She supposed he found it a rare good joke that his enemy Yanling should be in such a fix. Dolly made ready with a few swift motions. She caught up her own horse and was prepared to go before Mary even had time to thaw her fingers.

In spite of the cold, the uneven footing and the doubt of what lay ahead of them, Mary found it pleasant to be travelling down the dark valley with her friend. "Next spring, Dolly, will you ride with me back into the hills? But then we'll have our trees to plant, I suppose."

Dolly's answer was indirect. "You're a pretty girl, Mary, and you ain't very old neither. Are you goin' to spend the rest o' your life there, helpin' out your sister? Seems like you ought to get married."

I tried that, Mary longed to say. And it turned out so badly, so very badly. She would have liked to confide in Dolly, but she could not very well add "Don't tell Bert." And if Bert knew, the whole valley would know. Instead she countered, "Althea and I are in it together. We both inherited it from my father. We're both obliged to make a go of it. Neither one of us could do it alone."

"I hear you," Dolly said. "Say, why don't you go to Muldoons' and keep it warm and comfy for the old man and woman? There's going to be too tarnation many of us in Yanlings' house."

"I'll speak to Althea first." They passed the Hollister place, where Duke whickered, saying plainly that this was his nearest home, after all, and he would settle for it gladly. But when they reached Yanlings' he was delighted to turn in.

Mrs. Yanling's screams filled the house. Mrs. Muldoon sat beside her gripping her hand, and Althea, white-faced, stirred something on the stove. "There, there, now," Mrs. Muldoon said. "My John will bring the doctor, and it will be over soon. You'll have a dear little wee one."

"It's before her time," Yanling kept muttering, as if it were someone's fault.

60

It won't be like this when I . . . but of course, I'll never have a baby, Mary thought. *It's too bad my life is over.*

Dolly moved in at once, and Althea and Yanling took her orders meekly. She put water to heat, found the few baby clothes, and forced a spoonful of whiskey between Mrs. Yanling's lips. Above all she exuded confidence, as if everything was going to be all right. Yanling showed an interest in the whiskey bottle, but Dolly picked it up and carried it away. "No, you don't," she said. "We may need you to hold the baby."

The doctor got there in time. After a glance at the woman on the bed he said to Mrs. Muldoon, "Your husband's resting at my place. He was pretty tuckered. My wife will wait till he wakes and give him some breakfast. He was breathing kind of hoarse." Then he turned his attention to the writhing girl, and felt of her carefully. "Pretty close now," he said. "How are we fixed for clean blankets?" His voice was authoritative and kind.

Mary walked up the road and through the Muldoon orchard to their house to see what she could do. She revived the fire, poked in the cupboard, started to set the table for breakfast. Then she had an even better thought. Why shouldn't Mrs. Muldoon come home with them? and not back to this empty house. She was so sure that this was the right thing to do that she put the dishes back in the cupboard and tenderly took a few toilet things from the dresser. "See," she would say to Mrs. Muldoon, "everything's ready."

Dolly's words kept running through her mind. Now and then, though not as often as at first, she was swept with the frightened feeling that sometime, somehow, she must get away from here. Not for a long time yet of course, not while Althea needed her. But eventually she would go to some large city where she was unknown; she would do settlement work, or learn nursing. Her hair would turn gray prematurely and she would have some beautiful clothes—somehow this always got into Mary's picture of the future—very plain, very ladylike, but beautiful. Velvet gowns with the smallest possible pearls around her neck, and a bunch of violets pinned to her muff.

In her memories of that night everything was jumbled together, pearls and violets and the dark road and the smell of the horses and Dolly's shy voice, the gay red-flannel wrapper they found for Mrs. Muldoon, the stinging cold outside, and the crunch of freeze-hardened snow. But it was important only for two things, it was the night the Yanlings' baby was born and that John Muldoon came down with pneumonia.

The doctor would not let John come home for several weeks. "I want to keep an eye on him," he said. At last he brought John home in his own buggy. The Hollisters had made Mrs. Muldoon stay at their house as much as she was willing, and many a night when the lonely old lady could not sleep, they had beguiled her into telling stories of the days "before the river was open." She and John had come into the country by way of Robbers' Roost and Colockum Pass; they had let their wagon down with ropes. The girls went to the Muldoon place to do the simple winter tasks. They kept their guest fretting in an armchair. But when John came home she rose out of the chair and became a whirlwind. She sat John down where he could look at the orchard and made him bread puddings and hyssop tea, and redded up the house from front to back, and could hardly wait to scratch up a garden for the snap beans John liked.

John Muldoon sat docilely by the front window in his big rawhide seat. He looked gaunt, and he didn't have much strength. He would be all right by the time the spring work started, he said, and Ben Lucas would be back from Oregon and would come and do for him if he needed it. He kept his eyes on his six-year-old trees, due to bloom and bear this year. Already the sap was rising and the twigs glowed as if they had life in them.

4 THE LITTLE brown figures against the foot of the hill looked like people in a Breughel painting. They were two women with their skirts pinned up, and they were digging holes to plant trees.

It was time at last. Following Muldoon's directions, they had driven stakes around the edge of the plowed slope and down the ridge, and crisscrossed the ground with lines made by sighting from the stakes. Along the line of sight they had laid a hundred-foot steel tape, and along the tape they drew furrows. If the grid of lines was not entirely accurate, the trees would never know the difference. They had no level and transit, and would not have known how to use them if they had.

Because the spring rains and the Chinook wind would quickly erase the lines, they drove more stakes at the intersections. They had made stakes out of everything they could lay their hands on. Cedar firewood, the siding from the wrecked old privy, a few spare fence posts that Luther had left against the hill at the far end of the barbed wire—and still there was no end to their need for them. They bought costly mill ends from Bert Plew, and Mary split and sharpened till her back ached. It was work they would have preferred to pay someone to do, but the cost of the operation was beginning to frighten them. *We must learn to plan ahead,* Mary thought a little bitterly, *we could have been working on these stakes all winter.*

The Chinook started to blow in March, and it was like a wind from heaven. Coming in gusts down the canyons, it carried the sweetness of pine forests and raw mountain earth. It melted the snow on the open slopes; little streams coursed down every gully. On the shady side of the hills the snow drifts remained, buttercups and bluebells grew among them, and purple shooting stars clogged the ground around the spring.

The trees were to come in three shipments by steamer. As

63

the nurseryman had suggested, they began digging planting holes a week before the first crate was due. The work was simple, but incredibly hard. Picking out a marker stake, they made a little pit a foot deep, taking turns with the digging. When Althea's breath began to come in gasps, Mary would say "It's my turn now." When Mary's face was scarlet and her shoulders sagged, Althea would take the spade. At the end of each excavation they straightened their backs for a few deep breaths, and regarded it with love and approval, and went on to the next.

On the first day they tried it they only lasted a couple of hours. Sick with fatigue, they crawled to the house and lay down while the sun was still climbing the sky. But as they became inured to the work, and the deadline drew near, they put in longer days and developed a slow, dogged rhythm. They learned to sink down beside each hole and rest for ten or fifteen minutes before starting another. Washing and sweeping and trips to the post office could wait and they snatched meals the best they could. In the morning they built a fire for coffee, but the rest of the time they lived on cold snacks.

When the day came for the first crate to arrive, they rode to the Landing. Breathlessly they watched from their horses as it was put off the boat, and taken in charge by Bert Plew, who delivered it to the Hollister house with his nose in the air. Mary laid into it with the light axe, accurately knocking off a corner. They had bought, not seedlings to be grafted in the fall as many ranchers did, but year-old trees, already grafted to the right variety and healed with wax. As they lifted the first one from its packing of moss, there was reverence in their touch. These were their hope, their resource, their future. To plant them would be more than labor—it would be a deeply symbolic act.

Knowing that the baby trees had begun to wither from the moment they were taken out of the ground and packed, the girls unloaded them into the edge of the stream, where they formed a small militant row, damming one side of the water so that it made new eddies and swirls. The next morning at sunup, they began to set the trees. It was not as hard as digging the holes, but it was slow work. One of them held the tree in place and carefully spread the roots while the other pushed the dirt back in around it. Still scrupulously taking turns, one rested while the other picked up a bucket, walked into the house and filled it at the kitchen faucet, hoisted it out of the sink, carried it dripping to the tree, and poured it over the planting. Sometimes one bucket did not fill the hole. After the tree was gently lifted up and down a few times to settle the roots, they would kneel together and pull and press and firm the soil exactly to the root line. Another trip across the yard, a final bucket of water. The breeze usually died before noonday, and though the air was still cool, they could feel sweat running down under their clothes, and blisters scraping beneath the canvas gloves they wore.

The Muldoon orchard was in bloom for the first time. The six years of waiting were over. The trees, still no higher than a man could reach, were covered with sudden pink and white. The smell of the blossoms drifted out across the road and up the valley. John Muldoon sat in his window and drank the sight with his eyes. He seldom saw the Hollister girls go by on the road, but he knew what they were doing and he took a quiet satisfaction in it. If they were in trouble they would come. So it was a good sign that they never stopped in.

They might have startled him if he had seen them. Mary's cheeks had lost their plumpness, and Althea's eyes looked like two holes burned in a blanket. Their hands and arms were scarred and their fingernails blunted to the quick and they moved slowly, like sleepwalkers. All day they toiled across the slope, or drooped on the front porch till they could get their wind again. Above them on the hills, the wild phlox vanished and rank yellow sunflowers broke out. Pine Creek was running full, its sound was audible day and night. Mrs. Muldoon came up bringing a pot of stew and a couple of jars of jam. She hadn't bothered to saddle, she said, for in the spring she liked to walk. She thought, though John hadn't said so, that he would be glad to know how they were making out.

"We haven't been near you in ages." Althea's face was remorseful. "How is John?"

"Poorly," Mrs. Muldoon said simply. "Now don't you worry for being busy—we understand all about it. We done it together, John and I. I'll tell him your planting looks good, and that'll please him more than anything. You seen our trees in bloom?"

"They're lovely, lovely," Althea breathed. "We can catch a whiff of them up here if the wind is right. Oh, Mrs. Muldoon, it's all worthwhile, isn't it? When your orchard comes into blossom and you're going to have a crop. Will John be up and about soon?"

Mrs. Muldoon shook her head. "He don't eat much, though I try to cosset him. He keeps to his bed."

"Oh *no!*" Mary laid down the torn glove she was trying to catch together with a few quick stitches. "You . . . you do have the doctor, don't you?" Having the doctor involved money, and she didn't want to pry.

"The doctor *likes* John," Mrs. Muldoon reassured her. "He comes real often, considering what a trip it is from Indian Spring. John don't lack for care. But he don't seem to have any gumption. He just wants to set, or some days to just lay there. Well, you girls are over the hump, it looks like. You must come down to dinner as soon as you're through. We'll talk about it in front of John, and even if he don't spark up much, he'll enjoy it."

As Mrs. Muldoon walked down the weed-brightened road she was aware of the creeping approach of summer. In spite of the stone on her heart, she admired the faint green of the hills, the splashes of flowers, the swollen brown creek flecked with foam. Somewhere up the valley a cow whose calf had been taken away bawled faintly on the air. As she came abreast of their own orchard she heard the robins chirping and calling back and forth and she wondered where robins came from when you planted an orchard. You could go for years and nary a robin, but when you raised up an apple tree, and it got to be the right size, the robins were there, building their nests in its branches.

The Miller Boys passed her on the road, dropping into single file on their horses so as not to crowd her off the track. How many people there are that aren't mated, Mrs. Muldoon thought, and what a pity it is. Not that any woman hereabouts would marry a Miller Boy when there were so many to choose from, but somewhere, perhaps, there might be lonely women who would be glad of the chance.

It was too bad, in Mrs. Muldoon's forthright view, to go through life single. As for those silly Hollister girls, who set themselves up to be men, she loved them dearly, but she thought they were very foolish. They could learn something from the robins, Mrs. Muldoon said to herself.

A few petals were beginning to drift down from the apple-blossom branches; they made a faint white circular veil on the ground beneath each tree. Overhead, though it was not yet sun-down, the meat hawks were beginning to hunt. Where there are orchards, robins come—where there are robins, hawks come. Mrs. Muldoon crossed the little bridge over Pine Creek that connected the road with the southwestern half of their ranch and with the ranch house. There was a great deal to tell John; about the Hollister girls and their planting, the Millers and how she thought some women somewhere might be hard up enough for husbands to marry them, about the marmot she had seen sitting upright on a rock ("first one this year, John!"), and the hawks and the swollen creek running between stalks of yellow mullein that were like lighted candles. As she came near the door her footsteps quickened. She called out before she even got in the door. John was lying on his bed that had been moved into the sitting room. He said nothing, but he greeted her with his eyes.

The moon rose late at night in a clear sky, flooding the valley with silver. Down at Yanlings' the dogs barked, and at the Hollisters' Duke stamped restlessly in the lean-to. Mary heard him, though she had slept deeply the first part of the night. The tension was mounting as they raced against time to get the planting done ahead of hot weather, and she and Althea seldom failed to wake before dawn. She sighed, and pushed her pillow into a different shape and drew the covers up more tightly. It must be only one or two in the morning. She must go back to sleep.

The flood of moonlight penetrated every hollow and cranny of the valley, turning the granite rocks on the hill into ghostly castles and bleaching the peeled logs of the Plew corrals. It encouraged a coyote in Conway's woods to give a few long howls and the dogs at Yanlings' answered and Mrs. Yanling opened the door and bade them be quiet, they would wake the baby.

At Muldoon's it fell into a long perfect rectangle through the window onto the sitting room floor. John Muldoon, opening his eyes when the coyote howled, saw it and it came into his mind that it would be pleasant to see the blossoming trees by moonlight. He said softly and with some difficulty, "Mother!"

Mrs. Muldoon, sleeping on a cot nearby, started up instantly. "What is it, John?"

He pointed to his armchair, and made her understand that he wanted to sit there. She saw the moonlight and grasped the idea at once. Throwing her covers back, she helped him sit up and put her shoulder under his outstretched arm and got him to his feet. Together they labored across the room, and she eased him into the chair. Fetching his afghan, she tucked him in and asked, "A cup of coffee, John? A little warm milk?" He shook his head.

The orchard was like something in a dream. The moonlight took all the color out of the petals and they seemed carved from moonstone. Now and then a petal detached itself and floated toward the ground.

She sat beside him on the floor and leaned against his chair, looking out, happy because he was happy. But it was cramped there and finally she moved uncomfortably and he summoned his voice and said, "Go on to bed, Mother. I'm all right."

She obeyed him, crawling back onto the camp cot. Everything was quiet now, and the transfiguring moonlight took the earth to itself. It fell on the soil that John Muldoon loved, on the hills where he had roamed and the pinetrees that had sheltered him. It shaped itself into a shining road, down which he walked as if he were a boy again, strong and upright and glad.

When Mrs. Muldoon started up by daylight and saw him sitting there in the big chair and said quickly, "John, John!" he did not answer.

It seemed as though everyone in Tillicum County had come to John Muldoon's funeral. The crowd overflowed the Reverend Johnson's little church at Indian Spring, and stood around in the yard. It was added to by people passing and stopping to pay their respects to John, or just to satisfy their curiosity. Even folks from Wenatchee and Ellensburg were there, people John had dealt with, serious sunburned men holding their broad hats on their laps as they settled into the pews. It was a day of ripe heat and all the doors were open. Above the sound of the reed organ the clop of hoofs could be heard from the main street, and the voices of roaming small boys engaged in their own important business.

Mary and Althea sat one on each side of the shrunken figure of Mrs. Muldoon and held her hands. All too recently they had themselves known the shape of grief, the incredulity, the heartache that does not yield to reason. ("It was his time to go. . . . He had had a good life.") The words of the funeral service rang familiarly; Althea shaped them with her lips. Today for John Muldoon the Hollisters had put on their heaviest mourning; the clothes in which they had started west a year ago.

A year ago! Mary caught her breath. In a few days they would have an anniversary, and Althea would bake a cake, probably, and put a candle on it.

The pallbearers sat quietly in the front row. She knew none of them except Ben Lucas. Most were elderly, and a few looked prosperous. These would be the smart traders or the earliest settlers, men who had been "first in" at some favorable spot. Their sons and daughters would go outside to school, and marry over on the coast.

> For man walketh in a vain shadow, and disquieteth himself in vain; he heapeth up riches, and cannot tell who should gather them.

To hold back her tears and keep her hands from trembling, Mary looked out the high window at the end of the west wall of the church, which framed a little granite peak above Indian Spring. It was perfectly formed of its outcropping rock and falls

of gravel, as if an artist had painted it. No artist would paint
here. It's too big. Too frightening. Too far away.

> Therefore will we not fear, though the earth be moved, and
> though the hills be carried into the midst of the sea;
>
> Though the waters thereof rage and swell, and though the moun-
> tains shake at the tempest of the same.

The burial was in the little graveyard at Indian Spring. There
was no talk of sending John Muldoon's body to some far-off
family plot. Here he had lived, and here he would remain.
Afterward the Reverend Johnson drove them home, and took
Mrs. Muldoon straight past the empty house to the Hollisters',
where they put her in the rocking chair that by custom had
become hers. They gave the Reverend a bite to eat, and Althea
fussed pleasantly, filling the silence with the rattle of cups.

When he had gone, Mrs. Muldoon burst out suddenly, "I want
to sell. I want to go to my boy in Californy, and never come near
this valley again. . . . He didn't even see the fruit on the trees.
Only the blossom."

"Oh Mrs. Muldoon, we'll miss you so," Mary cried. "Are you
sure you don't want to live here with us, and let us help you
take care of things?"

"I want to go where I won't set eyes on them Yanlings," Mrs.
Muldoon said bitterly. "The boy was always asking us, why
didn't we come there where we could set on his porch, where
life was easy? John didn't *want* it easy."

"No, he didn't," Althea soothed her. "He wanted to do his part."

"There's all kinds of folks . . ." Mrs. Muldoon paused, feeling
for words. "Just people. They're all right and they get along. But
they'll take the soft road instead of the hard one. They'll do you
a favor if it don't hurt them, or if you ask. But they ain't looking
out to see that things go right. John was different. He wasn't
happy unless things went right. For himself and everybody. John
was a *man*." She stopped helplessly, for how could they understand?

"Mrs. Muldoon," Althea said gently, "I'm trying to learn to
make sourdough bread, and it doesn't seem to rise. Do you suppose you could help me?"

Mary wandered out the open door into the back yard. In the peace of late afternoon she could hear the murmur of the pipe sucking water out of the spring box.

A year. A year of stifling heat and searing cold. Of the river out there beyond the rocky gateway falling till it sulked in its bed, and then rising irresistibly till it was again in flood as it had been on the day of their landing. A birth and a death in Pine Creek valley, but nothing happening to Mary Hollister. New planting on the acres below the house, but nothing growing in Mary Hollister's heart.

PART TWO

5   THEY WERE in money trouble, though neither one liked to be the first to talk about it. They made glancing references.

Althea said, "It would have been nice to put siding on the house for next winter, but I don't suppose we can afford it."

Mary thumbed the pages of women's wear in the Catalog. "Here's a pretty blouse, Althea. But I guess we'd better wear out what we have."

Their financing methods were simple. They spent what they felt they must, always believing that this would be the last big investment and then they could economize. The horses, the curtain stuff and paint and window glass, Ben's work, the winter's supplies, the trees from the nursery; after each blow to their bank account they looked at what was left and roughly divided it by six (for the six years it would take the orchard to mature), and believed they could live on it still. They did not have much time to worry, for there was hardly an idle moment now in the day. A network of little ditches had been made across the slope and the water from the spring was being fed judiciously into them. Making the ditches with hoe and shovel had been the summer's first big job. Weeds grew fast in the friendly orchard soil and had to be pulled. They had resupplied themselves, reluctantly, with a few chickens, for Althea's hobby and joy was her baking and she felt lost without eggs for a cake. Besides, they could trade them for milk to the new family on Muldoon's place, who had brought several cows.

Dresses seemed limp and smelly after even a day out in the orchard, and needed constant washing and ironing. They no longer put flounces on their skirts and high collars on their blouses, but ran up work frocks of the simplest pattern and the plainest material. Even Althea stopped worrying about propriety

75

and abandoned her black for shirting stripes. At last, reluctantly, they bought some overalls (made for men, and tight in the wrong places), and wore them for some of the heavy outdoor tasks. They were self-conscious about it, though they need not have been; they were passably good-looking women, and in the rough clothes looked rather like short-legged boys.

On a delicious late July evening, when the water had been distributed into ditches for the night, supper eaten and the dishes washed, and they were sitting thankfully for a few minutes' rest on the front steps, Althea said suddenly, "Six years is a long time."

"I know." Mary's mind had been running so parallel that she picked up the thought instantly. "We're going to run out of money, aren't we, Althea?"

"I suppose so." It was hard for Althea to put the admission into words.

"As far as we know, Arthur hasn't sold the house yet." In this oblique fashion, Mary disposed of the fact that Arthur had said he would be glad to send more money. One Pillage naturally did not apply for a loan to another Pillage who might be short of funds.

"If they would build that railroad," Althea said, "they tell me there would be construction camps every few miles. I'm sure I could cook in one of them."

"Do you remember what Mr. Gillespie told us about teaching school?"

"Yes. But Mary, I'm not sure I could pass an examination. It's been so long, and things change, and there are new subjects. I looked at the books at the schoolhouse. Physiology—whoever heard of teaching children physiology? About their bones, and stomachs, and I don't know what." Althea's taste was offended, and her voice was crisp.

"You know very well, Althea, it would be my business to do it. I was in school for years longer than you, and why? Because you were at home taking care of us. It's my turn now."

"You're only a child," Althea said. "I won't have you out working for wages. I brought you here, and I'm going to look after you." Sometimes her native honesty transcended the creed that they were equal partners, and had both come there of their own free will.

There was a long pause. Then Mary said timidly, "I think I should like it. I really do, Althea."

"You don't know the first thing about it." Althea was fiercely protective. "Oh Mary, surely there's money enough. We can do without a few things."

"We can't put back what we've spent," Mary pointed out gently. "Actually, Althea, I've thought about teaching and I believe it would be fun—if I can get it. I wonder if the school here is taken? I ought to talk to Mr. Harris about it at once."

Mr. Harris lived down on the river and had taken Muldoon's place as chairman of the school board.

"I can't bear the thought that you should work while I stay home. I think it would be horrid." Althea's voice was so near to breaking that Mary said quickly,

"Althea, you can run the place and I can't. I'd be perfectly lost trying to plan and manage. But I *am* bookish, and you know it. Nothing about books scares me. And children don't scare me either. Sometimes at first I . . ." She hadn't ever meant to say this, but she had to make her point. "Once in a good while I used to wish I had stayed with Arthur and Hetty, just because of the children. I loved the children, Althea. I miss them."

It was the first word of regret that had ever passed between them for something they had left behind.

Althea was silent for some time. Finally she said in a slightly altered voice, "I don't doubt you could do it, Mary. And I don't know that I would mind so much if you could get the Pine Creek school, and live right here. I don't want to stay here alone."

"I won't leave you, Althea. I won't let you be alone. But if Pine Creek is the only school I can teach, I'd better speak to Mr. Harris as soon as possible."

"You could ride Duke and stable him at the school." Althea was happy to take refuge in practical details. "Some of the children ride, I notice. And the Deweys bring a load in their buggy—I've seen them on the road. But most of them walk. And if it gets too cold they just close the school, as they did in January."

"You think of everything, don't you, Althea? You'd be right in it with me. You'd help me study for the examinations. I expect I'll have to look very dignified. There's a new way to do your hair. I saw it in the *Household Companion*. It's called a Psyche knot, and it's up on the back of your head. You start with a little roll, and you coil it round and round. It's terribly smart, and very mature looking."

"It would be better to get to work on what's inside your head before we bother with the outside," Althea said austerely.

Five weeks later Mary found herself writing, with her heart in her mouth, answers to long pages of questions on arithmetic, grammar, and other rusty subjects. She had crammed day and night, for her interview with Mr. Harris had been propitious. He had given her the key to the schoolhouse, and said, "Use anything that's in there. It would be a relief to me to get a local girl, somebody that would want to stay on. Every fall we have to take a green girl out of Normal School, lookin' for some little outpost to get a year's experience, and every spring she says no, she won't be back, and takes her teachin' experience and goes som'eres else. I'll hold the job open for you till you see if you can qualify." Washington state history had been her biggest headache. She knew little of it except the fact that Luther Pillage had taken part in it. And things like square root and sentence parsing had faded with the years.

She was again at the Gillespies', for the family had become fond of the sprightly Hollister girls. Nancy Gillespie was going to be married. She showed Mary her hope chest and her little store of housekeeping things. Her father was glum. He would be left alone with the two young boys.

"Mary," Nancy said when they were alone in the roomy upstairs of the old Gillespie house, "do you think I'm doing right to leave? I *do* so love Pete, and I do so want to marry him. But what will Daddy do? He'll have to hire, I suppose, and it won't be the same. He can make the boys mind—too well almost. But he doesn't understand them like I do. Men don't understand each other very well, I often think."

"Of course it's right for you to go. What if you had been a boy too, Nancy? He would have had to get along somehow. Don't throw away your life on other people's children. Not even your brothers. It's very lonely after they grow up."

And you don't have a younger sister who will come home in disgrace, for you to be possessive about when you're middle-aged.

"Well, I'm glad I'm not a boy. Right now especially. You do like my blue willow pattern, don't you, Mary?"

"I'll get you a blue tablecloth to go with it," Mary said recklessly, for she already felt her teaching salary burning in her pocket. Then with a twinge of the superstitious fear of their luck that afflicts all Pillages, she applied herself to relearning the dates of the American colonies.

She squeaked through the exams by the barest of margins. Eyes red-rimmed from lack of sleep, her big straw hat askew on her head, she raced to the Gillespies'. "I passed!" she cried. "I passed! I can get the teaching job! I thought surely when I did that page of square roots and kept getting different answers, that my goose was cooked. But the ones I turned in must have been right."

Nancy hugged her, and Mr. Gillespie said warmly, "There now, Mary, we knew you could do it. It'll all seem simple when you get back in practice. I hope you'll keep a birch rod handy. Some o' those mountain young 'uns are kind of wild."

"I shall rule by kindness," Mary said firmly. "Do you realize," she added with a burst of irrepressible enthusiasm, "all there is in the world of books that's just *waiting* for those little minds to be opened to it? All the great stories, and all about our wonderful country and what's happened here"—she forgot that she had been a little shaky, five weeks before, on some of the things that had happened here—"and we'll make a game of the multiplication table, as Althea used to do with her brothers and sisters. You start saying it and as soon as you make a mistake you're out, and the next one begins. Oh, I'm going to *love* teaching school."

79

"You'll manage," Mr. Gillespie said. "Just remember, they ain't ready for Shakespeare. . . . Does your orchard look good Mary? It's the first summer that tells the story, pretty much. You got any ailing trees?"

"Not as far as I know. Oh, Mr. Gillespie, we never thought we could work so hard! But now the worst is over. I remember Ben saying—that's a handy man we had for a while—that you get a kind of a breather after you plant. I'm going to use my breather to teach. Teaching was your idea, you know, and I can't thank you enough. What would we do without you?"

"Just like I'm goin' to do without Nancy," Mr. Gillespie said dourly, "make out. She's got a good feller—that I'll admit. And it's not as if she was goin' to move clear away somewheres."

"Well, I want you to know we're grateful. Althea keeps saying we mustn't be beholden to anybody. It's such nonsense. Mr. Conway put up our cookstove, Ezra Miller helped us do the chickens, and the Plews loaned us the Catalog and taught us how to order. And Mr. Muldoon . . . Mr. Muldoon was like a father to us. We can't understand why he had to give his life for those no-good Yanlings."

Mr. Gillespie looked curiously at her. "The country's beginning to get under your skin, isn't it, Mary? All those names. Used to be, the only names we heard from you was your kinfolk back East."

The schoolhouse was the only building big enough to hold all, or almost all, of the population of Pine Creek. When Mary had seen it crowded to standing room, she had been impressed with its size. Not only church services and elections were held there, but holiday "entertainments" throughout the year. When she let herself in with Mr. Harris's key, however, and rummaged among the books from which she would have to teach, it had seemed small and dusty. Everything was as it had been the previous spring; sticks of chalk lay in the gutters of the blackboards, the map of the United States sagged to one side, Ralph Waldo Emerson looked disapprovingly down from the back wall. The teacher

80

was also the janitor, and the last one had apparently been in a hurry to leave.

The day before school opened, Mary and Althea rode down with mops and pails in front of them on the saddles, and cleaned and aired the place thoroughly. It was a golden early fall afternoon; the first crop at the Muldoon place was reddening on the trees. Mrs. Muldoon had sold to a family named Scobie. There had been no children at all in Pine Creek valley, but now it suddenly teemed with them. A bouncy girl of fourteen with red hair, several solemn-eyed little boys who wandered at large, and were always in the road, causing Bert Plew to swear profusely as he tried to drive around them with his wagon. There was one there today, squatting in the dust. His blank childish face looked up into theirs, and turned to follow them as they went on past.

"One of your charges, dear," Althea said.

"He looks awfully small. . . . Althea, what will I do if they don't mind me? I'm scared."

"Mary, listen to me." Althea's big-sister voice, the voice Mary had heard throughout her life, sounded firm and reassuring. "You're an able woman. You are well fitted to rule over these children, and their parents if need be, because you know more than all of them put together. That's not especially to your credit since it's not hard to know more than most of the people in Pine Creek. But above all you're a lady, and this is always recognized. You will be a lady no matter what happens, and instinct will tell you what to do. And if you get in a bad spot, go straight to the school board. You have authority, use it. But always as a lady, of course."

Bless the Pillages. They back each other up. "I'll come straight home every day," Mary said, "and tell you my problems. You're wonderful, Althea. I wouldn't have been able to do this if you hadn't remembered the difference between the indicative and the subjunctive."

"Well, now that you've used it in your examinations, you can forget it. The storekeeper's daughter will be a long time just learning not to say 'I done.'"

That had been yesterday. They had laid a fire in the stove

before they left, from the woodpile provided by the school district, and this morning Mary, shivering with cold and excitement, had touched a match to it. The room was comfortably warm now; by midday, she could let the fire go out. A little heat penetrated to the cloakroom, where the water pail with its dipper stood freshly filled.

The children had started arriving early too, rushing upon their fate. The red-haired Scobie girl brought two little brothers; not the one they had seen playing in the road, but older duplicates with their hair newly cut and slicked down with water. After she had got them settled the girl came to Mary's desk. "I would like to be called Florence," she said wistfully. "At home they call me Babe or Flo or Kiddo. Would you please always say Florence, please?"

"Why yes." Mary smiled at her. "Of course I will. What are your brothers' names?" She entered them in the battered book she found in the top drawer, for the Scobies were new. But most of the names of the pupils were already there; in a week she would know them all. There were one or two in almost every grade, and they ranged from Albright to Woczcek. She counted them—thirteen in all. She hoped none of the pupils or their families were superstitious.

And then as the hands of her watch crept toward nine o'clock, the door opened and a gangling figure appeared. It was Olly Miller, grinning a toothy grin.

"Ezra and 'Lias say I should come back to school," he said, squirming his feet in shoes that obviously hurt.

"Aren't you over sixteen?" Mary gave him a dismayed look. He towered above her like a young pine tree.

"Nope, won't be sixteen till April. 'Lias says it's my last chance. He thinks you can larn me if anybody can."

"Very well," Mary said. "You can take that highest desk at the back. What is that in your pocket?"

"My lunch," Olly said. "Cold pone an' hog meat."

"You may put it out in the cloakroom with the rest. Did you bring any books?"

"Yup." From another pocket he disgorged a battered reader. "This here is what I had last time. I didn't get fur in it."

82

"Please take it to your seat," Mary said. "And I think when you speak to me, you'd better say 'No, ma'am' and 'Yes, ma'am.'"

"Yup," Olly said. "Ezra done told me that, but I forgot."

He shambled to the back of the room, and Mary kept her eyes on her watch. At exactly nine o'clock she walked out to the cloakroom and picked up the hand bell. Stepping outside the door, she rang it till it reverberated off the river and the hills. Suddenly she was filled with a wild elation; she had *begun*. No matter how dependent she was on Althea, she was doing this herself. Surely it would be possible—surely it would work out. She rang and rang the bell till the echoes redoubled and clashed, and the children looked at each other in silent wonder.

She need not have worried about discipline. Most of the families in the district took schooling seriously, and expected her to give the little varmints the same strict treatment they got at home. When she heard the smallest pupil whimpering under the window at recess, and went out to find Jeff Porter poking him with a stick, she blazed out at Jeff with eyes and voice so fiercely that he slunk away to the hitching bar and was afraid to come back in the building and she had to go out and get him. The smallest pupil was so young that he did not always remember soon enough to ask to go outside to the boys' toilet on the hill. He was grubby and given to hiccups, but she could not scold him. And the first time that in a panic over some difficulty he put his arms around her neck and hugged her tightly, she felt a rush of tenderness that almost unstrung her.

A few scattered rains had begun, and the smell of wet coats and rubbers drifted in from the cloakroom. Hans Schlogl, who came from a poverty-stricken homestead up on Dutch Hill and who owned no rubbers and not much of a coat, had a loud, explosive cold in the head.

"Fourth grade geography," Mary said, shifting texts and pulling the right one out from beneath a heap. Fourth grade was Rose Lindsay, the storekeeper's daughter. She came up to the front row with her eyes glued to her book, stumbling over Hans' outstretched feet.

"Now, Rose," Mary asked persuasively, "what kind of people do they have in Africa?"

"Black," Rose said after some thought.

"Yes, black people. Negroes. Can you tell me something about how they live?"

"In huts," Rose murmured.

"What kind of huts?"

"Grass." Rose gave this gem of information willingly.

"Grass, or reeds, or the leaves of a beautiful tree called the palm tree. Can you find a picture of a palm tree?"

"Here, Misshollister. Right here." Her finger stabbed the page.

"Good. Now if a native of Africa needs a new house, he doesn't have a carpenter build it as we do. He weaves it himself out of whatever material grows where he lives."

For some reason Rose thought this was funny. She giggled, and several other pupils giggled with her. Mary sighed. It was impossible to keep recitations private. Everyone listened to everything.

"What else do you remember about Africans, Rose?"

"They hunt elephants. And giraffes. And . . ." It came with a sudden rush. "They don't know what is a picture. They think it's real. If you show an African a picture of a tiger, he runs away."

"All right, Rose. Did you color your map? Oh how nice! It's very neatly done."

"But Misshollister . . ."

"Yes, Rose."

"In my book, Egypt is pink. In Mom's Bible it's green. Which is right?"

"It doesn't make any difference really. But I would choose green, I think, because that is the Moslem color. The people of Egypt are Moslems."

"What's a Moslem?"

"Well, a Moslem is . . . They are different than Christians. Most of the people in this country are Christians. It's a different belief."

"What's a belief?"

84

"It's the way you think about God and . . . oh never mind. Tomorrow you can take the next two pages." Rose went back to her seat, and Mary called "Olly Miller!" She did not call him by grade number. Olly did not belong in any grade, nor did he have a wide range of subjects. He was stuck in the first reader.

She felt, rather desperately, that she ought to give Olly all the encouragement she could. This was to be his last schooling, no doubt. What right had she to wish he had not appeared? He was tractable and willing, it was simply that letters eluded him.

"Do you remember this word, Olly?" She stepped to the blackboard, and wrote MAIL. "This is what you get at the post office. What is it?"

"Mail," Olly said proudly.

"Do you see why it's 'mail'?" She sounded out the letters. "Except I, which in this kind of word is silent. Now. If I erase the M, and put a P, what would the word be?"

Olly thought deeply, but nothing came of it.

"PAIL," Mary said unhappily. "I would like to have you memorize that, Olly. Say it over and over to yourself. P. A. I . L. PAIL. Tomorrow I'll ask you again. Can you go back to the first page of the reader now and tell me what it says?"

Partly from recognition, and partly from memory, Olly made a fairly creditable job of the first page, then the second page. When she let him go, he returned to the back of the room and sat mumbling earnestly.

Behind and around the recitations rose the sound of shuffles, coughs, and suppressed hostilities. Now and then an "Ouch!" or the thud of a spitball made Mary look severe and advance upon some sinner. But she was holding her own, she was on top of it. To please Misshollister was the thing to do. At the moment that was all she wanted out of life.

"There's somebody knocking," Rose Lindsay said importantly. She was putting green over pink on Egypt, making it a ghastly mud color. "Shall I see who's there?"

"I'll take care of it." Mary rose and went out through the cloakroom. When she opened the door, Ben Lucas stood on the front platform, his hat in his hand. Bronzed and solemn, he looked all of one piece with the landscape. Mary was barred now all day long from the outdoors; she saw beyond Ben an etching of red sumac that her fingers longed to pick.

"Why, Ben, how nice!" She took a grateful breath of the fresh air. Then as she saw the loaded wagon in the yard, "Oh, you've brought the wood. Are you going to bring it all the time?"

"Yes," Ben muttered. "I have the contract."

"That's wonderful," Mary said. "You're so reliable, Ben. You won't let us freeze I know." Her light brown hair, with the crisp irrepressible life in it that he remembered so well, was pulled away from her face and twisted into a little heap at the upper back of her head. Ben thought it was charming.

A slowly rising tumult behind her caused Mary to turn back toward the interior. "Quiet in there," she called clearly. To Ben she said, "Would you mind if they helped unload the wood? They're so full of energy, it's a godsend if they can do something physical for a few minutes. Sometimes I have them just get up and march around the room. They study better afterwards."

"No, I don't mind," Ben said. "I can tidy it up later." It was not his first experience of the unorthodox Hollister way of doing things. Mary went in and spoke to the children, and a moment later they erupted from the building and fell upon his wagon-load with hoots and cries. They began eagerly to throw it to the ground, and Mary said smiling, "There now. I'll get them to stack it, later—they're perfectly able to. But one thing at a time."

She was really glad to see him, Ben thought; or else kind and gracious as always. Had she missed him at all? Not as much as he had missed her, that was not to be expected.

He had jumped at the opportunity to supply the firewood, telling himself that he was a fool, and remembering that he had resolved to keep away from the Hollisters. But at least, this was legitimate business. It was not asking for favors, or for work. On the contrary there was very little profit in it, and Mr. Harris had been surprised that he was willing to handle it.

Looking down at her bright face and the well-cut lines of the woollen suit she wore, he asked shyly.

"Do you like teaching the school?"

"Oh Ben, I love it. I didn't realize it would be such fun. I get rattled sometimes. It's awful to be the one who is supposed to know everything. But I keep ahead of them somehow."

"I shouldn't think it would be hard for you to keep ahead of a bunch of Pine Creek kids."

"That's what Althea says. But you know, a wrong answer could confuse them, or maybe stay with them forever. And I *don't* understand arithmetic very well. Not as well as Jeff Porter. He's naughty, but he's very sharp."

Lucky Jeff Porter, Ben thought, to have Mary care that he should get the right answers—to have that bright, pure look bent on him daily, encouraging him to learn. "Are you sure you don't want me to rick up the wood after they get through with it?"

"Goodness, no. It'll save me inventing something for them to do. They have these games, you know, Pom-Pom-Pullaway and Prisoner's Base. The way they play them at recess is absolutely brutal. And baseball! Ben, do you know anything about baseball? I have to referee, and I'm completely stumped."

"I'd be glad to come anytime," Ben heard himself saying, "and help what I could. I'm not too good about games, though. My folks kept me pretty busy with the chores."

"Then come and help invent some chores. Anything to let them blow off steam. Children! . . . *children!* It's time to go inside. Jeff! Olly! That will do. No, let Mr. Lucas' team alone. Inside, everybody."

To Ben's amazement, they all came. They straggled, but they came. "Would you like to visit school?" Mary said to Ben, smiling. "Listen to Ellen Dubois tell about the Indians of America? She's one herself, you know. Her father was a trapper at Fort Colville."

"I guess I'd better not," Ben said. "I'll be back next week, though." He had delivered enough wood to last a month, but Mary need not know this. It occurred to him that he did not have to bring such a big load another time.

As his wagon jolted down the grade toward the Landing, and from there took the dusty road upriver, he asked himself what in the world had got into him lately. He thought about gathering the wood on the unclaimed slopes of Beaver Mountain. It cost him nothing—he had always gotten his own firewood there. But the work of cutting and sawing it was hard and lonely. Life was hard and lonely anyhow. It was better to waste his time at the school than to be looking for an ax to sharpen or a pair o pants to patch just to keep from going crazy. He had come bac from the wheat harvest with a little money in his pocket, ar though no Lucas was ever careless with money, he was not in t desperate straits that had sometimes made his first four yea so difficult.

As he turned into his own yard, he saw several men on the railroad right-of-way which made a clean unplanted swat through the orchard. There was nothing wrong with the railroad having some of their men on their own property, if these *were* railroad men—but he thought he would look into it. He put the team away, and walked down through the dry gray soil to his own fence. All of the place was fenced, including the railroad boundary. The right-of-way was enclosed on both sides, in fact, and the orchard began again down below and ran to the river.

The surveying party knew that men must be ready to account for themselves when they are snooping about. As soon as Ben came up, the nearest man pointed to himself, and said, "Great Northern Railroad."

"Oh." Ben allowed himself to lean on the post that held up the barbed wire; there was a knack to it, so that the barbs didn't get your clothes.

"Hear they've discontinued construction," Ben said to the wizened little fellow who had spoken to him. The other men were younger and a little on the dudish side.

"Well, yes. There's a lot of argument about whether this spur will pay. Pay! Why, this whole upriver country is just waiting for a ride on a train."

"I don't know as I'd say that. The boats don't charge much, and they come right to your own piece of riverbank." Ben waved his hand toward the Columbia. "There's a natural highway. I was down in Oregon last winter, I crossed at Astoria. Whole river is plumb full of boats. If a railroad will do the job, why are they building this here Panny-maw Canal?"

The surveyor came to the fence and pulled out a package of ready-made cigarettes. "Smoke?"

Ben shook his head. "Not but what I'd like to see the railroad come. Every piece of land will go up in value the whole length of the river. I never aim to sell, but I like the idea that my place will be worth more."

"Right," the surveyor said. "And up at the top, where they make the *de*-cisions, they're bound to see this thing through. Construction will start again in a few months, and this time they'll stay with it till it's finished. It's a grand sight to see a railroad built. Once they know where they want the trains to run, there's no stopping 'em. If rock's in the way, they blast it. If dirt's in the way, they eat it out with a steam shovel. If they come to a little hole they fill it, and if they come to a big one they build a trestle across."

"Is it really true," Ben said, "that the Great Northern is a Wall Street outfit?"

One of the other men, a towering chap with a neat spade beard, spoke up instantly. "Certainly not. Our headquarters are in St. Paul. The road is operated by James J. Hill, who as you know is a western pioneer of the highest caliber."

"Way I hear it, Jim Hill owns the Great Northern and J. P. Morgan owns Jim Hill. I wish I could get the straight of it. And this trust-busting. Wasn't the Great Northern a party to a railroad trust?"

"The federal government saw fit to forbid us to enter a merger. It would have been for the benefit of all concerned. You're not one of those Socialists, are you? They say the woods are full of them out here."

"I'm just a farmer," Ben said. "I don't mix in politics. But I like to know what's going on. Have you any word of this flying machine? I've seen pictures of it in the papers."

"It's only a toy," the second railroad man said stiffly. "Why, it can hardly carry its own weight. Good for showing off in front of crowds. It'll never amount to anything for transportation."

He nodded toward the third member of his party, a boy in brand-new Levis and a large, carefully creased Stetson hat. "Here's our pipeline to the latest news," he said. "Robert Anthony, our new recruit, who is having his first view of the West. So far, he has not seen along the sky the smoke of a hundred campfires, nor has he slain a buffalo, but he is in close touch with civilization. Tell me, Bob, what is the name of that new dance you were telling us about?"

Robert Anthony's face turned the color of his clean red bandanna neckerchief. "The bunny hug, sir," he said.

The group of three surveyors broke up at Wenatchee and the two older men went on to a project in Montana. Bob Anthony, the green hand, would winter over as baggage smasher at the Wenatchee station. He wanted to stay in the area, he said, and be there when construction started in the spring. His two friends shook their heads.

"A railroad man's gotta learn to be footloose," the wizened litle chap told him. "What's this here locality got that anywhere else hasn't got? I can show you places where the mountains are higher, the women better lookin', and the joints are wide open seven days a week. You oughta try to get around some."

Bob Anthony said he guessed he'd stay where he was. He did not tell them that he had no intention of being a railroad man. There was much he had never told them, in spite of his willingness to share bits of information about the East.

They had insisted on showing him one real good time, anyhow, down below the tracks, before they left, and his head still ached a little from this as he finished his greasy supper at Mel Turner's cafe and started his long nightly walk through the poorly lit streets. Often he came to the end of town, and kept right on going. The apple harvest was at its height, and he strode down quiet roads among orchards where ladders had been left standing. There were piles of boxes among the trees, and the air was sweet with the odor of fruit. After a walk like this, he could sleep, putting his problems out of his mind.

He went briskly along the narrow street that he had come to know well in a few days, past the movie theater, where he had already seen the picture. For no good reason he turned up a hill toward the residence section, liking the feel of the changed pace and the tautened muscles carrying him up the slope.

90

There was a knot of people under a street corner light, around a window from which illumination was pouring. Inside the window a tall fair-haired man was desultorily playing the piano, its notes audible through the plate glass. Across the top of the window a sign said, "How Long Will He Play? Register Your Guess and Win a Superba Genuine Leather Music Roll."

A jolt went through Bob Anthony. His brother Lew had played the piano very well; not professionally, of course, but with a grace and facility that made it pleasing.

Bob came closer, and shouldered his way through the crowd. The man was *not* Lew. After the familiar jolt, the familiar let-down. How many times, halting his step, he had peered under some farmer's hat or into some window or down a counter, thinking he recognized a rangy man with yellowish hair; how many times it could have been Lew, working in his debonair way at some fribbling task! But it was never Lew.

The people on the pavement milled and jostled, restless, inclined to jeer, held by the unfamiliar sight and by the lack of anywhere else to go. "How long's 'e been playing now?" "Fourteen hours." "Nah, 'leven hours." "It says here, fourteen hours." "What I want to know is, how does he . . ." "He's got a tube, stupid." "Wisht I could ask him for "Alexander's Ragtime Band." "Who checks up on him?" "There's always somebody here." "Yeah, like you and me."

The man drifted into "Narcissus," lazily played, barely keeping the keys in motion. Lew had played "Narcissus." It was Lew's kind of music—engaging, wistful. How many times Bob had heard it, floating on the air through their turbulent household; Lew playing for his mother, or playing just for himself, after a row with his father. A year now, since their mother died and Lew had flung himself out of the house for good.

It had been for Bob a hard, instructive, man-making year. He had somehow stayed on terms with his father. His father had mellowed slightly, but not much. Bob had come to understand that the old man could conquer factories and banks, railroads and labor, but not his own stubborn contentious will. His father had been proud, though baffled, when Bob brought home prizes in science and set up a laboratory in the basement. He had gradually accepted the fact that neither of his sons would succeed him in his business. But on his deathbed, furious with his own weakness, autocratic and harsh to the last, old man Anthony had said suddenly to Bob, without preamble, "Find Lew."

"Narcissus" came to a soft, deliberate end. The man at the piano played a few chromatic chords, sliding down from key to key, as if uncertain what else to begin. Poor devil, how his muscles must ache. There was so much money in the world, and for the lack of it—surely for no other reason—people underwent tortures like this. Paid by the hour, probably, on a rising scale for the length of time he held out. Bob's fact-trained mind began coldly to estimate; hunger, fatigue, nervous tension. But while they watched, someone appeared from within the darkened music store, handed a cup of fluid to the pianist, who raised it with his left hand and drank. His right hand kept up a soft spare melody.

"Didja put in your guess as to how long he's goin' to play?"

"Naw, I never win nothin'."

Suddenly sickened, Bob turned away. He realized that he had been standing there for some time, a hick among the hicks, fascinated by the spectacle of human endurance. There was no heart in him for a long walk tonight. He turned back down the hill toward his hotel. A sudden spurt of minor notes followed him, and then, as if revived, the pianist began Cui's "Orientale." It's haunting pain-filled cry lay on the air. Pigs, Bob Anthony thought angrily. There's not a soul there it will get through to. No one is listening really.

"Orientale." His mother in her dark tapestry dress from Worth, the dress he had loved so because its formal beauty was so exactly right for her. Sitting with her eyes shaded by her hand, listening. Lew at the piano, handsome, reckless, no-good Lew, playing so effortlessly and so well. Overplaying a bit, pulling on their heartstrings, the melody too lush, the pauses too breathless. That was Lew.

His hotel room was stuffy and cold. He had doused it thoroughly with disinfectant the night he moved in—God only knew what might be lurking in the woodwork. There was no trace of himself in this room except the military brushes laid at precise angles on the dresser, the heavy outdoor garments hanging in the closet. ("Oh my dear Bobbie, what *clothes!*" his mother would have said.) And the little pile of math books and treatises that bridged him to his other world. They were not much good here; he was out of touch. When this was over, when Lew was found, he would go back to his laboratory. Marconi had carried his wireless telegraphy across the Atlantic. Madame Curie had established the atomic weight of radium. Sir Oliver Lodge was lecturing on the properties of the ether. It was an exciting time to be alive.

He had often told himself that it was not fair to have this search laid on him when he was eighteen. He would be too old to go back to college, and not to finish his training was unthinkable. He had made a show of resistance; he had told his father's lawyer, "I can't go parading out there asking questions of strangers, poking around. From what I hear of the West, they don't like that sort of thing." And old Mr. Pierce had said thoughtfully, "I agree with you, Bobbie. Get a job. Do you good. Where were those last cards of Lew's mailed from?"

It was obvious that the compulsion of old Anthony's authority still rested on them both. "Wenatchee," Bob said. "Chelan, Orondo, Waterville, Pine Creek, and Indian Spring."

"They're building a railroad there," Mr. Pierce had said. "I'll speak to the Great Northern."

Bob had spent the summer kicking his way through the dust, driving stakes, cutting brush. He felt that he had been miserably dealt with, that while his back was turned some one would make a discovery that he might have made. He had been lured away from the cold, dry, beautiful world of fact that he had found for himself; it was a shield against sentimentality, against money-grubbing, and everything that was wrong with the modern world.

He meant to lie awake with his grievances, but he was short of sleep and he did not even hear the sharp voice of the woman in the next room an hour later who complained that this was a long ways to come to Nancy Gillespie's wedding, and certainly not much in the way of accomodations when you got here.

6 "Now OLLY." Mary spoke with forced cheerfulness. She wrote some letters on the blackboard. "P. A. I. L. What does that spell?"

Olly groped among the sticks and circles on the board for some meaning, and memory came to his rescue. "Bucket," he said, pleased.

Mary gave him the encouraging smile that she kept for those who were really making an effort, but it was the end of the day and the smile was a little glassy. "We'll try it again in the morning," she said. "Put your desks in order, everyone. Rose, it's your turn to take down the flag. Fold it correctly, and put it on my desk. All right, children. SCHOOL DISMISSED!" She surged into the coatroom with the mob of them, helping to match up rubbers, quelling a squabble over a lunch kit, helping the littlest pupil into his dirt-encrusted jacket. Then they scattered, most of them scuffing off down the road on foot. The few horses were backed away one by one from the hitching bar, and when Mary came out with her jacket buttoned and a scarf around her head, only Duke was left, twitching with impatience.

Althea had seen to it that Mary's school suit was cut full enough not to look awkward on a horse. Mary wore the same outfit day in, day out, as did her pupils. There was an inkspot on Rose Lindsay's white collar, and Mary looked at this inkspot every morning, longing to make Rose a fresh white collar but afraid of hurting Rose's fragile pride. She found herself involved with her pupils' personal lives at every turn, worrying about Hans Schlogl's chronic cold and Florence Scobie's baffled, adolescent longings. "Oh, Misshollister," Florence would say wistfully, "I don't think I'm ever going to be pretty. My nose is too big. I *hate* my face."

But as Duke climbed the road and struck sparks from the half-

95

buried boulders with his shoes, the peace of the autumn landscape flowed over her. Everything was small and unimportant
beside the great tranquil acceptance of the valley now that
summer was over, that death and transfiguration were in the
wind. The sagebrush stood dry and ghostly beside the road.
Dried sunflower leaves rattled, and furry lichens coated the rock
of the Gateway. Yanling's fields were sere and stubbly, there had
been a touch of frost on the potato patch.

As she came abreast of Yanling's the door of the house flew
open, and Mrs. Yanling burst hurriedly out of it and across the
footbridge. She stopped beside the road and as Mary came alongside, she looked beseechingly up. Duke halted.

"Hello," Mary said. There was a moment's pause.

"Now that I've got you stopped," Mrs. Yanling said breathlessly, "I don't know what to say. I just wanted to pass the time
of day . . . Miss Hollister, would you come in and set awhile? . . .
I'm so lonesome," she added thickly, a sudden uncontrollable cry.

"Why . . . why, I don't see how I can. Althea expects me home.
She'll worry if I don't show up."

"It must be wonderful to have your sister to care and to worry.
I haven't got anybody. Any woman, that is," Mrs. Yanling said
with a deplorable lack of restraint. "Nobody but *him,* and it ain't
the same." Mary had grown used to the local woman's way of
saying *he,* without a name. It was how the women of Pine Creek
referred to their husbands. "Please, Miss Hollister, come in and
visit on me for a few minutes. I want to show you the baby."

A little dazed, Mary turned Duke into the Yanling yard. "This
is a very nice horse you sold us," she said feebly. "I do enjoy
riding him."

Mrs. Yanling, unlike Dolly Plew, was not in the least interested
in the careers of her husband's horses. She threw open the door,
and let her visitor go first; then hurried across the room to put
forward a chair. "I'll make some coffee," she said quickly, going
to the stove.

"Never mind the coffee." Mary was firm. "Althea will have tea
waiting for me at home. I mustn't stay too long. How have you
been, Mrs. Yanling? You look just fine." She was terribly em-

barrassed. "I'm teaching the school, you know. I was lucky to get the job."

"I see you go by everyday," Mrs. Yanling said. "Twice." She sat down at her own kitchen table and rested her elbows on it. "Often and often I've wanted to call to you, or run out and say something. And today I just did. . . . Oh, Miss Hollister, I do long for somebody to talk to. I know people hate us, because of— because of what happened last winter. About Mr. Muldoon. And *he* ain't friendly to folks. Men can get along by theirselves, I guess, or especially if they've got a woman around. But women . . ." She brushed her hair back with a bright childish gesture.

Her appalling candor left Mary helpless. "I'm sure you must be mistaken," were the only words that occurred to her, but having said them, she knew they were false and untrue. "I'm awfully sorry," she added impulsively. "How did . . ." No. She could not ask what had brought the Yanlings to their present pass. Anything reaching backward was better left unsaid. But there was one safe topic. "Do let me see the baby," she said with as much friendliness as she could muster.

Mrs. Yanling went into the second room and came out with a roll of blankets in her arms. The top corner was turned back and as she stooped with her bundle, Mary saw a delicate, tiny face with its eyes closed, a little knuckly hand with the tip of the thumb lightly thrust into a beautiful, small relaxed mouth. Something twisted inside her, as it had when she held the smallest pupil in her arms.

"He sleeps good," Mrs. Yanling said softly.

"Oh, Mrs. Yanling, he's darling, simply darling." Mary was thankful for the warmth with which she could speak. "He's just the sweetest thing I ever saw. How lucky you are to have a son."

"Yes." Mrs. Yanling's voice was sober. "He takes notice of me, if nobody else does." She began to croon tunelessly, rocking back and forth a little from the hips. Even with the baby in her arms, she looked like a whipped child.

"I *must* go," Mary said. "It was very nice of you to ask me in." Why could she think of nothing but these stilted phrases? "Won't you walk up and see us some time? Althea would be pleased I know." She knew that Althea would be nothing of the sort. "I'll see you soon I hope. . . . We'll try to . . ."

As she made her escape, she saw across the yard the humble shape of Yanling bending to some task. He looked at her with indifferent eyes.

"It's our duty to do something," Mary said dejectedly. "'Love thy neighbor.' Oh, Althea, she said all the things one simply doesn't say. It made me feel so queer."

"I know." Althea stirred her tea. The color was back in her face; she had been waiting for Mary at the foot of their road, white, frightened, for Mary was a full half-hour late. The schoolhouse could have burned down, Duke could have run away. After hearing Mary's outpoured story, she shook her head. "She's right, of course—we *are* lucky. Poor thing. Poor thing."

"We'll have to go there sometimes." Mary was resolute. "I will if you will. It might be a good idea to take turns, so we could make it seem more often. Would Dolly help us, do you suppose? She came when the baby was born."

"Yanling and Plew are feuding, you know," Althea said. Warmed by the tea and comforted by Mary's return, she put her feet up on the open door of the oven and toasted them pleasurably. "Would you like a turnover, Mary? Mrs. Scobie gave me some dried apricots. They're not very choice, I'm afraid."

"They're delicious," Mary said, nibbling. "Althea, we can't cut her off from the human race, just for . . . for . . ."

"For perfectly good reasons, which you know as well as I do. But it's not her fault," Althea conceded. "We'll bear it in mind."

Mary saw that if anything were done, she would have to do it herself. Between Althea and the school, she was already spread pretty thin. The shiny new magazines that came in the mail lay unread, and her wedding gift to Nancy, the promised blue tablecloth, was late and awaited hemming.

"Tell me about your day," Althea said. "Any budding genius? Any broken collarbones or mayhem? Has the written word caught up with Olly Miller?"

"I'm afraid not. I hate to send him home to 'Lias and Ezra with nothing gained. I think I'll concentrate on teaching him to write his name. . . . The Dewey children have chicken pox, probably everyone in school will have it. In the meantime the Deweys are not bringing their buggy, and all the youngsters that ride with them are absent, except Ellen Dubois—she walked five miles this morning. She got there late, of course. Ben Lucas came in and fixed the map, the big one that used to sag on one side you know, and I asked him to take Ellen home and told her she'd better wait a few days. I gave her some extra reading, and promised her everything would be just the same when she got back."

"I suppose," Althea said, "the school district pays Ben to look after things like that. Repairs and upkeep."

Mary knew this was not true, but there seemed no reason to make an issue of it. "We've had chicken pox, haven't we, Althea? They say it's hard on grown-ups."

"Indeed we have." Althea drew a deep breath. "You were just a baby. Kate was three, and Hank was five. Mama was already very poorly then. Arthur brought it home from school—things haven't changed much, have they?—and the rest of you all had it together. Poor Papa was so distracted. I'd run through it already when I was little, fortunately, so I could give you sponge baths and keep your temperatures down, and oh dear! you were all so cross, and Kate cried and cried."

Mary let her reminisce. It was good for Althea to remember the days when she was indispensable.

Directly after Thanksgiving she had her first visit from a parent. She had sent messages by the children that fathers and mothers were welcome at the school. But outside of Dolly Plew, who sometimes stopped in for a cup of coffee at noon, and Ben, and Mr. Harris who each month brought her sixty-dollar pay check, no visitors had come. There had been talk of an "entertainment" at Thanksgiving, but apple harvest was late, and in the end it had been decided to postpone all festivities till Christmas. The pupils materialized in the cold mornings out of nowhere; the buggy-load of Deweys pale after their fever, Olly and Hans on their horses, Lem Albright on his mule, Rose Lindsay in her furred boots, and the other walkers and dawdlers from up and down the river, some with chilblains that caused yelps of pain as they held their tingling hands toward the stove. For six and a half hours they were all hers, with their struggles, their discoveries, their transparent lies. In the morning the day stretched ahead interminably, but at night she wondered where it had gone.

One afternoon, however, she heard a wagon in the yard, and discovered on the doorstep a shrunken little woman with apple cheeks and enormous mittens. The resemblance left no doubt; she was looking at Hans Schlogl's mother.

Mrs. Schlogl cast one last glance at her team, standing at the hitching bar with their heads down. She followed Mary in and sat primly on a front seat, folding her hands. Hans shifted and fidgeted at his desk, his face shining with pride and anxiety, but he did not offer to move. He remained in his own rightful place, his seat, his schoolroom, his world, for his mother to look upon.

"You may all rise, children," Mary said. "We are very happy to have a guest today. All right, sit down. Second grade spelling!"

A Dewey and a Scobie were in the second grade; they advanced and put their words on the blackboard in round, trembling script. Mrs. Schlogl watched them absorbedly, her lips moving.

The school was always restive toward the end of the day, but today no one tipped over an inkwell, no one dropped and shattered the chalk, no boy untied a girl's hair ribbon with a tweak as he passed. Mary was proud of them. She sent Jeff Porter out to lower the flag, and said to Mrs. Schlogl. "Won't you stay and talk to me a while? Hans may tidy up the supply closet. He won't mind waiting for you, I'm sure."

Mrs. Schlogl looked helplessly from Mary to the door. Her voice was shy and uncertain. "Hans must go. He has the work at home."

"Then *you* stay a while. Take my chair, won't you, Mrs. Schlogl? I want to talk to you." She put some fresh wood in the stove. "May I warm you up some coffee? I always make it at noon."

"Thank you. No. I must not long stay." She sat gingerly in Mary's swivel chair. Mary fetched a packing box for herself.

"Hansi is a goot boy, *ja?*"

"A *very* good boy," Mary said warmly.

"He teach me the English. But I still do not speak it very goot. I want for mine self the school to see. Hans has tell me how it is beautiful here." She looked admiringly at the polished desks, the tall windows with their curtains of faded monk's cloth, the paper turkeys and Puritans and Horns of Plenty pasted to the window-panes.

Mary was touched. *Beautiful* was not a word she would ever have thought of applying to the Pine Creek school. "We do our best to keep it looking nice. And the children like to decorate it. They made those cutouts."

"Cutouts. Now I understand what is cutouts. Hansi studies goot? He learns much?"

"He studies just fine. He does well in arithmetic. He is good in reading. Grammar is hard for him, but he tries."

"*Ach,* so much to know . . . He plays the games? He is friend with all?"

Mary hesitated. In the caste system of the school, it was the aggressive boys like Jeff Porter and Rudy Scobie who dominated. She thought of Hans' wistful watery eyes, his thin wrists protruding from his sleeves. In the "sides" at recess, Hans was not chosen quite last; he ranked above the small boys and most of the girls. "Yes, I think everyone likes Hans. He's a very quiet boy, Mrs. Schlogl. But he works so hard! I wish everyone studied like Hans."

This brought a soft glow to the face of Hans' mother. Her eyes travelled from dictionary stand to maps to the heap of childish handwriting on Mary's desk. "It is *gemütlich* here . . . You are *Fräulein?* You do not marry?"

"I live with my sister," Mary told her primly. "We are ranchers. We have an apple orchard."

"Ranchers," Mrs. Schlogl said with awe. "Women of ranch-making. That is wonderful. You plow? You drive the horse? You shoot the gun? You are like Brunnhilde."

Mary felt abashed. "You drive the horse yourself," she said.

"Today I drive, because I must the school see. But a long time I wait. The father will not come. And I say I will come, he says no. Always I say I will come, and *endlich* he says yes, go, take the horses, be still. We do not need now for the wheat."

"So now *you* are like Brunnhilde." They laughed, and a sudden communion flowed between them. "I must see the school," Mrs. Schlogl continued, "because next year Hansi does not come. He is big enough to work in the field. The father has said it."

"Oh *no!* Hans mustn't leave school! Why Mrs. Schlogl, he's only eleven."

"Next year he is twelve, and strong. We have *Jünglinge* to feed. Hans must help."

"Hans cannot leave school until he is sixteen, or until he finishes the eighth grade," Mary said sternly. "It is the law."

"Law? *Gesetz?*"

"The law of America. Children must go to school until they are sixteen or graduate. That is five more years, Mrs. Schlogl. Hans can learn a lot in five years."

The light deepened on Mrs. Schlogl's face. "If we take him the school out, *wir sind verhaftet?* We are arrestet, *nein?* We go by the jail maybe?"

"Yes, indeed," Mary said. "First comes the truant officer. He is very severe. He tells you you must send Hans back to school."

"And if we do not send?"

"Then the sheriff comes. The County Sheriff." Mary was not completely sure of her ground here, but certainly *someone* came. "A big man with a gun. He says 'Hans must go to school. If he does not go I will take you to prison.'"

Mrs. Schlogl let out a long, happy sigh. They understood each other perfectly. "I must now go," Mrs. Schlogl glanced out at the gathering dusk. "I must make the supper." Her little rusty black figure gathered itself together. She put the mittens over her gnarled yellow hands. "Thank you," she said. "Thank you, and goodbye. *Lebewohl.* I am very happy to have meet you."

"*Auf wiedersehn,*" Mary said. It was the only German she knew.

She watched the wagon out of the yard. Mrs. Schlogl drove well. She guided the team down the schoolhouse road with care. Mary thought of a saying of her father's, "If you absolutely have to do something, God will show you how." Did Mrs. Schlogl have any inkling of the school law, and had she come to find out? And she had shown no surprise when she heard of the Hollisters' independence; we're common gossip, Mary said to herself.

It had taken courage for Mrs. Schlogl to come; it would take still more courage to tell Hans' father how matters stood. *But she'll do it. Or if she doesn't, I'll go up to Dutch Hill and tell him myself.*

Things were slack at the baggage depot in the winter, and Bob Anthony had a lot of spare time. Mostly he loafed, and flirted harmlessly with the local girls, who batted their eyes at him on the street and sometimes came down to the station in twos and threes on made-up errands. He knew and they knew that they were there to practice their wiles, to tease and be teased, and to entrap him if possible into dates that might lead to something. He always stopped short of actually inviting one of them out. He took weekend walks on the wet frosty hills, and in the evening lounged in a pool hall or the local library, where the librarian was sorry she had so few technical books to lend him. She tried to interest him in Jack London and Zane Grey, but Bob was living too much adventure to need to seek it in books.

He felt that he would have something to tell his grandchildren when the time came. He really did not quite believe in his own grandchildren. But one *had* grandchildren—one told them stories of one's youth in the West.

He never doubted that he would find Lew. There had been discipline in his life, but never failure. In the spring he would follow the railroad line upriver, and the brittle wilderness would close in on him again. Construction camps were being set up at intervals every few miles; he would make his way from one to another, and keep discreetly looking and asking. The area was not big enough to hide Lew indefinitely.

There were loungers at the station, drifting in and out, for Bob Anthony kept the potbellied stove full and was always willing to talk. But there was something about the woman who entered that caused the loungers to stop their joshing, though she was middle-aged and plainly dressed in heavy black that was several years out of style. She was dragging a very large bundle wrapped in burlap and manila rope, and her breath was short and her color high. "I should like to send this Christmas tree east by express," she said in a clear decisive voice, and even the few words held a civilized cadence that was grateful to Bob's ear.

He came out from behind the counter to help her, and hoisted the big package up to the counter. "I thought I'd never get it here," she said, triumph loosening her tongue. But then it never took much to loosen Althea's tongue. "On and off the steamboat—you can imagine."

"The *steamboat?*"

"Yes. It comes in at the dock near here, as you doubtless know. But not very near. And I scarcely trusted a hack to carry it."

"Well, you will trust us, I hope," Bob said. "The express company does the very best it can."

"I'm sure they do. My belief is that it will be quite fresh when it gets there. We cut it only yesterday and stood it in water overnight."

"You cut this tree yourself?"

"My sister cut it," Althea said. "She's really wonderful with an axe."

The loungers exchanged looks; they had all heard of Lizzie Borden.

"Though she thought it was a foolish idea," Althea went on. "I know it's not usual to send a Christmas tree so far. They can be quite easily bought in the backyard of any grocery, as my sister pointed out."

"But how much nicer to have one from the mountains of the West!"

It had been a long time since Althea had met a man who used the word "nicer" unselfconsciously. Her heart warmed toward him. "It is not only from the West, it is from the Pillages' own land, homesteaded by my second cousin, now deceased. We felt that it would bring us a little closer to our own folk, whom we miss very much at the holiday season."

"I understand," Bob said, though there was no one left back

104

East whom he had any reason to miss at the holiday season. "It certainly smells splendid. Do you care to insure it?"

"Well . . . there is no great monetary value involved. Will the recipient know for how much I insured it?"

"I believe not," Bob said. "It will be entirely at your own discretion."

"Then I should like to insure it for a very large sum, to encourage careful handling. Shall we say fifty dollars?" Bob blinked. "If they were to know of it, I would of course reduce the amount, lest they think we put too high a valuation on our efforts. . . . Do you think the knots will hold?" she added anxiously. "I am not very expert at tying things up."

"You did a wonderful job," Bob said. "Wild horses couldn't loosen them." His curiosity got the better of him. "I gather, then, that your sister cut the tree, and you packed it?"

"Quite. . . . I had a hard time convincing her that it would be practical. At first she said we had no good trees, which is not true, though our ranch is on the sunny and less timbered side of the valley. It has a short transverse canyon which we call the Gulch, and we looked there first." Althea unfastened her sealskin cape at the throat, for the room was warm. "The trees were all too small or too crowded to have a good shape. Finally we found one on the edge of the Rock Patch, a wasteland that lies immediately to the northwest of us. Though it was near the dividing line, it was actually on Pillage soil."

"That was very fortunate," Bob said.

"Of course, I am glad to get it off my hands. It has been a labor of love, as you can well realize. Most of all I regretted taking up my sister's time. She teaches the local school and is preparing for an entertainment at Christmas."

"She sounds versatile," Bob said.

Althea's hazel eyes flashed with pleasure. "Mary is a truly remarkable girl. I am very proud of her. She is perhaps not beautiful in the classic sense, but she is attractive. The children in the school are devoted to her, and she will in all probability continue to teach there, a light and ornament to the community. The chairman of our school board, Mr. Harris, is very happy to find a local girl who can qualify for the job; he has had to make do with a series of disaffected young women who could not wait to shake the dust of the region from their feet."

"Will you sign this, please?" Bob said, a little dazed. "And this is your receipt. I will do everything I can to insure its safe and speedy transit."

"You are kind." Althea took a last affectionate look at the burlap bundle. "Now I have shopping to do, for this is probably my last trip out before Christmas. I have commissions from the school, and a coyote trap to buy for the Scobies. I shall go home heavily laden tomorrow. May I wish you a very merry Christmas, young man, and a New Year in which you will find happiness and achievement."

"Why, thank you," Bob said. "The same to you, ma'am." He watched her march out, and then addressed the loungers generally. "All right, you can take those smirks off your faces. Can't any of you slobs move fast enough to open a door for a lady?"

Jeff Porter was making a snow scene. He had brought in some smooth sticks from the syringa bush at the foot of the schoolhouse hill, delighting in their straightness and cleanness. "Ya think these're good for anything?" he had asked Mary offhandedly, hoping that Misshollister might rescue him from the folly of having picked them just because they were pretty. Mary considered them, her head on one side.

"If they were trimmed up," she said, "they'd look quite a lot like logs. Could you build a little log cabin, do you think, Jeff? We could use it to decorate the schoolhouse at Christmas."

That was all he needed to know. For days he had cut and fitted, bringing in fresh sticks each morning and going to the corner where his project stood, as soon as he had done his spelling and his sums, too busy to be mischievous. Mary gave him a shallow box to fill with dirt, smoothed off for a yard, and around his cabin he planted a forest of twigs. When it was done, trying desperately to think of something more to add, he waited till he could get Mary's ear for a few moments and said in a hoarse

106

whisper, "I could rub two pieces of chalk together and it would come down like snow."

She looked into his foxlike face, and thought, *poetry is where you find it.* "I think that would be beautiful, Jeff. I mean, it would be very lifelike. I'll get you a box of chalk from the closet."

His own box of chalk! Jeff felt a foot taller. Rubbing two of the slender pieces together to effect a snowfall took a long time; he would tire of it, but by and by he would go back.

Ben Lucas, dropping by, was interested. "He could get the same results a lot faster with a cupful of flour."

"Now Ben, leave him alone." Mary glanced at Jeff's dreaming face. "It's *his* landscape, and I don't want him to get through any faster. What in the world will I have him do when this is finished?"

Ellen Dubois brought her nativity scene. It was badly worn and had several bits of plaster broken off. She said in her soft Indian voice. "Ma wouldn't never let me bring it to the school before. She thinks you'll take good care of it." It was missionary church art of the most gaudy and pretentious sort. The angels were gilded, the oxen and the asses simpered, and the wise men had a mildly startled look as if, Mary thought, it had suddenly begun to rain and they had forgotten to take down the wash. It would stand on one side of the tree, and Jeff's snowscape on the other. There would be lighted candles on the tree, and popcorn strings, and festoons of colored paper, and the gingerbread men Althea was making.

Christmas is love. Whatever you believe, wherever you are, Christmas is a tidal wave of love for somebody, for everybody, that catches you up and you have to do something. Mary stopped at Yanlings' with a present for the baby. Elsie Yanling's eyes told her she had been a long time coming. She stayed an hour, having warned Althea beforehand, and chatted about everything she could think of, and drank Elsie's bitter coffee, more cups than she wanted.

Christmas is love. She told the school firmly, "Christmas is all over the world, you know, not only here. Some of the things we have for Christmas are gifts from other lands and from very long ago. This manger of Ellen's came from France, and a priest of her faith carried it across the sea and the mountains. Perhaps he hid the Christ child in his robe so it would not be harmed. And in Hans' country, they have a beautiful Christmas. They gave us the Christmas tree, and songs like 'Holy Night.' Hans should be very proud."

Christmas is love. She said to lonely Ben Lucas, "You'll be here to help us, won't you? Those bracket lamps along the wall need to be polished and filled—I've never dared to touch them. And oh, Ben, we can't have anything catch on fire! The bracket lamps, and candles on the tree, and people crowding. We must have buckets of water, and put them where they won't show. Though Olly Miller will be sure to fall into one, no matter what we do. It's just got to be safe here. I'll leave it up to you."

The four Scobie boys were scrubbed to extremity and had on clean corduroys and checkered shirts. Mr. and Mrs. Scobie looked acceptable, Florence thought, in the clothes from the bottom of their trunk; though Mrs. Scobie had not had time to press her own dress at the last moment and it showed deep wrinkles from shoulder to hem. Florence's own dress was new, and it was her Christmas present. It had thousands of silver buttons—well, dozens at least—sewed down the front and along the epaulettes by Mrs. Scobie's hands at midnight. It was dark green stuff with a pleasant sheen and it would last forever. *I musn't grow any more,* Florence thought.

They walked to the school on Christmas Eve in the order in which the Scobies always walked; Florence ahead with Rudy, who carried the lantern, Mom with George, and Pop bringing up the rear with Tom and Archie. Archie was going to be the last, Pop said, but now, from the shape of her mother's figure under the long silk wrinkles, Florence could not be sure. There was a running mumble of talk among them: "Mind the puddles, Flossie, and try to keep in the track." "Them ruts are frozen hard as timber—there ain't no puddles tonight." "Archie, stop bouncing, or Pop will let go your hand." "Ain't the stars bright? You can almost see by 'em." "Rudy, the lantern's smoking—turn it down a little."

The rocky Gateway loomed black in the night. They marched through it, a small stout army. From just below the Gateway they could see the schoolhouse, its windows brilliant squares against the dark, its front stoop lit by Ben Lucas's gas-mantle lamp that shed a vivid blue light over everything. Florence shivered with bliss.

The schoolhouse was not the schoolhouse any more. It was a cave of lights, a Versailles, a Pantheon. The bracket lamps glittered in their sconces and threw a softened, humble look over the face of Ralph Waldo Emerson. The tree towered in glory almost to the ceiling, and in front of it, a spangle at her collar, a red ribbon in her hair, stood Misshollister, for whom Florence would gladly die.

Everything mundane had been hidden; the dictionary stand had a cluster of Oregon grape on it, the blackboards were crisscrossed with streamers of green and red. The place was already full of people, and the Scobies inserted themselves as best they could. Mr. Scobie, leaving the seats to the ladies, hunkered down in a corner and put his great weatherbeaten hands on his knees.

There was another Misshollister, whom Florence knew only by sight. This one got up from the front seat, where she had been bent practically double, and opened a book; and in a clear voice, a little prissy and quite sweet, she began to read "The Night Before Christmas." *Please do, Althea. Oh, Mary, it would be so silly. No, I want you to.*

Florence listened fascinated. Not to the words, but to the flowing voice. A Scobie could never talk like that. Or could she? *Nyah, nyah, Flo's stuck up.* She lost herself in a vision; Florence Scobie, queenly, with a better nose, speaking in a voice like music to a multitude. No, to a lover, who had ridden to find her through unimaginable dangers.

Merry Christmas to all,
And to all a good night.

The applause was tremendous. It made the candle flames waver and stirred the red and green streamers. Althea smiled, blushed,

109

smiled, and sat down in confusion. Orpha Dewey had a coughing spell, and the youngest Woczcek whispered to his mother and had to be taken out.

"Now," Mary said, "we will speak our pieces." Every child had a piece of some sort, rehearsed on Friday afternoons, polished at Thanksgiving, and brought forth at Christmas as his crowning achievement. Sometimes it lasted him more than a year, and Olly Miller was still saying "Thou, Too, Sail On, O Ship of State," which some patient young woman had taught him when he was in sawed-off pants. Mary let him wait, for he knew his recitation well. The little ones must come first, with their stage fright, their inaudible voices, their sighs of relief as they scurried back to their seats.

She did not watch the children; she had heard all they had to say, a hundred times. She watched the parents, and saw around the room, playing like a searchlight, the tension and concern on their faces. Mr. Lindsay, whose troubles with the Hollister girls had taken up quite a bit of his time at the store, saw nothing now except his little slender Rose, standing before them all, her head held proud and high above a clean collar at last.

Hans Schlogl had chosen his own piece. Mary had thrown him a hint, but he thought of it as his own idea. He made his way to the spot in front of the tree, and simply, with no hint of shyness, he began.

> Stille Nacht, heilige Nacht!
> Alles Schläft, einsam wacht
> Nur das traute, hochheilige Paar
> Holder Knabe im lockigen Haar,
> Schlafe in himmlicher Ruh!
> Schlafe in himmlicher Ruh.

Mrs. Schlogl sobbed openly, and Mr. Schlogl, far from Das Land and a stranger, sat behind his handlebar mustache with his arms folded, like a man turned to stone.

7

"IT WAS a great success," Ben said to Mary as he emptied the pails of water and patiently dismantled the tree.

"Oh Ben, I hope so. I do hope so. They're amazing people, aren't they? A year ago this time, I had no idea." She was tearing down streamers, piling them in the wastebasket.

"Better put those away and save them for another year." Ben carefully broke a candle loose from its drippings of red wax.

"I get so *tired* of saving and saving." But she rescued some of the streamers and began to wind them around her fingers. Ben proclaimed, with the air of a man who puts a self-evident thought in the best possible words,

> Use it up; wear it out.
> Make it do, or do without.

"Oh Ben, how *bleak!* Surely there must be better ways to look at life than that. One should create new things, shouldn't one, and not be always concerned with hanging on to the old?"

"Well, my folks didn't have much to create new things with." He left off what he was doing and came over to help her wind. His hands, for all their strength, were dexterous. He made a clean tight roll with no unnecessary motions. Mary watched him admiringly.

"Where are your folks, Ben? And how does it happen you didn't settle near them?"

"Best land was gone. A man's got to have land that will pay back. You put everything into it, you've got to get something out. . . . My family are in Oregon. They got there while the Willamette valley was still open. My pa was just a kid when he came. Things were rough. They had to clear before they could plant, and dig the stumps out of course. There was no market for the timber. They had years of stovewood laid up, and what they couldn't split they piled and burned."

"You don't think things are rough here?"

"Why, no," Ben said, surprised. "We've got roads and steamers and a store. And a post office. The way my family got their letters when they first moved in was by post rider—if he got through."

"Through what?"

"Through the Indians."

"Oh." Mary had forgotten that the Indians could be hostile. From what she had seen of them, they hardly troubled the white man's world any longer, but got along on the fringes of it the best they could.

"My family never had a lot of Indian trouble. My Pa was a peaceable man. He would palaver with 'em in Chinook—all Indians know a little Chinook, no matter what tribe they're from. He told me to leave the Indian graveyard alone, and I meant to do it. But one day I went back in where a creek had cut away a bank, and there were some bones sticking out. I didn't stop to think—I'd discovered something, like a kid will. I gathered 'em up in a box and put it under our front porch."

"Shame on you!" Mary said.

"I was going to study 'em. Show off in school a little. But before I had the chance, a very old man came. He was a 'pig-tail' Indian—had his hair braided down his back. He never bothered my father—he came right to me. He said, 'Memaloose halo kwann, yahka halo moosum. Tenas man kelipi.' The dead man wasn't happy—he couldn't sleep. I was to put the bones back."

"And did you?"

"Well yes, of course. I made a good job of it, and covered them proper. When I was through, I put a cross on it. Wasn't very appropriate, I suppose. He probably wasn't a Christian. But it was all I could think of." A little of the boyhood anxiety of long ago showed in Ben's eyes.

"I think that was fine. But you were on their land. *We* are on their land. It bothers me, Ben."

"It's always been like that," Ben said. "Those that can't defend their land, lose it." Mary looked so downcast, with her bright brown hair escaping from the Psyche knot above her ardent face, that he had a little trouble keeping the thread of his argument. "Maybe it's not right, but it's what happens. It's going pretty far to be sorry you were born because there was injustice and dirty work before you. Do you think the Pilgrim fathers shouldn't have come?"

"I don't know," Mary said honestly. "I've never faced it really. Couldn't we have *bought* the land from the Indians?"

"What makes you think the Indians would have sold their country? Would you?"

"I suppose not. . . . Ben, do you read a great deal?"

"No. My Pa gave me some books. When I left home they gave me the gear for my cabin, and my tools, and my clothes, and my horse. That's enough. It's all they had when they climbed down from their wagons."

"And were you very young when you left?"

"I filed on my homestead the day I was twenty-one."

"And you really do like it here. You aren't sorry you came, I suppose?"

"Of course not. I found it for myself," Ben said reasonably. "Though I had some guidance from my Pa. He said there was good land in these parts."

"You like it better than Oregon?"

"It's *mine*," Ben said.

He finished tucking rolls of crepe paper into a box and went back to stripping the tree. "Your cousin must have felt the same way. He came here on his own, didn't he?"

Mary was pleased that he should have remembered Luther Pillage. It seemed like a long time since the day Ben had come to measure for the plowing. "But Luther failed," she said. "I don't think you intend to fail."

"No ma'am."

Soberly he began to lop branches from the tree with a stout pocket knife and put them one at a time into the stove. The needles burned with a swish and a flare, their smoke puffing out through the cracks like incense. "At home," Mary said softly, "we celebrated Twelfth Night. We took the greens down and burned them. It felt different than any other part of Christmas. Sad, but lovely. Althea always let us sit up late that night and have lots of cocoa. . . . Althea wants to call our place Luthermere. Don't you think that a bit fancy? Such an awfully big name for such a little place. But when Althea sets her heart on something, I don't stand a chance."

"I can imagine," Ben said drily.

She remembered that she must not criticize Althea to outsiders. She had refused Althea's offer of help at the schoolhouse today, with the feeling that Ben was likely to show up, and that somehow he and Althea didn't get on too well, and that the easiest way would be to avoid throwing them together. She was not naturally secretive, but now her life fell into separate compartments, and Ben was part of school. It was surprising how she had come to depend on him. If something was out of order, Ben would fix it. If a crate of books or a few panes of glass were ordered by Mr. Harris and put off at the Landing, Ben would bring them up, and probably read the riot act to the boys who had broken the window that made the new glass necessary. This did not keep him from being popular with the boys; more than once they had dragged him to the playfield to tussle with him. He could handle Olly Miller, and any two of the others, and the fact that they knew it gave an edge to the discipline of which she was so proud.

She looked out at the lowering sky and the light film of snow across the sides of the valley. "If it gets any colder," she said, "we'll have to close the school. Last year it wasn't until near the end of January, and they only lost a week."

"In Oregon, we had school in a log cabin. I made out to finish the eighth grade, though it was a near thing. I expect my brothers are going to high school—there's one close enough now."

"And your sisters too?"

"Most likely." The ghost of a smile touched his usually grave face. "They can all be school teachers and earn a lot of money."

"Ben, how mean of you! I don't earn a lot of money. Just barely enough to keep us going."

His voice was politely impersonal. "You don't have enough capital to see you through, then?"

"We thought we did. Money is the most awful, slippery stuff." Althea would not like her telling him, but it was a relief to talk

114

about it. "There's been just one expense after another. The trees, and the horses, and fixing up the house." She stopped short, remembering that he had been part of the expense.

Ben remembered too. He covered it smoothly. "John Muldoon always said he'd bet his shirt on you to get along. No matter what it took."

"Oh *John!* I do miss him so tremendously."

"I miss him too," Ben said. "He was almost the only friend I had." He poked the smouldering remains of the branches. "We'd best put some water on this, though it's bad for a hot stove to have water poured in it. But it's getting dark out and I don't like to leave any coals. . . ." He took a deep breath. "Mary . . ." It was the first time he had called her by her name, but neither of them noticed it. "You wouldn't let anyone come and help you, I suppose, without pay?"

"*I* would," Mary cried. "But Althea . . ."

"Yes, of course. Well, it's cold out there for the horses. They'll be glad to get moving. You sure you'll be all right on the road?"

"In Pine Creek valley?" Mary looked at him in amazement. "Why, I'm as safe in Pine Creek valley as I am in my own house."

"I think it's time to close down," Mr. Harris said. His woollen cap was pulled over his ears and there was frost from his breath on his high-turned collar. "Last night the temperature took a drop, and it's still going down. I was hoping we'd have an open winter. Some years, it don't get much below freezing, and the roads are passable for those that will take the trouble. My own kids, now, never missed a day when school was in session. When there was need, I brung 'em in the bobsled. So what happens? They're all scattered and gone. Polly's on her husband's wheat farm in the Big Bend. Well, that's natural. Joe's in a sawmill with another fellow. It's all right, I guess. They're making a go of it. An' Pat, he was always an ornery little runt. He's over to Spokane peddling tea an' spice an' like that from door to door, and what d'you think, Miss Hollister, he's going part time to college. The little rascal. He's going to be a horse doctor, he says."

"Why, Mr. Harris!" Mary's face glowed. "Your children are your best crop! Far and away above anything you could raise in your orchard. . . . You want me to close *now?* Today? It seems such a shame."

She had poured him a cup of acrid coffee from the potfull kept on the stove during the noon hour. The children had bolted their lunches and dashed out to play; she had long since given up worrying about their digestions. The room simmered with warmth, papers overflowed from the desks and lay trodden on the floor. "Pick up and tidy up" would be the first order of business when they streamed in. The school was a going concern, and she hated to halt it.

"You only been here some over a year, Miss Hollister. You haven't seen the worst the weather can do. . . . You could get through an' I could get through, no matter how deep it gets, but if anything goes wrong with young'uns, they panic. You got a good feel for young'uns, Miss Hollister, if you think about it, you'll know that's true. We ain't going to lose any kids in a snow drift as long as I'm chairman of the board."

"Yes, it's true," Mary said. "I'll tell them just before they go home. If I tell them after lunch, I won't get a lick of work out of any of them this afternoon. . . . How will I know when to start again? I'll need word from you."

"You won't need word from nobody," Mr. Harris said. "Un-lessen it's the Chinook wind. You lock the place up good and keep the key. I've always got a duplicate, in case of elections and church services. When you wake up some morning and you feel in the air that there's going to be a thaw, you tell it at the store that school is open again. When you smell roots and grass, and your horse whinnies in the barn, you'll know. It might be only that you hear an icicle break and fall, but you'll know."

Ben Lucas went out every morning to a fresh untrampled flat place on the ground, and took a measurement of the snow depth and entered it in a notebook. Everyday the iron-gray sky let out a flutter of powdery white, and everyday the measurement got a little bigger. The snow gradually choked the roads, buried the fence posts up to the first wire, and fell into the shrunken winter streams to be thrown up again in gargoyles of ice.

There were many measurements in the notebook, for Ben liked to know the facts. He had hauled fruit that fall for some of the ranchers, hitching his team to his flatbed wagon, gathering the picked apples out of the orchard and taking them to the packing shed, and thence, wrapped and nailed up, down to the Landing and aboard the boat. He had kept records of how long it took to make each move, and how big a quota per day a man could handle.

After the harvest he had added a haymow to his barn, and done some rock picking along the riverbank where he expected his own boat landing to be. It was good to work in the bright winter sun between snowfalls, at the edge of the river, which was now at its lowest and most favorable for the job. And he could always drop it to do his self-imposed tasks at the schoolhouse.

When the school was closed because of the cold and the deepening snow, he found it out in the simplest way; there was no smoke rising from the chimney as he came up the road. It was only a formality that he tried the locked door, and put his head in at the store to be told what he already knew.

Somehow he did not feel like getting out his books. He checked every foot of his fences, trudging through the snow, watching for a sagging post or a down wire. He took excessive care of his team, currying them when they did not need it, and repaired his harness and polished his saddle. And often he tramped the riverbank or merely sat in the house, whittling or staring out at the charcoal sky and the relentless white waste.

He was obliged to face a fact that he had for a long time concealed from himself; he was gone on Mary Hollister. Completely gone. In love with her, if you wanted to put it that way.

The fact was disastrous. It was out of keeping with his plans, with everything in the hard bundle of beliefs and determinations that was Ben Lucas. He was not in a position to marry. His ranch would not come into bearing for nearly two years, and even then it would be a hard go at first. And when he was ready, Mary was not the kind of a wife for him. He had always supposed he would go back to Oregon, when the time came, and marry into one of the frontier families like his own. His mother would know the girl's mother, the fathers would be neighbors. There would be jollifications, sly jokes—Ben would be the man of the hour. It would all be simple and natural and uncomplicated.

Of this terrible tightening of the heart, this absorption in a woman, in the lift of her head and in the catch in her laughter, he had not had the least idea. He had never known that a man could be bashed senseless like a bird against a windowpane.

He thought about her, not constructively, not with anything particular in mind; he just thought about her. In the morning he opened his eyes to his cold house and rose and put his porridge on, and she was immediately in the world with him. She was somewhere, poking at her hair with her small hand, speaking to someone in those odd words she used.

In an hour and a half, say, he could ride up to her door. *Is there anything special I can do for you, Mary? Well, no, actually nothing much. Can I bring you food? fire? comfort? good talk? No, we have those things. Can I shelter you in my arms? Why, no Ben, I'm afraid not.*

No use to tell himself that they might be in trouble. The Hollisters were often in trouble, but not of a kind that he could help. He had given them his simple store of knowledge long since; how to bank up the house, how to de-ice the slippery paths with wood ashes, how to protect the horses with a windbreak. And they had money, or at least they spent money, whether they had it or not.

Nevertheless he had to see her. The closing of the school had caught him unprepared; it was not as if he had had time to think about it, to take off for Oregon or think of some other scheme. His folks would miss him this year, but it was too late now, it was not travelling weather. He had conveniently forgot that Mary had said, "If it gets any colder, we'll have to close the school." A man in love may be pardoned some lapses of memory and some flaws in his reasoning. He only knew that he was twanging like a fiddle string, and that a few more days of looking out at the snow would drive him daft.

He began to rummage in the box against the wall for his best clothes. It was powerful cold out, but he would wear them anyhow. No Lucas was expected to pay much attention to the seasons, and he had within him something that was better than a furnace.

To keep his team in exercise, he usually rode them alternately, but today he could not remember which one had been out last. He put his saddle on the nigh horse, and gave her a handful of grain to help her hold her own against the cold.

"You're twitchy," Althea said. You can't seem to settle down."

"I'm sorry." Mary stopped to try the effect of a jabot of thin white lawn she was copying from the *Household Companion*. It was true that she was not much interested in it, and that she had gotten up a dozen times to straighten a curtain, glance at the latest letters from Oak Point, or sample Althea's butter rolls which were laid out on the drainboard to cool. "Mr. Harris said to watch for a change in the weather, and I guess it's on my mind."

"I meant you to have a good rest," Althea said. "But all you've done is chop wood, and wash and iron, and fuss with your schoolbooks. My goodness, if you can't take a vacation now, what will you do when summer comes?"

"Work in the orchard, of course." Mary knotted off her thread and held the bit of lawn and lace at arm's length. "It doesn't hang quite like it does in the picture, but it's pretty, isn't it?"

"Quite *as* it does in the picture," Althea said automatically. Mary could not remember a time when Althea had not corrected her grammar, and that of their brothers and sister as long as they were where she could. It was not her fault that she had to concentrate on Mary now.

Mary smiled and nodded; that was automatic too. She did not have a sure instinct for such things. If Althea had not trained her, she would not be so good a teacher. She laid down her work and went to the door for the dozenth time, sniffling.

"It doesn't seem any different," she said. "It looks the same, and it smells the same, and there's no wind. Oh, Althea, who would have supposed it would hang on this long?"

Althea suppressed a hurt pang. She had enjoyed this interlude, it had been wonderful to have Mary at home. They had talked endlessly, looked at their albums. It had been like old times. Surely Mary might have said, *I hate leaving you again.*

"You may as well shut the door." Althea drew her shawl more closely about her.

"No, wait, there's someone coming. A horse just turned in from the road. Why, it's Ben Lucas! How awfully nice of him! He wants to see how we are getting along, I suppose."

"We're getting along fine," Althea said drily. "He wouldn't be looking for work, would he?"

"Althea no! And don't you mention it. Ben is my friend." Mary let the door stand open while the man outside dismounted, threw the rein forward over the horse's head, and came up to the step. "Ben, what fun to see you! Here, I'll fetch a broom for your boots. It's horrid out, isn't it?" He took the broom from her and dashed the snow from his heavy overshoes, certainly something Mary had never thought of requiring at the schoolhouse. He was in Althea's territory now.

"Good afternoon, Ben." Althea eyed him without warmth. He was wearing the same decent suit he had worn at John Muldoon's funeral, with a sweater under the jacket that she judged had been knitted a long time ago by some woman's hands, and a great-coat scruffy with age, which Mary took from him to hang near the stove. Before he let it go, he took something from the pocket.

"Brought you a paperweight," he said shyly to Mary. In his hand he held a water-rounded stone of palest gray-green, the kind that sometimes washed downriver from a different stratum and lay among the granite boulders. "Found this when I was working on my landing."

"Why, Ben, how beautiful! Rock is beautiful, isn't it? Are you sure you don't want to keep this?"

He shook his head. No need to say how he had racked his brain for a gift for her; how flowers were out of season, how bare his house was, how meager his pocketbook. It was enough if she were pleased.

It was not in Althea's nature to be really ungracious to a guest. She waved Ben to the big chair, still called "Luther's chair" though they had almost entirely rebuilt it with their inept fingers. "How have you been, Ben? You must have kept busy this year with orchard work. Your crop is near bearing, isn't it?"

"A year from next fall. I can't hardly believe, looking at the trees so spindling and so far apart, that they'll pick up that much in a year. I recollect what John Muldoon said, 'The time seems to go slower and slower.'"

They were all silent, thinking of how time had stopped for John Muldoon, and the silence threatened to engulf them. You talk to a farmer about crops and the weather, Althea said to herself. We've talked about the crops, and the weather doesn't bear thinking of.

Then she remembered that she had promised her brother Arthur to find out something. "Ben, who is the law in these parts? Who arrests people, I mean, and where do you report trespassing or theft?"

"We go right to our friend Mr. Gillespie, who has been so good to us," Mary said promptly.

Ben considered this. "A lawyer, yes, if it's a question of your boundaries, or something that a court can settle. But there's a certain amount of skullduggery, little stuff—horses run off, fencing stolen. The thing is, you generally know who did it, and if it's big enough to make a fuss about, you go and see the fellow."

"And tell him to give it back?" Althea was amused.

"Well yes. Stands to reason if you tell him you'll settle peaceable, he'll see the light and no more will come of it. The worst that ever happened to me, I got short weight on a side of beef, up in Indian Spring. The next time I went back, I dropped in and mentioned it. He says, 'It's your word against mine.' I says, 'I'm waiting here till you make it right.' After a while he gave me the money."

Mary could see him in her mind's eye; sober, inflexible, reproaching the owner with his presence. She laughed aloud. She explained, "I said something foolish to Mrs. Schlogl. I told her the sheriff would come if they didn't keep Hans in school."

"You certainly do care about those kids," Ben marvelled, neither supporting or contradicting her. "When the railroad is built, I look for things to be more chancy. There'll be a heap of strangers passing back and forth. I'm not really anxious for it to come, but I know it can't be helped. . . . The power of a big outfit like that is something to think about. Hundreds of people working for them, thousands, probably. And everywhere they go, they change lives. They'll change ours. Things won't be the same on this stretch of the river."

"But we can go to Wenatchee in a few hours." Mary said. "And from there to anywhere in the world." Her look was always candid. She gazed at him squarely, unlike most women, and he could look back and not take his eyes from her face with its winter-time pallor, its sweetly-cut mouth. "Do you long to travel, Ben? We don't expect to do it really, but we talk about it a lot. We believe the more one must stay at home, the more one should travel in one's mind. Althea has never decided positively where she would like to go. The South Sea Islands perhaps, or the Pyramids, or Switzerland. But I choose one place always." Her voice softened. "Greece. Always Greece."

There was a brief pause, and feeling that he was expected to, Ben asked, "Why Greece?"

"Because all the beauty of the world is concentrated there. A lifetime would hardly be long enough to enjoy the beauty that is Greece."

She spoke decisively, as if talking to a classroom. Ben wanted to answer her in her own language, but he did not know how. He only said, rather harshly, "I've heard you say it was beautiful here."

"Oh, well . . . yes! There's beauty anywhere, I suppose. One must not undervalue what one has. . . . You're right, Ben, the hills are bare, but they're lovely. I get an overwhelming sense, sometimes, of the flowering earth and the changing seasons." Why in the world, Althea wondered, was she talking to this yokel in such a way?

Ben tried to find words; he was not a wordy man. "I guess," he said, "the prettiest thing I know is a bluebell sprouting up beside a rock, when the snow is hardly off."

Mary rewarded him with a smile, but she was firm. "The beauty of Nature," she said, "is not exactly what I meant. Man-made beauty is purer, since it exists for its own sake."

122

Althea looked from one to the other; she was completely forgotten. It struck her as terribly inappropriate that Mary should be putting her deepest thoughts before Ben Lucas.

"You mean to say," Ben spoke slowly, "that a thing has to be useless to be beautiful?"

Althea could keep silent no longer. "Ben," she said, "would you like to see some of Mary's favorite places? We have Papa's stereopticon, and his slides." She went to the top shelf of the book-cupboard, and took down a box. He noted that though it must have been put away on a high shelf for a long time, no dust fell.

She showed him how to hold the little framework and how to put in the double picture. Before the slide was inserted, the two pictures looked just alike. But when he held the frame to his eyes, they merged, and they had depth. He was astounded. Sure as you were born, one thing was way back there behind another, just as it was in life.

"This is Delphi," Althea said kindly. "All the slides back to this marker are of Greece."

He saw a series of sunlit landscapes, a great deal alike. The buildings were in an incredible state of disrepair, sometimes only stumps along the ground. Mary came to sit near him to explain, to name the beloved names, some of which were vaguely familiar to him from his history reading. Mary's voice in his ear, her hand upon his sleeve occasionally, kept him from really concentrating, but he tried to comment and to praise. He was aware that once, seeing a row of statues that seemed to be lions against the sky, she began to speak and then swallowed hard, and was silent. Then she drew a deep breath and said, "I haven't seen some of these for quite a while. They always move me."

She talks to him as if he were one of us, Althea thought. A deep discomfort grew in her. She might as well have been in another room; they were alone together. She took refuge in housewifery and brought out the butter rolls. She was relieved when the showing ended and Ben began to speak of leaving.

But the stereopticon was a marvellous toy; he was reluctant to lay it down. He tried it wrong side up and peered into its recesses, and finally Mary said laughing, "No Ben, you can't take it apart. If you want to work something over, you might try fixing our coffee grinder. It's stuck and we've been using ready-ground coffee. We don't think it tastes the same."

Watching Ben as he carefully took the screws out of the coffee grinder and put them to one side, Althea thought she had a clue. Of course! Having a connection with the school, he did things for Mary all the time. He was one of her loyal retainers, like good Mr. Harris.

Ben was a worthy sort, really above the run of their neighbors. Perhaps they could do something for him. She and Mary must have a good talk about him as soon as he was gone.

The thaw began before dawn. When they woke, there was a current of air down Pine Creek valley. Up above, at the crest of the foothills, it was blowing a gale. They could hear it striking the great harp of the trees, an ominous and lovely sound.

"Althea, I think it's here. I do believe it's here. I hear wind in the treetops, high up. And Mr. Conway's flume is running full. There's quite a spill of water coming down to the road."

Althea came to look. There were runnels in their own driveway. The bite had gone out of the air, though it still made white clouds out of their breath.

The sun ate at the snow on the slopes, and the road became a quagmire. At evening the thawing slowed and stopped, but before day it began again, like the pulse of a heart.

Mary Hollister did not know whether to laugh or cry. She compromised by singing loudly as she strung new clotheslines from the house to the tree. Mr. Conway, in his cabin against the opposite hill, sighed as he heard her and wished he knew just what had gone wrong between him and the Hollister girls. They were good neighbors still, they spoke civilly, they never encroached their horses on his land. But they were not friendly like at first. He wished he had Laura back. Laura got along good with everybody—except him. But Laura was not coming back, and divorce was expensive, and he shrank from it somehow. So he picked up crumbs of comfort where he could, and in the spring nothing hurt too bad. It was enough to sit on a stump in the

124

sun, and listen to Mary Hollister's voice carolling back from the rocks. She had a mighty fine voice—had taken lessons, he supposed. "My luve is like a red, red rose," Mary Hollister sang, but of course it was just a song. It was well understood that the Hollister women didn't wish to be courted. They intended to stick together and farm their place.

Dolly Plew was of a different opinion. Riding down to the post office, she heard Mary singing, and remembered that she had seen Ben Lucas's horse there, one day, in the dead of winter. *Every woman's entitled to a man. The Lord sent me Plew, and I ain't complainin'. He was like a little game cock in them days, and I thought it was cute. I reckoned as how his rough tongue was the mark of a man. Nobody'll ever come it over Plew, I says to myself. Well, I guess nobody ever has. Least of all me.*

"I figured the thaw would bring you back," Ben said. He had come as soon as he decently could, and the children were hardly settled in. Everyone whispered. Jeff Porter softly kicked his desk, just often enough not to be reprimanded. Muddy overshoes stood in their puddles where they had been taken off. Olly Miller, who had reminded Mary of a young pine tree, fidgeted as if the sap were rising in him.

"We're having a little trouble getting organized," Mary said to Ben. "Rudy, you didn't hand in your sums before we closed, remember? I asked you for them several times. Did you do them?"

"Yes'm." Rudy Scobie's tone implied that it couldn't matter less.

"May I have them, please?"

"I left 'em to home," Rudy said after a moment's hesitation.

"Very well. You may be excused for exactly one hour to go home and get them. I will write a note to your mother." She scribbled on a sheet of paper. It would take Rudy just an hour to walk home and back. He would report that he couldn't find them, and she would say, "Then do them again and hand them in tomorrow." But no one would try that trick again.

Ben quickly found something to do—the front stoop had a

loose board in it. They were used to having him work around, and no one paid him any heed. He went in and out, to the drone of young voices. Florence Scobie read her theme on the "Causes of the War with Spain," and Frankie Dewey, who had never really understood fractions, had a sudden burst of insight and cried perspiringly, "I done it, Misshollister! I done it!"

Ben's chore took him almost until morning recess, but string it out as he might, he was finally forced to say to Mary, "Well, I'll be going."

"They're awfully turbulent today." Mary felt to see that her hair was securely up—a familiar gesture of which she was quite unconscious. "Since you're here, Ben, and if you have time, would you go out with them at recess, and see if you can wear them out a little? They love to have someone join in the games. I often do, but I have a feeling today that I might get trampled to death."

It would have suited him better to stay during recess and talk to her, lure her away from the papers she was eternally correcting. But he went out obediently with the jostling, yelling throng, who swarmed over him and tried to trip him and chose him first when choosing sides began. And after a while she heard his deep delighted laugh ring out; the laugh of someone, she thought, who had never really had a childhood.

8 AT FIRST it was scarcely a noise at all; they could not be sure they heard anything. But it grew vaguely louder, and had a pathetic, sobbing quality like the cry of lost children. Seeing Jeff Porter lift his head, Mary said, "Jeff, what *is* it?"

"Sheep," Jeff told her laconically. "Comin' through on the way to the range."

Mary went to the window and peered down the hill, but she could see nothing.

"They're most likely unloading 'em from the boat at the Landing," Jeff volunteered. "Or they might o' had to drive 'em up from Fraziers'. Boat men don't like the sheep."

Mary returned to her seat. The far-off wavering sound continued; it was unlike anything she had ever heard. At last she said cautiously, "How does it happen we hear sheep, Jeff? I didn't know our neighbors kept any."

"Range is open," Jeff said. Seeing that he was going to be allowed to have his say, he went on expansively. "The gover'ment don't let 'em use the same range except maybe three, four years apart. They eat everything. They clean the ground. It takes time for it to come back. Our range ain't been open for a long while."

Olly Miller raised his hand, and Mary nodded to him. "Six years," Olly Miller said.

"Five years maybe," Jeff contradicted.

"Six years," Olly said flatly. "Ezra went with 'em on their drive."

Mary rapped on the desk with her ruler. "One at a time. Olly, where is the range?"

"Up yander," Olly said simply. "A-hind of us on the ridge. Ezra went a fur piece to get 'em up to summer pasture, an' then he come back. He come down the other side, down the Kwikilat. He was gone about a month."

"Thank you, Olly. Lem and Rudy, we're late with your grammar. Come up and take your places, please. Lem, will you write the first sentence on the board?"

All the late morning the sound grew in volume, and at noon the hardier boys raced down to see the sheep and report that they were at the store, and headed up the Pine Creek road. Mary could see a cloud of dust and hear the continuous heartbroken murmur. When one strident bleat stood out above the rest, she gave up. "Ellen, you may stand at the window and watch. And when they get here, we'll all go outside and look."

No one paid any attention to lessons after that; words were misspelled and the simplest figures went wrong. The hubbub broke over them and through them, and presently Ellen gave a croak and pointed with her finger. Mary did not have time to dismiss—they had her promise that they could go. They streamed for the yard, with Mary close behind.

The sheep were dotted through the green brush. They looked thin and scrubby, and their dirty wool was the color of sackcloth. Behind the vanguard came a broad sea of bobbing backs, washing up against the hill on either side, and half-obscured by dust. At either edge of the flood was a mounted man leading a pack horse, and silent, alert, tireless dogs wove back and forth along the edge of the herd.

Their movement was inexorable, like a flooding sea. Seeing the schoolyard in their path, one of the men on horseback dropped the lead rein of his pack horse and with his dog clearing the way for him, came slowly through the herd and stationed himself at the edge of the yard. Together, man and dog, they divided the flow of the herd around the watching woman and children. The cadence of the bleating never stopped—it filled the valley with a vast mournful cry.

The herder was a small man, grizzled, covered with dust. Quirt in hand, he touched the brim of his hat to Mary and said above the uproar, "I've got to leave you now, ma'am. We got to get 'em through that there opening in the rock. If they start to close in, you and the young'uns had better go inside."

The sheep were refusing the Gateway, the tide of them washing helplessly up the hill. "There's one has got to go first," Jeff said. "The one with the bell." To the children it looked like a spirited game, but Mary watched with some nervousness as the two herders converged at the road, drove and divided, maneuvered and swung back and forth with short, efficient plunges, till suddenly the sheep started through the Gateway like water through a sluice. The volume of sound rose as the wretched creatures jammed and crowded each other and poured down from the hill. The grizzled herder gave orders with his arms. The tall one obeyed them and disappeared through the gap. Shaken, Mary saw the tide of animals diminish and narrow and after a timeless period, suddenly they were gone. Where they had been, stretched a vast desolation; ground nibbled to the quick, churned by a thousand hooves.

Then she thought suddenly, "Althea! There's no way to let her know."

Other ranchers had families to huddle with in danger; other ranchers were old-timers and knew about the passing of sheep. Only Althea, alone and unsuspecting, waited in their path.

"School is out for today," she said to the startled children. "I'm sorry. I must go to my sister."

Althea had been busy that morning. She had made butter, starched their petticoats, planted some nasturtium seeds, and written to Kate, the sister who was in between herself and Mary. Then she had walked down to the Scobies' after fresh milk. It seemed to her that she heard an unusual sound coming from down toward the river, but it might have been a freak of the wind. She had only been home an hour or so when she was startled to see Mary come riding in on Duke, her clothing coated with dust.

They met in the doorway, Althea's eyes full of alarm. Before she could say anything, Mary panted, "It's all right, Althea, it's *all right*. There's a herd of sheep coming this way. I stopped at the Scobies', after you'd been there, and told them to keep the children in. The sheep are . . . oh Althea, I was afraid you'd be scared silly. I mean, they make the weirdest sound, and they walk right over everything. Only the herder comes and holds them back. One of the herders took me around them so I could come home. He was very nice."

"Afraid of sheep? Oh, now really, Mary."

"Wait till you see. They're going up onto the range for the summer." She rattled off all her newly acquired information. "And they're going to spend the night on the Rock Patch. And start the climb up the Plew canyon tomorrow morning. They travel very slowly, like a glacier."

"Well, I'm glad you're home. Will it be safe for us to stand behind our fence and watch?"

"Oh yes. That is, I think so. They handle them very well. Althea, I *hear* them! Or maybe the sound is just ringing in my head."

"We'll go and see," Althea said composedly. She liked to feel that she was on top of any situation, but looking down the valley, seeing the cloud of dust approaching, she said suddenly, "It's just as well you're here. They sound like babies crying, don't they? I wish we had a gate across the bottom of our drive."

"The herders will watch it," Mary said.

Sitting on the steps after supper, they could hear the herd at the Rock Patch, the bleating coming muted but plainly through the gathering dusk. At this distance it was not so overwhelming a sound. Then a look of annoyance crossed Althea's face. "We're not through with them," she said.

Two stolid sheep were nibbling the weeds along the Hollister driveway, their backs turned, their dirty wool gray in the twilight.

Althea marched down and flapped her apron at them. "Shoo!" she said firmly.

It had not the faintest effect; the shabby bodies twitched methodically as the sheep went on grazing.

"This is *too* much." Althea drew back her skirts and kicked one of the sheep squarely on the rump. The creature gave a startled grunt, but went on snuffling in the weeds.

"They're lost sheep," Mary said romantically. "Like in the Bible."

This time Althea did not stop to correct her grammar. "We simply can't have them here. They'd be nothing but a nuisance. How do we get rid of them, Mary?"

"I guess," Mary said, "we tell the herders. It's their responsibility."

Althea looked dubiously up the valley. "I'm not sure I want to tangle with that."

"It's all right if we are on horseback. They don't bother anyone who is mounted, the herder said. They don't really want to bother anyone anyway, but they're rather simpleminded, and don't see very well. He said something funny, he said they reminded him of elderly dowagers."

"Bert Plew thinks all sheepherders are crazy. I should think they well might be. Well, Mary, are we obliged to ride up and let those people know that a couple of their charges have gotten away?"

"It's the only thing I can think of." Mary went in the house to put on her proper-looking riding skirt, and Althea followed. By the time they had changed and saddled, it was quite dark.

The road had dried out from the spring freshets and its entire width from fence to fence had been churned to dust. The feet of their horses padded in it softly. The air was chilly and the dark valley moonless. By the roadside, well up past the beginning of the Rock Patch, they could see the glow of the herders' fire. The ceaseless bleating, a low web of sound, grew perceptibly louder as they approached.

They rode with great dignity up to the fire and paused. Mary could hear one man say under his breath to the other, "Women, by God!" Then the older and smaller of the two, who seemed to be in charge, rose and came forward.

"We have two of your sheep." Althea spoke crisply. "Not intentionally, I assure you. I believe they are strays."

"Oh. Well. Thank you, ma'am. Are they very far from here?"

"The next place down, on the upper side of the road."

"I see. . . . Figured we were losing a few through those fences." The smell of their supper, in cans and pots on the campfire, came pleasantly toward the road. "I'm much obliged to you, ma'am. Though a few sheep more or less don't hardly matter when you're on a drive. But since we've made camp, and aren't real busy . . ." He turned back to the fire. "Go get 'em, Lew."

The other herder rose lazily and went a few feet over to his horse, which was feeding. He spoke to a dog, and man, horse, and dog together came to the road and joined the Hollisters. Together they turned southeast and started down the trace, neither Mary nor Althea holding their reins tightly, for the horses could find the way better than they could.

The stranger spoke to them out of the dark. "I guess you ladies don't know that ranchers usually keep strays from the flocks, and no questions asked. It was honest of you to report them."

"What else would we do with them?" Althea asked.

"Don't you like mutton? It's my impression that the rural diet is rather monotonous. Though no worse than that of a sheepherder. I spend a lot of time thinking about filet mignon and breast of pheasant."

"It was hard enough to cope with chickens. I wouldn't know were to *begin* on a sheep," Althea said. "Do you lose very many?"

"There is a certain attrition. Those that don't go into the homesteader's cook pot are probably relished by the coyotes." They ambled down the road and into their own driveway, and as the house came in sight he spoke again. "Could I trouble you for a drink of water? Driving is thirsty work."

"Why, yes," Althea said. "Please come inside." She opened the door and lit the lamp, and drew him a tumbler of spring water from the tap. He drank it slowly, looking about. In the light he was a tall man, rangy, with a blond beard scrupulously kept.

"This is delicious," he said. His eyes returned to the corner where the makeshift shelves housed their small library. "Books," he said softly. "The last sight one expects to see."

"We haven't very many," Althea said. "We brought them from the East."

"Have you been out here long?"

132

"Actually," Mary told him, "it's less than two years. But so *much* has happened."

"I wonder," the stranger said, "if I might exchange with you." He pulled from his pocket a small very battered volume. The lettering on the cover was almost rubbed away; it said *Virginibus Peurisque*.

"Written," the stranger said, "by someone like myself who was painfully young, and like myself was rather at outs with the world. I have kept it a long time, trying to memorize some turns of phrase that pleased me. I would be glad to leave it with you and take anything you can spare."

"*Do* choose whatever you like," Mary cried, "shouldn't he, Althea?" She knew very well the hunger for a new printed page. "There's some Dickens and Scott and Tolstoi—and Louisa May Alcott—"

A smile flickered across the herder's face. "If I may trade my very small book for a very large one, I would like to take *War and Peace*." He weighed the volume in his hand. "My horse will not approve of my choice, but it should last me through a summer in the mountains."

"Have *you* been out here long?" Althea thought it permissible to ask.

"Too long. And I am afraid, not yet long enough. . . . I have signed on for the summer as the result of an incident in an establishment of a sort with which you ladies are blessedly unfamiliar. I kept my companion from being, as the phrase goes, rolled, and he has given me a job." He tried to stuff the big book in a pocket, and failing, tucked it under his arm. "A thousand thanks," he said. They watched him step out the door and give the dog a few quiet commands, and the dog chivvied the sheep, their dream of freedom ended, down the driveway. The stranger rode back to the open door to lift his hand to them.

"But can you—can you *talk* to your friend?" Mary asked suddenly.

"In the open air at night," the stranger said, "under the stars, all men are much the same."

The new railroad construction camp was about five miles north of Pine Creek. The camp appeared there almost overnight. Fresno drags scraped and leveled, the upriver road was cut off for a few hours, and when the grading crew had finished, the road ran in a new place, under the cliffs. This impressed the natives more than anything else. For years they had built their roads painstakingly with spade and pickax. These people could scoop one out in a day.

Buildings sprang up; a bunk house, an office, a cookshack. On the slope below, facing the river, a cluster of cabins appeared. They each had a front porch, and someone had planted morning-glory vines below the railings. A red touring car halted in front of one of them, and a big man, a little overdressed in tailor-made khakis, helped a pretty woman out of the high front seat.

On her deep-piled coppery hair was a sweeping hat with long curled ostrich plumes of a shade of greenish blue that suited her exactly. She gathered her long skirts into a swirl with a practiced hand, and stepping daintily, walked the length of the planks that had been laid down on the bare ground to reach the porch. They went up the porch steps and into the house.

"This is what they have given us," the man said anxiously. "Will it do, Amie?"

She smiled at him. "Of course it will do. It's much better than some we've had. And after all, my dear Curt, when a man is doing important work, his wife must take what goes with it."

Curtis Loring sat down rather heavily on the only object in sight, a rough sawhorse that had been left standing in the cabin; but rose immediately and offered it to his wife. She shook her head, still smiling. "When will our furniture be here?"

"In less than a week, the camp boss said. Amie, I do hope you will be happy here. It's rather a forlorn-looking place, isn't it? I wish things would work out so that I could settle us in a city. I know it would be much more pleasant for you. But they seem to keep sending me into the field." He sighed. "Always into the field. I'm afraid I'm not brilliant enough,"

"You're doing very nicely," Amie said. "Stop fretting." Her eyes were going over the house, missing no part of it; the walls of upright planks, the square windows facing east and west, the new linoleum thrown down carelessly on the floor. "We'd best have this linoleum tacked down before they move our furniture in."

The house will creak and warp in the winter winds, there will be cracks to fill. The lumber is raw—we will have bedbugs.

"I'll take care of it immediately," Curt said. "We mustn't stay here too long today. It's a long drive back to Wenatchee. But come and see the view from the porch. It's rather special."

They stepped outside. "There is the river," Curt Loring showed her proudly. "Right at our feet. That's quite a river, isn't it?"

Swollen by spring floods, it ran and slithered a few hundred feet away, among rocks which she thought a most odious color. While they watched, a stern-wheeler came around the upper bend, looking very small and white upon the water, and skimmed toward them in a rush of speed that took Amie's breath away. She shivered. "I should not care to ride upon that boat."

"You will never need to. If I am busy, I can always find one of the boys to drive you. I am afraid I am going to be very busy, Amie. Perhaps not at first, but you know how it is when we are building. . . . Really, I admire those steamboats—they are very skillfully operated. I am sorry that we will probably put them out of business. Will you excuse me a moment? I'll tell the camp boss we will take possession as soon as our furniture comes, and I'll speak to him about the linoleum."

Left alone on the porch, Amie looked at the wide valley, the river, the scattered cabins. The section superintendent was to be stationed here; the superintendent's wife would rank her. The superintendent would be along in years, and his wife would be cheery and gray-haired and very proud of the railroad, and would have children married or away at school about whom she would talk constantly. She would say "What a pity you have no children, my dear." Amie would rank most of the other women because her husband was chief engineer of the camp. He would be a chief engineer in the field until he died.

In the meantime she would find her own amusements; she always did. She began to measure the cabin with her eyes. The phonograph could go in there below the east window, with her new records of "Pony Boy" and "Any Rags"?

135

> Any RA-AGS?
> Any bones? Any bottles today?

The bright voice would unwind its tinny length against the silence. A phonograph was wonderful company. She had Red Seal records for the other wives who would come to call, who would listen respectfully while Caruso warbled "O Sole Mio." And she had her own favorites: "Hug me, like you do your cello, When you play that mellow melody." "It ain't agonna rain no more, no more, It ain't agonna rain no more." "Frankie and Johnny were lovers, O my God how they could love." The boys liked these. Every camp had its quota of unattached young men, lonely fellows, nice fellows often, from good families. Surveyors, timekeepers. There had been dozens of them who had thought themselves in love with her—she could not remember how many. She kept nothing; no anguished letter, no lock of hair. It was good for them—it helped them grow up.

Curt came back with an armload of canned goods, a shiny frying pan, and a couple of stoneware crocks. "The cook is just getting set up, and these are things he couldn't find room for. I told him we would eat at the cookshack mostly. He said he was always glad to have the ladies aboard."

Amie put them in the empty kitchen. There was no point in having the cook ship them back. She was accustomed to accepting things as they came.

The big red touring car got under way with a little sputtering and coughing. It crawled up the dusty track among the cabins, and turned onto the main road, scattering people before it. Everyone understood that a horse would stop short before running over you, but a car could not; the driver didn't have that much control over it. Next to his beautiful wife, Curt Loring was proud of his beautiful automobile. In some places the road was almost too narrow for it; Curt handled the turns with care. As for meeting anyone and having to pass, it was very unlikely that in this up-river country they would encounter another car. If they met a team and wagon, the driver of the team would, naturally, back up until he hit a place in the road wide enough for them both.

It had been several days since Ben had appeared at the school-house; there was spring work to do. Mary felt that she needed him to speak to the boys. They had taken to playing in a new place, really not part of the schoolyard but not exactly out of bounds either; a thrust of brown rock against the hillside, just steep enough to be a challenge. The rowdier boys liked to scramble up this rock and hilariously fall back. They were silly with the warm air and drunk with the May sunshine. This was the time, however, when rattlesnakes emerged and sunned themselves on bare rocks. She had warned the boys, but a woman's word was no good outdoors. If Ben told them to keep off, they would keep off.

Perhaps he would drop by after school. She would wait a few minutes and see. There were often things to do after school, and Althea was used to it now. Althea no longer met her with a blanched face if she was a few minutes late.

Everyone had left except Olly Miller; he often dawdled after the rest had gone. She had taught Olly to sign his name, and to read the simplest of signs which might help him through life; "Water" and "Open" and "Closed" and—a real sticker—"No Trespassing." He had continued to grow—he was as big as his brothers. His mighty shoulders and rampant head of black hair towered at the back of the room.

She was glad he felt at home here, but she really must be rid of him—he seemed to get more dilatory every day. "Goodbye, Olly," she said cheerfully, looking around from the blackboard that she was wiping down with a damp cloth.

Olly turned on her a look of anguished indecision. His books were put away, but he sat on, and she turned back to her work. Then she heard him get up and his footsteps came toward her.

"I'm agonna kiss you," Olly Miller said thickly.

She could not believe she heard the words; they were so completely preposterous. She whirled around, with her back to the blackboard, and looked at him incredulously. He towered before her, and put his great arms around her, fumblingly, inexorably. She tried to scream, but all that came was a choking sound. She could feel his breath. He was pitifully awkward, he was searching for her face, and out of instinct she lowered it and turned as far down and away from him as she could, driving her closed eyes into his shirt with its male smell. *Oh where is Ben? Oh Ben, come, come.*

She had no strength against that massive embrace, that pushing head that tried to lift and nuzzle hers. She only stayed as rigid as she could, and waited wordlessly. And as if she had materialized him, she heard Ben's walk, on the stoop, in the coatroom, his gasp as he came through the door. A hand grasped Olly's collar and flung him backward, bruising his back across a desk. A sound came from Ben that she had never heard in her life before, a deep and terrible snarl like a charging bull. He went for Olly and gave him a series of thudding punches, a punch on the head, a punch in the throat. Olly slid off the desk, onto the floor.

"Now git," Ben said. "Your schooling is over." He did not wait to watch Olly pick himself up and head for the door. "Mary, did he . . . are you . . ."

"I'm all right," Mary said. "He scared me, though." She was shivering, and her voice was brittle. Her knot of hair had come unrolled and was hanging down her back.

"The bastard," Ben said. "Oh Mary, Mary. I couldn't put off coming today—something drove me here. What if I hadn't come?"

"Well," Mary's voice was shaking, "I guess . . . I guess he would have kissed me." She sat down carefully on the front seat. Ben knelt beside her, searching her face.

"Was that all? He didn't . . . he didn't try . . ."

"That was all," Mary said reasonably. "He said he was going to k-kiss me. He almost did. . . . I wanted you to come, Ben. I cried for you to come." Her voice was almost back to normal. She was amazed to see Ben's face working. He put his head down on his arms beside her and knelt there, utterly silent. She timidly put a hand out, and laid it on his hair.

After while he said hoarsely, "I'll see you home. Can you ride, Mary? Are you really . . . really . . ."

"I'm perfectly fine," Mary said breathlessly, with a touch of exasperation. It seemed to her that Ben was more shattered than she was. She had needed him, and he had come. It was perfectly simple. "Of course I can ride. And you don't have to see me home." She really wished he would, but there was propriety to think of.

Everyone in Pine Creek valley would see them. And what would Althea say?

"I'll see you home," Ben repeated. He got up and very gently helped her to her feet, and made himself let go of her hand. That little hand, so warm in his—he had thought of it so many times when he could not sleep at night.

The fire in the stove was out, the inkwells were closed. Ben checked methodically, while Mary did something quick and feminine to her hair. They left the schoolhouse together, and walked over to their horses. Mary's horse was on the right. They walked in between the two animals, so that he could wait while she mounted, and for a moment they stood and faced each other. He wanted desperately to reach out, to gather her close, but he would not repeat the violence that had just been practiced upon her. He laid his hand on Duke's neck to still him while she put a foot in the stirrup and swung into the saddle, and then he put up both their reins and got on his own horse.

As they rode, the heat, not yet fiery with summer, shimmered off the hills. The creek bed was green, and in the Scobie orchard the last petal had fallen. They paced side by side in silence; a meadowlark, clear and jubilant, trilled in Conway's field.

There seemed nothing to say; anything of which they might have spoken was too big to tackle, or too small to matter. It was not until they had reached the Hollister turnoff that Ben said, still in that roughened voice, "Mary, I've got to talk to you."

"Wait here," Mary said. She would always wonder afterward, with astonishment, how she had been able to take matters into her own hands so suddenly. "We'll ride on up to the Rock Patch. I'll tell Althea." Going briefly up the drive and to the door, she stuck her head inside. "Ben Lucas is here. I want to show him where they drove the sheep. He thinks of running a few himself." Without waiting for an answer, she turned away and rejoined Ben at the road. She had never known herself capable of such duplicity.

They rode on up the valley. It was like a journey in a dream. The cliffs of the Rock Patch looked warm and kindly in the sun. The remains of the sheep camp still showed beside the road, a charred heap among freshly blackened stones.

They found a patch of turf lightly scattered with fallen rock, among which the horses could pick their way. Turning aside here, they rode toward the cliffs, and in the shadow of an old and twisted pine tree they paused, still as if in a dream, and dismounted. And suddenly Ben knew that he need not wait any longer.

Their time was on them; they could not help it now. They moved toward each other and clung, and kissed and clung. He pulled her toward him till their bodies met and crushed; they felt each other's heartbeat. She was so warm, so exact of shape, so tangible, so headily sweet and fragrant. He had kissed girls before, and they had evaded or giggled or held their lips somehow self-consciously so you knew they knew what was going on. Mary gave him back his kiss wholly, willingly, so that he drowned in it, so that the whole world was Mary.

Somehow, the next thing he knew, they were sitting on a flat rock, and he was holding Mary's hand. Realization came to them both at once. Mary had read a story long ago in which a girl was called La Descarada—the Shameless One. *She* was La Descarada. He had not asked her to be his wife; he had not led up to this in any proper way. She knew what she must tell him, even if he had, but she had not waited for a declaration. She had kissed him, and she had a very strong impulse to do it again.

As for Ben, he was aghast at what he had done. He found his voice, though it still sounded queer to him. "Mary. Oh Mary." He knew there were words like dear, and sweetheart, and darling, but he could not readily bend his tongue to them—it would take time. "What are we going to do? I can't get married till my orchard starts to bear. I've got absolutely nothing. I work out by the day. But Mary, I love you. I do love you terribly. Oh Mary, you are so wonderful. I love you, I can't stand it not to see you and be with you." He ended as he had begun. "What are we going to do?"

It was time to tell him now. She made her voice as dry and impersonal as she could. "I can't get married either, Ben. I'm a divorced woman."

There was a pause so long that the shadow of the pine tree crept further away from their feet. The meadowlark cried and cried again, and there was some kind of rustling in the woods behind them. Wasn't he going to say *anything*? Anything at all?

At last he cleared his throat. "I think you'd better tell me about it." She found that he had let go of her hand. He shifted from the rock to the ground, where he could look up into her face.

Somehow it seemed that she was prepared for this. She must have known that she would have to tell Ben some day. The words were arranged in her mind. It hurt to say them, but they came readily. There was so little to tell. It seemed so remote now; her elopement, her father's shock, Althea's pain, her own stupidity and innocence, the discovery that he was not the kind of person she had thought. Anyone should have known, she supposed. He came from the town's famous old family, he was used to having what he wanted. He was cruel, and she had learned to fear him. At last she had gone humbly home, asking for asylum. That was all.

And then the flight from the small town, where everybody knew. "That's why I'm here," Mary ended simply. "I wanted to get away."

Again he was silent for a time, but finally he said, "You *must* have been wronged, Mary. . . . I don't know anything about divorce. Maybe we don't have it in Oregon. I never ran into it before. But . . . but anyone who knows you would take for granted you could not be at fault." His words were formal, his voice was a shade stiff. This was Ben who had said he loved her, who had punched Olly Miller black-and-blue for daring to lay a hand on her. Why was he not as hotly resentful that someone had laid a hand on her long ago?

Something prompted her to say, "At least, some good came of it. I'm here." She tried a smile, not very successfully.

Ben did not smile back. He said, "Mary, I must take you home. We must both have time to think. I wish . . . I wish you . . . I ought to want you to hate me, but oh, Mary, please don't. Think the best of me you can. I ought to be sorry that we . . . but I love you so much. If you want to forget about it, I'll try to let you. I'll stay away from the school if you want. If I can."

She looked at him in complete bewilderment. "Stay away? You mean you take it all back?"

"No," Ben said desperately, "I don't take it back. But it would be better I guess if I just left things lay. I'll try not to bother you, Mary."

He led her horse over for her to mount once more. The sun had dipped behind the high hill to the west; sunset was always early in Pine Creek valley. They rode back soberly, mutely. Nothing was settled. The memory of their caresses burned in Mary's veins, but she refused to think about it. La Descarada.

He left her at her own gate. The magic had gone out of the afternoon. She was unbearably tired. She greeted Althea, and went to her cot and lay down. Althea, baffled, unsaddled Duke and put him away.

They had said nothing about arriving early at school, but when Mary restlessly bolted her breakfast and threw on her clothes and reached the schoolhouse half an hour ahead of time, Ben's horse was already there. He was waiting for her inside. At the sight of him, at the tremendous joy that washed through her, she knew that she was lost, lost, that she would not give him up now.

Ben had something to say. He held himself stiffly, and his eyes were dark with distress and hunger. "Mary, can we be promised? I haven't any right to ask it, with things the way they are. I don't know how long it would be. It's just that if I . . . if I had something to go on . . ."

She had no idea how to answer this proposal, if it was a proposal. She only looked at him. Her faith in him was plain on her face.

"I guess I hadn't better try to bind you," Ben said miserably. "But I love you, Mary, I've fought it for a long time, but I love you."

So he had fought it! She did not know whether she resented this or pitied him or wanted to reassure him or merely needed to be in his arms again. But she made a small motion toward him and it was enough. The clock ticked away on the schoolroom wall while he held her, wrapped her securely, his lips upon her parted lips, her eyelids, her hair. The school day was coming nearer every moment, there were voices in the yard.

"We mustn't do this," Mary said breathlessly, having done it. "Ben, everything will be all right. It *has* to be. . . . Come back and ride home with me, if you want. Now run, run. I can't face these children if you don't. Hurry."

Misshollister was very gay that day; her voice lilted over the multiplication table, and when Jeff Porter said the tibia and fibula were rivers in Europe, she merely laughed. Florence Scobie would graduate this year, and Mary was getting her ready for state examinations. It seemed to Florence that she was going to be exiled from the only place she had ever loved. She cried quietly into her history book, and Misshollister came and hugged her and gave her a clean handkerchief.

9

IT BECAME apparent to Althea very quickly that kindness and tact were not going to solve the Ben Lucas problem. He rode home now with Mary every school day, leaving her at the foot of the driveway with a grave lift of his hat. How much more Mary saw of him than this, she could not tell of course, but she feared it was a great deal.

And Mary would not talk. To Althea's mild surprise that they had stayed so long up at the Rock Patch that day, Mary had said tersely that Olly Miller had misbehaved at school, Ben had given him a licking, and they had both wanted to go for a ride and take their minds off it. She did not say what Olly Miller had done, but on that point, at least, Althea was not to be left long in the dark.

Olly came dejectedly to their door one day just before supper. Though the Miller place was up and across from the Rock Patch and he could very easily have walked over, he had the inevitable horse with its dangling rein. Even more than the other Pine Creekers, the Miller Boys seemed to be part and parcel of a horse.

Mary was the one to open the door. She flinched a little when she saw him, but she said, "Hello, Olly."

"I done a terrible thing," Olly mumbled. "Misshollister, I want you to excuse me, please. 'Lias an' Ezra say I done a terrible thing an' after Ben whaled me, they whaled me some more. I should oughta learn somepin' from it, 'Lias said, like when the fireplace fell down on me."

In spite of herself, a smile twitched at Mary's mouth.

"I want to be forgave, an' I want to come back to school," Olly said. "I do want to come, Misshollister. Just till the end o' the year. You learned me more than anybody, like 'Lias an' Ezra

145

said you would. I ain't through yet with them signs. Please, Misshollister."

"I don't know what Mr. Lucas would think," Mary told him primly.

"I'll ask him." Olly snatched at this encouragement. "I'll go down an' ask him now, an' if he says I kin come back, kin I come back, Misshollister?"

"Why, I suppose so," Mary said. She felt that Ben's judgment was almost infallible, and she really held no grudge against Olly now, in the light of what he had caused to happen. If Ben thought she could manage Olly, she could manage him.

"I'll ask Ben would it be all right," Olly repeated. He raised his right hand solemnly. "An' I swear to God, Misshollister, I'll never try to kiss you again."

He was off down the road in a clatter of hoofbeats. She turned to meet Althea's eyes.

"So *that* was it. Oh Mary, how dreadful! I don't think you ought to have him back at any price."

"Olly's not really wicked," Mary said defensively. "He just hasn't had any bringing up." There was so much she could not say; it's spring, I am in love, men and women were meant for love, Olly is only human, I understand everything, the world is mine. She hummed a little tune as she put supper on the table. Jeff Porter had shown her how to whistle, delighted to teach Misshollister something. But she never whistled in front of Althea; it was not ladylike.

Olly Miller made excellent time on his way to Ben's place. He knew every foot of the Pine Creek trails, and he took a short-cut around the hill above the Gateway that brought him down a dry canyon below Ben's ranch. He got there just as Ben was putting away his supper dishes.

Ben was surprised to see him. Very few people travelled around the valley after sundown. He noted that Olly had the remains of a black eye, and a few abrasions here and there. But he found that he was not angry at Olly any longer. Perhaps, like Mary, he was obscurely grateful.

Olly began at once. "I ast Misshollister if I could come back to school an' she says it would be all right with her if it was all

146

right with you. Honest, I wisht I could, Ben, sir." The last word would have amazed Mary, who had never managed to teach Olly to say *ma'am* to her in all these months. But Ben was, in Olly's eyes, far above the ordinary fellow; he could wrestle, he could shoot, he could buck a tree, he was absolutely honest, he was a man's man. "If you say I can go back to school, I'll act good. Real good."

Ben considered him. It did not seem strange to either of them that Mary had given Ben the say.

"I never did wanta go to school before," Olly pressed his case humbly. "But now I got started so good, I wanta stay till the end o' the year. It's only a few weeks. I'd allus remember I was kicked out, and I'd allus figure I was no good."

This seemed to Ben to make sense. "If Miss Hollister wants you, you can go." He did not offer any stipulations; he put Olly on his honor. "You can tell her I said so. . . . How are you boys making out, Olly? I hear the game is getting scarce."

"You gotta know where to look," Olly said eagerly. "I'll take you hunting, Ben, any time you wanta go. We gen'rally go up south along the ridge, not too close to Bert Plew's. Bert an' us has kind of got it divided up between us. There ain't nobody else left, much, that lives off the kentry. Ezra says the day we gotta plant crops, he's gonna leave for Alaska. If you was me, Ben, would you go with him? Or would you stay here an' try to git along? I don't know how to work in the sawmills, an' like that."

"Why, now that you've had some schooling, I should think you could get along here." It was a deadpan joke, the only kind Ben ever made, but Olly thought it was terrific; he threw back his head and roared. As he climbed into his saddle, he gave further proof of his acumen. "If I'd o' knowed you was her feller," he said, "I never woulda tried it."

Once before, Althea remembered, there had been a time when Mary had withdrawn like this. The years had not erased the memory of it, of how it had hurt and how terrible the consequences had been.

147

She must speak to Mary, she had no choice. She dreaded it and put it off from day to day. Althea had won from her brothers and sisters some of the responsive love that mothers live for; it had filled her life from the time she was fourteen, and one by one they had outgrown it and gone their separate ways. Only Mary had been given back to her, only Mary was still her child.

But there had been that time when Mary had drawn away. Taking these thoughts out of a compartment where she would have preferred not to look, Althea evaluated them soberly. She knew this change in Mary. It could only be a man; it could only be Ben Lucas.

Ben was well enough, no doubt. He was knowledgeable and useful, he worked hard, he did not drink or smoke, his speech had some traces of gentility.

But for *Mary!*

It was impossible; that was all there was to it. She made up her mind to talk to Mary, and decided when she would do so—on Friday after school, when they would have the weekend to mull things over.

In the meantime she tended the irrigation system, and began the summer weeding with a hoe. As fast as she undercut the milk-weed and the China lettuce and threw them away, and left a clean orchard floor behind, they began to prickle up again with new growth. The whole orchard ought to be harrowed with a team, but she did not want to spend the money.

When Mary came unsuspectingly home on Friday, telling Ben goodbye at the road, Althea was taut and nervous. As they went through familiar motions, Mary changing to a housedress and Althea stoking the fire for tea, Althea said as casually as she could, "You're seeing a lot of Ben Lucas, aren't you, Mary?"

Mary paused and lifted her head, like a deer at the sound of a distant shot. "Why yes, I am."

Bless her honesty, Althea thought; but she won't open up. I'll have to get it out of her bit by bit.

"Is Ben in love with you, do you think?"

"Yes. Yes, Ben is in love with me." The timbre of Mary's voice warned Althea that she must be careful.

"I suppose that's natural." She ventured to add lightly, "Olly Miller is in love with you too, no doubt."

"There's no comparison," Mary said dangerously.

"Well," Althea sought for familiar ground, "this country is full of lonely men. We know that. It's a pity, but it can't be helped. There's only one thing I'm afraid of, Mary. You're very tender-hearted. You hate to hurt people."

"Ben isn't people." Mary took her stand. "Ben is . . . Ben is . . ."

Althea abandoned any notion of being trivial. Her voice came out strained and chill in spite of herself. "Don't be impetuous, Mary. *Remember*."

It was the wrong thing to say and she knew it at once. Mary began to cry. "Do you think I'm not remembering? Do you think I don't *know*? I promised myself I'd never look at another man. I can't help it, Althea. I just can't help it."

"Have you . . ." Althea felt herself completely at sea. "Have you and Ben talked of marriage?"

"Some." Mary wiped her eyes. "I told him I couldn't. I guess I didn't even wait for him to ask me. I told him about my being . . . about Albert." The name, so long unheard, caused both sisters to wince. "Ben *can't* marry. He has to wait until his orchard grows up."

"So of course he hasn't proposed to you." Althea did her very best to make it kind, to take the edge from her voice. The effort tightened her body and brought a fine mist to her forehead.

"Yes. No . . . I don't know exactly. . . . Whatever Ben has said is honorable. He respects me, Althea." She knew this was true, in spite of the fact that she had let him kiss her.

Althea moved uncomfortably. "I think you should have told me this before."

"But there's nothing to tell. Nothing has happened. I suppose I should have had him call on me on Saturday nights, or something like that. But I didn't want people to talk. There hasn't been anything . . . anything . . ."

"Formal." Althea supplied the word.

"Yes. You do understand, don't you, Althea? Ben's not courting me. He can't." A tremulous smile came to Mary's lips. "I don't think Ben wanted this, any more than I do. If Ben were courting me, he'd have come to you straight off. He's so *decent*, Althea. And so strong, and so good. And so reliable." This word, once applied to Ben the hired man, now came readily to her lips to describe Ben the lover, and Althea shuddered.

"Well, I think he had better come to see me now. I think Ben and I had better have a talk." Her tone was as mild as she could make it, but Mary took fright instantly.

"There's nothing to talk about. I've told him, Althea. I've told him I can't leave you. That we have our plans, and all that. He knows how it is."

"Mary," Althea said sternly, "what kind of an ogre do you think I am? Do you think I'd hold you to anything, for one moment, if it wasn't for your own good? I can't have you talking like that. Don't think of *me*. Don't blame it on me. Please don't."

"Althea," Mary took a deep breath, "I'm not so changeable as all that. This place comes before everything, it always has. Since we decided to take it." She must be very careful what she said. She could hurt Althea so badly. "I answered your questions because it was only right that I should. But I'm not trying to get away. We'll go on as we have, and . . . and Ben will do the best he can."

"If there is a reason why you shouldn't marry Ben," Althea found herself saying distinctly, "it's not because of our project. I wouldn't buy success with your happiness, Mary. And it's not because a divorcee can't marry again—I believe it's quite the thing nowdays, in some circles. It's because he's not good enough for you."

They were silent a long while, and then in a low voice, Mary spoke the final thing, the irretrievable thing. "That's not for you to decide, Althea."

There was nothing more to say. "The tea is getting cold," Althea brought it to the table. They ate, or pretended to eat. They began to plan the weekend—Althea made a grocery list, Mary sorted the wash. Before going to bed they read a little, as they usually did; Althea in a novel of Robert Chambers' that Mrs. Scobie had loaned her, though she thought it rather trashy, and Mary in the *Household Companion*, which had just come in the mail. There was no anger in the air; anger washes out quickly between two people who are tremendously concerned for each other. They bade each other an affectionate goodnight, and slept, or pretended to sleep, among the wreckage of their little world.

If she could not talk to someone, Althea thought, she would lose her mind. She was alone all day, with the hills staring down at her. The hills were companionable when you were doing what they wanted, when you were keeping the rhythm of planting and gathering, of glittering snow and parching sun. But when your thoughts were alien and troubled, they were like scornful eyes. . . . It would hardly do to lay the matter before Arthur or Kate by mail; it would be betraying Mary's confidence. When a Pillage had something to tell, he was allowed to tell it himself, in his own way. Besides, it would alarm them needlessly—the whole thing might blow over. If Mary recovered from her infatuation, it would have seemed pretty silly to write to Oak Point about it.

In the meantime she was lonely and wretched and afraid. Her thoughts formed a circular pattern that repeated itself endlessly. I must leave Mary free. But then what will she do? Make a disastrous marriage. *Another* disastrous marriage—it would finish her. No, she can't marry him, she says he hasn't even asked her. A short interlude here, to be furious with Ben, who had trifled with Mary's affections. And always after this the realization, I must be fair to Ben. No one could help loving Mary.

She tried to keep her own needs out of it. She tried to avoid the thought, and what will become of *me?* They could sell, she supposed, and she could go back to Oak Point. A planted orchard would always find a buyer; the boom was still on. She could go back to Oak Point with a little money in her pocket to cover the taste of defeat. And if Mary received half of the money, Ben could afford to marry her. But again she had to be fair to Ben—he would not take a woman's money. He was, as Mary had said, decent.

There was no answer. She was weary of trying to find one.

151

Perhaps she could talk to Mr. Gillespie. He was fond of Mary, and he had a daughter just Mary's age. She had always found him perceptive and she would not have to spell out the fact that Mary had been very forward, very indiscreet. She would not have to say in so many words, "Mary has accepted his hand," or "Mary has refused the poor fellow." This was, in fact, one of the aspects of the situation that bothered Althea most. She liked things tidy, she liked to know where people stood.

She made up her mind to go to Wenatchee. It was not unusual for her to go alone now; she took care of all the shopping and since they were out of mourning, really out, she liked to pick up little bits of lace and bright buttons, and try on hats. She had bought a pink bonnet on her last trip which she had never worn. It was slightly frivolous for her, but she would wear it this time, to raise her spirits. She always saw the Gillespies anyhow, to report on the progress of the place. She never forgot that Mr. Gillespie had encouraged them to plant their orchard, and had set Mary on the road to becoming a teacher. If she were lucky, if the opportunity offered, she could bring the talk with Mr. Gillespie around to Mary; and she hoped she could touch on the problem without in any way criticizing Mary, or seeming to say that Mary had lowered herself.

She was aware that Mary was glad to see her go. They were living gingerly with each other, afraid to say anything except commonplaces. Ben continued to see Mary home each afternoon, and certainly no one in Pine Creek valley could miss the fact. Perhaps no one cared, but Althea could fancy bulging eyes behind every window.

Mary could not even go with her down to the boat, since school was in session. Althea tied Rusty in the schoolyard, and walked on alone. She would get out of her riding habit on the boat, in the Ladies' Place; but she wore a frilly new blouse, and the pink bonnet. Dear Althea, Mary thought chokingly as she stood on the little stoop to wave. I would do anything else in the world for her, but I can't give up Ben. How nice she looks. That pink bonnet will do Althea more good than the vote.

The last days of school were a frantic time. Those who were behind hurried, and those who had finished their work dawdled and made trouble. Olly, a model of behavior, printed out enormous letters with his pencil. He was learning to write, by rote, "Pine Creek, Washington." Florence Scobie, the only graduate, practiced a little speech to make when she was presented to guests on the Last Day.

Mary seemed deeply tired when Ben met her each afternoon, or perhaps it was not fatigue. The first time he had come after her talk with Althea, she had blurted out, "Althea *knows!* Ben, she asked me a lot of questions about you. She *knows.*" She looked at him anxiously, to see how he would take this. To Ben, it did not seem very important. He looked at her rather blankly; he was a long way from understanding the tremendous feeling, significance, response that went into all contacts between the Hollisters and their kind. But he had learned to recognize the Hollister touch; as when Mary said to him, "Everything will be all right. It *has* to be." Ben knew it did not have to be. If his experience had taught him anything, it was that life was very haphazard, and things were as apt to turn out bad as good. Year after year there on the river, watching for the trees to grow, picking up work in the wheat harvest and the box mill, he had learned to take nothing for granted. He could not take Mary for granted, since he could not give her his name. Beside the weight of all this on him, the fact of what her sister knew or thought seemed trifling indeed.

She had stipulated that he not try to see her on Saturday or Sunday; she saved this time for Althea. On the weekend that Althea was to return, she was alone in the house. She made a ritual of getting it as clean and seemly as she could. She had read in Althea's face that Althea felt it best to be away for a few days; they were getting on each other's nerves. But she did not want Aletha to feel unwelcome on her return.

She made their cots beautifully, smoothing down the covers. She put a fresh pat of butter under the glass bell, set the table carefully, and put a tumbler of wild flowers on the sewing machine. She fed the chickens so that Althea would not have to do it that night. Then she saddled Duke and Rusty and set out for the Landing.

There were a few loungers as usual; some of them she knew, and the rest she ignored. She belonged here now, she had met many boats. The long summer day was just turning into evening, making the boat seem late as it beat its way around the lower turn and crawled across and drew into the bank. Althea was on the foredeck, waiting to get off. The pink bonnet made a glow of color against the dingy white housings. The gangplank was thrust out, and Althea with her suitcase came down it.

Her bonnet was on the back of her head, and her face was pinker than the bonnet. She set the suitcase down, and looked around as if not quite sure where she was.

"Althea," cried Mary in alarm, "what *is* it?"

Althea took a few steps forward, and stopped again, and put out her hands.

"Mary, I . . . Mary, I am betrothed. . . . I am going to marry Mr. Gillespie."

They talked most of the night. Occasionally Althea would say, "I must let you get to sleep, Mary. You have to teach tomorrow." And Mary would answer impatiently, "Oh, never mind that." There was so much to think about—everything would be changed if Althea married. If Althea married! It was preposterous.

But why? It had seemed very simple as Mr. Gillespie explained it. Althea quoted him, blushing and trembling. He had esteemed her from the beginning; she had always seemed to him the most courageous and competent of women, at no sacrifice of those qualities that an old-fashioned man like himself, Mr. Gillespie said, found so rare nowdays.

He knew, of course, that the Hollister girls did not plan to marry; that each was dependent on the other for the success of their venture. But now that . . . now that . . . Here Althea found herself in deep water, and was suddenly silent.

"Althea," Mary said ominously, "what did you tell him about me?"

154

Why, nothing much dear. Just how you're getting along, and . . . and . . ."

"You told him about Ben, didn't you?"

"Well yes, sort of. Is there any harm in that, Mary? You're just like another daughter to him, he says. You would always have a home with us, if you wished it, and Nancy is fond of you—they're all fond of you. Oh Mary, he is so *kind.*"

"I don't *want* a home with you. Not that way, I mean. Oh Althea, I was willing to stay with it. Why weren't you?"

"I know you were willing, Mary. You're very loyal. I might have had to take advantage of it. But now, of course, I need not." There was in Althea's voice an unmistakable timbre, the note that is in young girls' voices when they tell of their beaux. Mary could not sit still. She rose and began to walk about the room. *Althea!* The heavens had been shaken, the earth had removed out of her place.

Crushing relief and pity and guilt swept Mary as she paced the floor. Guilt because she had forced Althea to this step; pity because it would be dreadful, she thought, to be married to that bumbling old man. And yet . . . and yet . . . Althea did not have the look of a woman about to be sacrificed. She looked breathless and beatific and possibly just the least bit smug. Mary longed to stop in front of her and say, *Answer me just one thing. Do you love him, Althea?* But it would have been a graceless question, an unkind question, and possibly one that Althea could not answer.

"I wish you would get some sleep," Althea said. "You'll be dead on your feet tomorrow."

"All right." Mary suddenly capitulated. "We've got a lot to talk about still, Althea. All your plans, for heaven's sake. Did you make any?"

"We thought we ought to tell you first," Althea said almost timidly. She came and put her arms around Mary. "Mary, I'm so happy. I hope you are pleased, dear."

But whether I'm pleased or not, *it's not for me to decide,* Mary thought, remembering her own words. She hugged Althea as warmly as she could. The constraint was still there, the little stiffness that made them careful what they said to each other. They braided their hair and put on their flannel gowns and went to their

155

cold and narrow beds, and how Althea might be making out she could not tell, but Mary felt that she would never sleep again.

So I'm to be thrown at Ben's head . . . I won't even tell him. That's silly. I'll have to, of course. But I'll make it very light. I'm not going to compromise him. Oh Ben, Ben, I wish things were different.

. . . I'll go right on teaching, and I'll board somewhere. Mrs. Scobie would be glad to have me. Or the Lindsays. It would have to be near the school . . . Althea can't do this to me. I didn't do it to her, and she can't do it to me. Let's be honest. If Ben had asked me, no power on earth could have kept me from marrying him. Sometime. Somehow.

There was something so reminiscent about these words that she began to grope in her memory. Their first night there; the dreadful little dirty house, the impenetrable dark outside. She had promised herself then that she would not stay there. She would get away. Sometime. Somehow.

And now she was free to go. It would be simple. Mr. Gillespie would look after the place, or hire someone to do it, and she could go back to Oak Point. To Hetty and the children. Or anywhere else, of course, that she wished. They would not let her go empty-handed. Mr. Gillespie was generous. He would probably offer to buy out her share, and keep the place in his wife's name.

So I can get away. There's just one inconvenient thing, I'm in love.

I'm not engaged to Ben. All he's asked me to do is wait. Ben, this is ridiculous. I love you, and I know you love me. All that's standing in our way is money.

That's all that stands in anyone's way, really, isn't it?

She had a strong impulse to call out to Althea, to say as she had so many times in the past, "Althea, are you awake?" To talk some more, and keep on working things out. But if Althea were having pleasant dreams, asleep or awake, she had no right to disturb them. Althea suddenly belonged to her, only to her, no longer. It was odd how different it felt.

I've never been so lonely in my whole life. I must think. I must think about Ben, about what to do. I must try to think straight.

But it's hard to think straight about Ben. When I think of him

156

there's this humming in my wrists, and this feeling that I want him to hold me tightly, tightly. I've kissed him a thousand times more in my thoughts than I have really. . . . I can't help it if I've had knowledge of a man, I can't help knowing what it would be like to belong to him, to let everything happen.

Mary Hollister, for shame. You are a good girl, you are respectable, you are a light in the community. Women have gone to their graves without what you are asking for, and been useful and blithe and led good lives. . . . I thought Althea would. I really thought she would. I ought to be glad for Althea and pray God that everything will be wonderful for her. I'll try. Dear God, let Althea be happy. Make marriage sweet and pleasant to her. Don't let her be afraid. Oh, God, let being married be wonderful for Althea, let her not be timid or ashamed, let her be rewarded. She has done so much for so many people, let her have a little happiness now.

I could do with a little happiness too, God, if You have some to spare. But take care of Althea first. She's waited longer.

The end of school was only five days away. Mary made out report cards, and reminded those who threw their books at each other that the same books would fetch good money next fall when new classes needed them. "It's like running a menagerie," she said to Ben when she went out to meet him at the hitching bar.

She had herself severely in hand. Her gray school suit, soon to be put away in mothballs, had never been more crisply pressed, her hair was neat, her little chin was in the air, and her voice was the voice of Miss Hollister. They rode out of the schoolyard up the road, on which summer dust was beginning to rise. Through the Gateway, and along the clover-scented Yanling meadow. Precisely opposite Yanlings' house she said as if she had just thought of it, "Ben, I have news. Althea is going to be married. To Mr. Gillespie in Wenatchee. He's our lawyer—we had him investigate the place before we ever came out here. He's been very helpful to us."

"I know him," Ben said. "He took care of my water rights."

He had turned on her the fixed and hungry look with which often, as they jogged along, he was apt to study her face—as if he could not get enough of it, as if he were continually imprinting it on his memory. "He's a fine man, I believe," he added after a moment. "Has a family, doesn't he?"

"His daughter is married. There are two younger boys. Althea will be simply wonderful with them. She raised all the rest of us, you know."

"It sounds," Ben said unexpectedly, "like a put-up job on your sister."

She stared at him. Never in the course of all her wildly jumbled thoughts about Althea had it appeared to her in this light.

"He gets a housekeeper and a mother for his boys," Ben went on. "What does Althea get?"

"Lots," Mary cried. "Ben, Althea is *glad*. Every woman wants . . ." No, she could not say that. Her face turned rosy as it always did when he looked so intently at her. There was no use being decorous and trying to say the proper thing with Ben. He cut through to the essentials.

"I understand he's well-to-do," Ben mused, as if that might have some bearing.

"That isn't it at all. Ben Lucas, I've never seen anyone so stuffy. Althea's not marrying his money, or his children, or his big stupid house. I've been mean to her, though I never meant to be, and she's lonely. She wants somebody to adore her, and make a fuss over her, and spoil her. And he'll do it. He's lonely too, and he's kind. Althea said, 'Mary, he's so kind.' I wish you could have heard her. She's rattled, but she's happy."

"I'm glad he will be good to her," Ben said simply. "Althea doesn't like me overly, but I like Althea. At least, I think she deserves well. . . . Mary, you can't stay here alone."

"I can board," Mary said. Her chin went up in the air again. "I have no intention of giving up the school."

"I see."

Ben lapsed into silence; he never talked just to be talking. She was painfully aware of what must be going through his mind—there was no way to stop it. Yes, there might be one way. "I think I would like to spend the summer with them in Wenatchee. I would always be welcome, Althea said."

"Who would look after the place?"

"Does it matter?" Mary said wildly. "We can find someone to look after it." She did not say, We might get *you*, for she hated him, but she also loved him dearly.

For once he agreed with her. "If this really means Althea's happiness, I guess it doesn't matter. . . . You get used to thinking of an orchard, sort of, as if it were a person. Yours is too good to be ruined."

"Thank you," Mary said stiffly. "I'm glad you think so. It's the first time you ever happened to mention that you think we're managing it well."

"I didn't think so at first. But now," Ben stopped his horse at their driveway and looked critically at the wheeling rows, "it seems to be coming along OK. You've kept the weeds down wonderfully. A good harrowing wouldn't hurt it."

"Harrowing costs money," Mary said bitterly.

At the pain in her voice, Ben suddenly jerked the horse back and reached to cover her hand with his. "Mary. Mary, you don't understand. I'm trying to get my bearings. I know Althea has a right to get married, but I can't stand it to have you go away. It's all I can do to live with things the way they've been. If they get any worse, I might as well give up. Don't be hard on me, Mary. I just can't stand it."

His brown hand bit into her wrist; it was hurting her, but she did not want him to take it away. The horses stood patiently waiting—they had all the time in the world. These people would tell them when to turn up the driveway or go back down the road.

The horses were surprised, but philosophical, when by common consent they seemed to be urged on past the driveway and up toward the Rock Patch. Well, they had been there too, at least once before, and had found some rather choice nibbles of grass behind the rocks.

Ben released Mary's wrist, and she rubbed it unobtrusively. Dear brown hand, dear brown face, dear voice that goes to such unexpected depths of grief and passion. *I am sorry I am such a trouble to you, Ben. I have never meant to be.*

The horses ambled past the sheep camp and in among the trees. They stopped in the shadow of the old pine, and as they had expected, the people climbed down.

159

"Mary," Ben said, "will you chance it with me? Before God, I will do my best to take care of you. Every way I can."

She could never remember afterward that she had answered him in words. She did not think she had. It was just that it was settled, and when he put out his arms she could fling herself into them, could give the whole self of her to his embrace, could grip the back of his coat with fingers that dragged him close. Could say against his warm throat soundless things that were darling, darling, darling.

"Mary," he said. "Mary, my love. Oh Mary." He did not know all the words, but when he spoke her name, it was in itself a caress.

The horses felt it safe to wander a little further away, looking for tufts; they might be here for quite a while.

There was some talk of a double wedding, but neither of the sisters felt that this would be in the best taste. Althea's marriage date was set for early August, and Mary's for a week later. Wedding dresses and trousseaux must be sewed, and the house put in order for closing. Althea preferred to be married in the church at Wenatchee to which she would belong, and it was considered a nice touch that their attendants would be Mr. Gillespie's daughter Nancy and her husband. The new Mr. and Mrs. Gillespie would then "stand up" with Mary and Ben before the Reverend Johnson at Indian Spring.

In the meantime the multiple news was sent to Oak Point, and produced a shower of letters. Hetty and Kate sent ecstatic love and asked a thousand questions. As for Arthur, he informed them that he would be pleased to send something for each of them to remember Mama and Papa by. He asked, in a businesslike manner, for the delivery addresses of their future husbands. Thus it happened that the Gillespie house received the old hand-carved walnut secretary with the pineapple knobs, while at Pine Creek Landing, to everyone's astonishment, a bulky crate, which was found to be billed as a piano, was wrestled off and pitched in the sand.

It produced a furor in the neighborhood. Bert Plew declared he could not handle it; Ben would have to come down to the Landing with his flatbed wagon. Mary was summoned from the orchard where, ever since school was out she had been helping to do battle with the spreading weeds. She flung down her hoe and saddled Duke and clattered, unbelieving, down the road. Her piano! It was too good to be true. Oh, wonderful, wonderful dowry! She had never expected to see it again. She sank down beside it and put her cheek against the crate, imagining the long smooth reach of ivory keys for which her fingers had never lost their hunger.

She would not be able to play it, of course, until she was in Ben's home. But next day when he made his trip down with the wagon she was back again at the Landing; she could not stay away. By this time a number of people had stopped by on horseback and in buggies to view the wonder, and there were many willing hands to help hoist the big crate aboard, and half a dozen fellows to ride along and disembark it at the other end. Mary rode too, on the seat beside Ben. She was speechless with happiness.

The bevy of helpers broke open the crate in Ben's big, bare living room. When it actually stood there, dusty in its dark case, there were cries of "Give us a tune!" But Mary, conscious of being months out of practice, could hardly be prevailed on to touch the keys. When someone brought a packing case to sit on and she finally settled down and groped for a few chords, she was so flustered that they soon stopped teasing her, and gathered in the yard, where they talked about fertilizer and cover crops. Only Ben remained, watching her with his deep somber eyes, as she sat and sometimes struck a few soft notes, trying it, feeling it, making it come alive.

He had spent quite a bit of time and some of his scarce money putting in a water pipe, to give Mary what he knew she was used to—running water in the house. She had thanked him, and kissed him, and been very pleased. But she had taken it more or less for granted. Whereas this piece of frippery, this relatively useless piano, seemed somehow to have for her the quality of a miracle. Well, she was Mary, and he loved her, and soon they would be alone together and some of these confusing situations would straighten themselves out. When she gave up at last with a sigh, he was ready to take her home, having saddled both his own horses. It gave him great comfort to see her in the saddle, managing a strange horse well. Mary had had a poor raising, but she was smart. A little guidance, a little experience, and she would make a wonderful rancher's wife. He would teach her everything she needed to know.

And Mary, looking at him adoringly, thought what tremendous potential Ben had. She would introduce him to all the finer side of life, the things he had been cheated of. Music, pictures, poetry. "We needs must love the highest when we see it." She thought she might read to him evenings, those winter evenings that stretched ahead down the years.

She got home to find Althea packing, trying to separate their possessions, and to divide fairly the things that belonged to both. The rocker was Mary's, of course, and the pink lamp was Althea's. What about the sewing machine? "You'd better take it," Althea said. "I'm sure Nancy has one I can use." She was careful not to intimate, in any way, that she was going into a rich household and Mary into a poor one. But the Gillespie house was already overflowing with dishes, blankets, linens—it was only sensible for Mary to have the larger share.

One box had never been unpacked since they came. They knew what was in it; a few pearly shells from Mama's trip to Pacific Grove, a burnt-wood glove box clumsily made by little Kate for Althea, a New England primer, water-stained and yellow with age. Althea thought it was time to get into it now. She came up presently with a silver cup. "This is yours," she said to Mary. "From your godparents, at your christening."

"But what will I *do* with it?" Mary asked.

"Use it, perhaps," Althea said in an odd voice. "Mary, when you have a child . . ."

Mary gave her a startled look. This was not like Althea. But nothing was like Althea these days.

"*Don't* name her Althea," Althea finished her sentence hastily. "Name her something of her own, and God bless her. Something lovely. Like Helen. 'Helen, thy beauty is to me . . .'"

"What if she's a boy?" Mary said, greatly daring.

"Pillage is a good name," Althea said promptly, and then they looked at each other and burst into gales of laughter, as they had in the old days. It had been so long since she and Althea had laughed together! Suddenly, she felt that they had each other back again; the breach was healed, there was nothing now to forgive. Women did not make this world, their laughter seemed to say, and no woman is to blame for what happens in it. "Oh Althea," Mary cried, "I wish you weren't going so far away."

"Pooh! A day's ride on the boat . . . Mary, try to do something for that Scobie girl. Don't let her become a drudge for all those little brothers. And keep an eye on Dolly Plew, she's not as young as she used to be. I leave Pine Creek valley in your hands," Althea said magnificently. Dear, dear Althea. This was their real parting. All the bridal business would leave no chance for talk. She went over and laid her cheek on the silvery wing at the side of Althea's dark hair.

The collapse of the Hollister enterprise was the talk of Tillicum County that summer. People who had not even met the girls knew all about it. "Remember them two old maids that had the ranch up Pine Creek? Hear they both got married." "Yeah. Both to once. Smartest thing they ever done. Women can't farm." "Dunno. The place looked good. I was up to Bert Plew's and I seen it." "They say this Gillespie's got money." "Hee-hee-hee—wonder who popped the question, him or her?"

It was generally conceded that the women had only been biding their time. "Got good catches, both of 'em. Hell, if I'd known they was in the market, I'd of tried my luck myself. But I heard they was so prissy, a fellow didn't hardly know where to begin."

Thus male sovereignty was reestablished in Pine Creek, and everybody breathed easier. Only Mr. Harris, faced with his annual problem, regretted the turn of events. It was, of course, unthinkable to hire a married woman. "It would of been nice," Mr. Harris said wistfully, "if just once we could of got a teacher that was willing to stay more than a year."

PART THREE

10

THIS RAILROAD camp would be just like the others, Bob Anthony thought. He had been transferred in and out of several of them, advancing from brush cutter to head chainman. Usually he could have the transfer for the asking; building this railroad was a rough-and-ready, go-to-hell operation. Never once had he had to write to Mr. Pierce, the administrator of his father's estate, who had "spoken to the Great Northern" about taking him on.

And never once had he had a word or a glimpse of Lew. He had searched each area thoroughly, dropping in at the packing houses, attending the dances, talking to postmasters and justices of the peace (for there was always the possibility that Lew had gotten into trouble). He had become acquainted here and there with nice people, and ruthlessly dropped the acquaintance and moved on. There was, for instance, Joanie, the girl for whom he had carried the box of peaches. He had wandered into an orchard, on an early July evening when it was still light; he hated to dawdle around the quarters, and often took a long walk after supper. The girl was just down from a ladder, a heavy thing which she had obviously managed and tugged about for herself. As she brought the peaches down from the tree in a small basket she had been adding them to a box on the ground. Now she was trying to lift the box. Bob walked toward her, and said, "May I help you?"

She had not known there was anyone near. She had given him a frightened look, and when she said yes, she had stammered.

Bob fetched the box up off the soft ground, squaring his shoulders, showing off just a little. They walked to the ranch house with the box, a distance of a quarter-mile. How these people did treat their women! He was tired himself by the time they got to the door. The girl had thanked him profusely, and said "Won't you come in?" She was rangy and thin and her face was scarlet with embarrassment, but pretty in a nubile way. He had spent the rest of the evening with the Varners.

Joanie was smitten with him at once. They had sweethearted that summer, roaming the hills, waltzing and two-stepping in the lodge hall on Saturday nights. He could have had anything he wanted from Joanie, and he was at an age when he wanted a woman badly. But Joanie was a virgin, and he was not altogether heartless. He had thought he'd better get out of there.

That had been the camp before last.

There was only one thing different about this camp above Pine Creek; it was built against a cliff. Usually they lay on dusty flats, with sprawling fringes of sheds and cabins. This one was laid out along the rocky slope that lay back from the river. He thought it rather pretty. And he was pleased to find the engineers' quarters nestled under the cliff, above the road, where it would get what coolness there was in the hot months. Right now, it did not matter; it was winter and the crews were drearily working, out in the sloppy snow, only because this section of the work had fallen behind its contract.

He reported to Curt Loring, the chief engineer, and then went to the shack under the cliff to wash up. Most of the engineers and survey crew were single, and they always had a digs of their own. They ate in the management dining hall, too, tiny and stuffy, instead of out at the long tables with the crews. In the dining hall he met Curt Loring again, and Loring's wife, and some other company people who were eating at the cookshack. He noticed that the men did the talking; it was all shoptalk. Longer track was needed for the dump trains. The fill was completed south of the Pine Creek bridge. The powder tunnel up the road was coming along, but it was slow; they were into bedrock.

The women nodded and smiled and waved to each other, and set up small eddies of gossip. Loring's wife spoke little. She was a striking-looking woman with dark auburn hair beautifully dressed, and a creamy skin. She sat listening politely, with her chin in her hands; but near the end of the meal she said, "The coffee is very bad tonight. Worse than usual. Perhaps Mr. Anthony would like to have coffee with us down at the cabin."

"Good idea," Loring agreed. He had taken the new man on recommendation from Lawrence at Bailey's Slide Camp, but he liked to size people up for himself. Bob walked with them along the rocky path toward the river. Amie Loring made coffee in a handsome percolator, the kind a man might give his wife for a present, and Loring offered, "I have brandy, if you like it. Dry around here, local option. Horrible condition, isn't it?"

"Thank you, sir," Bob said. "I'll take some." He dribbled brandy into his coffee while Loring noted that the boy knew how to go about it. In this work, you got all sorts. Green college types mostly, hardly dry behind the ears.

Loring said, "I see you've worked in several of the camps. Any special reason for always moving on?"

Bob was surprised. No one had ever taken notice of it before. He had not talked of his mission to anyone, but then no one had asked him. Even Joanie had not questioned that he had to be transferred.

These people were friendly, and of a type to be discreet. "Yes sir," Bob said. "I have. I'm looking for someone. My brother."

"Interesting," Loring said. "Been looking long?"

"A fairish time." Bob lifted his cup and drank. Amie Loring studied him levelly. Underneath the sound of their voices Bob could hear the murmur of the river down below, an endless, ghostly whisper.

"Won't ask you any more about it," Curt Loring said generously. "That sort of thing is a man's own business. Sorry to intrude. Good luck."

"No, I'd just as soon tell you." The cognac was warming, and so was their civility. "There's an estate to be settled. Lew left home in a huff. It wasn't the first time. And then my father died, and things are tied up."

Amie Loring made a small sound of concern. They were pleasant people; they sympathized readily.

"As soon as it's straightened out," Bob said, "I have to go back East. This thing took me out of school. I'm interested in wireless."

Loring smiled. "Some of us have to claw our way up," he said, "without benefit of schooling. I've been with the railroad since I was twelve years old. Water boy. Learned on the job. Wireless, you say? Great thing for communications. If the Titanic had had it, she needn't have gone down."

"She had it all right," Bob said bitterly. "It was the listening stations that were at fault. We need more of them, and manned around the clock. They're being built now. And I'm not there to help do it. . . . Not that I don't like working on your railroad, sir."

It was true. The country had drawn him in; his muscles had hardened and his walk had lengthened to a stride. But he was friendless and alone. He had been a fool to spend that summer with Joanie—or perhaps he had been a fool to leave her.

"Would you like to listen to some records?" Mrs. Loring said kindly. She had already discarded, in her mind, "Pony Boy" and "Everybody's Doin' It." Red Seal, certainly, but not the heavier sort; not Bach, not Brahms. Something lyrical.

She put her hand on an old album. It took only a few moments to lift out a disk, wind the crank at the side, and place the needle.

As the rocking, gentle, insistent accompaniment to the "Barca-rolle" began, she watched him. She saw his eyes lift and fix themselves on something far away as the throaty voice came in. She could not know that the "Barcarolle" had been typical of Lew in his best moods; reasonable, reconciled, trying to get along. Its simple counterpoint came to Bob laden with peace, with the smell of late summer flowers coming in through open windows.

But she knew that she had chosen well. She had guessed right about him the very first time.

Mary Lucas (née Hollister) had learned to cut water sprouts with a big two-handled pair of pruning shears—unwanted twigs that came up from the strong, vulgar roots to which the choice little trees were grafted. She had learned to milk (though Ben usually did it since the cow was temperamental). She had learned to pitch hay, to drive the team and wagon, to wash out flour sacks and convert them into curtains and dish towels, to hive bees, to hold a board steady while Ben drove a nail, to sun-dry fruit on the roof with a piece of netting between it and the buzzing hornets.

She had never been so busy in her life, and so happy. In a year and a half she had not had a new dress, a new pair of cotton stockings, even a new ribbon for her hair; and she did not care. She would manage to keep decently covered somehow until Ben's second crop came in.

In the basket on the table by the wall was her crowning achievement, which she dropped everything constantly to go and look at, to touch, to bury her face blissfully in the baby's warm sweet midriff. To marvel over the small thing that lived now apart from her, after all those collaborative months; the entity with warmth of its own, which it communicated to its blankets—decisions of its own, whether to breathe shallow and peacefully or in infuriated squeaks. A little scarlet caricature of a human being, intact in every bone and blob, and alive, ALIVE.

Even not counting the baby, their household had grown. Ben needed another man on the place now, but he could not afford to hire. He had sent for his brother Fletcher, who was ready to leave home. Fletch would work for his keep while he looked around for a piece of ground for himself.

Fletch had arrived by steamboat, proudly stepping down at the new Lucas Landing, with his carpetbag and his own gun. They had finished off the first of the rear rooms for Fletch, and when he had made up a bed with the blankets they gave him, and hung the gun on the wall, he was at home. He was scared to death of Mary. For days he said nothing but "No," "Yes," and "Thank you." Mary was entranced with him. He was Ben all over again, thinner, more awkward, with a higher timbre to his voice. He appeared at meals and then vanished, either to the outdoors or to his own room, where he whittled or read. "I've given Fletch my books," Ben said one day to Mary, who had missed them from the top shelf of the kitchen cupboard. "And he brought a few of his own. About Kit Carson and Fremont. Fletch wants to get to know the country."

Mary made up her mind to win him over. "Fletch," she said one evening at supper, "are you interested in girls?"

Fletch considered this while he broke off a piece of corn bread and buttered it. "Kind of," he said finally.

"Did you have a girl down home?"

Fletch shook his head. "Last one run out on me. She married a fella that tans hides in Portland. City fella."

She could not resist asking, "What do you think of the city, Fletch? Are you curious about it? Do you want to go there?"

"I been in Portland. Stayed nigh a week. Couldn't seem to settle down. One street was just like another. And boat whistles all night long, and they never put the lights out. I couldn't sleep."

"We must see that you meet some girls here," Mary said. She thought of Florence Scobie. Who else? The community was rich in growing families, but they reached marrying age only a few at a time and there was never a wide choice. In Pine Creek, Mary thought, quite unconscious of any relevance to her own case, you marry whoever is there.

She was glad in a way that Fletch had come along for Ben to teach and guide. She had been all the help he had at first, and he needed help badly. But he wanted things done right. He was very patient, showing her over and over where she had made a mistake. Though she loved him deeply, and was eager to please, she had had a sudden mischievous thought in the ache and lassitude that followed the baby's birth: "There, I've finally done something that Ben didn't show me how to do."

The baby had cost money, of course. Most of the money from Ben's first crop. Mary had gone to Indian Spring to the doctor as soon as she was sure. She had made several visits, in the jolting wagon, and finally Dr. McClellan had said, "You'd better not ride that wagon any more, Mary. You're fine. Just send for me whenever you need me."

She had had a good birth, relatively easy for a first child. She was young and strong, intelligent, utterly healthy. She had followed orders, eating lots of fruit, drinking copiously the milk from the newly fresh cow. The milk had dwindled now and the cow had been bred again. But there was still enough for Mary to drink it every day and help to keep her own breasts full. This was fortunate, for baby Helen was a pig. A lovely, pink, heavenly, insatiable pig. She nursed with passion, went to sleep happy and distended. Ben would come and stand beside the basket at odd times, his face such a well of love that Mary wanted to throw her

172

arms around him and cry. He adored the baby—they both adored
the baby.

"I like you bein' a Missis," Dolly Plew said, lifting up the pot
lid to see what was cooking on the stove. "I allus figured it would
come. And I allus figured you'd take Ben."

"You did?" Mary raised her face in astonishment.

"Why sure. He was the best pickin's."

"Oh Dolly! I don't think you're very romantic."

"Would you be romantic in my place?" Dolly demanded. "Don't
get me wrong, Mary. I think Ben'll be a good husband to you.
But he ain't a very fancy package, accordin' to the way you
was raised."

"Ben is *real*," Mary said quickly. "He's part of this earth. Part
of the hills and river. It's as if they had come alive for me in Ben."

"Sounds kinda like book talk."

"Well, is there anything wrong with book talk?"

"No. Only I ain't sure it fits Ben Lucas."

"Of course it does. It's given me the feeling that I belong. To
Ben. To the valley."

"You sure needed it," Dolly said. "You needed a man, an' you
can fix it up with yourself anyway you like. I useta watch you,
that fust year. I wouldn't o' been surprised for you to go tearin'
down to the river on them cute little feet an' stand an' scream for
the boat. . . . *You*, not Althea. She's the stayin' kind. It seems
funny, now, that she's gone an' you're here. You see her much?"
Dolly opened the bread bin and sniffed. "I see you've got to be
a better cook since she left."

"I'll never bake bread like Althea's. . . . Why yes, I go to Wenatchee quite often. It doesn't cost much, you know. The boat
stops here now—you should see how wonderful our landing looks!
I used to help Ben on it, before . . . before I got too big with the
baby. He would carry the rocks over, and I'd help put them in the
wall. It's a beautiful wall. We're very proud of it."

"I'll bet Ben told you where to put every pebble, too. Mary,
don't you go runnin' off to Wenatchee too regular. You got a job,

now, an' you tend to it. You sure know how to pretty up a house."
She looked appreciatively at the curtains, which hung straight,
and the wall cupboards in which the Lucas belongings were neatly
arranged. She moved over to the piano, that stood grandly apart
at the other end of the room, and laid a finger on an ivory key. The
piano spoke softly, a single note. "You play this a lot?"

"Well, yes," Mary said a little defensively. "Mostly I play it
when Ben is out at work. I'm afraid he'll get a little tired of my
same old pieces if I play them every evening. But *I* never get tired
of them. I improve everything a little bit every time I play it. At
least I think so. My fingers were awfully stiff! And I'm working on
something new—a Mozart sonata. It's *hard*—it comes terribly
slow. Oh, if I were just really good on the piano! I didn't study
long enough. I don't get out of the keyboard what I put into it."

"That's where a washboard has got it all over a keyboard. You
get out what you put into it. You need more chairs, don't you,
Mary?"

"We'll have them soon. Ben is awfully clever about things like
that. The big old chair is from his folks, and the rocker is from
mine, but Ben made the cowhide chair himself. And he's working
on one with a splint seat. Ben can do anything with his hands."

"You don't really need a lot o' chairs to give a party," Dolly said
hopefully. "Most folks would just as lieves set on the floor between dances. You could carry out the bed an' push back the
table, an' you'd have room for two sets o' square dances." She
ended her walk at the baby's basket, as everyone did. "Sleepin'
like a charm. How 'bout *her*—does she mind the pianny?"

"She loves it," Mary said. "I can quiet her that way. Dolly, have
you been up to the railroad camp? Lately, I mean. It's getting
bigger and noisier every day. When the wind is right, we can hear
the cook beating on the triangle at mealtime. And of course the
steam shovels are into our right-of-way, right here through the
orchard. They'll soon be opposite the house."

"I rid by up there last week," Dolly said. "Just to see how they
was makin' out. Some o' them cabins are real tidy. They was a
woman on a porch, starin' up. Beautiful hair she had, dark red.
I waved to her, but she didn't wave back. I won't take *her* no
piece o' my yellow rose."

174

A whimper came from the baby's basket. Mary went over quickly. The whimper developed into a string of imperative sounds. "I'll have to take her up," Mary said. "It isn't time to feed her, though. I know I shouldn't do it, but if she gets too desperate I give her a soda cracker. There are zwieback wafers especially for babies, I've seen them advertised in the *Household Companion,* but I don't know where to buy them. And Ben would probably think it was foolishness."

"You mean you feed her by the *clock?* Now I've heard everything. Mine, when they was hungry, I give 'em suck."

"Doctor's orders," Mary said serenely. "And she's getting along just fine." She cuddled the baby to her, brought out a bright rattle with which Helen hit the admiring Dolly in the eye, turned over the meat on the stove, carried in a pan of milk and skimmed it, and shook the ashes down, all with her right hand, holding the baby on her left hip in the immemorial stance of women, and keeping an anxious eye on the time. When Dolly had left, and the feeding was over and Helen back in her basket, Mary opened a jar of wild black raspberries and was trying to decide whether her hungry men would need cobbler cooked on top of it, when Fletch burst in the door.

"Ben," he gulped. "Ben . . ."

He thrust his thumb toward the outdoors, and turned and fled, and Mary dashed after him. "Fell off the roof," Fletch said panting. "Shingle let go in his hand."

She could see Ben lying, flat out, in the east shadow of the barn. He was unconscious; he looked young and defenseless, like Fletch. There was a long gash on his face and his eyes were closed. She knelt over him. *Oh Ben oh Ben.* She did not dare to touch him, but she must. Her hands went over him gently. His arms were whole. His legs were whole. *Oh God I always knew that roof . . .*

"Bring something to cover him," she said over her shoulder. She could get help up the road in twenty minutes if she were swift. The man with the big red car. Ben could not die in twenty minutes. "Saddle Duke . . . no don't bother. Don't leave Ben. Don't let him move around. Only tuck the cover under him if you can. If the baby screams, give her a cracker." She was already leading Duke out, her own dependable Duke. She had seldom ridden him bareback, but he would understand. She was up on him and out of the yard, clinging, not taking time for a backward look. Along the new road, the fast hard-packed road, through Piggott's old place, to the end of the bench. Up and down across a thrust of basalt, Duke's great shoulders rising. Into the midst of the railroad crew, where with a sob of thankfulness she saw Curtis Loring standing, talking to some men. She jumped off, in front of him.

"My husband is hurt," she said. "Can you come?"

Loring looked at her disheveled hair, at the unsaddled horse. "Why yes," he said. "I will come at once." He spoke a few more words to the men and turned, and Mary followed him across the oozing side of the fill. Everything took so long! Seconds were passing, whole minutes were going by. Ben was there on the cold ground—asleep, surely that was all, asleep. Loring led her to the big Locomobile, the great powerful car that had passed the Lucas place so often. He opened the door, stuffed her into the seat, and went around and got behind the driver's wheel. Mary hoped that someone had Duke by the bridle rein and was leading him to a safe place.

The roar started in the massive engine under the red hood; the brasswork shook. The car began to crawl like a powerful beast up the road. The woman with red hair came to a window, and looked out. They left her creamy face suspended there as they moved down the road, around the turns, down off the basalt hump. There was nothing now for Mary to do but twist her hands and pray. *God, thank you for this car. For this man, for having him waiting there.*

"Our place," she indicated to Loring before they reached the gate. "He's knocked out . . . he's . . . I don't know. He fell from the roof of the barn, mending some leaks." She had not been able to start talking; now she could not stop. She babbled as they halted the car and climbed out and crossed the yard.

Ben's eyes were open. His face was contorted with pain. "Get me up," he whispered, and Mary, used to obeying, reached for him.

176

"Not so fast, young fellow," Curt Loring said. He got down and in his turn felt Ben over, his hands knowledgeable, his face concerned. "I think you can be moved, all right. Where is your doctor?"

"Indian Spring," Mary said. "Oh, can you . . . will you . . ."

"This kind of thing goes on all the time around a railroad," Loring said. "Last week we . . ." He decided not to finish the sentence. "Going to be a problem getting him into the car." Fletch had retreated into the background, but Loring beckoned to him. "Better take his other side. This is going to hurt, lad." Fletch came over, and with skill and caution Loring directed Ben's raising. Ben gave one gasp, and set his teeth. His gaze locked with Mary's, and while they got him off the ground she urged and pleaded and lifted him with her eyes. When he was on his feet, and they paused to let him rest, she ran to the car and opened the rear door, twisting the handle as she had seen Loring do. Loring nodded. His authoritative voice said, "Easy, now. This will be the worst part."

Somehow they got Ben laid on the back seat with his head in Mary's lap, the cover over him. The sun had gone down and it was bitterly cold. "Get a few more blankets in here if you can," Loring said to Fletch.

"And oh, Fletch, take care of the baby," Mary said, her voice breaking. "Hug her if she cries. Give her something to chew on. Bread. See if you can pour some water down her with a spoon. She'll fight it, but try. Do the best you can."

Ben had had a sedative. His gashed face was bandaged, and his ribs were taped where Dr. McLellan had found fractures. Mary had a set of instructions as long as her arm. "His back is wrenched, but not too badly," Dr. McClellan said. "There will be some pain. Make him take his capsules. And hold him down. If he frets about the work, don't give in. Make him stay in bed till I say he can get up."

Ben smiled crookedly around his bandage. "She's been plumb

177

longing to boss something ever since she gave up the school. Wouldn't be surprised if she tore out the orchard and put us in the chicken business."

In her relief, Mary could smile. But it was going to be very difficult. She and Fletch would have to manage, for how long she did not know. And somewhere in the back of her mind hung the dreadful image of old John Muldoon, never getting up.

Dr. McClellan studied her face. "Mary, you're very lucky that he didn't fall five feet further. Or come down across a saw horse. All he needs is care, if you can make him accept it. Don't get into a swivet, don't try to do more than you can. I'll come by every two or three days, and help you lay down the law."

It was pitch dark when they started back from Indian Spring. Fussing with the mound of blankets, trying to take the jars of the road with her own body so they would not get through to Ben, she wondered about the man in the front seat. Silent, imposing, he went about this as if it were his everyday business. The lamps of the car flickered before him on the road. She could think of nothing to do that would show the depth of her gratitude. She had seen the big car go by their ranch almost every day, had learned to know Loring by sight, had seen the red-haired woman with him, or with some other driver, the driver erect and mannerly while the woman sat beautifully in the back, a long veil flying.

Mary sighed. For years she had dreamed of riding in an automobile. And when it came, it had to come like this. She brought herself up sharply. It had come to save Ben from disaster. She could never be thankful enough that it had come when it did.

She could see, through the isinglass of the curtains, the sparkle of the winter stars. She tried to calm herself with remembering how her father had shown them to her—Taurus, Orion, the Pleiades. Her slippers had crunched in the frost of the front lawn. That *could* not be Mary, that awestruck child with a braid down her back. Or if that were Mary, who was it that was riding now through this bleak night with the cold numbing her face, the broken body of her husband in her arms?

She went to Wenatchee no more that spring. She did not play the piano, for Ben was lying there, reproaching her with his eyes. Rest, he could understand; anyone needed rest. But he could not see how a body could frivol with the piano when the spring work needed to be done. He was thoughtful of Mary after his fashion. He said, "Let Fletch handle the ditching, Mary, and if it gets behind, we'll live with it." "Fletch, you'd better milk for Mary, the cow is a little on the mean side." When she was tired she would come and lie beside him, and he would ease his arm out, though the movement hurt him, to cradle her head. His enforced stay in the house brought them very close. "Familiarity breeds contempt"—whoever said that had been stupid indeed. Familiarity breeds certitude and peace, and a sense that things are as they ought to be.

Along the river, spring came so fast that even in her second year on the Lucas place, it took Mary's breath away. In Pine Creek valley, the snow had let go reluctantly, lying in drifts on the upper slopes till late March. But here it seemed as if she looked up one morning and it was gone. The wide foothills lay open to the sun; they swiftly changed from dun color to a shallow green and almost immediately the bunch grass began to wither. What was left of it, in stubborn clumps, would graze the horses and cattle the rest of the year. The Lucas cow was not dependent on forage, however. Ben had kept track of the milk, and determined that she should have a ration of alfalfa hay the year through. She was driven out, bawling, after milking time in the morning, and seldom went farther than the upper flat. Mary or Fletch, scarlet-faced and out of breath from the hasty climb, would retrieve her at night if she had not dawdled in by herself.

Every day, Mary thought of going to the railroad camp to thank Curt Loring for his help. It was something she *must* do, though her natural shyness was growing on her in these years of having so few contacts with strangers. At last on a Sunday afternoon late in March, when the house was in order and Ben as comfortable as he could be made, she baked a couple of pies from her blackcap raspberries and put them in a box and set forth on Duke, the box before her on the saddle. Her heart was beating hard. It was one thing to ride into the camp when Ben was hurt, without stopping to think—it was quite another thing to pay a formal call.

Wild buckwheat foamed along the road as she took her way north. The box handled badly, resting on the pommel of the saddle. She wished she had bought one of the beautiful baskets she had seen in Wenatchee. No, she didn't really. It would have been terribly extravagant.

The camp was sunk in Sunday sloth. Without the accustomed shouting of men, the belch and grind of the steam shovels, the rattle of rock, it seemed deserted. In the shade of the bunk house a line of lazy figures sat or lay just out of the warm spring sun, and one of the men whistled softly, "Oh! You Beautiful Doll." She was a lady, Mary reminded herself, and no one who behaves as a lady ever comes to any harm. To the first man she met who was upright and walking, she said, "Can you direct me to the Lorings'?"

He pointed down across the rocks to one of the cabins, indistinguishable from the others, but now she remembered; this was where they had gone after Loring's car. She guided Duke down the cabin road, and dismounted with her box and set it on the ground while she tied him to a railing of the porch. Picking up the box again, she summoned all her presence, and climbed the plank steps and knocked on the door.

Loring answered. He was resplendent in a uniform (or so she thought of it) of dull brown. His face was blank—for a moment he did not recognize her.

"I came to thank you," Mary said in a rush. "For the ride that night. You may have saved my husband's life. It was so very, very kind of you, and we will never forget it." She added anticlimactically, "I . . . I brought you something."

Loring took the box from her. He opened it carefully. "Pies, by Jove. They look like pies. . . . You baked these yourself?" He raised his voice slightly. "Amie!"

The red-haired woman came up behind him. "Amie, this is Mrs. . . . Mrs. . . ."

"Lucas," Mary supplied. She had a panic moment. I've done the worst possible thing, I've reflected on his wife's cooking. What will she think?

Amie Loring did not seem to be thinking anything. She put out her hand, below a beautiful lingerie cuff with row upon row of lace and lawn cobwebbed together. The hand was cool, her voice was cool and pleasant. "How do you do," she said.

"Pies, by Jove," Loring repeated rather helplessly. Amie took the box from him.

"Don't leave Mrs. Lucas standing there." If there was anything at all in Amie's voice, it was amusement. Mary followed Loring in, and gave a gasp of pleasure.

There was a small bright-toned Oriental rug across the linoleum. Mary had not seen an Oriental rug since she left Oak Point. The windows were veiled in gauze. A lamp with a shade of leaded glass stood on what Mary recognized as a phonograph.

"And how is the young man?" Loring boomed. "Recovering, I hope?"

"He's doing just fine," Mary said eagerly. "He'll be up and around in a few weeks." She had said the phrase so often that it came of its own accord. "He's had a good deal of pain with his back, but it's mending. We're very lucky that it was no worse." Phrases, phrases. Where did they come from? She sat politely on a sofa, gripping her hands together.

Amie brought in the big silver percolator; it made a sort of entrance of its own, as when the Ark is borne in. "Oh, how beautiful," Mary cried, speaking naturally for the first time.

"My husband gave it to me." Amie set the tray down deftly and went back after cups and saucers. From the kitchen she called, "You'll share one of your pies with us, I hope? It's nice to have something to eat on a Sunday afternoon. What we get at the cookshack will be strictly leftovers."

Mary was a little puzzled. Sunday supper was leftovers anywhere, but did this mean that Mrs. Loring ate with the men of the camp? Her hands were so white, so pretty.

"Why, no, I . . . Yes, if you like. I meant them for you, but . . ." Mary felt herself relaxing. She was at home here, with the rug and the lamp and the small courtesies. She smiled at Mrs. Loring as the auburn-haired woman came back. "May I cut them for you? We practically live on pie. My husband adores it. So I cut them continually." They did not live on pie. It was a graceful

181

exaggeration—Amie Loring would know. Mary rose and went to the kitchen.

She wondered, as she cut the pie generously and put it on plates that Mrs. Loring handed her, how anyone could resist cooking in a kitchen like this. It was compact, charming—it had everything. Just as she had seen Althea do a hundred times, she passed the plates around adroitly and settled herself with her own. The coffee came from the percolator amber, hot, and strong.

"Good, good," Loring said as he bit into his pie. "*Damn* good. Local fruit?"

"Wild fruit," Mary told him. "All over the cliffs. We raise some tame ones too, but we like these especially. We go berrying for them every summer."

"Berrying!" Loring said. "Haven't been berrying since I was ten, eleven years old. Went to work for the railroad when I was twelve. Water boy. Learned on the job." He sighed. "Haven't got as far as I should. Ought to have a desk job by now."

Amie gave him a patient look. "You wouldn't like a desk job, Curt. . . . You've done extremely well."

Mary thought so too. She was beguiled by the quiet comfort, the soft light. She supposed she should have gone straight home. She looked about surreptitiously. No books. Yes, there was one. Elinor Glyn's *Three Weeks* lay under the lamp.

Curt Loring looked humorously at her. "A railroad owns you. Body and soul."

"Oh, so does a ranch!" Mary cried. "You think of nothing else. You just try to keep up with it. Days go by, and you don't stop to write letters, you don't play your piano, you don't think about anything but that the crop is coming, and it must be a good one."

"A one-crop economy," Curtis Loring said. "Can't help thinking that's very bad. What do you do when the apple crop fails?"

"It never fails." Mary was on the defensive immediately. "We have everything just right for it here. The soil. The climate. And the market is bigger than we can supply."

"Well, it's good to be young," Curt said. "Full of faith. If a man loses faith in what he's doing, he hasn't got much." He saw Mary's eyes light suddenly on the clock across the room.

She rose to her feet. "Oh, dear! My baby . . ."

"Baby too, eh?" Loring was jovial, interested. "Baby crop coming right along with the rest."

Amie said nothing. Impassive, she gathered cups and plates and put them neatly together. After she had made a trip to the kitchen she put out her hand.

"It was very good of you." Her voice was as correct, as lifeless as her words. "Please come again."

I wish she really meant it, Mary thought as she disentangled the reins that Duke had pulled about in reaching for the morning-glory vines. She saw to her dismay that he had one crumpled blossom between his leathery lips.

11 BEN PUT HIS whole mind on getting well. When the pain in his back began before it was time to take the capsule, he bore it quietly. He closed his eyes and listened to sounds, concentrating on them, trying to sort them out. Every day the track-laying crew came nearer in the right-of-way, laying down a railroad through his orchard. Traffic passed; it was a lot heavier than it used to be. He could tell the creak of a wagon from the light rattle of a buggy, and by the clop of a horse's hoofs he could tell something about the size and style of the horse. The night the new calf was born he strained his ears, helping Fletch and Mary with all his heart, willing them to do the right thing. He need not have worried. Fletch knew how to run a calving. Soon afterward there was the daily sound of Mary stirring oil meal into milk in a pail, and the calf's head butting the pail as it tried to learn to drink.

By the end of April he was taking a short, gingerly walk every day. On his walks he inspected the beat-up old sprayer he had instructed Fletch to buy, and watched Fletch put it in shape. Alone among all the apple ranchers along their part of the river last fall, Ben had not been surprised to see a few worm holes in the crop. Sawyers had some; Scobies had some. Ben had estimated pretty closely how long it would take the codling moth to work its way up the valley, and he was ready. The machine had cost something, but he figured he and Fletch would make it back in one season, going out with sprayer and team to treat the orchards of the neighbors who didn't have their own rigs. The time? He would find the time somehow. He could always find time for things that would put money in their pockets and make Mary more secure.

She was in and out all day, flashing him a smile sometimes but seldom stopping to talk. She left the baby alongside him, however, and in those weeks he got happily and diffidently acquainted with his daughter. He watched her go to sleep, resisting to the last, popping her blue eyes open just once more, making diminishing sounds of rebellion. He saw her grapple helplessly with the air and caused the small aimless fingers to close around his brown calloused one, looking down with awe at the fragile flesh in which his flesh was wrapped. He was happiest when Mary came to sit beside him and nurse the child, or when at night she came to lie carefully on the other side of the bed, going to sleep with the whole series of sniffs and cover-twitchings and pillow-punchings that he knew well. He could not possess her now, his aching frame would not do the work. Desire was in him often, and his body responded hotly under the covers. But the time would come again. Ben was a patient man.

When the trees burst into bloom in May, it was time to evaluate the crop, and see what harvest they could reasonably count on and how much it would be safe to spend for spraying and cultivating and how much box lumber to buy. He thought he could very well make up the boxes himself, standing all day in front of a rack, hammering and turning. It was really boys' and women's work, but he accepted it without fuss, knowing that he could not yet lift heavy objects or bend or stretch.

His slow progress through the orchard carried him from one end to the other of every row. The trees were noticeably bigger this year. It was a pleasure to see the straight trunks and the rounding out of the limbs. He went out after breakfast, and did not come in till nearly time for mid-day dinner. Mary was starting to think about dishing up when she heard his deliberate step.

"We're going to have a good crop, Mary." There was relief in his voice, but not the jubilant note she might have expected. Turning quickly, she saw that he carried in his hands the long-handled pruning shears, dull with rust.

"I found this under a tree down in the south end," he said.

Mary's heart jumped into her throat. She knew who had left it there, and when. Last fall when she had been learning to prune, more playing than working really, hating to give up, but finding herself too heavy with child to be comfortable. She had laid down the shears, thinking she might be back.

"Oh Ben, I'm sorry." Shame engulfed her. She knew how Ben valued his tools. The pruning shears looked dreadful—they were stuck fast, the blades were pitted, the handles soaked and swollen.

"Mary," Ben said a little desperately, "We *must* take care of our gear. It's all we have."

She knew, she knew. She would have clawed her fingernails to the quick to clean it—would have washed it in her own blood, if that would make it like new.

"It'll cost about two-seventy-five for another one. That would buy a sack of flour or a hundred feet of hay-rope," Ben said, moving to the sinkboard, where he laid it down carefully behind the dishes.

"Ben, I . . . oh, I *am* sorry. I won't do it again." There were no words for what she felt. There was a lump in her throat that almost strangled any words at all.

"I'll take some oil and emery to it," Ben said more cheerfully, "and see if I can save it." He sat down at the table, and she brought the chicken and noodles, of which he was fond. They were her own noodles, dried in long strings over the oven door. She took her place opposite him, but she could not eat. The chicken was flanked by a dish of pickles, and some rather dry cake that had crumbled in the spring heat, and scalding coffee. Ben chewed methodically, and when he took a piece of cake he said, "The crop looks wonderful. The trees are loaded with bloom."

"That's splendid," Mary said. She would have been rapturous at some other time, would have given him back his exultation. But now she felt speechless. This was the worst thing she had done; worse than leaving gates open, worse than breaking a dish in the sprigged set that had come over the Oregon Trail. Worse even than letting a kettle of jam boil away while she struggled with the Mozart sonata, destroying both kettle and jam and filling the house with a dreadful reek.

Ben seemed to have dismissed the whole matter from his mind. "Fletch has to go to the store after a nozzle for the sprayer. Is there anything you want?"

"Some lard," Mary said, "and a spool of number fifty white thread. I'll write it down." From somewhere she fetched up a smile, based on their common understanding that Fletch wouldn't remember what thread size to get, and Ben smiled back. He got up refreshed, and stretched cautiously.

Doctor McClellan was still enforcing a rest after eating. Ben lumbered over to the cowhide chair, sinking into it gratefully. Mary carried the dishes to the sink. The pruning shears stood there horridly, and she did her work around them. Ben had built her a screened cooler on the north side of the kitchen area, away from the sun, and she put the butter and what was left of the noodles in there. She had ironing to do, but the stove had cooled; the fire would have to be built up again for the sadirons to heat, and she had no heart for it. She knew what she needed— she needed the baby in her arms, for comfort.

Ben dozed lightly, but he was up and out within the hour. As soon as he was gone and everything was put away, she scooped up Helen, who was sleeping soundly, and left the house and took a different path than the one Ben had taken. Hers led to the highway and across it, up a steepening rise, and finally along the last short sharp climb to the upper flat, a hundred feet or so above the orchard.

On the edge of the flat was a tumble of rock, one of the many outcrops that dotted the hills. It made a seat with a sort of back-rest, and the view from it swept up and down the river. She could see past Pine Creek Landing, though not the Landing itself; it was hidden within a curve. To the north, the basalt hump cut off a sight of the railroad camp. The scene was all river, and fields and slopes and sky; it was infinitely peaceful. She liked to come here when she was troubled, or to rest after a morning's work. Ben and Fletch had both seen her there, and teased her, and called the outcrop "Mary's Rock."

She sat a long while with the baby in her arms. Helen had roused, grumpily, when her mother picked her up, but she went back to sleep again and her shallow, regular, earnest breathing was lovely to listen to. She was a good baby. She was healthy, and clean, and intelligent, and beautiful. Beside having such a baby, did anything else matter?

Yes, it did.

She must try to get over this deep hurt, this panic, at being criticized or held less than perfect. She must try to figure out how Ben's mind worked. It was essential to their marriage that she should know.

But perhaps Ben's mind worked about like everyone's else. . . . The Pillages never took each other to task. Maybe it was the Pillages whose attitude was wrong. *It's such a lovely way to be,* Mary thought, her heart aching. *Right or wrong, it's wonderful. Althea and I always backed each other up. If one of us did something stupid, the other one said it's all right, it doesn't matter. Until I got involved with Ben. And even then, she didn't blame me. She saw how it could happen. She only said to be careful.*

I made my choice, and I'm not sorry. I'm happy, married to Ben. Very happy. I'm leading a normal life, married to a normal person. I must forget all this business about being so touchy when he scolds me.

"Dolly," she said to her only confidante, "do you think people who love each other ought to forgive each other everything?"

Dolly Plew's eyes twinkled, but her face was impassive. "Don't know as I ever knowed a couple that didn't git riled up at each other once in a while. You still havin' a little trouble gittin' to be a Lucas, Mary?"

"They're so *righteous,*" Mary blurted out.

"They're a hard breed," Dolly admitted. "They git along, though. Ben'll never take his eye off the target. There's worse things than bein' took care of in your old age, Mary."

"But if you love a person, naturally you do your very best. And the other person knows it's your very best, and if it isn't perfect, he understands. He doesn't criticize."

Dolly laughed outright. "That may be love, but it ain't marriage. Marriage is when you're stuck with each other, and know it. A man's gonna complain about somethin', an' you might as well give him somethin' to complain about. You should hear Plew!"

189

Mary saw that it was no use talking about such things to a woman who had made out a life with Bert Plew. But Dolly surprised her by adding,

"Don't give up, Mary. With people like you comin' into the kentry, our men are gonna learn some manners, whether they like it or not. I notice my Dan is a lot politer to his Sally then Plew ever was to me." She cocked her ear toward the sound of track laying, now beginning to diminish as the men worked their way south. "*That's* what's gonna bust up the old ways—that railroad. No more splashin' ashore with stuff—no more freightin' over the trails. Plew'll be out of a job."

"Oh not really, Dolly! Bert can do so many things." She was suddenly contrite; the little brown woman had problems that were real. How to go on eating, how to buy shoes and gunpowder, and liniment for an old, creaky body.

"Plew an' me lived off the land before the orchards come," Dolly said, "an I guess we kin do it again. Oh, we was goin' to make a big killin' when we fust moved in! Our land had timber on it, an' we brung in some cattle, an' Plew had his team . . . a better team, his fust one was. Look, Mary, you kin treat Ben Lucas any way you like, but don't you never git too uppity to take care o' them good horses o' hisn."

Now that the cow was fresh and there was lots of milk, Mary soured some of it and made cottage cheese, hanging it all afternoon in a drippy sack above the sink. She dangled the old silver christening cup by a string from the ceiling above Helen's basket, where the baby watched it twirl with gravely delighted eyes. She cut leather patches from the tongues of Ben's wornout boots and fitted them onto the elbows of his work jacket. His face had a little color now, and there was more spring to his step. He began to take over the chores from Fletch, who was right glad to let him. Fletch had his eye on the old Piggott place, so long abandoned. There would be a lot of red tape, tracking down the title; it had been put up for taxes, and some stranger had bought it, probably for a song, and might be willing to let it go at a slight profit. Fletch and Ben conferred together under the evening lamp.

You had to hand it to the Lucases; they knew how to take hold. They had populated their share of the Willamette Valley, and now they would start to possess the Columbia. Fletch would work in the wheatfields that summer, and make a payment on the place. There was no homestead land left in the area that he really wanted. Mary found it pleasantly feudal to think of Fletch on the next place up the road, with his own orchard in due time, and his own family. Determinedly, she told herself that she would see things Ben's way.

She was whistling gaily as she knelt with trowel and claw, putting in the last of the tomato plants that had been started in a flat in the south window. (Now that she was out of Althea's hearing, she whistled when she felt like it.) There was a rumbling sound behind her, and she turned to see, resplendent in the driveway, the big red car.

Her heart leaped. Whatever came of this car was good. She saw the red-haired woman in the back seat, and an erect young man behind the driver's wheel. She was conscious of her earth-stained dress, her flushed face, her flying hair; it could not be helped. She brushed herself off the best she could, and walked toward the car.

The driver opened the door and the red-haired woman climbed down and put out her delicate hand. "I have come to see you," Amie Loring said. "To return your call, and to observe this woman who has a piano and a baby and a cliff full of wild raspberries."

A little flustered, Mary said, "What a memory you have! Or else I must have talked too much."

Mrs. Loring turned to the young man. "You may come back in about half an hour," she told him. The red car started and grumbled and backed, turning around in the soft earth at the edge of the driveway. By the time they were indoors, it had freed its wheels and was moving majestically away.

"There's the piano," Mary waved her hand at it. "It looks silly in here, doesn't it? And over there is the rest of my house.

And this is my baby. That's all there is, there isn't any more."
This phrase from a play had been current when she left Oak
Point, and she had never used it since. Amie Loring smiled.

"I adore Ethel Barrymore. . . . Is all this orchard yours?"

"Forty-five acres of it," Mary said. "And all made by my
husband with his bare hands." She had known at once, up there
at the camp, that she could talk to Amie Loring if she had the
chance.

"That's rather tremendous, isn't it?" Amie murmured. "Or does
everyone have holdings like that?"

"Goodness no. This is the best ranch on this part of the river.
With the best trees. And the best soil. And a steamboat landing
on the best sandbank. And we have a superior cow, who gives
nothing but cream. Except eggnog at Christmas, of course."

Amie laughed. "You're not native here, are you?"

"I was the schoolmarm," Mary said demurely. "In that little
white building that stands all by itself, on a bench above Pine
Creek. . . . Oh Mrs. Loring, it was so good of you to come."

"I felt that I should like to see you again." Amie carried a
purse of white linen, which she fingered as she spoke. "We are
unfriendly there at the camp, or so I have heard. I thought I
would do something to redeem us."

"Unfriendly?" Mary's eyebrows went up. "Why everyone knows
how your husband took Ben to the doctor and probably saved
his life. And all the men that work along the right-of-way are
very nice. We watch them work and they wave and smile, and
we wave back. It's been very exciting for us. I don't suppose you
realize what a quiet place this is ordinarily."

"I shall tell Curt that the labor crews are making a good impression. . . . Mrs. Lucas, will you play for me?"

"I'll be honest with you," Mary said. "Since Ben was hurt, I've
hardly touched the piano. And my old pieces, from the days when
I studied . . . I'll be more honest still. I wasn't sorry to give them
a rest. I read music badly. I play by ear a little. But mostly I
practice what I learned, and now and then I hack away on something new, but it's always disappointing. It always sounds terrible."

"You don't play ragtime?" Amie said hopefully.

192

"No. My teacher said . . . well, never mind what my teacher said. But I have heard of it, and I'm dying to know what it's like. Will *you* play for *me*, Mrs. Loring?"

"If you haven't practiced for months, I haven't practiced for years. Come to see me, and I will let you listen to my phonograph. How cozy you are here, in this house that looks as if it were built to last forever!"

"Why yes," Mary said. "We'll add to it of course, but essentially I suppose it's the house we'll always live in."

"Not like our cabins at the camp, which will be dismantled when the railroad is done. It has been so pleasant to see your trees in blossom. The orchards were blooming two years ago, when I came. They are delightful."

"You have been here for two years? And I haven't known it? Oh, Mrs. Loring, it is *we* who are unfriendly. I'm ashamed of us."

"I should judge it has been a full two years for you." Amie looked toward the basket where Helen slept. Mary was startled; she had momentarily forgotten the baby. But she *never* forgot the baby! She must watch the clock. The child's schedule governed her day. "I haven't been here all that time," Amie added. "It is not, perhaps, dutiful of me, but sometimes in the summer, when your heat here is almost unbearable, I go away to the city."

"And what do you do in the city?" Mary's voice was eager.

"*Je m'amuse*," Amie said drily. "Tell me, what is the odd thing which horses draw through your orchard, with men beside it holding wands?"

"That's Ben and Fletch running the sprayer." Mary began a glowing account of Ben's enterprise, but the car could be heard approaching; the driver rapped lightly on the door. "You've only just come!" Mary said. "Will I see you again, Mrs. Loring? I can ride Duke up to the camp someday, like I did before."

"It will not be necessary," Amie said. "I will send the car for you. Shall we say a week from today? I am afraid you will find it dull, though perhaps you are the temperament that never finds things dull. Goodbye, little Mrs. Lucas."

She opened the white linen purse and took out a bit of red stuff, which she touched to her lips. Mary watched fascinated. There had been a few society women in Oak Point who were said to "paint," but she had never seen it done before. "There," Amie said lightly. "I must keep my looks, you know. This climate of yours is not exactly the Fountain of Youth."

"It's dreadful, isn't it? . . . Oh dear, the baby's crying . . . goodbye, goodbye Mrs. Loring, don't forget me." Mary did not stop to watch the red car out of sight. When Helen was nursed and comforted and put down, a tarpaulin hastily flung over the tomato plants to keep them from wilting, she went irresistibly to the piano. It felt so good, so responsive, after all this time. The keys obeyed her, the delicate fractions of the sonata fell together into a soaring whole. She did not stop to correct her mistakes, but rose and rose with it to a full satisfying climax, a statement that was firm and final. She was something more when she played the piano than Ben's wife, Helen's mother, Althea's sister; she had a purpose of her own. Without her, Mozart's music would lie on the page forever silent.

The sound of an explosion woke Bob Anthony, though he did not know till afterward what it was. He only knew that he was sitting bolt upright in bed in the middle of the night, with the quarters pitch dark around him. A moment later the emergency whistle began to toot, a series of short sharp yelps. A yellow glow appeared beyond the window, and by the time he had on his shirt and pants and boots he was across the room and out the door.

The vast black night was split by a wall of flame, out on the flat where the fuel shed had stood that housed the gasoline supply. The smoking fragments of the shed lay among dry, greedy sagebrush that was burning brightly. It was far out from camp, but not far enough, Bob calculated swiftly, and on the windward side. The soft breeze of night was blowing up the valley, carrying sparks and fiery brands. The cottages lay in its path, their huddled shapes and dark corners painted a sickly red in the firelight. As he raced for the strip of crackling sagebrush, he saw Loring and two other men running among the cabins calling "All out! Everybody out! Grab what you can."

From the cookshack came a huddle of men, carrying a hose

out of which trickled a little water. It fell far, far short; the nozzle did not reach to the end of the bunkhouses. "Put it on the roofs," Bob shouted back without stopping.

He converged with other men on the open ground, stamping as they went, blotting out patches of smoldering grass which smoked evilly and soon grew bright again. "Buckets!" Loring directed a mighty bellow at the cookshack. There was a confusion of dimly lit figures there, but soon they emerged with armloads of pails, cauldrons, cook pots, stumbling with them toward the open space and sprawling down and getting up again, dropping things as they ran.

The bunkhouse men were coming too, a frowsy army in denims and torn underwear, smelling of sleep—Poles with wild shaggy hair, Italians with frightened eyes. They fell into line toward the river as Loring barked orders, scrambling down the cliffs, picking their way blindly, yelling with pain and indignation as the sharp rocks bit into their shins. Presently there was a ragged line of them, beginning to pass up buckets from the dark river. A bucket on the nearest blaze, extinguishing the tall torch of a burning greasewood. Another bucket, coming with agonizing slowness up the path from hand to hand, sizzling into the teeth of the fire.

Bob had taken off his shirt and was flailing the flames with it, having no other tool. The gray-haired superintendent appeared beside him with a still smaller and more grizzled man in tow. Their arms were loaded with shovels and mattocks. "Firebreak," the superintendent said quietly. "Across in front of the cabins." He seemed to gather a group round him out of nowhere, and led them across the seething ground. He knows his business, Bob thought suddenly, and Loring doesn't.

With a few swift motions, the superintendent showed them where the clearing should run, and how widely. Bob took a shovel from the grizzled little man and began to scoop and throw, going deep enough to get fresh earth, turning it over. He put his back into it, the hard rangy back that had developed in him over these outdoor years, Scoop, throw—scoop, throw.

The fire had a head start. It had been scattered by the gasoline explosion and was eating at outlying fences and boardwalks.

The line that was chosen ran behind these, and already a few embers had crossed it. Bob saw the superintendent's wife and several other women going methodically about, stamping them out. Without breaking his rhythm, he glanced back at the cabins. The women and children stood far back in the shadows, reluctant to leave, and some of them were crying. The superintendent's dog barked incessantly from the darkness.

It was good to have a concrete thing to fight, something besides frustration and loneliness. Bob dug with zest. His soles were blister-hot, and his lungs were beginning to feel the smoke. Fire country, they called it, and this was what they meant. The stories men had told around the bunkhouse stove suddenly came alive. "Took out eight hundred acres up above Baldy Mountain." "Lost all his buildings, but saved his corral." "The bridge burnt out and they ain't never bothered to replace it."

Scoop, throw. His muscles were beginning to feel it, and there was a tender place at the base of his ribs. The smoke from the sagebrush smelled like incense. He turned his head this way and that, trying to avoid it. Changing his stance, he saw beyond the huddled figures a low flat bastion of rock. On it stood Amie Loring, her phonograph records piled around her feet, and on her sharply chiseled face, unguarded in the ruddy light, was a look that said plainly, *Let it burn.*

Startled, he bent to his work again. The glare was dying down behind him and the big timbers of the fuel shed were burning themeslves out. It was guerilla warfare now, man against flame. A pine seedling kindled and exploded, throwing hot resin in his face.

What if the fire should win? What if this were the end of his mission? I'm sorry, Lew. I tried. I really tried. "Narcissus." The windows open in the drawing room, the scent of the summer flowers. His mother in her Worth gown, her face shaded by her hand.

Thought ceased in him, and the primitive need to keep going welled up and took over. Scoop, throw. The dirt on his face was streaked with tears from his smoke-filled eyes, and in his nostrils was the stench of his charred shoes.

When a shout went up, and caps were tossed in the air, he

dropped on his hands and knees, and began to crawl away slowly toward cooler ground.

Ben Lucas heard the far-off thud as the fuel shed blew up, and the toot of the emergency whistle at the railroad camp. He came awake quickly; Ben had sentry blood in his veins. He did not know what the tooting meant, but he was pretty sure it was trouble.

He shared Mary's sense of obligation to the "railroad people," but he was shy of them. Was this a call for help? Would he make a fool of himself, rushing up there? Well, it had to be risked. A favor is a favor. He stretched cautiously in bed, though he knew he was pretty well mended now. To his amazement, nothing twinged, nothing ached. To wake from a refreshing sleep, and find himself a whole man again, felt glorious. He could hardly believe he was really free of pain.

Mary stirred softly, and with her movement a rush of passion took him. He was able now, and it had been so long, so long. The railroad camp and everything else faded out of his mind, and he was aware only of her closeness, her dearness, the soft familiar outline of her body. He turned over and began covering his wife's face with kisses.

Bob Anthony, who had been nobody, was suddenly a hero. To be sure, he was not the only one. Every fellow who had a bandaged arm or a scraped shin was made much of, and the women fussed over them all. Dr. McClellan came down from Indian Spring to put on dressings and give advice. But Bob's face and feet had been badly burned, his voice was only a croak, and the doctor advised laying him up for a few days.

The superintendent's wife baked him cookies, and Amie Loring came to bring him letters and read him the paper. The letters were nothing special; they were mail-order offers and a bulletin from a science club, that had somehow followed him from camp to camp. "Nothing from home?" Amie said.

Bob shook his head. "There isn't any home," he whispered hoarsely. "I told you about that."

"Ah yes. The parents are gone. The brother has run away. Will you find him, do you think?"

Bob shifted restlessly. "I don't know. It seems so stupid, just to give up. It would be years before he could be declared legally dead. . . . I thought about it, during the . . . the fire. It was the last thing I thought of. I guess I was light-headed. It seemed to me that Lew was here."

"And what will you do when you find him?"

"Take him back, I suppose. Lew needs looking after. He just never grew up. I've come to see it so clearly. Perhaps he wasn't allowed to. Perhaps some people never do."

"He is the older, is he not?"

"That doesn't seem to make any difference." Bob spoke slowly. He had not had occasion to try to put some of this into words before. "Your parents give you . . . well, certain things. I don't mean material things. It's like the gifts the fairies brought to the christening." Bob's furious blush rose to his face—he felt that it sounded very juvenile. But Amie regarded him steadily. She did not smile. "Things weren't evenly divided between Lew and me. I got what seems to be useful. The . . . the . . ."

"The brains?" Amie supplied helpfully.

"No, Lew isn't dumb. He was a terrific reader, but a poor student. He was dropped from two schools. Not for being bad, but just for not coming to grips with things. Dad tried cutting off his allowance; he got along somehow, and of course Mother wouldn't let him lack for pocket money. A couple of times I stood up in my little boots and tried to lecture him. It must have been quite a sight."

"Go on," Amie said. "I'm sure it does you good to talk, though we must think of your throat."

"I'm supposed to gargle . . . I will, after you've gone. . . . I've lived with this all my life, you know. I've been pretty bitter about being the plodding good boy, while everybody worried and stewed about Lew."

"You're still pretty bitter," Amie said.

"No, I've accepted the facts objectively. I'm just tired, that's all. Awfully tired."

"Then I shall leave at once," Amie said. "Curt will send you some of his cognac, I'm sure. Would you like it?"

"If he wants to. But please come back. You've been so kind. Everyone has been so kind."

"Everyone owes you a kindness. You fought the fire like a tiger."

"By the way," Bob croaked, "how does it happen that the fuel shed was built so close, and south of the camp? Every fool knows that the wind blows upriver."

Amie's face closed up. "It is not known who is to blame," she said.

The care of the Hollister place had devolved, of course, upon Ben. Mary supposed this could not be helped. The girls had talked halfheartedly about selling, but neither of their husbands would hear of it. Mr. Gillespie thought the place a good investment, and was indulgently pleased that Althea should have a bit of property in her own name. As for Ben, he would as soon have sold his right arm as a piece of prime land already planted to orchard. He knew the ranch, he pointed out. It was near, the work cycle was the same as his. When he had finished a task for himself he could easily take the ditching plow, or the harrow, or the sprayer, and go down to Pine Creek valley and do what was needed. The Scobie boys were growing up and looking for work. They could watch the irrigation water during the season, for very low hire that the Gillespies could pay if they liked.

The catch was that Ben himself would not take any money. He needed money, yes, but he would not take it from the Gillespies. Mr. Gillespie, who would have liked to have done something for Ben and Mary, was hurt. The two women anxiously kept their mouths shut while the men argued it out. At last Ben said that if Althea was not going to need a riding horse in town, the Gillespies could give him Rusty. Rusty was a horse that Ben esteemed. Ben had known Rusty since he was foaled. He had picked Rusty early, as a colt that was apt to turn out well. He was, as Ben said, a lot of horse for his size.

So now they had four horses, and could feed them all, or nearly all, on the crop of alfalfa from the east piece. They had to buy a little hay and a little grain, but this was like buying groceries for the family. Mary thought that next to herself and Helen, he was fonder of Rusty than of any living thing. It was a pride to him to ride Rusty into town or over to a neighbor's. Rusty would be the best stud in Tillicum County, Ben said, and he would breed him far and wide.

Mary rode Duke, as she always had. Ben's work team had been a little jealous at first, and nipped Rusty when they got the chance. But they were middle-aged and tolerant and it had been only a few months before Ben had been able to graze them all together. When there was no need to catch them up, as sometimes on a Sunday, he liked to see them headed up across the threadbare slopes, their feet broadly planted in the gravel, their long necks beautifully arched toward the ground. All day they snuffled out the bunch grass and the small tender weeds, and Ben thought them the finest sight a man could rest his eyes on.

12 THE RAILROAD line was nearly finished. The crews were getting smaller and the camp buildings were beginning to be torn down. Amie Loring sent the car for Mary as she had promised, and the two women spent several agreeable afternoons, sitting on the tight little porch above the river, listening to the sound of Amie's phonograph as it seeped out through the gauze curtains. Amie returned the visits, prowling about the big room like a bright bird who refused to light. *She'll leave, too, like a bird, when her time comes to migrate, and I shall never see her again.*

She ventured to ask, "What are your plans, Mrs. Loring?"

"Who knows? Curt will be reassigned."

"Your husband is very brilliant, isn't he?"

"Brilliant? No. He is faithful. He is earnest. He has had long training. The railroad is his life. But he has poor judgment. He cannot be given great responsibility. He does not understand why. It has nearly broken his heart."

Mary felt uncomfortable. "He is so good to people. He was awfully good to us."

"He is good to *me*." Amie made a little grimace. "Except, of course, that he cannot do the only thing I would like. He cannot leave the railroad."

"Where else could he work?" Mary said.

"Some dull job, some clumsy job. Something without glory. But it would be a settled life, knowing the neighbors, the tradespeople. . . . I make friends well. I could make friends. . . . But it would destroy Curt's image of himself. I cannot do it."

"If you don't mind a dull, respectable job," Mary was surprised to hear herself saying, "why don't you get one yourself?" She could not imagine what had gotten into her. A wife's place is with her husband. But the memory of her own brief independence flared pleasurably in her.

"Look at me, Mrs. Lucas. Who would trust me as a governess? Or a clerk? Who would have me for a seamstress? Men would always look at me a certain way. As they do now. No woman would keep me in her house to make her gowns or teach her children. And I do not want some other woman to buy me, anyhow. I want my own life. When Curt is gone, I shall have it. I can wait."

"That's a dreadful thing to say," Mary told her severely.

"I thought you would find it so. You are a child, dear Mrs. Lucas, an angelic and really very simple child. Nothing worse ever ought to happen to you than to be sent to bed without your supper."

"Some very bad things *have* happened to me," Mary said defensively. "I have been . . ." No, it sounded pretentious. Amie Loring would laugh at her.

"I make a life for myself," Amie spoke more tranquilly. "I like to watch the world. Things interest me. Things entertain me. I am glad to be not bad looking and to make the most of it. One gets accustomed to being noticed, to turning a few heads. . . . I like to go about with my big car and have everybody stare."

"Wouldn't you like to drive it yourself?" It seemed to Mary that in the wildly improbable event that the Lucases ever bought an automobile, this would be her first desire.

Amie shrugged. "What for? A driver can always be found. And some of them are very charming young men."

Mary said, troubled, "If you talk like that in Pine Creek, someone will misunderstand you."

"To make myself understood to the people of Pine Creek is not essential to me. Since as far as they are concerned, I am here today and gone tomorrow. Ah, little Mrs. Lucas, it is nice to talk to you, with your good, forthright mind. You refresh me, and I am very fond of you. Nurse your baby, now, and do not be shy with me. She will cry if you don't."

Mary obediently undid her blouse, and gave the baby her breast. "Enchanting," Amie said. "You are an absolute picture. . . . When the nursing time is past, do not forget to firm your bosom for a while with a handful of snow or a pat of ice. Nothing is so unattractive as a woman who droops. It is time for my car. You are coming next Saturday?"

"Saturday will be fine." Mary's heart leaped unreasonably. She would take Helen along, of course, but Helen was always good. A few hours apart from the orchard and the house, a meal perhaps at the cookshack, where no matter how many people dropped in, there always seemed to be food enough. She would leave a snack for Ben. Even had he been invited, she wasn't sure he would have gone with her. He liked to be in the orchard in the cool of the late day, switching the irrigation water, keeping a watchful eye on every tree.

Amie turned at the door. "I should like to give you a dress," she said. "It is a little large for me, and perhaps tight for you. But you are clever about fitting things, are you not? It is a good blue, the color of your eyes, and would look very nice on you."

"Oh dear!" Mary hesitated, greatly embarrassed. "Ben wouldn't like me to take it, I'm afraid. I mean, I wouldn't like Ben to think that I took it. Ben is so proud."

"*Quelle folie!* Who is to tell him? Say you bought it at a great bargain with your egg money. All farmers' wives have egg money, don't they?"

"They do not. And it's darling of you, and I'm sorry I can't accept. I could use a new dress." Mary added simply, "It means a lot to me that you should offer it." She laid the baby down and readjusted her clothing.

The driver was waiting. "This is Bob Anthony," Amie said. "Curt has appointed him to drive me because his foot is still tender from the fire. Till Saturday, then."

Mary thought the boy was, as Amie had said, charming. All the railroad people were charming and had manners and gave her a faint nostalgia for Oak Point. Bob Anthony placed his passenger in the back seat and drove off waving gaily. Mary put her washing to soak overnight in the copper boiler and went to pull a few radishes and green onions from the garden. It was her day to do out Fletch's room, but it was too late. She would have to put it over till tomorrow.

Althea's elegant handwriting skittered down the envelope; the letter looked as if it had been opened and resealed several times. Mary took it eagerly out of Fletch's hands.

> Mary dear,
> You simply cannot imagine what I have heard from Arthur. Mary, he is coming out here! He wants to see his sisters settled in their own homes, he says, and meet their husbands. Oh Mary, I am so rattled. Of course I will be delighted to see him. And we have the room that was Nancy's, which we keep always ready for guests. Charles has so many old friends who pass through town, and we would not think of letting them go to a public lodging.

It took Mary a moment to remember who Charles was. Althea, whose manners stemmed from an earlier generation, always called her husband Mr. Gillespie, even to his face. She *must* be rattled.

> Now as you know, dear, Arthur will expect to see everything. Our little home in Pine Creek Valley, and our present establishments.

Mary looked around at her present establishment. The bare room, with only three chairs and a footstool, the "corner kitchen" with its sink and range plainly visible. The other corner with the plain old bed, and the far end with nothing but the piano. I can finish the new patchwork spread if I hurry, and put it on the bed.

> I thought I would forward this as soon as possible. Arthur is so methodical, I am sure he wrote to me because he thinks of me as the head of the family here, and will duly write to you. Mary, he does not realize that there is no family! He does not know that Luthermere is just another farm that Ben looks after. I used to be very faithful about writing to him, and when I spoke of Luthermere I suppose I painted a rather rosy picture—I wanted to cheer him, and myself too.

I wonder what she has said to him about Ben and me? Maybe it's just as well I don't know.

> We must make the best of it. I am ashamed that I even hesitate to have him come. Arthur is such a dear, and he and you are so like—you are the rosy-faced ones, the quick ones, the easy-

going ones. You are a family within a family. And when I begin to really think about Arthur, I could almost weep. I missed them all so dreadfully at first. In the bottom of my heart I miss them still. I wonder if he will bring Hetty. How fashionable she must be, for Oak Point has grown they say, and Arthur's firm is very busy.

I shall want your reply as soon as possible, so we can decide what to do.

Your loving sister,
Althea

Then there was a postscript, written with a different pen.

I wonder if it might be best for us to keep Arthur here and plan on daylong trips upriver.

And still another postscript below, small, hasty:

If there is anything possible I can do to help you, Mary, let me know.

Dear Althea. She has managed to keep from saying that our house is poor and small and we have no place to put a guest, but she knows. . . . We could put him in Fletch's bed, I suppose, and Fletch could sleep in the hay. . . . That last postscript means that she'd like to offer me some money to fix things up, but doesn't dare.

And I wouldn't take it. I am Ben's wife, and this is Ben's home, and he built it himself and I am proud of it. . . . Am I?

She looked at it dispassionately for the first time. Before this it had always been simply the place where Ben was. She saw the cupboards and the cooler built of box lumber. In Oak Point, there were iceboxes, and ice was delivered to the door. There were bathrooms, too. Perhaps the little privy out back would amuse Arthur. Arthur was a good sort. He would take everything in his stride, and if he was shocked at anything they would never know it.

All this swivet on Althea's part is for my sake. She can entertain very well, and knows it. . . . Perhaps we could get in a few borrowed things. I wouldn't be above doing that. Oh, dear, why doesn't Arthur stay where he belongs? I love him, but . . .

Ben came in to the noon meal. She had it ready, a pot of stew and some early June peas. She was so busy with her own thoughts that she did not chatter lightheartedly at the table as she usually did. As for Ben, he never spoke unless he had something to say. She had the dishes washed up and he was settled in his big arm chair and had finished glancing at his seed catalog before he said hesitantly, "Mary . . ."

"Yes, dear?"

"Mary, I'm afraid your friend Mrs. Loring is fast."

"Nonsense," Mary said. "She's just so pretty and such fun that people won't let her alone. . . . What makes you think so?"

"A man can tell." Ben sighed somewhat heavily. He was not trying to make Mary unhappy. He was only doing his duty. "Besides, I've heard . . . things. Hints here and there."

"You'd better tell me what you've heard."

"I can't exactly, Mary. They don't come right out and say it."

"So for hints here and there, I'm to lose my only friend," Mary said, forgetting Dolly, forgetting the Pine Creekers who had loved and supported her in her school. All that was not the same.

"I didn't ask you to give her up," Ben said, though it was obvious that he wished she would. "Just be a little careful, about getting your name mixed with hers. People talk, you know."

"I've been through that once," Mary said bitterly. "Indeed, people *do* talk." She had never mentioned her past to Ben except that one time, up at the Rock Patch. She only mentioned it now because it was a left-handed way of defending Amie. "Well, I have good news for you. She's leaving in a month at the most. And what I'll do without her I don't know."

Ben made one more try. "You're so *believing*, Mary. You think the best of everybody."

"Isn't that a good way to be? I'm not suspicious, and self-protective, and worrying about my own skin." She knew that by implication she was accusing him of these things. She did not care; she was sharply hurt, grievously hurt. "I'm gullible. I know it. All right then, I'm gullible. I wish you'd stop trying to make me over."

It was the nearest to a quarrel they had ever had. Ben, with the air of a man who has just tangled with a hornet's nest, came over and kissed her goodbye, quickly, before he went out. This was not part of their noontime routine. Mary gave him back his kiss; she must never, never forget that Ben loved her and that whatever he did was for her own good. If she could not get from him the kind of fierce endorsement that ran in the Pillage blood, she could at least give it to Althea. She rummaged in the kitchen shelf for ink, pen, and paper, and she did not have to choose her words.

> Althea, dear, I am sure whatever you have said to Arthur is exactly right . . .

So this was the end of it. Bob Anthony watched them disassemble a big ugly yellow crane and put its vitals on a flatcar. The end of his job, the end of his search which had netted nothing; above all, the end of his nearness to Loring's wife, which had become (he said to himself) torture to them both.

There were times when he almost believed this. And there were times when his innate honesty told him that he had merely happened to be there when Amie Loring was lonely and bored. She was graceful about it; she pretended to be very concerned for him. He had gone to her cabin the first time with his ardor and his chivalry flying like banners. He had intended to ask her to run away, but she had been so beautiful, in her wisp of silver lace, that he had forgotten about it. And the next day he had had second thoughts. Did she know he would have them? Was it obvious that he was very young and at cross-purposes and in no position to elope with another man's wife?

On the long drives when he had been for some days her steady escort, the thing had become palpable between them. Then Loring was called to Wenatchee, and Bob, waking at three o'clock in the morning in the stuffy shack under the cliff, had seen her light burning, and known that it burned for him. . . . He did not feel guilty toward Loring for anything that had happened. Loring had not trusted him really, in the sense that one man trusts another; he had merely thought it inconceivable that one of his underlings would lift eyes to his wife.

Perhaps Bob had turned to her because of the taste of failure in his mouth. He needed comfort; it was not only his body that had been long denied. He was hungry to hear himself speak, to have someone say "Yes, you are right." Amie was a good listener. Without ever accusing him of a quixotic act in coming out here, she agreed that he had done his best and should go back and give the case to Pinkerton, and forget it.

In the last few days he had seen to the packing up of the transits and levels, the timekeeper had given him his last card. By now he understood that he would wake up some morning to a half-empty camp and that the Lorings would be gone.

He was lounging on the cookshack porch, wondering what to do with himself, when a party of visitors came by, walking loosely grouped and stopping to look at everything. They had the look of sightseers, a so-this-is-how-they-build-a-railroad look. He recognized Mrs. Lucas, whom Amie had often stopped to see, and a man he thought was Lucas, and another woman and two more men, nicely dressed. Beside Mrs. Lucas strolled the oldest of the men, stout and dignified. They resembled each other greatly.

"Oh, there's Mr. Anthony," Mary said. She liked this polite young man. "Mr. Anthony, I want you to meet my brother, Arthur Hollister. And my husband, and my sister and brother-in-law from Wenatchee."

Bob bowed. There was something about Althea that brought out the Easterner in him. Surely he had seen her before, and the same thing had happened. He said, "Ma'am, did you once send a Christmas tree from the railroad station in Wenatchee?"

"Why, yes, I did. Arthur, the tree, you remember? You said it came through very well. And I believe Hetty made up the needles into a pillow, and embroidered it 'For thee I pine.'"

Bob turned to Mary. "Then you must be the fearless young lady who cut it down."

"Oh, what *fun*," Mary cried. She was having a wonderful time. The dinner she had cooked for them had turned out very well, and the baby had captivated everyone. She had left Helen with Fletch and was spending the afternoon like a lady, showing her little realm to her guests.

"I'll be glad to show you around," Bob said. "Only there's not

208

much left to see. Maybe you'd like to take the trail to the top of the bluff and look at our waterworks."

They followed him single file, Arthur gamely planting his feet in the tracks of the others, the whole party raising a little cloud of dust which settled on the shrubbery beside the trail. At the top stood a squat tank of weathered wood with a trolley wire soaring up to it from the river, and a windlass at the top. Bob loosed the windlass and a bucket swung and lurched down the wire, plunging into the river. The contraption groaned aloud as he turned the drum and hauled it back, dripping, and tipped it over the edge of the tank, making a sullen splash.

"Good God," Arthur said, "how many hours a day does some poor soul have to wind that thing?"

"You are on the last frontier, sir." Bob hooked the bucket back into place. "It's a disciplinary measure, among other things. When the crews run out of culprits, they take turns."

"All that water down there," Mr. Gillespie grumbled, "and miles of land up here without a dang drop. It's enough to make you question the ways of Nature."

"Down here on the Entiat," Bob said, "they're giving Nature a hand. They've dammed the river and are using the power from the dam to pump water where they need it. This river in front of you could be dammed."

"You're joking," Mary told him.

"Not at all. You'll most likely see it in your lifetime."

Ben Lucas listened with painful attention. There ought to be some way to irrigate his upper flat, just out of reach of gravity water. Summer and winter it reproached him with its acres of rich soil, some of the best on the place. Time and again in his mind, he had planted it to trees and thrown a road along the hill there, just under Mary's Rock. Sometimes as he was going off to sleep he would think about a little steam engine, fed with scrap wood from the nearest mill; but in the morning he always knew that he had neither the skills nor the money.

"I'd like to see the Lorings," Mary said. "Are they home, do you know?"

"I really can't say." Bob glanced involuntarily down at the

camp. Arthur Hollister took out an already ruined white hand-kerchief and ran it around his collar.

"I don't suppose," he said hopefully, "that there's an ice cream parlor at the nearest crossroads?"

"They can usually whip you up some lemonade at the cook-shack." Bob offered his arm to Althea. "Shall we go down and find out?"

"I want to see the Lorings," Mary said stubbornly. "Please take us there, Mr. Anthony."

"Very well." Bob sounded more formal than ever. He guided them down the slope and to the head of the boardwalk, but there he muttered abruptly, "Will you excuse me? I've got some reports to write." Waving off their thanks and farewells, he continued on the road, up around the turn, and found a seat on a boulder dark with lichen, just out of the sun.

The great cliffs stretched away to the north, following the sweep of the river. He had climbed one once, on an idle after-noon. The cliff was like his mission in the West; endless, and difficult, and full of slippery places. And when you got to the top, what was there? Nothing.

The Lucases and the Gillespies and Arthur Hollister had coffee on the Lorings' crowded porch. Arthur exerted himself. He asked Loring questions about the financing and legal aspects of building a railroad, most of which Loring could answer, and listened respectfully to Caruso singing "O Sole Mio" on Amie's phonograph. Mary sat and fanned herself and looked very pretty. This was unquestionably her day.

She followed Amie into the house and as they fussed with their hair, and Amie put a little rice powder on her creamy skin, Mary said, "Amie, about that dress . . ."

"Yes, my dear?"

"I've changed my mind. If I may." It was Ben's pride she was putting in her pocket, but it had become necessary. "My sister is going to give a big party, for Arthur, and ask all her friends in Wenatchee. We are to go, and I . . . I need it."

"I am glad for you to have it. There is something about it that is just right for you." Amie went to the shelf with its cretonne drapery that served as a clothes closet, and pushed aside the hangers and took down a frock. It was a clear, bright blue, and it rustled.

"Oh Amie, how lovely. How marvellous. I can't thank you enough. I could have asked Althea to loan me something, but since you offered . . ."

"You will look sweet in it," Amie said. "It is a sweet dress. I have worn it very little. Save your qualms. It is better that I give it to you than to throw it out when we move."

"When will that be?"

"Any day."

"Come down to the house, Amie. Come and tell me goodbye. I don't want it to be casual like this."

"This way is best," Amie said. "But I will come if I can."

"Does Curt have his new assignment?"

"Tentatively. He is not happy about it."

"Are you?"

Amie shrugged her shoulders. "What difference does it make?"

"Aren't you ever going to break out, Amie? Can't you tell Curt?"

"What would I tell him? That I propose to destroy him? . . . That is something you do not understand, Mary—that Curt could be so easily destroyed. Your Ben could pick himself up and go on. Curt cannot. He needs to be needed, to give, to be thanked. I am thanking him, sufficiently, for what he has done for me. It was a great deal."

Mary gave it up. "Can I hide this under my coat, do you suppose? I'll need it quite soon."

Amie laughed. "I will send it down this evening. Go and have your festive day."

"With you going away? Oh Amie."

"You did quite nicely without me for a long time. Mary, are you with child again?"

Mary was startled. "How did you know?"

"I was not sure. But I thought so."

"I'm not sure myself. If I am, it will be in the winter. February, probably. I had Helen last December. I'll scarcely have her weaned. Oh Amie, I'm a little bit scared!"

"You will get along," Amie said. "You will always get along." She kissed Mary's rosy cheek. "Go to your guests now. If you want to know, I had planned to vanish while the brother was here. I thought it would be simpler for you. But you came to seek me. Well, I am not sorry. One likes to be valued. So, you see, I understand Curt."

"You were going to all that trouble to make it easy for me?"

"That is nothing. The only other one I must part from will be infinitely more trouble, I can assure you."

Taking Mary's hand in hers, she drew her gently back into the tiny front room. Althea, impressed with the silver urn and the Oriental rug, was saying goodbye. Arthur had provided a livery rig; it would be a long trip for them back to town.

They left Mary and Ben at the Lucas gate. Nothing had changed. Fletch was conscientiously minding the baby, who was hungry and cross. The cabin was clean, as she had left it. The cow was part way down from the bench. The irrigation water was running in the orchard in long, trickling rows. The nasturtiums on the chicken wire drooped in the heat. A cricket rasped under the front porch, and in the cooler, though the sun was off it, everything smelled faintly stale and the melted butter had a dingy rime of salt. In the quiet kitchen corner she set out some hastily found supper, and the men, without speaking, sat down to eat.

Ben watched the party at the Gillespies' and felt that he scarcely knew this Mary in the blue dress. She moved among Althea's friends with a kind of wistful grace. Or had Mary always been like that, among her own people? If these *were* her people. They said a great many overly polite things to each other in bright voices, and they shook hands with limp arms held high. There was waltzing, and Mary revolved on the floor in the arms of his brothers-in-law, and sent him several beseeching glances, but he shook his head. He literally did not know how. It was all he could do to make out in a square dance, without getting involved in this fancy twirling.

She danced mostly with Arthur. Arthur's feet kept excellent time, and his frosty eyes twinkled. He was immaculately clean, with the kind of pink-and-tan cleanliness that no farmer who puts his hands in the earth can ever achieve.

Ben wished he had skinned down to the General Merchandise Company and got a collar that was really white, like Arthur's. The one he had on, saved from his not very festive youth, was frayed and yellowed, though Mary had done her best with it. Perhaps he could replace it tomorrow. *Whoa, boy, don't let yourself be stampeded. Tonight was the night for a collar, and when will you ever need one again?*

He caught the eye of his other brother-in-law and felt better. He had always thought Gillespie something of a stuffed shirt, but at least he was a Westerner, a pioneer, he was just folks, and Ben understood him. Gillespie's look said as plain as day that the women had the bits in their teeth tonight.

Lawyers. They're both lawyers. I wouldn't be a lawyer, I don't want to make money out of peoples' troubles. . . . I suppose that's not fair—there have to be lawyers. If something happened to my claim or my water rights, I'd need a lawyer, and need one bad. But that doesn't mean they're so all-fired important. Who cuts down the timber and rassles the rock and starts the deals, so lawyers can come along and help them out?

The dancing stopped and Althea disappeared into the kitchen to supervise what, if he knew Althea, would be a round of refreshments that would leave them groggy. Mary and Arthur walked slowly toward the porch, where the Gillespies' wicker furniture, the very latest thing, stood behind screens that held at bay a cloud of bumbling moths out of the summer night.

"Well, Mary?"

"Well, Arthur?"

"Mary, are you happy? Is this what you really want? Up there, I mean."

"Yes. Yes, of course it is. Arthur, I wouldn't trade my life for anyone's."

"I see. . . . You girls didn't have it too easy. . . . We used to wonder . . . we couldn't get much idea. I think," Arthur said gently, "that you could have let us know."

"We did. We wrote and wrote."

"Quite." Arthur nodded. "Well, let that pass. . . . What's going to become of your children, Mary?"

"They'll grow up strong. And good. I'll give them books, and play them music. I'll teach them. Everything."

"I wish you luck," Arthur said. "I'm glad I came, Mary. To see for myself. We always thought, for such a long time, that . . . that some day . . ."

"We'd fail."

"I suppose so." Arthur was silent, and Mary knew he was thinking of the weatherbeaten houses, the long dangerous roads, the unruly river, the pitiless sun. There was nothing she could say.

"I believe you'll be all right," Arthur said finally. "At any rate, I'm proud of you, Mary. You're a Pillage through and through."

Glowing with pleasure, Mary said, "I'll get along. That's what Amie . . . oh, Arthur, compared to other women, I am so well off! I . . . I love Ben, you know." It was hard to overcome her shyness, but it must be said. If only to make it clear to herself how much better life had treated her than it had treated Amie.

"Of course you do. . . . Mary, there is something I would like to . . . I wonder if you would . . . I've done awfully well the last couple of years. I invested the money from the house—I've never felt that that was exactly mine. . . . Did I tell you I got Hetty an electric stove? She's very pleased with it."

"I'm so glad."

Arthur drew from an inside pocket a compact roll of bills. "Mary, I want to leave something with you. I'd appreciate it if you'd take it."

Mary's eyes watched him as he stripped off ten ten-dollar bills. "This is for the baby, if you like. Or to put away against a rainy day. Just to feel that you have it, if anything should happen."

"Althea tried to give me money too," Mary said with faint bitterness.

"Now, Mary, don't spoil my visit. I've looked forward to doing this. What good is money, if you can't share it? You're my little sister, and I want to make you a present, and I'm too clumsy to think of anything else to give you."

Mary looked at the money. To have it hidden somewhere, to know that sickness or catastrophe would not strike her unprepared. Her voice was unsteady. "You're very nice, Arthur."

He pressed it into her fingers. "It isn't much."

"It's a fortune. . . . Arthur, where shall I put it?"

Arthur was feeling jaunty. "I believe," he said, "that ladies sometimes hide money in the tops of their stockings."

"Why Arthur!"

"It's only hearsay," Arthur said hastily. "You could ask Ben to carry it for you, I suppose. But I thought of it as being sort of a secret."

"Till the right moment comes. All right, Arthur. I'd better go upstairs then, if you don't mind, and tuck it in my bag."

The smell of fruit cake followed her up the stairs, and a light wash of voices came from the dining room. A secret. Arthur did not want her to use it for feed for the horses, or lumber for the packing benches. But of course it would be awkward to spend it on herself, it would lead to explanations. Her sewing basket had a false bottom, quilted to hold pins and needles. She would put it under the quilting of the sewing basket and forget it was there. As long as she could.

She was restless after her holiday, and one day seemed exactly like another. To get up while Ben was still rattling the lids of the stove, to give the baby a crust for chewing while she made Ben's mush (she must put Helen on solid food, now, as soon as she could, for there was no doubt that she was pregnant again; she had passed her second time-of-the-month). To take the milk pail from Ben's hand and strain and cool the milk, put the bread to rise, bathe the baby, wash or sew or can rhubarb or peas, or scrub the bare wood floor according to the exigencies of the day; and to have everything caught up, for Fletch was to leave soon for the wheat harvest to make his stake, and Ben would need some help in the orchard again. After this fall, if the crop was good, he could take on a Scobie boy as a hired hand.

215

There was no word from Amie; she supposed the Lorings had left. That had been goodbye, then. Amie wanted it that way, and Ben, though he would say no more, would want it that way too. She bore Ben's good name. She must not keep running up to the camp if that would compromise it.

It was only by accident, sitting on Mary's Rock with the baby in her arms in one of her rare free moments after noonday dinner, that she caught a glimpse of the big red car in the tangle of willows and seedling pine down by the river. There was a stub road leading to the river across the stony land north of Ben's homestead—it was almost never used. How cautiously the car must have crept along it, jouncing in the ruts, brushing the sagebrush with its burnished sides.

She could not contain her curiosity. She walked down the hill with the baby in her arms, and crossed the highway. The sun was very warm. She took off her apron, and laid it lightly over Helen's head.

It was none of her business. Yes, it *was* her business. She skirted the Lucas orchard and walked quietly along the old ruts, coming to the little dry scrubby grove in which the road ended, and saw the empty car, below which the beach began with its worn rocks and sibilant water.

Amie was sitting on a piece of driftwood, and young Anthony in the sand beside her had his arms on her lap and his face buried in them. She did not need their tracks from the grove to tell her the story. While she watched, the boy raised his face and said something, and Amie, with her thin white hand, pushed back his hair.

They were tranced. They would scarcely have heard her had she spoken their names.

It is my business, because they are here. And they are here because they have no other place to go, and because this is the Lucas place, and Amie is my friend. They do not feel safe anywhere, but they feel a little safer here.

She was not surprised, and she was not shocked, though she felt she might be when she began to realize it. *Shall I be like Althea, saying we must not let Mr. Conway help us any more because of his Indian woman?*

216

Bob Anthony made a sudden gesture; he flung out his arm and got up. Hidden by the screen of trees and sand dunes, Mary was afraid the baby would cry. But Helen lay content and quiet on her mother's shoulder, drowsy in the heat, her weight making Mary's arm ache a little. *I must go. I have seen what I came to see.* Yet she watched until they closed in a sudden, forlorn embrace, and then she turned away her face. At this point she had no right. She did not need to look to know the mouth seeking mouth, the body pulsing against body, the moment that is endless.

When the engine had started and the car had gone, she turned along the lower edge of the orchard and found the barbed-wire fence where it ran along the riverbank, and laid the baby through it and let herself between the rows of wire as Ben had taught her. The baby, taken from her snug place against her mother, began at last to fuss. Mary soothed her and walked up between the orchard rows, in the dusty soil. She opened the gates along the right-of-way, closing them carefully. She was sure of only one thing, no one must know. Not Ben, who would be justified; not Althea, who would judge. The secret she had felt so oppressive, the money from Arthur, was trivial compared to this.

She came into the shade of the house and sat down, not looking at the clock, forgetting that the peas needed to be picked and the eggs gathered. From down in the east piece she could hear faint sounds of Ben and Fletch cutting the alfalfa.

She tried to tell me. Over and over. I can think of so many different ways that she tried to tell me. But I could never understand. I'm just a child, dear Mrs. Lucas, an angelic and really very simple child, and nothing worse ever ought to happen to me than to be sent to bed without my supper. At the memory of Amie's crisp voice her heart began to ache, as if she were coming out of an anaesthetic.

And where is my loyalty to Curt Loring? To Curt who helped us in our trouble? Who is good and kind and stupid and futile and loves his wife?

Not to talk of it was torture. Mary had an open heart and mind. She assailed Ben's habitual silence with endless chatter. But she

217

knew that if she said one word about Amie, she would have to take sides. She would either have to defend Amie or blame her, to Ben who was prone to say "I told you so." She was not ready to give him the chance, and Ben would see no need to be wholly discreet; he already knew what other men knew. If there was gossip about Amie, she would not pour fuel on it.

But if she condoned by her silence, it meant that she was flying in the face of everything she had been taught; it meant that she forgave and overlooked. The forgiveness they talked about in church? "Go, and sin no more?" No. Amie would sin again. "I amuse myself," she had said drily of her summers away from the camp.

If she had forgiven Amie, must she not forgive Mr. Conway also? It seemed to her that this was so, perhaps because it offered some concrete thing to do. She would see Mr. Conway and right an old wrong.

She told Ben that she was going up into Pine Creek valley, and he nodded. Ben could understand an attachment to places; it appeared natural to him that she should wish to see Luthermere. She would take the baby, she said—Helen was old enough to sit before her on the saddle. And Helen's was a special kind of companionship; it was precious to Mary to be greeted with smiles and glad cries, to be wholly and uncritically adored and welcomed. Helen never tried to make her mother over, to offer advice, or to pass judgment.

Mary saddled Duke immediately after breakfast, for it would be cooler then. On the oilcloth covered table she set out covered dishes of hard-boiled eggs and cheese and cold baked beans, in case she were not back by noon. Helen's diapers went into a sack behind the saddle. The baby herself, fresh and fragrant in clean clothes and full of early morning joy, was handed up to her by Ben. "You sure you'll be all right?" he said. It was true that his folks had started him out on horseback when he, too, was about seven months old, but it seemed more precarious now. Almost everything he valued in the world was perched up there in the saddle.

"We're fine," Mary said. With the baby in front of her she could not stoop to him, but she put her hand lightly on his shoulder.

Proudly and a little apprehensively, Ben walked with them up to the gate and let them out.

Mary rode to the inner side of the highway against the hill, drawing Duke on to the shoulder whenever a buggy or an automobile appeared. The air, not yet heavy with heat, smelled of the newly falling river, that had passed its early summer crest and was now slowly uncovering its sandbanks again. The Sawyer house between Ben's place and Pine Creek had a scraped cowhide nailed on the logs to dry. Mica glittered in the freshly broken rock where the road had been moved uphill to make room for the railroad.

Well, there it was. The railroad. Running arrowlike among the orchards and bare graveled slopes, through cuts that were still like open wounds in the landscape. A shiny black train ran each way everyday along the river, making a tremendous racket. The horses were getting used to it, and no longer shied and pranced. And at Pine Creek when the train stopped, though the station had not yet been built, the loungers gathered as they used to gather at steamboat time.

Mary waved at Mr. Lindsay in the front door of the store, and took the long curving road around the bowl, past the schoolhouse and up to the gate of Pine Creek valley. It *did* seem rather good to be climbing this road again. She remembered how Duke's shoes used to strike sparks from it before the road crew had worked it over. It was a better road now, and Duke was older, and so was she.

In Pine Creek valley the shadow fell narrowly along the foot of the southwest hill. She did not turn in toward Luthermere, but took the opposite road, up across Mr. Conway's field. There was a rustle of insects in it, and the hay had not been cut.

Mr. Conway's door stood open. She dismounted carefully and took the baby down and into her arms, and walked up and looked in, expecting to see his stooped figure somewhere about.

The house was empty, and so was the yard. Inside, the meager furniture held dust and a few drifted leaves, and a pack rat had built a nest in a corner, from which protruded a shiny silver spoon.

The odor of habitation had almost disappeared; the house had the clean, woodsy smell of a deserted building. Mr. Conway had gone. He had not merely stepped out for a day or a week, he had gone and taken his troubles with him. From a nail beside a small cracked mirror a towel hung limply. The sound of the water in the flume outside came peacefully into the house.

Mary looked for a long time, and then she stepped back and sat down on the square-hewn log that formed the doorstep. And here, at last, she wept—clean healing tears that fell on the baby's fresh muslin dress as Helen dozed. Not only because she was too late, but for all the too-lates, the cross-purposes, the empty hands and hungry hearts of mankind. For Mr. Conway, for Curt Loring, for faithless Amie and bewildered Bob Anthony, for her disenchanted self. For what we have left undone, and what we have done that we should not, but cannot help.

A chipmunk ran across her feet, and wild bees soared through the clearing. At last she dried her eyes, changed her baby's diaper, got back on the horse with some difficulty by putting Helen up first and holding her there, and went on up the road to see Dolly Plew.

"Dolly, I'm in the family way again. Oh Dolly, so soon!"

"That's how it goes sometimes," Dolly said philosophically. "Some women, when they git started, they just have 'em and have 'em. What you goin' to do with *her*," she jerked her thumb at Helen, who was sitting precariously upright on the floor, "give her to somebody else? Like maybe me?"

"Dolly, this is serious. What shall I do? I've already got my hands full."

"Well, they do say it helps if you tell your husband to go hang his pants on some other bedstid." Dolly watched Mary's ladylike color rise, and laughed. "It's a far cry from teachin' school, ain't it, Mary? Have you told Ben yet?"

"No, I haven't. I've only just admitted it to myself."

"Seems to me I've heard as how Ben was one of six or eight kids on a stump farm, an' I don't think any of 'em ever went hungry. You just tell Ben, an' let him cope with it. Ben may be a little hard sometimes, but he don't scare easy. Ben's a family man. He'll be *glad.*"

Mary felt a surge of relief. It was true. When Ben had said he would take care of her, he had meant it all the way. This, as far as Ben was concerned, would be expected in the scheme of things.

"I'll come down an' do for you for a few days," Dolly said, "when the time comes, or before, for that matter. If you get took down bad with morning sickness, you have Ben come up an' git me."

Mary kissed Dolly's withered cheek. Would Amie Loring have done this for her? She doubted it very much.

13

"Mrs. Lucas, I'd like to speak to you, if you're not busy."

Mary looked at the nervous young man on the doorstep, and said, "Why yes. Come in." She did not tell Bob Anthony that no one was ever too busy to talk to anyone in Pine Creek. She showed Bob to a chair and laid down the carrots she was scraping and sat regarding him with a friendly gaze. After a moment or two she saw that she was going to have to break the ice, and she did so warmly and directly. "I suppose she's gone."

Bob flinched a little, but he said, "Yes, she's gone." Perhaps it was a relief to him to find that Mary knew. "I'm leaving the country, Mrs. Lucas. I can't stand it here any more. I just thought I'd drop by and say goodbye. And ask you . . . and ask you . . ."

"You can ask me anything you like." Mary rose and looked out the window and came back. "I heard my husband in the yard, and I just wanted to see if he needed me out there. He's lost his other helper. . . . Would you like a cup of coffee, Mr. Anthony? Or a glass of buttermilk?"

Bob shook his head. "I just . . . I've got something on my mind. And you seemed the best . . . She was very close to you, wasn't she?"

"Not awfully," Mary said honestly. "But I miss her a lot. I don't expect I'll ever hear from her."

"I know damn well *I'll* never hear from her. . . . It's all right I guess. Part of my fool's errand. You know why I'm here, don't you, Mrs. Lucas?"

"I've heard a little about it. You're looking for kinfolk, I believe."

Supper would be late, and the baby might claim her at any moment. But Mary knew well the passionate need to be heard, to get something straight by talking about it. "You'd better tell me the whole story," she said.

She listened while the sunlight crept lower in the west window and fell on the piano, turning its mahogany to a somber red. "The longer I waited to give it up," Bob said, "the worse it seemed to leave without accomplishing anything."

"You had the bear by the tail, as my father used to say." Mary was sorry for him. With all his youth and promise, his good looks, his virility, you still could not help being sorry for Bob Anthony.

"Well, I'm letting go now. Right now. If Lew doesn't show up in a few more years, he'll be legally dead, and I'll inherit."

"A lot?" Mary said.

"You'd call it a lot, I suppose. . . . That's one reason I hung on so. I won't have it said that I profited by letting Lew disappear."

So he was rich, too; and she was sitting here wondering how they were going to support another child. Mary smiled. "Who would say it?"

"It would be true, whether anyone said it or not."

"I think," Mary said, "you're a little hard on yourself. You've tried to stick by him. Families feel that way, or they ought to. Were you very fond of each other?"

"We fought like cats and dogs. But kids always do, don't they? We rode our bicycles together, and sailed boats on the pond. Only Lew's generally sank."

"How did it happen he never married?" .

"Oh, he married. Off the cuff, like he did everything. She was older than Lew and terribly attractive. My father had it annulled. It wasn't long after that that Mother died, and he lit out."

Mary sighed. "It sounds very difficult. And yet you're wasting all this time over him. Did you really want to come?"

"I guess I did. When my father said 'Find Lew,' I put up a little fuss, but I guess I was kind of glad. . . . It hasn't been any use. People disappear here like rabbits into the brush." He put his head down on his hands. "*Where do you suppose he is?*"

"Don't think about it now," Mary said. "Go back where you belong. Find some work to do. Didn't Amie . . . didn't I hear that you're a scientist?"

Bob said with a rather thin smile, "That's a big word. I'm just getting a toe in the crack, but Mrs. Lucas, there's an awful lot to do, things are opening up fast. I had some plans for a laboratory —a place that people could come in with ideas. Perhaps if Lew never . . . I guess I could endow it in his name."

He gave her a wistful look. "Anyhow, you've made it easier to ask you something. I wanted to just walk out, but I can't. It's been too long, and I'm too committed. . . . You'll probably always live here. I'd like to leave you an address. If you hear anything. . . . If anyone mentions Lew Anthony, or you think there's a lead, will you let me know? Right away? I don't suppose it would be a lot of trouble to you, and I'd like to think there might still be some way. . . ."

"I'd be very glad to." Mary thought it a rather pathetic hope. She excused herself to shake down the fire and put fresh wood on it, and turned back to suggest, "You might talk to Ben. He knows the country pretty well. But it's too late for that, isn't it?" She added in accordance with the custom of the country, "Will you stay to supper? I'll lay an extra plate."

"Thanks, but I'm headed down the river."

"The train has already gone," Mary said, surprised.

"I'm not going on the beautiful new train." Bob stood up. "I'm leaving the country the way I came into it. On foot. Somehow I'm fed up with trains."

He towered over her as she came to put out her hand. He could probably have bought and sold them with a few scratches of the pen, and he had asked her a favor, something money could not buy. Sweat-stained, young, discouraged, washed up, he stood there like any tired youngster, and it was part of the unreality that she was taking the hand of Amie's lover. It ought to scorch her fingers somehow, but it didn't.

He fumbled in an upper pocket, and took a slip of paper from it. "This will always reach me. You can't imagine how much I appreciate it. Goodbye, Mrs. Lucas. I don't expect to be back, unless I hear from you."

Ben came in as the dust rose about Bob Anthony's feet along the litle road up through the orchard. "That young fellow want something?" he asked, lifting from a lower shelf the box where he kept his pipe wrench and blow torch.

225

It would take her too long to tell him, and supper was hardly started. "Just to say he's leaving," she answered. Perhaps after supper, when the dishes were washed and the baby asleep. Though she would keep Amie's name out of it. And though Ben, who was rather glad the railroad building was over and done, might well yawn and decide to go to bed in the middle of it.

Arthur wrote that he had had a wonderful time on his visit. He was sending something to show his appreciation, he said; and Mary understood that this had nothing to do with the hundred dollars he had put in her hand. He had found a chance to pick up something pretty for Mary at a bargain, and it would arrive by freight shortly.

Mary doubted that he had picked it up at a bargain. Money was on her mind these days, and if there was such a lot of it floating about, she wished Ben did not have to work so hard for it. She did what she could to help him; she chopped her own kindling and pulled down hay for the horses and drove the cow out in the morning. When Ben felt that they must put on one more spray, she drove the sprayer, not very successfully, for the whole thing depended on keeping going with the team so that the spray machinery would revolve, and the horses, feeling an unfamiliar hand and lacking Fletch's accustomed bellow, would stop and look around inquiringly. And Ben, who knew now that a baby was on the way, was dubious about letting her do it. Still, they managed it, and the fact that they did not have to hire a driver was important.

It was not easy to make their budget stretch from harvest to harvest. Ben would not borrow unless the need was dire. He knew too many ranchers whose crop was in hock before it ever left the trees. But he was shyly pleased about the baby. And though he came from a family where childbirth was not made much of, instinct told him that this outlander wife of his needed something more in the way of pampering than his mother and his aunts.

After her third month, he did not ask for her help outdoors, and he carried the wash water for her on Mondays and filled the copper boiler for their baths on Saturday night and got out the tub and set it up by the stove. For himself, he preferred to stand out in the yard after dark and sluice himself down, but Mary liked a tub. Being a reticent man himself, he retired behind a newspaper while she took it, but he allowed himself a peek now and then, and the sight of his wife's rosy pink body, soaped and glistening, lay at the bottom of his heart among his few treasures.

The late summer heat quivered on the land like a living thing, and the orchard was thick with green fruit that seemed to get bigger overnight. Little trees for their first couple of years bore sparingly—big perfect apples that sold for a premium price. His trees were trying hard; the load was exceptional for a second crop. He thought he ought to pluck a few off, to lighten the branches, but he did not have the heart. He needed every penny they would bring. Anxiously, for the responsibility was his alone—to balance present gain against the future welfare of the orchard—he placed a few props under the most heavily loaded boughs, and hoped for the best.

Arthur's gift arrived uncrated, which made it even more spectacular than the piano. On the cinder platform at Pine Creek stood a leather-topped surrey, slenderly black and shining, with two beautiful brass lanterns. It was a sort of Cinderella coach, and Mary gasped when she saw it. The shafts, wrapped and tied alongside, were quickly untied and fitted on by all the bystanders who happened to be there that day. It was getting to be a real occasion when Miz' Lucas got these here presents from her brother.

Ben admired the surrey. He suppressed a twinge that often assailed him because he could not be the one to give Mary everything. This was a graceful gift, and he did not begrudge it to her. They didn't really have a horse fit to draw it, except Rusty, and Rusty was not broken to harness. But Ben made up his mind at once that Rusty and the surrey belonged together. He began in the intervals of all his other work to hitch Rusty to a drag and then to a two-wheeled half of the wagon frame that would have the draw and feel of a vehicle, and Rusty learned quickly and was proud.

It was September before Ben felt that the whole thing was far enough along to turn it over to Mary. In the meantime they used the surrey occasionally to take Mary to Indian Spring to the doctor. Ben drove, for the work horse did not like the sway of the tall unfamiliar shape and was skittish. The visits to the doctor were not frequent. Mary had had a baby before and felt that she knew how to do it. She let some gathers out of the blue dress that Amie had given her, turned the skirt upside down, redraped it, and it became a maternity dress, the only one she would have.

She felt very elegant in it as she started out on a September afternoon, with Helen beside her in a nest made of a bedquilt and several pillows. Helen wore a floppy silk bonnet that Althea had sent, and Mary had a pair of old kid gloves with which to handle the polished black reins. It was almost like going driving in Oak Point. Except that in Oak Point she had never had a companion so talkative and so in need of a watchful eye. If the baby so much as put a foot over the edge of the quilt, she said "No, no," automatically, and put it back without really taking her eyes off the road. Helen spoke a gibberish which, though it was not words, plainly explained that she found her seat confining, that the horsie made interesting whickers when they met another horse, that she loved her mama, and that mealtime was never far away. The communion between them was so intense that Mary could not tell whether it was conveyed by sounds or by a telepathic stream between mother and child. This must end, she supposed, when she had another baby. Or would it reach further, and include both children? She was past her resentment of the pregnancy now. It seemed natural and right. But her condition was beginning to show, and no nice woman continued to go about in public after it became too obvious. She had promised herself that the first time she took the surrey out without Ben, she would visit the school. On her comings and goings to Pine Creek she had passed it often enough, and never without a twinge of possessiveness. Perhaps it was not tactful to go there so soon after school opened —she could imagine the confusion, the new teacher's qualms (for there was still a new teacher every year). But she felt that her time was running out.

It was an afternoon of tawny splendor. The leaves of the cottonwood trees beside Mr. Lindsay's store were like gold coins. Mary took the great curve of the road that climbed from the store to the schoolhouse, and crickets stopped chirping as she passed and then began again behind her. She drove into the school yard, maneuvered the surrey smartly, and tied Rusty to the familiar rail.

Nostalgia swept her as she saw the scarred desks and smelt the chalk and library paste. The room seemed dingy, darker than she remembered, and Miss Stacy, who politely asked her to take the swivel chair, seemed very young. Miss Stacy had round black eyes like marbles, and wore a starched blouse formidably stiff and white.

Ralph Waldo Emerson was gone from the rear wall and in his place was an enormous map, the continent of Europe, with red and blue pins stuck in it. "We're keeping track of the War," Miss Stacy said. "In Current Events. The red pins are the German lines. The blue ones are the Allies."

"Oh, yes, the War," Mary murmured. She knew about the War. Though they saw few newspapers nowdays, you could not help but know. It was a bad dream, from which everyone hoped that Europe would soon awaken.

"Do they like it?" Mary asked doubtfully. "Are they interested in all that?"

"Why yes," Miss Stacy said. "It's like a game, you know. The Germans have stopped advancing now and the rows of pins don't move much. It was pretty exciting at first."

There was no reason, Mary told herself, why she should find it a slightly shocking game. Henry Hollister had taught his girls the same great stories he had taught his boys; Thermopylae, Balaclava, Valley Forge. But a war that was safely tucked away in history was somehow less horrifying than the homes and libraries of Belgium, still smoldering.

She did not expect to find the faces of the students familiar; little Indian Ellen was graduated of course, and restless Jeff Porter, and Hansi. She was rather glad, in view of the row of red pins, that Hansi was not here. And the rest would have grown beyond recognition—children change so fast.

But *they* remembered *her*; she could tell by the stolen glances, the whispering. She was dislocating their world—two teachers in the room were like two norths on the compass. "Your arithmetic, Thomas," Miss Stacy called briskly, and Thomas was surely the smallest pupil, scared and grubby, who used to throw his arms around her neck. He was still grubby, and breathed through his mouth—adenoids, no doubt.

At recess Miss Stacy turned to her with a rather forlorn smile. "A bit dismal, isn't it? Not quite what I expected when I went to Normal School."

"I didn't go to Normal." Mary said. "I really don't know what one would . . ." She wanted to sympathize, and at the same time was a little dashed to find Miss Stacy's job so thanklessly regarded. "I had some superior pupils I guess. Florence Scobie . . ."

"I board at the Scobies'," Miss Stacy said. Plainly, she felt that Florence was no genius.

You have to love them, Mary wanted to cry out. *Or be mad at them, or something. You have to care. And of course you don't have Ben waiting for you at the door. That made a difference too.*

"You must come and see me," she said. "Talk about it sometimes. I don't know if I can be of any help."

"I'd like to." Miss Stacy spoke quickly. "I'm lonely here."

We're all lonely here. At the prospect of making a new friend out of this unlikely material, Mary's spirits rose. Perhaps Miss Stacy liked books, or embroidery, or classifying wild flowers. Perhaps she could find Miss Stacy a young man.

She put Helen carefully back in the heap of pillows, and turned Rusty and the buggy in a wide sweep around the schoolyard. *I'm as bad as Elsie Yanling. Oh, dear, I have to see Elsie soon. If I don't give, how can I expect to get? I'll make it next week, and I'll stay an hour. A whole hour.*

Stopping briefly to see if anyone was coming down the winding road before she drew out on it, Mary turned toward home. The children were trooping back in the schoolhouse; their cries diminished as she went around the hill. The thin wheels of the surrey made a dignified creak against the hard-packed road. From the top of the big curve she could see down across the Landing to the river. There was no brake on the surrey, since it had not been built for mountain roads, but Rusty held it back skilfully, putting his haunches firm against the harness.

And then, just as the ground fell away below them in the big curve, the fragile hold strap broke, and the buggy rolled down and slapped Rusty forcefully on the buttocks.

Rusty sprang forward. It was a new kind of signal, and he did not know what to make of it, but it seemed to say go. He jumped as far as seem safe, but the surrey jumped too, and the moment he paused it hit him again.

He began to go down the hill in short leaps, with the surrey careening behind him. Doing his best with a totally new situation, he managed to keep it upright, but it lashed at him over and over. He tried to keep ahead of it, dodging and bounding, but each time he tried to stop it came at him once more.

Mary had put her arm tightly around the baby, and her other arm was tugging back with all her strength, but she might as well have been pulling on a skein of yarn. The incredible thought forced itself into her mind—*Rusty is running away.*

They came down the side of the big bowl in a fury of motion, the wheels spinning, the top swaying, Rusty settling down to the blind lope of a frightened horse. At the middle where the road was steepest, his thumping hoof dislodged a big stone that went bouncing and crashing down the hill.

Oh, God, don't let anything happen to my babies. Not now— not before one has even had a chance to be born.

The road began to level off. Rusty felt the change in his panic-stricken feet, and the surrey began to draw back, not hitting him as hard. It was time to end this nonsense. He stopped suddenly, planting his shuddering hooves in the road. The surrey twisted sideways and keeled over into the brush.

It was Mr. Lindsay who found them. Puttering around outside the store, he could hear at a little distance the screams of a frightened child, and he dropped his bits of rope into the dust and set out toward it, his walk quickening to a lope as the baby's cries assailed his ear.

He found Mary half-sitting in the sagebrush, with vacant eyes; Helen lay a little distance from her, howling with rage and fright. He picked the youngster up at once, cradling her against his shoulder, and walked quickly to Mary and laid the child in her arms. "The baby's all right," he said, "the baby's all right." He was pretty sure it was true; and the fixed look on her face scared him.

Mary seemed to come back from a great distance. "What about me?" she said in a voice barely above a whisper.

She doesn't mean herself, Mr. Lindsay thought, she means the new 'un. At that moment the last shred of Mr. Lindsay's grudge against the Hollister girls vanished forever. "I dunno," he said. "I ought to get a woman to tend you, in case you start to have pains. Can you hang on all right while I fetch my wife?"

"I'm not going to have pains," Mary answered him firmly. "I'm going to be fine." She strained Helen to her, running her lips over the child's hair, burying her rigid face in the warm contour of neck and shoulder, and Helen's cries quieted to a whimper. Mary's eyes fell on the battered vehicle and a few tears squeezed out of them. "My surrey," she said thickly.

"Now, never mind about that fancy hack." Mr. Lindsay looked at it with disfavor. "Just take it easy till you know if you're OK. I been rolled in a buggy myself, and it didn't hurt me none, except a few bumps and bruises, but it might be different with you. How come you let go of the reins?"

"I didn't," Mary said. "The hold strap broke. . . . Oh, poor Rusty. Go and tell him it's all right."

The little horse, shivering with shame and confusion, still stood in the roadway where he had stopped. "Where did it happen?" Mr. Lindsay asked.

"At the head of the grade."

"I guess he done all right," Mr. Lindsay said heavily. "He brought you down."

"But he doesn't know it. You must go and tell him. . . . All right then, I will." She felt that otherwise she might sit there for days. With infinite caution she handed the baby to Mr. Lindsay and got up, and when she stood on her feet she waited anxiously for cramping, but it did not come. She walked slowly to Rusty and petted him and stroked his neck and whispered in his ear. Then she turned back to Mr. Lindsay. "Can you get Ben?" she said. "Oh, I want Ben. Please have Ben come."

Mr. Lindsay looked around for help. To his relief he saw a wagon coming slowly down the grade, giving off a cloud of dust. That would be Bert Plew, coming to meet the afternoon train. He hailed Bert with a lifted arm. Mary's strength was ebbing, she found, and there was one shoulder that hurt rather badly and several other sore spots. She leaned forlornly against Mr. Lindsay as the wagon stopped.

"Gor!" Bert Plew said, taking in the situation at a glance. "Is she hurt much?"

"She don't know," Mr. Lindsay said, and they understood each other perfectly. How sweet they are, Mary thought weakly, these men that used to think of me as an outlander. I'm not an outlander now. They act as if I belonged to them.

"I'll take her home," Bert Plew said promptly. "I got hay in the wagon bed here. Reckon she can make out. Her an' the young 'un. Think you kin git aboard, Mary?"

"She wants her husband," Mr. Lindsay said.

"Well, git him. Don't stand there dodderin'." Bert let down the tailgate of the wagon, and with the help of both rough, sun-scorched pairs of hands, Mary half-climbed and was half-lifted in, and the child restored to her arms. Bert Plew disengaged the surrey and tied Rusty to the rear of the wagon with a few encouraging rubs and slaps. "Now you go on ahead an' tell Ben an' head him down here," Bert said. "An' don't scare him. Mary's in good shape. I seen my old woman through wuss times than this."

The motion of the wagon was soothing. Helen was now furious with hunger, and as they jogged along, under hillsides frowning with rock and through orchards loaded with ripening fruit, Mary gave the child her breast, under the open sky, like any peasant woman riding in a cart. Mary Hollister, she thought. Late of Oak Point. Raised to be a lady.

Harvest was upon them suddenly; it came as it always came, seemingly without warning, though Ben had been braced to meet it for weeks and had done everything possible to prepare for it. The picking boxes were stacked in the orchard. The packing bench was ready with piles of wrapping paper and racks of rubber stamps. The railroad was scheduled to set off a refrigerator car at Pine Creek siding. Ben was one who would miss the steamboats skimming by, but he could not afford to be sentimental. The rail lines gave him better transportation and better handling. Fletch was back from the wheatfields, and Ben had sent him up to the Scobies' to learn to pack, a responsible job. Mary saw to it that Florence did the teaching. She scolded herself for being a matchmaker, but the temptation was irresistible. They were such nice kids, and she was so fond of them both. When Fletch felt that he understood the way of it, she insisted that he take Florence a box of candy as thanks for showing him how. She noted with satisfaction that he was gone all Sunday afternoon, and was late with his chores.

Between other concerns, Ben worried about Mary. She seemed perfectly all right, but you never could tell. The broken surrey was stored in the end of the barn, and sometimes Ben stopped to look soberly at it as he walked by. If he could help it, he would never have it fixed. He had suffered a near thing; it could have cost him Mary and Helen and Rusty all at once. A man should not have confidence in anything newfangled, anything beautiful or seductive. He should stick to plain ways, and to what he knows best.

His crop of apples was the one thing in which there was no flaw. There were not many wormholes; that last spray had done the work. He carried Helen out in his arms to see and feel the pretty things, tasting a rare delight in showing his daughter his achievements. Standing at the furthest reach of the orchard, looking down the bulging rows, he inwardly saluted old John Muldoon who had encouraged him so greatly and taught him so much. He wished John were here now. The orchard, and its opulence, John might have foreseen, but Ben had a sudden longing to show him this bright laughing child, spatting her hands together for pure joy, chattering in her wordless speech. John had loved children.

To his loyalties, so few and so deep, Ben had added lately one shapeless concern that was properly none of his business. He read all he could lay his hands on about the conflagration in Europe, the invasions, the shattered treaties; and he wished, formlessly, that it could be set right. His winters spent with the old *History of the World* churned in his mind, and he tried to make the tramp of armies congruous with the fresh, confident, rewarding world in which he lived.

Mary cooked enormous meals for the harvest crew, hung out washings, bound up scratches from tree limbs, and made out Ben's bills of lading in her neat legible hand. As the lush little crop rolled in from the orchard, and departed again for the freight car, she indulged in a few daydreams. Toys for Helen at Christmas. Perhaps a rug. A sheepskin jacket for Ben with a high collar against the coming cold.

But just at the end of harvest, Ben came in with a letter in his hand. "Pa is ailing," he said simply. "He wants to see me. I think I'd better go, Mary."

She knew that Ben had not been down to Oregon since they were married, because of the cost which would be even greater for the two of them. She did not hesitate. "Of course you must go. And don't try to take me along, Ben. With sickness in the house, it's no time to bring home a bride."

"Fletch ought to go too," Ben said doubtfully.

"Dolly will come down and stay, if you'd feel any better about it. She was to come anyway when I have the baby."

"I don't know about Dolly. It hardly seems fair to do another man out of his wife every time we need a bit of help."

"Bert can come too if he wants. I'll stuff him with pound cake, like Althea used to make."

"I thought you didn't have much use for Bert."

"Oh pooh. I can handle Bert. I understand him. The trouble with Bert is that he has to live with his own inadequacy."

She knew Ben's heart was heavy, but she was not prepared for the look of displeasure that crossed his face. Somehow she had erred again. Perhaps he did not understand her; she had to be careful about this. A proud man does not like to have his wife talk over his head. Or perhaps she was not supposed to criticize

235

someone Ben had long known and who was wiser than she in the ways of the country. Her gaiety blew out like a candle. "Will you ride, Ben, or will you take the train?"

"Fletch and I will ride," Ben said soberly. Even with money in his pocket, he must still be thrifty. It had to last the year out.

He and Fletch were gone for six weeks, and when they came back, Mary put on mourning again, awkwardly making an old dress do, for a father-in-law she had never seen. The color had faded from the canyons now, the sun was rising late and setting early, and Bert Plew had won a turkey shoot and had treated them all to Thanksgiving dinner. And in the crowded house (for Bert and Dolly took Fletch's room, but they were underfoot all day), there was suddenly the most miraculous of happenings—Helen began to say words. They could not believe it, they seized each other with delight, the three silly and adoring adults coaxed and pestered her all day. She could say "choo-choo" when it went thundering through the orchard, and several other useful things, especially "dinner." She was weaned now, and they vied for the job of feeding her with a spoon.

Ben felt that he had got home none too soon. Mary looked peaked, and there was a tired set to her shoulders. He sent the guests packing with many thanks, and settled down to watch over her. Mary was restless, and he could not keep her quiet. She went out to walk in the dour weather, and when there was a fall of sleet she insisted on polishing all the windows. In December she felt the quickening, the sudden flutter of movement that was proof the "new 'un" was there and alive. Though she remembered well from before how it felt, it gave her a moment's awe. She stopped ironing, and then went on, smiling a little to herself.

Dr. McClellan was concerned. He came to the ranch occasionally instead of letting Mary go to Indian Spring. It was a nice outing for him, he said, and he could admire the new railroad. He suggested that Mary come a couple of weeks ahead of time to the rambling old house that served him as home, office, and hospital, and that she have the baby there.

" Oh no!" Mary protested. "The expense . . ."

"Shut up," Ben said.

Dr. McClellan looked a little startled, but Mary understood.

236

She knew when to let Ben take charge. "I'll do whatever you say, doctor."

It was a good thing she had gone. David was born with far more difficulty than Helen. Dr. McClellan had a few sedatives and some whiskey, and he did the best he could. Mary hemorrhaged badly, and had to be kept in bed for days. Whether it was the runaway, or the fact that this time it was a boy, or that he had come too soon after Helen, was not clear. Mary tried to put up with her pain as patiently as Ben had endured his throbbing back, and by and by it went away. She worried about what was going on at home, but there is something about the presence of a newborn baby that makes other things seem unimportant. She had the baby beside her, in a lying-in crib where she could reach out and feel his aimless little hands and feet, the warm roundness of his head. A son. She had borne a son.

Perhaps now, if God was really very good, she would not have any more babies for a long while.

PART FOUR

14

To HELEN LUCAS, three years old, the sound of the piano was one of the sounds of Mama. You could tell where Mama was and what she was doing by listening for the rattle of dishes, the creak of the clothes wringer, or the dull whirr of the sewing machine. But most of all, when she played the piano, the presence of Mama filled the house. The "Old Spinning Wheel," "Monastery Bells," the tender beginning of the "Fifth Nocturne" and the place where it began to hurry and argue with itself. These were the things Mama played when she first sat down, and though Helen did not know their names, she knew every note. Then Mama would begin to play more slowly and the music would become confused. Sometimes it would end by Mama just sitting there, with her face close to the music, poring over it. Putting her face close to the page was somehow connected with a saying that "Mama needs glasses."

"Well, get them then," Papa would say, and Mama would murmur inconclusively,

"Not just yet."

There was something illogical and grown-uppish about this needing a thing, but not trying to get it. When you need something you need it badly and right now, as Helen knew well. She had made the word her own; she never said "I want." But, "Mama, I need a drink of water," "Papa, I need my dollbaby buggy fixed," "David, I need your Mother Goose book. I can read it and you can't." This was not strictly true, but she could gabble it off from memory, which served the same purpose. She had an enormously retentive mind, an iron will, and a bubbling charm that put everybody at a disadvantage except David, who hated her.

But this morning Mama was doing something to the piano that sounded bad. She was dusting it and washing down the yellowed keys with a wet rag—grump, gramp, grimp, scrash, scrish, SCREE! Helen quickly left for the outdoors, where she had a bug hole that she was watching. For many minutes, now, nothing had gone in or out of the bug hole—not since she had put a stick down it to see if it would make it go faster. Ergo, you cannot stir up a bug hole—you merely ruin it. Her life was full of such lessons. She could not take time to worry about them. Papa was shaving just inside the kitchen window, and she went over to watch him.

Papa did everything with great seriousness, one thing at a time. He held his nose to one side while he ran the huge razor blade down his cheek, and then wiped it on a round sheet of colored tissue that hung beside the mirror—the "shaving ball" that Mama had given him for Christmas. Seeing Helen outside, he flipped a bit of foam out the window, and she squeaked gleefully and ran away, but not far. Uncle Harve was working the grindstone, pumping the treadle steadily to make the wheel go around while he held a scythe blade against it. Uncle Fletch was gone now and Uncle Harve had come, and though he looked almost exactly like Uncle Fletch, and was about the same size, he was not the same person. She was shy of him, and kept her distance, though she wanted to see the grindstone spin and the scythe strike sparks.

Uncle Harve had a can of water with which he doused the spinning stone now and then. He watched her eyes travel each time to the can of water as he picked it up and splashed and set it down, and by and by, as if it were the most natural thing in the world, he stopped and got up and handed the can of water to her and took her compact, hard, warm little body in his arms and held her high over the grindstone. She dumped the water on the stone, drenching them both, and the little girl and the new uncle laughed delightedly together.

Fletch had taken his time. He had traced the title to the Piggott place and bought it for a fair price, on a contract that would run till after he could put it back in shape and begin to get some income. Piggott had raised soft fruit, for which there was little market. Fletch ruthlessly tore out the peach and plum trees, and put in an apple orchard. He had it good, compared to Ben, for Ben advised him and loaned him machinery. Even before the contract was signed, he was up there grubbing out greasewood and repairing the house. To Mary, who had the Greek superstition about tempting Fate, this seemed like a bad idea. But she would not have ventured to tell him so. The Lucas men had no use for such notions.

He had taken his time about courting Florence Scobie, too. Once or twice, Mary thought he had lost her. Her ribboned basket of fried chicken and fresh gingerbread was bid away from him at a box social by Olly Miller, and Florence vivaciously ate supper with Olly and danced every set with him afterward. For a while, Olly's horse could be seen tied up at the Scobies' on Sunday; but Mary thought, or hoped, that Florence would think twice about marrying a Miller Boy. Dr. McClellan took an assistant one summer, a medical student whose nose was forever in his books. He took a somewhat more than clinical interest in Florence, but he had no immediate prospects, and he earned Florence's scorn by shinnying up a tree when he heard a cow bawling.

When it was time, Fletch put on his best suit, and pulled a Michaelmas daisy from the bush by the door and put it in his buttonhole. Looking at his fierce, scared, proud young face, Mary thought she knew what was up, and realized how thoroughly she had disrupted Ben's life by leading him to propose before he was good and ready. The next morning Florence came flying down on her pony, her orange hair brilliant in the sun.

"Oh, Misshollister! I'm going to be your *sister-in-law!*"

Mary hugged and kissed her warmly. "You must learn to call me Mary," she said. "Oh, Florence, I'm so glad. Fletch is very lucky. And it will be simply wonderful to have you living right up the road here."

They were married after harvest, and Florence was expecting a baby late in the summer.

Then there was the War. It had crept closer, though no one seemed to know exactly how. When Mr. Lindsay declared to the group at the store, "Well, we ain't goin' to get mixed up in it, and that's for sure," there were fewer cries of assent, and more heads doubtfully shaken. Althea was deep in bazaars and bandage-rolling, and in the last few months Ben and Mary had sub-scribed to a newspaper so that, as Ben put it, they could get the bad news faster. The paper was delivered a day late, but it was better than rumor.

The trees at Luthermere would bear their first crop this year. Mary wondered why this was not more exciting. Ben would have charge of the harvest, of course. The small yield of fruit would probably be hauled down and packed out with their own. She had a sudden pang for the little orchard, for all it had cost, for Althea and herself digging holes and carrying water. She must be crazy—did she want those days back again? Of course not. She did not want Luthermere back, she did not want the school back, she did not want to be back in Oak Point. As for the question of what would be done with the money from the Luthermere crop, it more or less answered itself. Half would be sent to the Gil-lespies, for Ben was scrupulous about such things. And since he had done all the work, taken all the care, and never bothered to keep it separate from his own affairs, the other half would barely repay him for his time. She had no claim on it.

And the money would go for their common welfare; it wasn't as if she were being deprived of it. Ben would use it for their best good. He was not selfish. On himself, he spent almost nothing. He wore old clothes, he carried his father's heavy gold watch that his mother had given him at his father's death, and she had only been able to get him to buy a good saddle by pointing out that Rusty ought not to acquire bad habits with broken-down or worn-out gear.

I wish I had some money, she thought sometimes, if only to buy Ben a present, something to be gay about.

But she had only what he counted into her hand each week for groceries—a just amount, based on their income and their station in life.

Nevertheless she thought she would go up to Luthermere and see "her" trees, old enough this year to put forth fruit. She went to Pine Creek valley very seldom now. With the two children, it was hard to manage. But Harve offered to keep the young 'uns for a few hours, and she accepted gratefully. "Don't take your eyes off them for a minute, Harve. Don't let David go in the hen house—he loves the chickies, but they don't love him. Don't let Helen climb the wood in the woodshed. Have you ever taken a little girl to the toilet? Well, she can manage, if you haven't. Keep them off the road, and away from the bee hives, and out of the toolbox. And give them all the bread and butter they want."

It was late March, cool in the shadows, but softly warm in the flat spring sunshine. Mary had wound a scarf about her head and neck, but as Duke ambled along, and the hills began to reflect back the heat, she undid it and let the breeze blow through her hair. She thought it would be an early summer. There was already a little shimmer on the distant hills.

She did not stop at the store, for she and Florence usually shopped together now, and gossiped as they rifled Mr. Lindsay's shelves. Here was the turn where her buggy had crashed; she seldom thought about it. It was a spot only to be recognized in passing, like any other familiar place. The schoolhouse looked as it should, with the big outcrop of rock behind it where the boys used to play King-of-the-Mountain.

But there was something not quite right about the rock outcrop itself. She saw that there was a figure on top of it, half-hidden, and her heart skipped. There were still a few outlaws in the hills, and what more likely place for one to try for food and water than the schoolhouse, with its defenseless teacher and children? But she was almost sure the figure was a woman—there was something about its lightness, the way it crouched.

It would bear looking into at once. Anything that might happen at the school transcended any errand of hers. She rode clear past, keeping her eyes resolutely turned away, and tied Duke to a serviceberry bush near the Gateway and set foot carefully across the slope. She could stalk along a hillside as quietly, by now, as any hunter with his gun.

When she saw who it was, she stopped treading softly, and plowed across the slippery gravel. Elsie Yanling heard her coming and raised a ravaged face.

Mary sat down. "Hello, Elsie," she said as casually as she could.

245

Elsie did not seem surprised to see her. She belonged there; she was to Elsie's mind still some part of the doings down below.

"Oh, Misshollister," Elsie said, "they've taken Sammy away. They've made Sammy go to school."

"Why yes," Mary tried to sound cheerful. "It's time, I guess, isn't it Elsie? It comes so fast." She thought of how it would be with her when David went.

"Sometimes I think I can't stand it. He's all I got, Misshollister. And now he's got to go to school."

"But you live so close," Mary said. "Just around the turn here. He's not very far away. You can think of how he's here, just the other side of the Gateway. And when school is over, he can be home in minutes."

"I worry if a car would hit him. Coming through the Gateway."

"There aren't very many cars that come into Pine Creek valley."

"It would only take one," Elsie said.

Mary was silent. She knew.

"That house is so quiet. Oh God, it's so quiet."

Mary reached out and took Elsie's hand, which was scrabbling at her dress.

"So when I can't stand it no more, I come down here. At recess time. I can see him, playing with the other kids. It's like I was keeping him safe. Just watching. Nothing can happen to him with me looking."

"Elsie, it's going to get a lot worse. He's going to be a big boy and climb the hills. And go hunting with the men. And ride a horse. And fool with machinery. And with girls."

"I don't think about that," Elsie said. "All I think about is now. I reckon that's my trouble—all I ever thought about was now. I done some foolish things."

"We've all done some foolish things," Mary answered sincerely.

There was a sudden racket down in the schoolyard as the children streamed out of the school and began to run about the yard and shout and bicker and set up games and play them passionately, not wasting a second of their fifteen minutes of freedom. The two women watched silently. *That was what I taught. Everyday. As if it were nothing. Other people's children. Each one*

246

wrapped around some woman's heart. Bought with some woman's pain.

Following Elsie's eyes, she saw Sammy, a stocky little boy with coarse pale hair, his face flushed, his voice raucous with the rest. He looked all right; he looked as if he might grow up whole and useful. *He'd better,* Mary told herself. In her way of thinking, John Muldoon had given his life for this child.

When the hubbub had died and Elsie had breathed a long sigh, Mary said hesitantly, "Elsie, perhaps you could have another child." *I'm not taking my own advice, but never mind that.*

Elsie flung her a bitter look. "With *him?* No, thank you."

"Why did you marry him, Elsie?" The question seemed natural; now was surely the time to ask it.

"He said he'd take me away. He said he'd bring me to the States. We didn't even wait to come in legal." She clapped her hand over her mouth, and then said, "It's all right. *You* won't tell. But look what he brung me to. *This!* And I'm ailing. I've got pains in my chest."

"Have you seen a doctor?"

"Doctor! Ha! If doctors was growing on bushes, I couldn't afford to pick one."

"Dr. McClellan is very kind. He'll wait for your money as long as necessary."

"It would be forever, I guess. And anyway, sometimes I *want* to die. If it wouldn't hurt too much. Oh, Misshollister, I ain't got nothing. Nothing but Sammy. And he's gone, and like you say, he's never coming back. He's goin' away further an' further."

Mary said resolutely, "You're young yet, Elsie. You mustn't just lie down and let life run over you like this." She looked at Elsie's bony hands, her yellow teeth with a few gaps in them, her slack jaw. Surely there was *something* the girl could do. She seized on the first thought that came to her. "Who makes Sammy's clothes? Where do you get all the little shirts and pants he looks so cute in?"

"From the Mail Order."

"You could make them yourself, you know, and it would be cheaper. And it's a lot of fun. I love to sew for my children."

247

"I cain't sew," Elsie said with finality.

"It's very easy. I'll show you how if you like." How smug it sounded! *O teach the orphan girl to sew.* She hurried on, "Just something simple, like play pants for Sammy. Come down to my house, and I'll cut out a pair of pants for Sammy, and you can sew them up on my sewing machine."

"I'm kind of scairt of it," Elsie said, but her fingers stopped twisting her skirt. "Do you really think I could do that, Misshollister?"

"Anybody can do it. And if you spoil the first pair, we'll cut out another."

"I'll bring my own overhauls," Elsie said with sudden dignity. "I got plenty of old stuff layin' around. Oh, Misshollister, you never did come to see me no more! It's been a couple o' years since I seen you."

"I don't come to Pine Creek valley now. Not with two little folks to lug along. I was just going to run up today and look at our orchard, but it will keep. I didn't leave lunch for the men, so I've got to go back."

"I done you out of it, didn't I? I'm sorry."

"It doesn't matter. . . . But Elsie, there's one more thing." She pressed her advantage. "If you're in the country illegally, you might be found out and sent back. You'd have to get on a quota then, and it's hard. It would be considered how you'd spent your time here, and what kind of a home you'd made for Sammy, and all that."

She saw Elsie turn white. "They couldn't take him away from me, could they? Because of being born here?"

"No. I'm sure they couldn't. Some judge would work it out. But just try to make a good impression, Elsie. Redd up your house, and keep Sammy clean and teach him to be nice to folks. And don't ever, ever, no matter how you feel, get him to play hooky from school."

"I won't. I won't. Oh, Misshollister, you can read my very mind."

"You *will* think about the sewing, won't you? Bring some material, and spend the day with me. Some day when you think you can't stand the quiet house any longer."

She had had a long reprieve from Elsie, she thought as she un-

248

tied Duke and turned him around, but it was over now. This was the price she paid for living in Pine Creek, and being Ben's wife, and it was not too much. Pine Creek owned her pretty thoroughly now. It had her, as Ben would say, by the short hair.

"It's not that there's anything so great about sewing," Mary said to Althea. "It just happened to be the first thing I could think of."

"Well, I don't know." Althea tucked back her hair, which was getting quite white, and snapped a rubber band around the graduation invitations she was addressing for one of her stepsons. "It used to say in the *Ladies' Garland*—you wouldn't remember the *Ladies' Garland*, Mary, Mama took it when we were little— but it said that there is practically no feminine ill or unhappiness that the needle cannot cure. . . . Mary, what are you laughing at?"

"I'm laughing because I'm so happy to be here. Oh Althea, it's been a long time."

It was, in fact, her first visit in nearly a year. To transport the children and their clothes and their favorite toys was quite a task, and David did not eat well away from home. David was a ritualist, he wanted his own highchair and his own bowl and spoon. At the moment, however, the youngsters were contented and quiet, on their hands and knees in front of the outside door, where they could look through different panes of colored glass, making the whole world yellow, or red, or green.

"Did I tell you," Mary said, "that we have Ben's brother Harvey with us now? Pine Creek is filling up with Lucases, they'll soon be everywhere you look."

"Are there many more to come?"

"As a matter of fact, no. Harve is the baby. The father died, you know, and Ben is sort of the head of the family now. I sometimes wonder about them, about my children's kin. Will Helen be like you, or Kate? Or will she be like some woman I have never seen?"

It was the kind of easy, heartwarming talk she could have only with Althea. The telephone jingled on the wall, and Althea went to answer it, pulling the mouthpiece down as far as it would go.

The telephone had been installed for a man, and no one had ever thought to lower it.

"Yes, we're taking volunteers. Yes, you must come a certain number of hours a week. Can you knit? Do you know anything about hospital supplies? No, we don't wear uniforms. I know they're charming, and of course it does help in keeping things clean, but we don't think the expense is justified. . . . Yes, Mrs. Cole is a member. . . . I see. . . . Quite a few of your friends. . . . Why don't you ask Lucy to bring you to a meeting, then, and we will see what we can find for you to do?"

She turned back to Mary. "Red Cross business. Honestly, Mary, *women!* You know I'm a stickler for women's rights. I think they can do just as well as men, if they try. But so many of them are *ineffectual.* I often feel like knocking their heads together. . . . Most of them want to do it because it's fashionable, and they'll meet the right people. Would you like a cup of tea? For old times' sake? I seldom make it now; Mr. Gillespie prefers coffee. And some pound cake perhaps?"

"I'd love it," Mary said. The two children were trying to peer through the same pane of glass, and beginning to squabble. "I'll put them down for their naps, in the spare room, and stay until they're quiet. And then I'll be right back."

When she came out of the bedroom a half hour later, the tea service was on the table, and Althea was busy in some other part of the house. She went idly to the book case. She and Althea had divided their books when they left Luthermere, and though she knew Althea's as well as she knew her own, they might seem a little fresher after this interval, and she might borrow one to take home. Althea had the Mrs. Humphrey Wards, and the Walter Scotts, of which they were both so fond. And here was the battered copy of *Virginibus Peurisque,* left with them by the sheep-herder on that long-ago day. She had re-read it at the time (though nothing of Stevenson's was really new to any Hollister) and then stuffed it in the shelves with the rest. It was perhaps the least familiar thing there. She took it down and opened the cover.

Across the end sheet in a sprawling, flamboyant hand was written, Lewis Anthony.

A tingle seemed to travel upward through Mary's body from

the floor. There *was* a Lewis Anthony. He *had* been here. He was doubtless out in the hills with a band of sheep. From being a bit of pathetic hearsay, which had caused her to be sorry for young Bob and to look leniently on his behavior, it suddenly became a tangible thing, in which with any luck at all she could take part. She could help find Lew, and keep the promise that had seemed so futile when she made it.

Heedless of the sleeping children, she raised her voice. "Althea! Althea! Come and see what I've found! Bob Anthony's brother I mean, I've *practically* found him. Here he is. Right on this page."

Althea came in with the pound cake. "Who?" she said. "This is such a nice tea set, Mary, don't you think? It was in Mr. Gillespie's family."

"Do listen," Mary cried. "You remember that nice young man that used to drive the car for Mrs. Lor . . . that showed us around the railroad camp? Of course you do. The one that lost his brother."

"Suddenly?"

"No, no. *Lost* him. Mislaid him. He disappeared. I told you all about it."

"I remember something," Althea said. "I wasn't close to those people, you know. But I remember the young chap that was hunting for a brother. You mean you think you have a clue?"

"Right in this book. Why, I've as good as got him located right now. I'll leave word at all the sheep camps, and I'll send a note to Jeff Porter—Jeff will be tickled to help. Some of the herds haven't even gone out yet. We might get hold of him tomorrow."

"Are you sure he wants to be gotten hold of? People don't just disappear for nothing."

"You're right. That would be up to him I suppose. Perhaps I'd better not let Bob know I've found him, until . . . but Althea, he has a right to know. That his father left him money. That Bob wants him back. Oh, it's all so romantic."

"*You're* romantic," Althea said. "You always were. Don't you think you already have enough projects going, with teaching Elsie to sew, and harboring Ben's brothers, and raising your babies?"

"This will be different. Something new to do. Althea, it will be fun."

Althea sighed. "I can remember when I was the one who was always thinking of something to do. I'm getting old, Mary."

"Oh Althea! You're worth any half a dozen women I know. Where would the Red Cross be without you? And the Firemen's Fund? And who raised the money for the Everett boy to go to medical school?"

"I do what I can," Althea said, gratified. But her thoughts were elsewhere. After a while she spoke again. "You didn't see the trees in bloom, after all."

"No. By the time I got back, it was too late. The petals had fallen."

"Neither of us saw it," Althea said lightly, as if it were of no consequence.

"I know. . . . Do you remember, Althea, how hard it was to get the rows straight . . . and the day we found we'd laid the tape over too far, and dug a couple of those dreadful holes for nothing?"

"And we sang, to keep from crying."

"And Bert Plew went by on the road, and thought we'd taken leave of our senses."

"Mary," Althea said suddenly, "for once women did something worthwhile. Not because we were women, but because we were *people*. I'll never forget it."

"I guess I won't forget it either."

They were silent a while, thoughts running unspoken between them as in the old days. Then Althea went to the window. "What in the world brings Charles home so early? He hardly ever leaves the office before five o'clock." She set down her cup, and went to meet him.

Mr. Gillespie had his hat in his hand when he came in, and his face was grave. He looked around at both women. "I thought it was best you should hear it from me," he said, "and not from the newsboys in the streets. The United States has just declared war on Germany."

Before Mary could get home with the news, Ben had it from the day-old Wenatchee paper. He got it out of the post office box, passed the time of day with Mr. Lindsay, and spread the front page out before him. When he saw the headline, something rose in him, and quickly died again. It would be pure foolishness to suppose he could go. He was a family man, with a wife and two children; he was a farmer, tied to the land.

Food would win the War, they said. Ben cleared the last foot of his property that could be reached by irrigation water, the space around the barn and corral, and the swath next to the road. He planted what he knew would grow; vegetables for canning, and sunflowers whose seed would feed chickens and turn into eggs that could be dried for the Army. Unlike Mary, he did not try to read and remember every day's events in the paper; he was obliged to let the generals fight the war, whether he liked it or not.

Harve enlisted at once. He said he guessed he'd get in a few licks before it got too late and the whole thing was over. This left them shorthanded, but Ben knew it was only the beginning. The time would come when an able-bodied hired hand could not be had for love or money. Getting up at half past four, when a tremendous burst of robin song was filling the orchard, he put in twelve or thirteen or fourteen hours a day, and slept the sleep of exhaustion at night.

This helped to keep his mind off things, for Ben was of the belief that what could not be helped should not be dwelt on. It had not been the same between him and Mary since David's birth. He knew why, and he tried not to blame her. She was afraid of getting pregnant again, and the joyousness was gone from their mating. A man does not like to see fear in his wife's eyes. Often he forebore to touch her, and when he did, they practiced the only kind of birth control known to their time and place—Ben withdrew before he was satisfied.

Well, if this had been all . . . men learned to live with such situations, he supposed, and he didn't want to take it out in chasing other women—he was too busy, and too involved with Mary still, no matter how she treated him. But lately he'd had the feeling that they were living in two separate worlds under the same roof. He in one world, and Mary and the children in the other. That was what hurt.

Those foolish stories she read to them, about princesses in

253

towers, and knights and dragons, and Crusaders. . . . When his Pa had told stories of an evening, they were about real things—hitting the trail and crossing the prairies and fighting the Sioux. . . . And the laughter and chasing and pointless delay when they were dressing and undressing, the choosiness at meals—David was downright silly about eating. His own parents would have been appalled. Lollygagging, they would have called it. The word came bleakly back to him across the years.

Mary was spoiling the children; that was what it amounted to. He wondered if he ought to talk to her about it. For a long time, he had been able to teach and guide Mary; she had been a wonderfully docile and understanding wife. But now sometimes, when he tried to explain something to her, there were flags of rebellion flying in her eyes, or still worse, she wasn't really *listening*. The next minute, the children would be giggling, and Mary like as not giggling with them, and he could never understand what the joke was.

And this thing of riding around to the sheep ranches and leaving messages for Bob Anthony's brother. He thought it unbecoming. He didn't object to tending the children while Mary was gone—he liked to have them plodding after him through the orchard or scrambling over the wagon and sprayer. And he tried not to worry about Mary's riding alone on the long roads up and down the river—she was as perfect a horsewoman as you would ever find. But it embarrassed him, somehow, to have his wife involved in a manhunt. If he had known the words to use, he would have said it was in poor taste.

15

THE EVERLASTING sound of the sheep had begun to rise as daybreak crept along the ridge. The helpless, silly creatures, complaining in that sorrowful tone which is like a troubled human voice, were spread across the hillside, bunched in watchfully by the dogs. A little way to one side, the remains of a campfire made a red eye against the slope. A thread of smoke still rose, twisted occasionally by the light wind before dawn. The three men beside the fire were wrapped in their blankets; here at four thousand feet it was cool at daybreak, even in late summer.

One man still slept with long, easy snores; the other two were talking in low voices, though not steadily. The big blond man with the beard leaned on his elbow, staring at the embers. Presently the slightly smaller dark man turned over, sighed, and sat up. "You might as well get an early start."

"I might as well," the big man answered rather sadly.

"I should of knowed they'd send somebody that snored up here to take your place."

"I'm sorry, Paddy. I don't expect to have much to say for myself at the Day of Judgment, but I will remember to cite the fact that in the years we pardnered, I never kept you awake with my salutes to Morpheus."

"I'm gonna miss your crazy talk." Paddy cast aside his husk of wrappings and climbed out, shivering.

"You old mountain billygoat, I'm going to miss you so much that I'd just as soon not think about it. Nor about what I owe you for my being here. Nor the trouble I'm making leaving in the middle of the season. I ought to have stayed till we took the sheep down."

"Ever since the grub-train brought that message up, you've been as itchy as a cow with her tits in a thistle. . . . I ain't goin' to keep you, Lew. . . . Funny thing . . . I never believed them yarns of yours before. About your rich family in the East, and all that."

"I don't know why you should. I've told you a lot of tall tales. But the part about my running away was true. And the old white house with the hollyhocks, and all that."

"Was the ones about the wimmin true?"

"Some . . . not always."

Paddy began to rebuild the fire, putting the coffee pot in the coals. "The only thing that worries me about your pulling out, is that Rafe won't like it."

"He has no business not liking it. I wish you were rid of Rafe."

"It's all right for you to talk, Lew. I ain't smart enough to corner the wheat market, or own Standard Ile, or sell somebody the Brooklyn Bridge. Like them big-money folks you come from. I got to take it where I find it."

"If I should send you some money, would you break up with Rafe?"

"Let's not start counting your chickens. You just get out o' here, and let me handle it."

"You sure you won't come with me?"

"Too chancy. Besides, I can't leave the sheep."

" 'Conscience doth make cowards of us all,' hey, Paddy? You can't abandon a herd of sheep, but you can drive off a few at a time to Rafe's herd—"

"Sh-h!" Paddy gestured sharply at the sleeping man. "Don't say it, Lew. It's better not to think them words, or they might pop out when somebody else is listening. . . . *He* don't know yet. Maybe he never will."

"Don't tell him," Lew said in an urgent whisper. "Look, Paddy, no promises, but maybe I can bail you out. Like you once did me. . . . I don't know what to expect, when I get in touch with Bobbie, but my God, there must be something in it for me."

"That note didn't tell you much," Paddy agreed.

"*Lewis Anthony: Your brother is looking for you. Contact Mrs. Ben Lucas at Pine Creek.* Whoever Mrs. Ben Lucas is. Paddy, when the time comes, will you be sure to draw my pay? I'd rather you'd have it than let O'Brien put it in his own pocket."

"You got any money on you now?"

256

"Some change. . . . Put away that purse, lad. I'll ride my mare as far as I can, and then sell her. I'll be all right."

Paddy put flapjacks on Lew's plate. "Eat your grub. And keep a straight face. That there is Rafe, coming over the ridge."

"He didn't lose much time, did he?"

"I think we was a little careless what we said last night. Rafe ain't dumb, he can't afford to be."

Rafe's hat was pulled down and he wore a poncho against the chill. He stopped his horse by the fire and said, "Cold, ain't it? Got a cup of coffee?"

"We always got a cup of coffee." Paddy filled a tin cup and handed it up. Rafe drank it scalding hot and quickly.

"Good for a man's bones," he said. He watched Lew smooth out his saddle blanket and tighten the cinch. "Goin' somewhere?"

"I've got business down on the river."

"Stayin' long?"

"Don't know."

"Beats all how some sheep men can go off an' leave the herd." Rafe climbed down and stretched his legs. He took a carbine from its place along the stirrup leather, looked critically at it, and put it back. Walking to the fire, he spread his hands to the little blaze. "Still, I suppose it's up to the ranch boss. O'Brien know you're comin' down?"

"He sent me a replacement." The sun was up now, and it seemed to Lew that he was gaining nothing by waiting. Each minute made it more awkward for Paddy and for himself. "So long." He put a foot in the stirrup.

"I wouldn't be in a hurry if I was you," Rafe said. "You got somethin' special to tell O'Brien?"

"No, not a thing. Why?"

"Wisht I could be sure o' that."

"His word's good," Paddy said in a reedy voice. "Let'im go, Rafe." Lew leaned from the saddle, and wrung Paddy's hand. Then he started down the draw and into the canyon. The slope was open and scrubby, with a few stunted pines, and two short granite cliffs showed where the canyon began, with a spring in the tangled growth at their foot.

Just as Lew's horse reached the granite, Rafe snatched his gun,

257

put it to his shoulder, and fired. Paddy knocked it upward from his hand. "You dang fool," he said, " 'sposing those people that's looking for him come looking *here?*" They saw the horse rear and disappear into the brush.

It was very quiet in the canyon. The mare lay where Lew had shot her, for obviously she could go no further, and you do not let a horse die more slowly than need be. The little stream from the spring trickled by, and Lew bathed his face and hands in it and filled his canteen. The stream would peter out below, no doubt, and he did not know when he would find another.

From where the sun stood at this hour, he judged that the canyon bore north and west. It came down into one of the smaller valleys, then, to be gathered up later into the great skein of the south-running river. "Just keep going downward," Paddy had always said. "Don't be lured off to take no shortcut. It don't buy you anything in the long run."

He supposed that they had heard his shot, up above, but he did not think Rafe had the hardihood to follow him. He had a whole skin—some scratches where they had brushed the rock, but the horse had taken Rafe's bullet. He had had this little mare for a couple of years—she was well trained and smart. On top of that, she was worth something. The loss left him strapped.

There was nothing with which to dig a grave, but the coyotes and the brown bears would spare him that trouble. And time was precious. It is a long way down out of the high range for a man on foot, without a poke of victuals, without an axe, without a map except the one he carries in his head. There was no way to take the saddle, but he put it up in the nearest tree. It might do somebody some good. He checked his canteen, his compass, and his matches before he started out.

Mr. Lindsay weighed up Olly Miller's five pounds of dry beans, and put them with the sack of raisins and the chewing tobacco.

"Well, Olly, be you goin' to Yurrop to fight the Huns?"

"I reckon so. My name's on that there list. I ain't in such a dad-burn hurry that I can't wait till they call me."

Mr. Lindsay cleared his throat delicately. "Harve Lucas's already enlisted."

"Yeah, I heard. Harve ain't got anybody to look after. . . . 'Lias an' Ezra is gittin' old, Ferd. Ezra can't see to shoot game no more, an' 'Lias has got the misery in his legs."

"Pshaw now, Olly! They'd both lambaste you if they heard you talk."

"They lambasted me good for my twenty-first birthday," Olly said. "An' give me a bottle o' whiskey an' a rabbit's foot. I'm gonna have that rabbit's foot sewed into my uniform someplace. Don't git me wrong, Ferd. I ain't afraid o' fightin', if I can just git to where it is. But that feller at the draft board says you got to go to camp first. That'll be fine, I says, I can camp real good. I can bring in my own fresh meat everyday, an' I can find dry wood to start a fire even on a sozzlin' morning. No, he says, it ain't like that. Camps has got thousands of men in 'em, he says, an' you have to stand in line to get your chow. Now how in hell am I gonna know what to do in a place like that?"

"They'll tell you," the storekeeper said, not unkindly. "You kin be sartain they'll tell you, Olly. How . . . how about readin' an' writin'? Did they allow you was good enough?"

"I put down what Misshollister larned me," Olly told him simply. "But they never ast me could I shoot. I can shoot pretty good, but nobody ast me."

"You can shoot the best of anybody I know," Mr. Lindsay said, almost reverently. "If you can hang on till they give you a chance to shoot, Olly, you'll come home with a medal."

"What's a medal?" Olly started to make his groceries into a double pack that would fit the rear of his saddle.

The screen door behind him opened, and someone came in. Olly turned to see a tall man with a matted blond beard and blistered face, who walked uncertainly to the counter and fumbled in his pocket. Putting down a few coins, he said thinly, "Something to eat."

"What sort o' something?"

259

"It doesn't matter really." The stranger pointed a finger at a package of wafers. "Those."

Mr. Lindsay handed them over, and went to the drawer to make change. The tall man tore the end of the box off and began to eat the wafers one by one, chewing each one thoroughly. He did not pause. When they were gone he pushed his coins to the front again. "More."

"I ain't got no more vanilla." There was something in the man's face that caused Mr. Lindsay to add hastily, "I guess you'll take choklit." Again he put a package down.

"May I have a drink of water?" the stranger said.

"Help yourself at the tap." Mr. Lindsay waved his hand at the front porch.

Olly, who had watched fascinated, moved quickly. "I'll git him some." He banged out and in the screen door, and came back with a dripping cup.

"Thank you," the stranger said. He drained the cup and set it on the counter. Finishing the second box of wafers, he looked about. "Am I in Pine Creek?"

"Yes, you be," the storekeeper said, as if his words came at so much a dozen, like the cookies.

"Then perhaps you can direct me to a Mrs. Ben Lucas."

"Second place up the river. Just go down toward the Landing and turn left."

"You can't miss it," Olly said. "There's a sign on the gate that Fletch carved, only he didn't do very good. I could do better myself. But you can read it."

"I am greatly obliged to you." The tall man went out with slow and regular steps, negotiating the door carefully. They could see him setting one foot ahead of another in the direction of the river.

"Jehoshaphat!" Olly said. "What was that?"

"Some galoot down on his luck." Mr. Lindsay took a toothpick from the glass dish behind the counter and chewed it thoughtfully. "If he wants a job, he can't hardly miss. First time in my life I ever saw it where there was more jobs than people."

"And I'm just leavin'," Olly said with what sounded like a real note of regret. Mr. Lindsay looked up surprised.

"Don't kid me, Olly. You don't want a job. You Miller Boys live off the kentry."

"That's right," Olly said stolidly. He gathered up his groceries and took them out, lashed them to the saddle, and in one long flowing movement was up and headed for the Gateway at a gallop. Inside Pine Creek valley, however, he slowed his horse to a walk, and past Yanlings', past Scobies', between the Conway place and the Hollister place (both deserted now), he dawdled as if he had no destination. Olly Miller was a troubled man.

He wasn't afraid of the Dutchies. 'Lias and Ezra had fought the Modoc Indians when they were young, and had done fine. Olly wondered if they would let him carry 'Lias's old Krag—'Lias would be real proud. But likely not. Everything was different out there.

He could hardly remember when his brothers had brought him into the valley. What he could recall of his parents was little more than showed in their charcoal portraits, in many-ringed oval frames of walnut, hanging in the Miller kitchen. This was his place, his world, the only world he had ever known. The old men had done right by him always, and it was only fitten that he should stay and do right by them. He didn't know how they could make out, and he could not even tamper with their fierce pride by talking about it.

In his moment of truth, riding along mumbling to himself and to the marmots who flicked in and out of the rocks, Olly admitted that that wasn't the whole trouble. Not by a long shot. What would the old fellows have said if they'd knowed that in his heart he wanted plowed and planted ground, like the outlanders—a nice house, maybe even a wife? They'd of haw-hawed, or they'd of whaled him to get the fool ideas out of his head. And he didn't get no encouragement, neither. He'd lost out with Mary Hollister, he'd lost out with Florence Scobie. But there had always been plenty of time to look ahead and to daydream.

Until now.

"Mama said to give 'em back to me." Mary could hear the desperation in Helen's voice, and she went to the door. It was not true, she had said nothing of the sort. Perhaps this was the time to remember Mr. Ingersoll's warning, that he would have no use for a child who did not occasionally, in a hostile world, throw up a little breastwork in the form of a lie. She listened long enough to determine that Helen had loaned her precious box of crayons and was regretting it bitterly. "He *breaks* them," Helen said as soon as she caught sight of her mother. Such was the awful power of all-seeing Mama's name that David had given the crayons back and was standing dejectedly, like a lonely sparrow, in the middle of the yard.

"Give me the crayons," Mary said, merely to keep the moral issue straight. "You can have them back at suppertime. David may help me turn the churn." Only in the case of downright disobedience did she spank, and then she struck quickly and hard, like a mother bear with a cub, and listened to the howls and dried the tears.

But it was surprising how seldom this happened. They minded her well enough. Perhaps it was the calm assurance in her voice. They were good children. And intelligent, and lovely to look at and to touch. She kept them in shirts and overalls, but Helen must have a dress soon. Preferably a pink one, and a pink bow in the hair that curled into her neck.

It was almost more than David could do to force the handle of the churn around, and after a few turns he subsided and sat listening contentedly to the rhythm. After a while he began to sing to it, tunelessly, like a medicine man. "Nah nah *nah* nah, nah nah *nah* nah." Mary laid her cheek for a moment against his rough head. When she played the piano, Helen danced and clowned, but David sat in a kind of trance, gathering the chords like arrows to his breast.

The sunshine pulsed in the dry air. In the yard, the snap beans awaited picking. Mary wished she had some meat for supper, but it would not keep in this weather. She would slice and fry salt pork, and make a kind of apologetic gravy from the drippings. And boil some potatoes, and cook a mess of the snap beans. The beans were ready for canning, and she was worrying as she worried every year since the old couple down in the coulee had nearly died from eating home-canned beans. But there was no other way, they had to have green stuff. Some of the wives had told her to add vinegar to the beans, or a lot of salt. She didn't think Ben would eat them if she did.

She gathered the butter out of the whey and washed it under running water and packed it in a crock and put it in the cooler. Then she counted out a load of empty glass jars for the wash boiler, and went to see if there were really enough beans to fill them. When she came back, a big man with a blond beard and blistered face was standing by the door, supporting himself with an arm against the house.

"My name is Lewis Anthony," he said. "I believe someone here wishes to get in touch with me."

"Oh *yes*," Mary cried. She had done it, she had brought Lew Anthony out of the mountains. She forgot all about the beans. "Oh, I'm so glad to see you. Your brother . . . I'm to tell you . . . won't you come in?" He pushed himself away from the wall of the house, and Mary saw with alarm that he wavered a little on his feet. "Are you ill, Mr. Anthony?"

"I could do with a drink of water," Lew said politely. He leaned against the house again.

"Of course." Mary flew to get it, and he took it from her hand and as he drank it down she said joyously, "You asked us for a drink of water at Luthermere. I've thought of it often. You left your book. . . . Mr. Anthony, you're not feeling well. *Please* come in and sit down."

He followed her and sank gratefully into the big cowhide chair. "Now," Mary said, her voice trembling, "I won't keep you in suspense. Your father is gone, Mr. Anthony. Your brother came here to look for you. He left again because . . . He was here for several seasons. All over the valley. He never . . . I have the address he left, and everything. He wants you to come back." Staring into his gaunt face, she added breathlessly, "Am I talking too fast? Can you understand me? Would you like another glass of water?"

"Have you any food?" Lew said simply. "If it's not too much trouble."

She looked at him aghast. Taking down a loaf of bread from the cooler, she crowded it thickly with the fresh butter and with jam and thrust it into his hands. Then she turned away, unwilling to watch him eat if he were in extremity. When she came back bringing a linen napkin, she saw that he had finished and was leaning back, looking through half-closed lids at the long living room and at the two children who had come in and were watching round-eyed from over by the piano. "Thank you," Lew said. "It's a far walk from the sheep range."

"You *walked* out? How long did it take you?"

"About a week, I think."

"What happened to your horse?"

"Lost her. . . . You might go on, Mrs. Lucas, and tell me about Bobbie. You *are* Mrs. Lucas?"

"Yes. And you must have some coffee . . . milk if you'd rather."

"Do you have whiskey?"

Mary flushed. "We don't keep it in the house. I'm sorry."

"Coffee would be fine. You're going to a lot of bother."

"Nonsense," Mary said vigorously. She felt the coffee pot from noontime dinner. It was cold. "I'll make some more."

"I'll take milk," Lew said. "You were going to tell me . . ."

"I hardly know where to begin." She brought the milk, fresh and cool, and sat down across from him. "Your brother was here with the railroad. I've come to the conclusion that it was a contrived business somehow, though a lot of young fellows drift in and out where there's construction going on. I got to know him finally and he told me about you. That you had . . . you had—"

"He came to look for me," Lew said wonderingly. "That's more than I would have done for Bobbie. . . . No, perhaps not. What sort of fellow is he? Upright, probably, and a little preachy?"

"Why no, I wouldn't say so. He had a few problems of his own."

"Bobbie with problems? How refreshing."

Mary said, nettled, "He's tried his very best to do right by you, anyhow. . . . I'm supposed to let him know if I hear of you. May I write to him now, at this address he left?"

"Kingsbridge Street?" Lew said in a tired voice. "It isn't by any chance Seventeen Kingsbridge Street?" In his thin face the eye sockets showed hollow and dark, and under the blond beard was a mouth that plainly twitched.

The enormity of what she had done came suddenly home to Mary. She was always meddling in people's lives, Ben told her.

She had meddled in this one with, perhaps, shattering effect, and she was a little frightened. "There's no harm done," she said quickly. "He asked me to send him word if I ever heard of you, and of course I . . . When I found out where you were, it seemed . . . I guess I thought you ought to know. My sister Althea said people don't disappear for nothing." A fresh embarrassment overwhelmed her. "I always tell Althea things. You mustn't think I've talked to a lot of people about it. There's no one to talk to really."

As Lew Anthony did not answer, she went on, "Now that you know, if you want to forget what I've told you and go back to the range, I'll never say anything. Never."

His look focussed on her with an effort. "Thank you, Mrs. Ben Lucas. I'm sure you are discreet. The fact is, I think I've burned my bridges."

"Then I may write?"

His eyes closed, and his mouth fell a little open. She saw that he was asleep. She hurried out through the orchard to tell Ben. Fletch and Ben were laying up a corral on the stony ground north of the fence, for the horses Ben hoped to sell to the Army. She took a child by each hand and dragged them across the hot dusty ground, making them stumble in her haste.

She saw to her relief that the two men were working a little way apart from each other. She poured out her story to Ben. "And we must keep him till he's fit to travel, mustn't we, Ben? A little rest and some food would do wonders. Imagine, he . . . There's something very peculiar about it."

"You never know about sheepherders," Ben said. But he understood the duties of hospitality as well as anyone. "Of course, keep him. He can have Harve's room. If you're sure you want him around the house. Or he can sleep in the barn."

"He looks perfectly harmless," Mary said. She plucked Helen from the bars of the corral, which Helen had managed to climb almost to the top without being noticed. Protesting, the children were borne away. It was always much more interesting out here where Papa was.

Ben looked after them through the trees, and shook his head. The canning was coming on, and in this sweaty weather Mary's wash lines were full almost everyday. And he had come in more than once to find the Yanling woman, sullen and shy, pumping the treadle of the old sewing machine under Mary's direction.

He went back to hammering together the corral. Selling any of the horses came hard to Ben, but it was time. He would not let Rusty go. Rusty was his stud, and he would never find a better one. Nor would he part with Atalanta, the high-strung two-year-old that Mary had named. He had asked her what it meant, and she had said it meant "fleet-footed." It seemed like an odd name for a horse, but he liked to humor Mary when he could.

"I'm afraid I'm a good deal of bother," Lew Anthony said, handing back the cup into which Mary had put a little of the broth from the chicken and dumplings she was readying for dinner. ". . . Mrs. Lucas, who plays the piano?"

"I'm supposed to," Mary said. "I'm not very good at it. I used to take lessons. In Oak Point. From Miss Lytle. She was a pupil of a pupil of a pupil of Paderewski."

Lew threw back his head and laughed. She was startled, but it sounded pleasant. Almost no one had ever laughed at anything she said since Amie went away.

"And you're no bother," Mary went on warmly. "Are you comfortable in the Uncles' Room?"

"The what?"

"Ben's brothers used to stay there always. I expect the children think you're an uncle of some sort. They don't seem to mind you being around."

He lounged over the back of the big chair, watching her work. "Mrs. Lucas, in my place, what would you do?"

She looked at him, the big spoon poised above the pot. It had not occurred to her that there was any alternative.

"I'd go back East, I suppose. And see . . . and find out . . ."

"The position is awkward," Lew said. "I haven't any money."

"Oh. . . . Well, there's a lot of work going about, if that's what you need. Especially now with the draft and . . ." She did not say that Ben would give him a job, for she was not sure that Ben was

266

ready to hire. "But it seems silly to just trade one kind of work for another when they . . . when there's supposed to be . . ."

"I can't see myself asking to be sent for." Lew's voice was grim, and again she was swept with the feeling that she was to blame for all this.

"*I'll* write," she said. "I'd be very glad to."

"No, I'd better do it myself. Perhaps you'll be kind enough to loan me some writing paper and a pen."

He settled himself at the low shelf that Ben used for doing his accounts. Leaving the chicken to simmer, Mary went out to the garden, where she was trying to defend her tomato plants against an invading column of caterpillars. Everyday she found a few, and everyday she militantly plucked them off and hoped there would be no more. She had scarcely got settled on the ground with an old tin can beside her, half full of kerosene, and was reaching for the first plump hateful creature, when she heard, soft and hesitant from the house, the sound of her piano.

Her scalp prickled. No one ever played her piano. There was no one but herself to play it. It felt very queer, as if the keys were speaking by themselves.

There were a few chords, fumbling and awkward, as though the fingers that felt for them had almost forgotten where they were. How strange, this moment of discovery. How well she remembered it . . . the revelation that the notes are still there, the instant, affirmative answer. She sat back on the soft earth to listen. Probably it would not occur to him that she could hear him—at any rate it did no harm. Mary Lucas could not think of anything else while someone was playing her piano.

He ran a few scales, lamentably bad. She knew the futility, the anger at one's own fingers. A melody picked out, defiantly, with one hand. And then silence. Was he going to stop there?

No. After a while he began, very slowly, the rocking bass of the "Chinese Dance" from the *Nutcracker Suite*. At one time he had surely known it very well. A little fumbling for the rhythm, a moment while the hand adjusted to the octave span. And then, a note at a time, the simple plaintive melody, groped for, more or less found. The trailing thirds, repeated and repeated. The children had heard it too, and were standing by the barn, fixing startled looks upon her, as if they had just found she was capable of being in two places at once.

"It's Mr. Anthony," Mary said. She tiptoed into the kitchen corner, afraid the chicken would scorch. Lew heard her and turned upon the piano stool.

"Mrs. Lucas," he said, "I didn't ask if I could use the piano."

"Anytime," Mary said inadequately. "As much as you like. It seems like a life time since I have heard anyone play." Twelve o'clock was upon her, the exact and ruthless noon of the farmer's wife; Ben would be in at any moment. "Dinner is ready. You can wash up at the bench outside the back door." The coffee came to a boil, and she put a dish of radishes on the table and some of the crisp pickles Ben liked.

She had David on one side of her at the table in a highchair, and Helen on the other in the seat with the extra cushions that Ben had devised. She had taken great pains with the children's table manners, and with pride she saw that David kept things strictly on his tray, heard Helen murmur, "Excuse me, p'ease," before she slipped down from her seat. Did the stranger know what momentous things these were, how hardly they had been earned? Of course not. He answered Ben's few civil questions in an abstracted way. Immediately after dinner, he went back to his letter, and while she washed up, she heard him crumple sheet after sheet of paper and drop it on the floor.

When she had stowed away the dishes and hung out the towels and put the children on cots on the porch for the afternoon rest, and was quietly darning socks in the corner, Lew said suddenly, "Mrs. Lucas, this is impossible. 'Lewis Anthony announces his return from Limbo.' I don't know what to *say*."

"It must be difficult," Mary agreed. "Maybe you'd better think about it for a couple of days. We'd like you to stay until you're rested. . . . Are you *sure* you don't want me to write it?"

"I suppose you could." He conceded defeat by getting up from the writing shelf. Mary laid aside her darning and came over.

She sat down and drew the pen and paper toward her, and began without hesitation,

268

Dear Bob,

The reason you could not locate your brother was that he was herding sheep up in the hills. He is at our house in Pine Creek now, and would be glad to hear from you.

Sincerely,
Mary   Lucas

She handed it to Lew, who read it through, and looked at her with respect. "How direct and sensible you are! It practically says itself. . . . Besides, it gives him the option of not answering if he doesn't want a sheepherder for a brother."

Mary flushed painfully. "I didn't mean it that way."

"Of course not. But I have reason to think . . . You might as well know this, Mrs. Lucas—I'm scared to death of the whole thing. If I don't like it, by Jesus I'll turn around and start back! I beg your pardon. I've been living with men too long."

"That's quite all right. Perhaps talking will help you."

"Then tell me what Bobbie is really like."

"Well," Mary considered this, "to begin with, he's not the sort of person you'd call Bobbie. He's extremely serious and rather charming. My sister Althea liked him, and she has very old-fashioned ideas."

"I see. Any vices?"

"Am I supposed to know?" said Mary primly.

He broke into a laugh. She thought it was very nice to hear so much laughter in such a short time, especially as she was causing it. "All right," he said. "I will be prepared to give Bobbie . . . Bob . . . the benefit of all doubts. Did he talk to you about . . . about what went on before I left?"

"A little. He spoke sometimes of his mother. She must have been very lovely."

Lew's face tightened. He went to the door and stared out. At this time of year it stood open, and the windows too, to catch any thread of breeze that might be stirring. There was a faint sound of hammering from the corral, and out on the highway an old Ford clattered by.

"Forgive me," Mary said. "I've been out of the world quite a

269

while myself, you know, and I'm getting tactless. Tell me how you travelled West and where you've worked. But please talk." She had brought him this far, and she was obliged to help him further now, like a Chinese who has fished a man out of the river.

"I haven't done anything very distinguished. I think perhaps," Lew said thoughtfully, "I've spent my time hunting for jobs where I wouldn't have to shout at anybody."

"*Shout* at anybody?"

"From the time I could remember," Lew flung himself into the chair again, "I'd been shouted at. It was a matter of principle with my father. It was how he got things done. He shouted whenever he noticed I wasn't busy at something, and then if I tried to do anything and it turned out badly, he shouted in a different key, as it were, and *fortissimo*. I left home with the idea of turning out to be as different as possible from my father. A rather negative ambition, isn't it?"

"Has it made you happy?"

"Who is happy, Mrs. Lucas? St. Simeon on his pillar? Peary at the North Pole? Beethoven writing symphonies he would never hear?"

There was a sound of small naked footsteps, and Helen came in the front door, dressed only in her cotton panties. "You're talking and talking and talking," she said accusingly.

"Oh dear!" Mary caught the child up in her arms. Over her shoulder she apologized, "It's usually so quiet here. I must find some clean rompers for this poor little girl and go gather the eggs and get my sheets down from the line."

"Can I do anything to help?" Lew asked gravely.

"Yes. There's *always* something to do here." She thrust a basket into his hands. "Go around to the garden east of the barn and pick beans."

16

IN SPITE OF what Mary had said, it *was* a bother to have Lew Anthony in the house. After the children were put in their trundle beds at night there was no place for him in the living room. Fletch and Harve had always gone to bed early, and since these were the only house guests they had ever had, the question of a stranger underfoot had never arisen. Each night after supper Lew took a book from their scanty stock and disappeared; she doubted if he always read. He probably stared at the low raftered roof of the Uncles' Room and wondered what was going to become of him. Or perhaps he did not try to figure out. It might be easy, too easy by now, to have the habit of leaving everything to chance. There was some lack of drive in him, some failure of the brisk captaincy of one's soul that she was used to in the people of Pine Creek.

In the daytime he followed her about, or went for desultory walks, and he was forever at the piano. At first he would not play when anyone was in the room, and Mary tried to leave him alone there, going outside to peel her vegetables or pit cherries. But it was a necessity that she go back and forth constantly, and he soon accepted her presence, and that of the children, too, who went about their own affairs.

He played Chopin preludes and Viennese waltzes and "Liebestraum" and "The Kerry Dancers" and "Humoresque" and Handel's "Largo" and "Last Night a Nightingale Woke Me," and (while Mary held her breath and the bread dough clung to her motionless fingers) the "Bacchanale" from *Samson and Delilah*, piling chord on chord till the mighty ending hammered out and there was a crash and silence. Mary let go her breath with a long sigh, and began to knead again. He gained skill hour by hour—he must have played excellently at one time. Had his father shouted at him when Lew spent time on such foolishness?

When he was not playing the piano, he and Mary, as Helen accurately put it, were talking and talking. He made fumbling efforts to earn his keep, but there were few chores either she or Ben could give him that he knew how to do. At last, to his daily inquiry, she suggested, "You can help me pick caterpillars off the tomato plants, I guess. It isn't very nice work for a guest." She took her can of kerosene out to the garden, and showed him where the enemy was hiding among the green leaves. "You're supposed to pinch them, but I can't do it. So I drop them in this kerosene, and go bury them later."

"And blame yourself because they suffer, no doubt. It's hell not to want to hurt anyone or anything, isn't it, Mary?" He knelt beside her, and began a businesslike search.

"One can't always afford to think about it. But I *do* think about it. Watching the boys go to the War. Kind boys, tenderhearted boys, like the ones I know, having to learn to hurt and kill. After you get home, Lew, will you go to the War?"

"Very likely," Lew said. He looked humorously at her across the vines. "You like to have things settled, don't you, Mary? I'm really not able to settle anything at the moment."

"I know. And I'm so sorry. I've really disrupted your life terribly."

"You did the best you knew." Lew watched her out of the corner of his eye.

She looked so ready to cry that Lew said, "Mary, I'm teasing you. I must never do that, must I? Of course I'm grateful. I always expected to go back sometime. When I had made some kind of a showing. But I've never made a showing, and I never will. I'm perfectly fitted to be rich and to dawdle."

"That's ridiculous. You could do a lot of useful things. Build hospitals. Give scholarships."

"All you can do with money is to give people a chance to be more the way they already are. I'd like to send Paddy enough to get him out of this racket he's in, but what else could I do for him? Find him some unicorns to herd?"

"I suppose," Mary said conscientiously, "we shouldn't keep speaking of your . . . your inheritance as if you already had it."

272

"It's there. I have Bobbie's word, or your word anyhow, that he's not trying to do me out of my share. You're right, though—I'd better wait till I get my hands on it. I shall miser over it, pouring it through my fingers. . . . No, I won't. I'll buy first editions and spend summers in Maine and winters in New York, and keep a ballet dancer."

"Won't you marry?"

"I had a jessamy bride once. They took her away from me. It was a long time ago."

"How could they do that?"

"They could do it, all right. I was under age. *God*, it was a long time ago."

"How old are you, Lew?"

"Don't I think I'm old enough to settle down, you mean. Let's say I was sailing boats on the lagoon when you were born. Out there by myself, too, without my nursemaid."

"Bob told me about the boats. He said yours always sank."

"That was unkind of Bob. Even if true." Lew dropped a long green worm in the kerosene can. "Did he have any other little biographical gems to offer?"

She did not know how to answer this. Tell him he must not be bitter? In his place she would be bitter too, and confused and wary.

"He said hardly anything that you haven't told me yourself." The sun was beating down on them. Stinging sweat ran into her eyes. She wiped it away with the back of her hand.

"And that's far too much. . . . What about *you*, Mary Lucas? Haven't you any skeletons to rattle? Any blighted hopes? Any secret wishes?"

Mary considered this. "I did want very much to go to Greece, once upon a time."

"What for?"

"Just to be there. To look about, I suppose, and put my hands on the old stones. To know that they were real. I used to care tremendously about it."

"And you don't any more?"

"Not so much. Or perhaps I care for other things."

273

"What sort of things?"

"My family, and the ranch, and . . . goodness, I don't know! You fluster me, Lew."

"What would you like that money would buy, Mary? Providing I do come into some."

"Why, nothing really," Mary said, and she meant it. There were hundreds of things she needed, but none that Ben's wife could take from Lew Anthony. To soften the ungracious sound of it, she added, "Ask me again when the children are ready for college. Perhaps you can give us some of those scholarships."

"And in the meantime, no Greece."

"No."

"No Parthenon against the sky."

"No."

"No ragged old theater cut into the hillside, with crumbled seats."

"I'm afraid not."

"No row of stone lions looking down the valley of Delos with vacant eyes."

"I like to hear you talk about it," Mary said. "Since I don't see Althea much any more, I never hear those things. We used to have jokes about them. You can, you know. You can make jokes about something and still respect it. . . . I can't find any more caterpillars. Can you?"

"I think that's about it," Lew said. "Want me to do the disposal job?"

"If you don't mind. There's a spade in the barn, over against the grain sacks. It's very kind of you."

He picked up the can, and whistled a few bars of the "Funeral March."

"Really!" Mary said, a little shocked.

"You can make jokes about something and still respect it." He started for the barn, bearing his smelly burden carefully in one hand.

Florence's baby boy was born on a sizzling August morning. Dr. McClellan arrived before daybreak, and Mrs. Scobie came at breakfast time to take charge of her daughter's household. Mary ran back and forth all day with food, hot water bottles, and advice. It was strangely moving to see Florence's damp red hair spread out on her pillow, above a radiant face. Little Florence, who had cried because she was graduating from the eighth grade and nothing exciting would ever happen to her any more. Mary stooped to kiss her swiftly. "He's beautiful. Beautiful. Oh Florence, I do love you."

"I love everybody," Florence said. "Mary, will you please find Fletch and tell him it's *all right?* He's outside somewhere, having the shakes."

Fletch was sitting with his back against a disreputable old shack that had been built by Piggott for a corncrib before he discovered that his land would not grow corn. Mary sat down and slipped an arm around Fletch's shoulders. For awhile they sat in silence, watching the heat shimmer up from the valley, the road wind away to the north past the dismantled railroad camp. Lew Anthony had said, tactfully withdrawing himself from this day of family crisis, that he was going up to Indian Spring. On foot, she supposed, catching a ride where he could. She had taken time to make him a sandwich and insist that he thrust it into his pocket.

She thought of him, adrift, aimless, helplessly whiling away his time, and of the harried boy beside her with this fresh responsibility thrust upon him. "Fletch," she said, "Florence will have a lovely time with the baby, and it doesn't cost much more for three than for two. Ben and I managed. A Lucas can always manage."

Fletch looked at the far line of hills, beyond which lay the upland wheat fields. "I ought to be over there right now, making my stake. I only waited till the baby was born."

"Well, you can go now. We'll all look out for Florence and take care of her. And when you come back . . . oh, Fletch, what a homecoming that will be."

"He's awful small, isn't he?" said Fletch as if he were almost afraid to mention it. "I guess they all are. I guess I never noticed before."

"Yes, they all are. In a month, you won't know him. He'll be twice as big and hitting out at people and hollering for his food so you can hear him down at the Landing. But he's all there. Don't be afraid to pick him up and look. You've got a son, Fletch. You're a taller man now."

"Is *she* . . . all right? She'd say so, whether she was or not."

"She came through it fine." Mary knew he was thinking of her own last confinement, the illness, the long anxiety. "It doesn't often happen the way it did with me, Fletch. Women are pretty durable."

"Then why did you quit?" Fletch asked unexpectedly.

Mary was startled. She had not supposed that anyone noticed she had quit. There was no privacy in Pine Creek, no making of lone decisions, no solitude. Everybody belonged to everybody.

To be late for meals was, in the Lucas household, a sin. *There are so many sins,* Mary thought bleakly, as she filled the milk pitcher and set it beside Ben for his bowl of mush. Breakfast was proceeding in silence, as it always did; even the children were subdued in the morning, and gobbled their food so they could be out at play. They had finished and had left the table by the time Lew appeared, breezy and freshly scrubbed, coming from the washbasin outside the back door. She dished him up some mush while Ben traveled on through his bacon and eggs. He greeted Lew with a slight inclination of the head.

We're feeding and sheltering him, he should mind our rules. Ben is right. Ben is always right.

Ben rose, and stopped by the sink a moment. "I'll be down in the south piece. If Fletch comes by, you can tell him."

He put on the frayed straw hat that hung by the back door and went out. Mary poured herself a second cup of coffee and brought it to the table. Meeting Lew's eyes across the dirty dishes, she said unneccessarily, "It's our way. Life is pretty serious here. I sometimes think—I think of something I read a long time ago, about how serious life was in the Middle Ages, how they were afraid to enjoy themselves, for fear it would displease God." She spoke haltingly, for she was not used now to expressing such thoughts. "There was a philosopher—I forget his name. When anyone laughed in his presence, he said 'Christ was crucified—and dost thou laugh?'"

"A very proper attitude," Lew said. He began to stack the dishes nearest him and carry them to the sink.

"Oh never mind those. I'll wash them while the water for the tubs is heating."

"I see. Every moment accounted for." Disregarding her words, he continued to walk back and forth till the table was cleared.

"Yes, I suppose so. It's the only way to get through the day." A dreamy look came over her face. "Althea and I didn't always wash the dishes right up. Sometimes we just sat awhile, and talked about what was on our minds."

"Fine," Lew said. "Let's talk about what's on our minds." He sat down again across the table; for a moment she was touched with the feeling that she had said something imprudent, had sounded forward. But he went on, "What's under that utterly devastating little topknot of yours?"

His tone was so light, so casual, that she could not take offense. "Oh lots of things. I must start to dress Helen in little girl clothes, I don't want her growing up a tomboy. . . . I must make something for the Bake Sale at the railroad station—it's for the overseas YMCA. I must see if I can nerve Elsie Yanling up to ask for her money back on the hatching eggs she bought. She got eleven roosters and one hen."

She meant to evoke his easy laughter; but Lew was grave today. "So you keep an eye on all the social life in Pine Creek, including the poultry. I like your presiding spirit, Mary Lucas. I'm glad you're in charge of my affairs—and by the way, you haven't heard any word from the eastern connection?"

"I'll tell you instantly when it comes. Don't get discouraged, Lew—it's only been a couple of weeks since I wrote. Waiting is horrid, I know."

He was her ward, her charge, her shorn lamb. She did not need to look at him to know the peaking of his eyebrows over the dark caverns of his eyes—thank heaven, not quite such caverns as when he came to them—and the spatulate firmness of his hands on the table. A pianist's hands.

"Play something for me, Lew. I've been meaning to ask you—will you play my Grieg? It helps to hear it from someone else. If one makes the same mistake a few times—and I know I do—then one learns the mistake, and it's awfully hard to correct it."

"I've never heard you play it."

"And you never will. The piano is yours for as long as you're here."

"That's silly."

"It is not. I'm bashful. I can't bear to bring out my little wares and parade them and have you say, 'Why, that's very nice, Mary.'"

"Do I strike you as being so patronizing?"

They were flaring out at each other like children. She felt apprehension, terror even, lest his endurance might wear thin and he might blow up and spoil everything.

"Very well, I will try to play it for you." She got up from the table, but Lew said quickly,

"Never mind. I do nothing but put you to trouble. Oh Mary, be patient with me. I'm out on a limb."

And she had put him there. She was never without this consciousness that the whole thing was her doing. Unsteadily she said, "It can't take much longer. *Wouldn't* you think that they—It's just not knowing, isn't it? Do you wish you were back on the range, and had never heard of me?"

"No," Lew said crisply. "I don't wish I had never heard of you. Can I wash the dishes for you, Mary? I promise not to drop them—not more than two or three, anyway."

She hesitated. The work of the house was so uniquely hers, she was so accustomed to have it completely in her hands, that it would be inconvenient to have someone else puttering about. Moreover, it was an infraction of his dignity; she did not want him reduced to doing the household chores. And for some obscure reason it would be far better to have him out of the house for a while. But meeting his bright gaze, aware of the napkin he was rolling into a careful cylinder, she said only, "Why yes, I suppose you could."

She knew the splashy, imperative handwriting, though she had barely seen it before. Lew knew it too. His eyes flickered in his bearded, impassive face.

The letter was addressed to Mary. She tore it open with nervous fingers.

Dear Mrs. Lucas,

I don't know how much of a hand you had in this, but I'm everlastingly indebted to you. I'm at camp, and can't get home in the foreseeable future. Pierce has charge of everything. Lew will remember him. I hope Lew will come back. He's all I've got —except a wife, whom I acquired just before joining the army.

Please make it clear to Lew that he and Pierce can work things out anyway they like. I can't tell you how glad I am not to have to worry about it any more. There's a fair amount to worry about right here.

When this war is over, I'd like to show Janice the West.

A thousand thanks,
(Lt.) Robert Anthony

Army Signal Corps
Camp Dix, New Jersey

She handed it to Lew, and went to get some crackers for the children, who were begging for a snack. She did not want to watch him while he read. Afterward she found him sitting in one of the dining chairs, with his chin on his hands, looking into space.

"Well," Mary said brightly, "nothing stands still, does it? . . . It's a very decent letter."

"Yes."

"In fact it's a very *nice* letter," said Mary resolutely. ". . . Remember, it's just as hard for him to write to you as it is for you to write to him. . . . Who is this Pierce?"

"My father's lawyer and right-hand man. It's amazing that he's still around."

"Were you good friends?"

"In a way. You can hardly be enemies with old Pierce."

"That sounds promising," Mary said. She began to clean and

cut up the eternal snap beans for dinner. ". . . I wish I could think of some new way to cook these. . . . Should you start east, do you think, Lew?"

"What with?" He put his head down on his hands.

"With harvest money," Mary said. "Everybody works in the apple harvest. It's only about a month away. . . . Oh, Lew, that would seem like a lifetime, wouldn't it? I have a better idea. If this is going to be handled by lawyers, I'll send you to my brother-in-law. Charles is a good attorney, and he's also one of the most wonderful people I know. Althea and I depended on him so much, and Althea finally married him. I sometimes tell her it's so we could keep his services in the family."

She tried to smile. She was talking against time, waiting till he raised his head, waiting until that look should leave his face. Of all the things that could be said, most of them did not bear uttering. "I think the dignified thing would be to have Charles write to your Mr. Pierce, and suggest some . . . some . . ."

"Handout," said Lew's muffled voice. "Peace offering. Dole."

"Now Lew. Family things are always difficult. I remember when Althea and I . . ." No. She could not tell him how she and Althea had quarreled over Ben, how sorely it had hurt them both. "Charles will know what to do. You'll like him, I'm sure. You're among friends, Lew."

"If you're talking about yourself, I'm among angels." He straightened up, and drew a deep breath. "I guess legal advice wouldn't hurt. I'm eating your bread and salt, and incidentally your husband's, who doesn't much approve of me. . . . Mary, what's the matter with me, that I don't tell them to go to hell? Have I slept by too many roadsides, knocked at too many doors? Why do I want to go on with this thing, anyway?"

But he did want to go on, she was thankful for that. She thought she could not have borne it if he had stormed out of the door and gone his derelict way again. This much she had accomplished. He would go home and things would work themselves out. At least she hoped so.

She did not waste time in argument. "I'd like you to see Charles before you make up your mind. I'll give you a note to him, and one to Althea. If she asks you to stay with them, please do. Tell her about the theater in the hillside, and the Parthenon against the sky. She'll know who you've been talking to."

Did he have money for railroad fare? She did not dare to ask. "If you walk down to the store, you can nearly always get a ride into Wenatchee. Mr. Lindsay goes in often, and Bert Plew, and a lot of others. It's so different now! With the good road, you can make it in a matter of hours. When Althea and I came into the country, the way wasn't fit to drive—at least that was what they said. We came in by steamboat. Everybody did. Oh, Lew, the steamboats were lovely. I was afraid of them, but they were fun. It makes me feel like a real old-timer to remember them now."

Somehow, she kept up this chatter until he had brought his bedroll from his room and made his simple preparations. With dinner boiling on the stove, she wrote the notes she had promised. They only took a few moments. She was full of what she wanted to say.

"There." She gave them to him, sealed. In the one to Charles Gillespie she had enclosed Bob's letter; it was no time to be finicky. This *must* succeed. Offer him food for the road? Possibly not this time. She must not seem officious. But she brought him a glass of milk and a slice of bread and cheese before he started.

Mary had gone to sleep as soon as her head hit the pillow. She nearly always did. To rest was blissful, after the day's furious course. She hardly had time to savor it and to be aware of the familiar presences in the room. Was that Helen, snoring faintly? She must be taught to sleep on her side—a woman who snores is an unseemly thing. It was the last thought she was conscious of.

But toward morning, some passing wagon, some shrieking mouse or bird caught in the owl's claws, made a sound that woke her. She came up gradually through layers of drowsiness; identity returned to her. She was Mary Lucas, drudge and dreamer, chatelaine of this house. Mother of the two most important people in the world. Busybody, strategist, befriender of the passing guest . . . No, she had no guest. He was gone—the Uncles' Room was empty. . . .

Ben slept earnestly, systematically; he approached it as he did all his tasks. The earth had turned to the point where their side of it was in shadow; it was time for sleep, and Ben slept. She tried to think of the turning earth. Somewhere it was day, in China no doubt. The dawn was coming up like thunder out of China 'crost the bay. In Henry Hollister's house, they had read the poems of Mr. Kipling as fast as they were printed, tasting on their tongues the East, and hearing the temple bells of India. When Kipling had received the Nobel Prize, Henry Hollister had felt it as a personal triumph.

Behind her closed eyelids she could see her father plainly. Good, gentle, tolerant. He had left her a legacy, a gift of compassion. "Don't rub it in," Henry Hollister had always said of those who failed or made mistakes. "He feels bad enough already."

For this reason and no other, she told herself, she had become involved with Lew Anthony. . . . There was something about the night hours that made one uneasy, that questioned one's motives. *Mary Lucas, would you be just as interested in doing something for Lew if he were ugly and old and didn't have a tongue of silver?*

No, of course not. He's only pitiful because he's young. The old aren't pitiful, they've learned to live with themselves. I want Lew to learn to live with himself.

Are you sure you're entitled to care, one way or the other? Isn't it true that Ben doesn't approve of him?

Oh, what does that matter? Ben disapproves of so many things.

She wished it was time to get up and start the fire and put the kettle on and watch the children tumbling out of bed. Things always looked better, more reasonable, in the light of day.

"What's this?"
"What?"
"This."
"What?"

282

"This."

She had no idea how long Helen and David would keep it up. Whichever one collapsed first from curiosity, and came over to where the other one was, would lose face. It was the chief business of their lives for each to hold his own in a society with only two members, and they were pretty evenly matched. Helen was older and smarter, but David had a gentle tenacity that would carry him far. When he grew up, Mary thought, he would be a rallier of lost causes and a holder of beseiged places.

She never interfered with their bickering, unless it became an open quarrel. But she ought to shoo them out of the driveway; not that there was any traffic to speak of, but she thought that the floor of the orchard, with water running among the rows, was safer from rattlesnakes. None had been killed near the house for the last few summers, but it was her habit to be watchful.

When Lew walked into the yard, she gasped. His beard was gone. Around his bitter, humorous mouth was an expanse of pale skin, sharp against the sunburn, like the big light-colored patch on a clown's face.

"It was your sister's idea," Lew said drily. "She's rather . . . definite, isn't she? She thought I ought to start looking like a city man again."

"Then . . . then there *is* . . . you *did* . . ."

"Everything is being more or less taken care of," Lew said. "They were very kind to me. Your brother-in-law wrote a letter. Owing to the need of settling my affairs, and so forth. Then they exchanged some telegrams. And there will be a bank draft at his office for me in a few days."

"Oh, I'm so glad," Mary said. She was, in fact, dizzy with relief. It was done, now there would be no further hitches. She had brought Lew Anthony out of the wilderness and delivered him into safe hands.

"I think I'll stop thanking you. It gets monotonous. Besides, how do I know you've done me any real favor? I may miss the feeling of pine needles in my bed."

"You're teasing me again," Mary said happily. ". . . Oh Lew, I couldn't be more pleased. . . . Did you always have pine needles in your bed?"

"No, it wasn't always pine needles. Pine needles don't bite. There's plenty I'd just as soon not tell you, Mary. Or would you insist on knowing?"

"*Would* insist? . . . How do you mean, would? Under what circumstances?"

"Never mind," Lew said. He certainly looked, though she wasn't used to it, more civilized without his beard. She kept giving him covert looks, making sure this was Lew. He declined to come to dinner. He said he was not hungry, and went to walk up toward the highway, at least that was the direction he took. When she was putting the children on the porch for their naps, she saw him sitting on Mary's Rock.

She took her mending out to the coolness and quiet of the orchard. Harve had found an old Indian dugout, carved from a single log, on the riverbank and had brought it up and filled it with water for the children to play in. When mosquitoes began to breed in it, it had been turned bottom side up and left there. It made an excellent seat. She spread her work out; dungarees and the patches to put on them, socks that would bear mending once more, shirts with the elbows out. A cicada shrilled in the distance, and an irrigation ditch gurgled nearby. She did not hear Lew's footsteps till he stood beside her, a spray of gummy yellow flowers in his hand.

"Oh, those are 'stickums,'" Mary said. "Press one on your lapel and it will stay. The children love to pin them on each other. They drop off in a few moments, of course."

He did not follow her suggestion, but sat down on the other end of the old canoe and let the flowers fall in the dust. "Mary," he said, "I seem to keep wanting to ask you questions about Bob. Once in a while you say something that makes me think you knew him rather well. Anything I could find out now would help me. Does Bob dislike me?"

"Perhaps. I rather think he did, when he was growing up. You left him in the lion's clutches, after all, didn't you?"

"Yes, I did. I can see how he'd have to be hardhearted to survive."

"He's *not* hard-hearted!" Mary's work dropped in her lap.

284

"Whatever he thought, he came out here to get you. . . . Oh, every young man wants a junket to the West, I suppose! But he's vulnerable and easy to hurt, like everybody else. And when he got hurt, he went home. . . . I don't know that I have any business talking about it. I don't know that he'd want me to."

"You'll have to do as you think best."

Perhaps it was right to tell him; perhaps she could enlist his sympathy. She began to describe the railroad camps, the bleakness, the makeshifts, the air of exile, the feverish small seekings for gaiety, the getting acquainted and being wrenched away again. "And hardly any women. Oh, there were girls around the countryside. Girls that want a proper courting—he was in no position for that. I think he was always just about to give up and leave, but it was an adventure. Maybe the only one he would ever have."

Lew watched her intently. "You seem to understand it pretty well."

"Well, it was an adventure for me too. Having them come. I'd never seen anything like it. And I was lonely. Everybody in this country is lonely. All the time."

"Yes," Lew said.

"So then there was this woman." Imagine describing Amie as "this woman!" But she managed to get on with it, to tell him about Amie, about Amie and Bob. The things she had promised herself never to tell a living soul. Her voice showed that it was urgent in her, that she had forgotten nothing, that the price Amie's friendship had cost her was still being paid.

"I've got to understand it," Mary said. "If it takes the rest of my life. She was so lovely, I liked her so much. I can't make it seem right, and I can't make it seem wrong. But that's not the way I was raised. Or rather I was raised two ways at the same time, like most of us I guess. Most people that get a good education. What was beautiful in poetry and the myths, was horrid when it happened next door."

"You were concerned for your friend," Lew said gently. "What did you think of Bob's share in the business?"

"He was a fool," Mary said succinctly.

There was a barely perceptible pause. "I'm a fool too," Lew said. "Mary, would you like to go East with me?"

She just looked at him. The ditch trickled noisily and a magpie chittered among the trees.

"I didn't mean to throw it at you like that. I don't want to scare you, Mary. I didn't intend to speak of it now. But it's . . ." He paused, and wet his lips. "It's hard not to try to find out how you feel."

She said the first thing that came into her head. "I don't want to be your ballet dancer."

"Mary!"

Then she was ashamed; she could hardly look at his dear, crazy, bi-colored face. "I . . . I know you didn't mean that. But I . . . No, Lew. No."

"Why?"

"Because I . . . because a woman in my position . . ."

"You just finished telling me that a woman in your position could do as she pleased. You said you couldn't make it seem wrong."

"It would be wrong for *me*. I've made promises . . ."

"Everybody has made promises, one time or another. What makes you suppose yours are any different? . . . Mary, I'm only frightening you. That's what I wanted not to do. Don't panic. Don't suddenly feel you can't talk to me. You can always talk to me. Can't you?"

"I don't think so. Oh, I don't mean I can't say the words! I've done nothing else, for days. Words I never thought I would use again. I know how terribly I'll miss you."

"But haven't you thought at all about . . . You're not stupid, Mary. You're surely not going to tell me you had no idea. You're not going to put me off with a lot of platitudes."

"I don't know anything to say that's *not* a platitude. I *am* stupid, Lew."

"They've taught you to devalue yourself pretty thoroughly, haven't they? I won't put you to the trouble of defending your husband. I'm sure you could do it very well. I don't want to hear it. . . . I've been making love to you on the piano, Mary. Didn't you know?"

She shook her head.

"I could kiss you and I think I could make you like it. Shall I try?"

"No," said Mary faintly. She did not doubt he could make her like it. That was the whole trouble.

The tawny ground around them darkened under a thin summer cloud, the cicada stopped singing.

"I have to laugh," Lew said. "Do something for people, make somebody happy. . . . It's perfectly obvious that you're in a bad spot here, Mary. I'd like to have a go at making *you* happy. Could I, do you think?"

She did not answer.

"Well, *could* I?"

She said between stiff lips, "I don't want another failure, Lew. Another divorce. I don't want to keep going from place to place and man to man and thinking this time will be better."

If there was anything surprising to him, any news about her past life that he had not heard, he did not choose to show it. Perhaps . . . no, there was no one that could have told him. It might be the missing piece in his picture of her, perfectly fitting, perfectly explanatory.

Into the silence she said softly, "I want to hold my head up, Lew."

"You don't realize, do you, that everything could be arranged in time? Quietly. Nicely. Money takes care of Mrs. Grundy. That's one of the things it's for. . . . Mary, I think you're beating about the bush. Making excuses for doing what you think you ought to do. Just be honest with me. Do you love me at all?"

"Oh *love!* Love is not enough. Love can't stand alone. I know a lot about love, Lew. It's trapped me twice. I'm a plain little woman with mousy hair—no, don't interrupt me—I'm just a very ordinary person, but I know about love. Love is your own need, made visible in somebody. Love is what makes you start something that you have to finish if you can. Maybe you can't, but you have to try. I don't *want* love. I can't afford it."

"You poor child," Lew said softly. "You poor lost little Passion-ate Pilgrim."

Somehow at this point the sense stole over Mary that she had not seen or heard the children for too long. When this feeling came, nothing else mattered. She turned to him a face suddenly gone blank.

"I must check up on Helen and the boy," she said.

He knew it was not a feint nor an excuse—all consciousness of him had left her. In her ceaseless war against the wilderness for her children, he had become for the moment just an obstacle, just somebody sitting there. "I'm sorry," she murmured as she might have to a stranger she had brushed against. She pushed aside her work and went toward the house.

If anything had happened, if they were not where she could find them readily, she would go from riverbank to the edge of the hill and up and down the road, and if by then she did not see them, she would call everybody out with the cry, "Lost child!" She had never had to do it yet.

She did not have to do it today. David was still asleep, sprawled moistly on his cot, his arms and legs flung out. Helen was playing in the shade of the house with a grubby doll, trying to make the poor thing sit up on its hinges. With angry patience she picked it out of the dirt and jammed it into place and watched it fall over again. Her mother turned and left, making no sound.

When she came back, Lew was standing beside the log. He had gathered her mending into a neat bundle, which he handed to her. "I guess that was my answer. . . . Come along, Mary." They began to walk toward the house, and though she preceded him through the soft loamy ground, it was as if they went hand in hand. At the edge of the yard he made her a dry, ironic little bow.

"I think it might be better, under all the circumstances, if I left here at once."

She nodded. She avoided looking at his face. She would never have any trouble remembering it, if she needed to. She did not say that she knew it was awkward for him; he did not say that he knew how abrupt this was. Neither of them had any cause to apologize to the other. Things were the way they were.

"I'll be in Wenatchee a few days, if anything comes up. Till your . . . till Mr. Gillespie hears from Mr. Pierce. It sounds like a comic song." He had his nonchalance back, his voice was level.

"Yes. . . . You've decided to see if you can go and hurry things up." Mary's voice was level too, if a little strained. "You'll take Duke, my horse. The saddle is on the rack to the left of the feed boxes. You'll go straight to Charles and Althea . . . won't you, please?"

"If you wish."

"You'll need . . . When you first came, I remember you said 'The position is awkward.' " She choked a little on the phrase. From that time on, she had never been unaware of him. "It's still awkward. You must have . . ."

She did not know how to say it. Walking to the shelf where she kept her basket of spare needles and braid and ribbon, she took it down. She pushed all the contents to one side, and lifting the tightly fitted bottom pad, brought out Arthur's one hundred dollars. "You'll need this."

He looked at her blankly.

"It wasn't enough to send you East," Mary said breathlessly. "But now . . ."

"Where in God's name did you get this money?"

"My brother gave it to me, Lew. To do something with that I might want to some day. This is what I want to do with it. Do you mind?"

"Of course I mind."

"Please," Mary said.

"To save my face," Lew said slowly. "Before your kin. Sometimes I understand you, Mary. Suddenly. Better than you'll ever know."

She slipped it into his hand.

"I'll send it back," Lew said. "Not that it would matter to you. You have a singular quality of dedication, Mary."

"I'm going up to see Florence. I haven't seen her today. I'm taking the children. When I come back, you'll be gone."

He bent his head. He picked up her nerveless hand and she thought he was going to put it to his lips, but his bravado left him, and he started for his quarters, not looking back.

As she plowed up the road with the children, she did not feel virtuous, or heroic, or relieved, or any of those things. Numb, that was all. Just numb.

17

THEY WERE DESPERATELY shorthanded for harvest. Skilled sorters and packers, assured of all the work they wanted at the long-season sheds in Wenatchee, could not be lured to Pine Creek. At the Scobie place, Rudy and George and Tom and Archie were all old enough to help, and Mr. Scobie said he thanked God for his boys, who took their places uncomplainingly with the grown folk, though Archie was only ten. The Sawyers drove to the coast and came back with a carload of small brown men who turned out to be Filipinos; they made their camp along the riverbank, and Mrs. Sawyer testified at the post office that they did *not* eat snakes and crickets, as Bert Plew had reported.

The Lucases would have to have a second packer—the crop was bigger. Fletch could not possibly handle it alone, and Mary said that if Dolly would come and cook for the help and keep the children, she would learn to pack this year. She had always done the bookkeeping and the boarding and kept the coffeepot on and the bandages ready, and listened to both sides of the quarrels that broke out under the pressures of the season. But now the children were old enough to leave with someone else, and if Fletch would teach her, she would try to be ready when the main part of the crop began to roll.

She threw herself into it with an energy that astonished Fletch. The lean-to against the barn, with its slanted bench and open boxes facing upward, had been ready since the first of September. Here Mary stood, in the denim apron that packers wore to take the rubbing against the boxes, and began to learn the simple motions of wrapping and stowing. She was careful; she made few mistakes. And though her shoulders started to ache within the hour, she kept it up till Fletch begged her to lay off. "You've got to harden up to it," he said. "Give your muscles a chance."

If it hurts tonight, so much the better. It'll keep my mind off things I don't want to think about.

Florence was entranced. It was the next best thing, she said, to working out here herself. She came down bringing the baby, laying him tenderly in an apple box while she gave Mary a few pointers. After while she was back again, carrying fresh gingerbread. "I just can't stay out of it," she said. "I wish I were you."

And I wish I were you. With a new husband and a new baby and complete faith in the way everything is going to turn out.

The first load came in on the flatbed wagon on a morning as clear and dazzling as crystal. It was perfect picking weather. A few cool nights had brought on the color, so that every boxfull glowed red, and the sorting was easy and could be done by Mrs. Slocum, the wife of the California picker who came to the Lucases every year after he had finished with the tomato crop. The Slocums came in a covered truck, fitted up for sleeping, and the other pickers were Jerry Gillespie, Althea's stepson, who was marking time till he got old enough to join his brother in the Navy, and—to everyone's surprise—Bert Plew. He still didn't believe in the apple business, Bert said, but if Dolly was going to be down on the river, he might as well come too, and join in the general foolishness.

Ben was deeply thankful for every pair of hands. There were ranches where the crop would drop this year before it could all be harvested. He did the nailing up and stamping himself, between haulings with the wagon, and every time he brought in a load he looked anxiously at Mary, packing like a dervish, trying to keep up box for box with Fletch. She looked awfully pretty, he thought, with her hair under the blue kerchief, and there was something about the tilt of her little chin that brought back Misshollister. Ben sighed. He had a mind to tell her to slow down, but he knew as well as she did that the crop had to move. Besides, Mary didn't seem to pay much attention to what he said any more.

If they didn't make enough progress, toward the end, they would have to work on Sundays. Ben resisted this as long as he could. His folks had taught him to remember the Sabbath day, to

292

keep it holy, and though his religion was a thing so mixed up with the love of his land that he thought God would very likely overlook any conflict, he knew his people cherished their weekly day off and needed it. He knew very well that the Slocums and the Plews passed the whiskey bottle on Saturday nights, and he was glad that young Jerry took off for Wenatchee the moment the shed closed down on Saturday. As the taskmaster of this perilous, exacting enterprise called a harvest, he had more responsibilities than just to get the fruit collected and shipped.

I let Lew think it was the children. Just the children. Well, isn't it? Isn't that about all that's left of my marriage?

I wasn't the kind of a wife Ben wanted. I made him marry me because I could, because I knew how. Nature tells you how. Nature wanted me to want him so I would have the children. And I have the children and look at me now.

But I gave my promise. I gave my promise. I gave my promise.

"You're a good packer, Mary," Fletch said, looking over from his own set of boxes. "Never thought you could catch on so fast. But don't wham 'em in like that. You'll bruise a few if you don't look out."

"Eat it up and I'll give you some cookies." Dolly sat the children firmly down on the edge of the porch and handed them the bowls of bread and milk with which she invariably began their supper. David had never heard of starting supper with a bowl of bread and milk, and he was dubious. It was not Mama's way, which as far as he was concerned was The Law. This little old lady was kind, but she wasn't Mama. Mama was out there in the lean-to, mysteriously putting something into boxes.

He was very hungry, but the bread and milk kept catching on something in his throat. He put down the spoon, and listened to a robin giving a few sleepy chirps as the sun went down. Papa had lifted him up and showed him the inside of the robins' house last spring, with the baby birds in it being fed. There was some confusion here—when Aunt Florence had a baby, it did not look the same at all.

A freight train went by, the refrigerator cars flashing yellow in the openings between the trees. The railroad track was something to stay away from. Mama had taken him as close as he was allowed to go, to the barbed-wire fence. Then she had pointed through the fence and said *"No!"* many times. As long as you were with Mama, things fell into place. And if you were not with her, and something scary happened, you had only to open your mouth and bawl "Mama!" and suddenly she was there.

But it hadn't worked like that in the last few days. All during the long hours, now, if you called for Mama the little old lady came. She said, "What's the matter, child? Are you hurt? There. There. Big boys two years old don't cry."

I would only have to write a letter, and say Lew, I've changed my mind. And then it would all begin again. Of course, I don't want it to begin again. I did the only thing I possibly could.

Mary, I think you're beating about the bush. Making excuses for doing what you think you ought to do.

I wish I wouldn't keep hearing his exact words, in his exact voice. And I wish I wouldn't keep hearing the music. I can't get it out of my head.

I'll never play the piano again.

A little hand fumbled at her skirt. "Lift me up, Mama. P'ease."

She never refused the children anything reasonable. Helen loved to be put on the bench alongside the boxes where she could watch Mama's quick hands going in and out. "I try to keep the children out from underfoot," Dolly had said ruefully. "But they want to be out there with you. It stands to reason, I guess."

Of course. That was where they belonged. "I'll be in the house next Sunday," Mary assured her daughter. "All day. I'll rock David on my lap until he goes to sleep. And then I'll rock you."

"A long time?"

"Yes, a long time."

"Till *I* go to s'eep?"

"Not necessarily," Mary said, sensing a trap. "But a long time, anyhow."

Helen picked up an apple, shyly, and felt of its coldness and hardness. "Not to eat," Mama said. "Too green. If you want an apple to eat, go ask Mrs. Slocum to find you a ripe one."

"I p'ayed a game," Helen offered conversationally, after while.

"Yes?"

"I p'ayed I eated people up."

"People?"

Helen nodded, her eyes enormous.

. ."*Well!* That wasn't a very nice game, was it? I don't think I'd play it any more, if I were you."

Helen looked relieved. Her guilt was assuaged. She had told Mama. Mama was shocked enough to confirm her feeling that she had been bad, but not shocked enough to withdraw her love and favor. Mama went on putting squares of paper around the apples with a little swish, and adding them to the rows in the box.

When the box was full, she signed to Uncle Fletch to come and carry it away, and before putting up a fresh one, she stopped to give the warm, sticky child a reassuring hug.

But who can I tell when I have naughty thoughts?

The ladder was tarnation heavy, it seemed to Bert Plew, and by the time a man drug it around in the dust for a few hours, and went up and down with sacks of apples, he was tireder than if he'd druv a team and heisted freight all week. When Dolly first put it to him that he ought to come and help out the Lucases, he had said that he wasn't no dang farmhand. What had happened to the feller they had staying there, Bert asked—him with the beard? Dolly said tartly that she guessed he wasn't no dang farm-hand neither. The last she knew, Mary had been trying to help him get in touch with his family, and then he had lit out sudden.

Bert took a simple and earthy view of human nature. Had there been any hanky-panky between Mary and the stranger, did she think? and Dolly had near taken his hide off. Which was hardly fair, considering that in their young days he'd had to black

Dolly's eye a couple of times for letting some of the other teamsters get too close. She was a live one, Dolly was.

It had been a good while since him and Dolly had been live ones, either of them. Bert did not like to think about it. But as he fought back the leaves and went through the arm-racking motions of reaching in among the limbs, he thought about it some. He guessed it wouldn't be too long before they had to give up and go live with one of the children. He knew what that would be like. He could hear Danny's wife saying, "Now, Pa, we got this bathroom, you can take a bath everyday if you like." Or whether he liked it or not.

It eased his heart to look across the tops of the trees and see the outlines of the valley, the land rising shelf by shelf across the river, the big notch to the south where Pine Creek came in. They looked exactly the same as when him and Dolly had taken up their Pine Creek claim. Funny thing, he could hardly remember what happened last week or the week before, but everything from them old days stood out clear and separate, like mountains on a bright morning.

He cast a sour look at Jerry Gillespie, whistling like a blackbird in the next tree. Jerry finished loading a picking sack and came down the ladder, and opened the bottom of it and let the fruit carefully out into a box. "Fine morning, isn't it?" Jerry said out of sheer high spirits.

"It's all right for them as likes it." Bert ran his fingers under the straps, which were killing him. He searched his pockets till he found a bandanna, and slipped it between the webbing and his shoulder on the side that hurt the worst.

If anything happened to him, Mary would look out for his old woman. Mary was a good girl. A little flighty. But Dolly wouldn't hear a word against her. It was men's country, after all, and he supposed the women had to stick together.

I could have made a tolerable life for Lew, who has never had a tolerable life. Could I really? Is it his own fault that he hasn't amounted to anything? Ben would say so. Lew is a Pillage. Something Ben would never understand.

But I have Pillage blood. I know how it is to go through the world defenseless, pushed around by things, defeated by things.

It isn't too late . . . Lew, I have changed my mind. . . .

It would even go in a telegram.

Mary Lucas, you ought to be ashamed. Oh, I am, I am ashamed. But women are so used to being ashamed. It doesn't make much difference to them finally. Shame is their daily bread. Asking give me this, and help me with that. I'm sorry I can't work quite as hard as you, I'm only a woman. I'm sorry I don't think very straight, I'm only a woman. I'm sorry I choke up and cry. I'm sorry I forgot to latch the gate, my mind was on something else, my mind was on the children, I'm only a woman. I'm sorry I'm moaning on the couch today, I've got that thing that women get, you'll have to excuse me, you'll have to forgive me, I'm a woman.

She tried to think about the plans she had made last spring, when it became apparent they would have a good crop and that prices would be sky-high. They would add to the house again, for the children, Ben had said. Helen could have the Uncles' Room, and they would start building out a wing on the other side—a bedroom for themselves, and a guest room where David could sleep, except when he was turned out by company coming. This was the Lucas way, and the house followed the Lucas design. It was a sensible design, she could not think of anything wrong with it. It was plain and substantial, like the Lucases.

They're a good family. My children will grow up honest and decent. And successful. That's what I want, isn't it? That's all I have a right to want, isn't it?

I have the man I chose, the one I went to so much trouble to get. And a good home and beautiful children and friendly neighbors. I have no complaint. She died smiling, saying, I have no complaint.

Everyone knew the meaning of the white mist that began to gather along the top of the valley. The temperature dropped abruptly, and the yellow glow of the maples in the canyons was quenched. Winter had a foot in the door.

"We'll lose a few, but not more than we can help," Ben Lucas said. He scraped up every ladder he could find and put his shed crew out in the orchard. Everybody picked. The women were given the easier places around the trees, and the men toted for them, and climbed inside among the slippery branches. Jerry Gillespie stopped whistling. The fruit was stacked on the ground and covered with tarpaulins.

To Mary, the change was a relief. Her restlessness was such that anything new was good. She was strong and agile, and there was challenge in the frosty air. When the needle-sharp rain began, the pickers retreated to roofs and doorways, and as soon as it was over they went back to their dripping posts. They got most of the crop. It lay in great, rough, crimson heaps of treasure under the wet canvas. It would take until almost Thanksgiving to pack and load it out.

Everybody was exhausted, everybody was white-faced, talkative, gay. There was money in their pockets—the mail-order catalog was thumbed nightly. Ben paid a fair wage, exactly the going rate. He would have plenty left over to operate with next year. The Lucas ranch had turned the corner. He wondered wistfully if Mary understood this. She had never had a grasp of money matters and he had known it when he married her. He wanted her to exult with him, to have that radiant look on her face that came suddenly when something pleased her very much. Perhaps he could make their good fortune visible, with gifts for her and the children. He would try to find something when he went into Wenatchee to sell his horses to the Army.

He started out on a bleak, chilly day toward the end of November. The harvest was so nearly over that he could leave the last details to Fletch. And he knew from reading his day-old paper that the buying depot was currently open. His horses had been cut out of the herd and were roped loosely together for leading down the road. A few years ago, he would have driven them ahead of him, unattached and free, trusting to their good sense to keep bunched together in strange territory. They would have been able to fan out here and there and snatch a little grass. But now there were almost as many automobiles on the road as horses, and it was a lot of trouble to get a bunch of loose horses past a motorist, who sat there with his engine running. Ben did not care much for automobiles. It had dumfounded him when young Harve said he would like to own one.

Harve was a good lad. There was deep, mute satisfaction to Ben in having brought Fletch and Harve to the valley. He had seen them lay hold, helped to shape things for them. When Harve came back from the War, he would marry and settle. If he could find a good girl, of course.

A girl like Mary, Ben said to himself automatically, and then he knew that it was a hollow saying. A girl like Mary could dazzle you, overwhelm you, make you stake everything you had. And some fine morning you could wake up to the fact that she simply wasn't there. She sat across the table from you, she lay in the same bed, she carried on conversations and answered questions, but in some important sense she was gone from you.

He had asked a few questions about the stranger, the man from the hills. Mary had answered them evenly and briefly. Yes, he had left, thanking them for their hospitality. He was anxious to be gone—it was the money, she supposed. He was to come into some money, and Charles Gillespie was advising him. He had been so impatient that she had loaned him Duke, whom she would go to Wenatchee and get, someday shortly. It would be an excuse to see Althea. She smiled at this, remotely, as if it were a little joke on herself.

There, he had put his finger on it. Mary acted as if someone had played a monstrous joke on her, and she was taking it gamely.

A thin, melancholy sunshine had succeeded the rain. There was no wind, and the only sound as he rode was the clop of the horses' feet behind him and the murmur of the river where the road overhung it, around the cliffs. Between the cliffs the stripped orchards were carpeted with fallen leaves. Everything was bleak, inside him and out.

It would never have occurred to Ben to suppose that Mary had been unfaithful to him. She was good, she was a gentle-woman, she was . . . she was Mary. *She* might not know the difference between herself and that red-haired trollop she had set such store by, but Ben knew. A man knew.

But Mary can change her mind. Remember? She changed her mind before she ever met you.

He must have groaned aloud, for Rusty pricked up his ears. Ben leaned forward and patted Rusty on his sleek, dusty shoulder.

When Mrs. Loring left, Mary had complained. She had been angry and sad . . . Mary had been greatly taken with this stranger. They had talked and laughed for hours together. Why did she not mind his going away? If she minded, why did she not say so?

Ben did not want fidelity. He did not want virtue. He wanted his wife's love. It was part of the world he had built around himself with such difficulty. He could not lose it now and remain whole.

At noon he loosed the horses beside a stream and allowed them to drink and graze a little, and gave them a ration of grain. This steady travel would bring him to Margett's ranch about sundown, where he planned to spend the night. Margett had plenty of corral space, and hay. Ben would sleep on the hay, in the nearest corner to the horses, where any unusual kicking or whinnying would rouse him instantly.

This was the last night that he would own Billy Bones, the big gray, or the little cayuse called Pedro who was Rusty's get, and as smart and dependable as Rusty.

There was a lot to look at on the way to Wenatchee—the white boat crossing the river at Hallowell's Ferry, the skeleton of the old tram line coming down from the wheat fields, the bluffs changing gradually from bleached granite to dark basalt rock. Ben did not see any of it. He looked inward, at his unstable and crumbling universe.

"He ain't very big," the sergeant said, letting go of Pedro's jaws and standing back.

"He's got more gumption than nearly any horse I ever raised. His sire is my own saddle horse, there." Ben indicated Rusty with a nod of the head. Selling off some of the herd wasn't any easier than he had figured it would be. But he liked the little sergeant. They understood each other.

"He's built, all right. . . . We got rules about size, y'know. . . . Oh well, he might squeak by. That would make four. You understand about cashing the government check, and all that?"

"Yes," Ben said. He looked with favor on the intricate system of corrals and chutes alongside which they stood. "I figure you'll let them stay in a bunch till they get used to it. The gray is the boss horse. The others will do what he does."

"Yeah." The sergeant called to a lank private in fatigues. "Take these critturs to number nine."

Ben stood with his hands in his pockets, bracing himself to watch them led away. His horses were tractable—they handled well. Billy Bones twitched off a fly, and the ripples flowed across his smooth gray hide.

"I wish I was going with them," Ben said involuntarily.

The sergeant, busy with a tally, stopped and looked at him. Ben's tone was something more than conversational. The sergeant had found Ben an agreeable man to deal with; experienced and eminently fair, and with a natural savvy about horses.

"Ever think of joining the Army?" the sergeant said.

"No . . . not till just now."

"How old are you, Mac?"

"Thirty-one. I could fudge a little."

The sergeant thought this might well be true. Ben was the sun-dried and wiry type that does not show the years. "It's done all the time," the sergeant said. "Only mostly, they fudge the other way. Sixteen-year-old kids, trying to bust in. It's a young man's war."

"So I've heard," Ben said.

"You'd most likely never get to the front."

"Don't they need men anywhere but at the front?"

"You're goddam right they do. . . . Tell you what—I could make it a little easier for you. I'm sending a shipment to Fort Riley at the end of the week. I need a man to go along with the horses. Haven't got anybody right now that knows the north end of a horse from the south. You report back here, along about Saturday, and I'll send you to Riley with a note to the adjutant.

He'll find a way to swear you in without making too much fuss about it. After that it's up to you."

"I don't know the first thing about drill, and all that."

"Your drill will be with a pitchfork, Bud. You won't be up there with the flags flying and the bugles blowing. You got a wife and family?"

"Yes."

"And a farm, huh?"

"An apple ranch. We just packed out this year's crop."

"Well, don't count on being home for the next one. Things ain't going that good." The sergeant eyed him curiously. "You just make up your mind after you walked in here?"

"Good a time as any."

They grow 'em poker-faced in this part of the country, the sergeant thought. "If you mean business, I won't bother to find somebody else. See you Saturday?"

"See you Saturday," Ben confirmed soberly. He mounted Rusty, and rode up through the town and stopped at the bank. When he came out, he left Rusty tied to the hitching post, and wandered along the main avenue.

It bothered him that he did not know what to bring home for David. The boy was too young for his first jackknife, his first fishing tackle. The Christmas goods were already in the windows. There were toys, bright with nickel and enamel, but they looked flimsy to Ben. His own few toys had been whittled from the felled pine trees in the clearing, and had smelled of pitch as long as they lasted.

There was a small plush animal that caught his eye. It stared squarely at him with its yellow glass buttons. It looked stubborn and thoughtful, like David. He knew what they called them: "teddy bears." He went in and bought it.

Then he looked around the store. Most of the stuff was shiny and false-looking. The dolls had rigid golden wigs and spangled clothes. Was this what little girls liked? He puttered so long that the saleslady lost interest in him and went away. Finally he found one that had clothes that came off and a cardboard trunk to put them in. This tickled Ben. Someone understood the tireless energies of a small child. He called the woman back. "I'll take this."

He realized that he had put off choosing something for Mary as long as he could. The part of the store devoted to woman-things daunted him. He did not know where Mary got those lace-trimmed pink layers that clung to her body like cornsilk. Besides, she had not encouraged him lately to think about such things. His native reticence smothered an impulse, that any man might have felt, to insist on this intimacy by bringing her something intimate. It was too serious, too crucial, for that.

There was a counter of jewelry, and he looked at it for quite a while, turning some of it over with his awkward, careful fingers. Gew-gaws. Mary hardly ever wore them. She had a pin of garnets (she called them) that had been her mother's, and a string of beads the color of a robin's egg. Otherwise nothing much but her plain gold band, which might be considered orna-ment enough for a wife.

He kept poking, under the distrustful eyes of the clerk, till he saw a thin gold chain, very fragile, with a little pendant of pearls. It was unlike anything he had ever seen on a woman, but it looked like Mary. The price of it startled him. He counted out the money, and had his purchases made up into a pack for the ride home.

There was a long plank left over from the building of the corral gate, which, with other odds and ends of lumber, had been stored under the barn-roof overhang. The children had found it, and they wanted a seesaw. Mary, appealed to, said she would see what she could do. There would have to be a round log or something to teeter on, just big enough and the right height off the ground. They went to the woodpile, the children running in excited circles.

Some unsplit rounds of pine were in a heap at one side, drying. They chose one, and Mary threw aside the chunks from the top of the pile until she uncovered it. They were heavy; her face flushed brightly and her loosely pinned hair came down. The three of them began to tug it toward the open space between the house and barn. It was only a little harder for Mary to drag it with the children's help than it would have been to do it by herself.

Ben, coming to the corner of the house, saw them and stood still. They were short of breath and hilarious; their cries and laughter rang out, and defied the cold and sullen day. It was like coming into a circle of firelight out of the dark.

When they saw him, there was a moment's pause, and Helen ran over to be picked up and tossed in his arms, a ceremony she loved. David toddled after her gravely, and Mary, between gasps, came and gave him a kiss. Was it a duty kiss? He could not tell.

For a few moments he let himself bask in the gayety, the irresponsibility, the ease. They had wrecked the wood pile, and from the house came the unmistakable evidence that Mary was letting something burn. She smelled it too, and began to dash for the door. "Wait," Ben said. . .

He must let them know at once, it was only fair.

"Mary," he said, "I am going to this War."

18

THE CHILDREN were asleep at last. Feeling tension in the air, they had tossed on their cots and demanded drinks of water, David had insisted on taking the teddy bear, for which he had formed an instant affection, to bed with him, and Helen had therefore felt obliged to do the same with her doll. Ben watched all this with somber eyes. They were old enough to have their own rooms—he had been planning on it. He was always behind with things, it seemed, and whatever decisions he made were never quite the right ones or soon enough. Well, he would not be making any more for awhile now.

He spoke into the long silence, not trying to lead up to what he had to say; that was not Ben's way. He merely began at what they must both be thinking.

"If I didn't suppose you could handle it, Mary, I couldn't go. You did fine when I was laid up so long with my back. And when I was down in Oregon, when Pa died, you made out. And you'll have Fletch."

"What if Fletch decides to go too?" There was not exactly bitterness in Mary's tone, but it was dry and troubled. The lilt was gone from it, and her face looked anxious and very young. He had to remind himself that Mary would soon be twenty-nine.

"I had a long talk with Fletch before supper. He'll stay. He said it was one or the other of us, and since I'd made the move, he would abide by it. Turned out he'd been thinking some about it, though. The Lucases have always gone when there was a war, Mary."

"The Pillages too," Mary said. She would not speak one word to dissuade him, not if she had to bite her tongue out. No Pillage woman had ever asked a man to stay at home. But she could not resist asking, "What made you decide right now?"

"The chance came," Ben said simply. "I'm over-age, Mary, or near it. I didn't expect there would be a place for me."

That wasn't all. Men did not go to war only when some chance offered. They went when things were not right at home. To get a fresh start somehow. To fight a Crusade, or conquer Gaul, or lay siege to Troy. But Ben was not going to tax her with any fault, and she was not going to diminish his deed by suggesting any.

"They told me not to expect to be home for the next harvest," Ben said. "Or maybe other harvests. The orchard is in good shape, Mary." Thus he dismissed, lightly, his days and nights of unremitting labor for ten years. "And prices will stay up while the war is on. You can hardly lose."

"I see." Mary made a nervous gesture, pushing back her hair.

"I'll send you my pay; it won't be much. But it might help out. And you'll have to keep the books—like you do at harvest time, only more, I'm afraid—pay taxes, and the like. You can get help from the bank, or from Charles Gillespie."

"Oh, stop talking about money!" Mary cried. "It doesn't matter that much."

"I know. The Hollisters never liked to talk about money." There was something new in Ben's voice—it was almost gay. "We'll have to, though, before I go. And I'll want to—there are some papers— the title to the place, and so on."

"Oh Ben!"

"It's only sensible." Ben's voice did not waver. "We can't count on. . . . you know."

Mary felt as if a block of ice wrapped her, paralyzed her thoughts, stilled her tongue. She had thought of almost anything that might happen, except this. She sat looking at him silently, intensely; the steady eyes, the cleft chin. Ben, as ever was. So familiar as to have become, in the way of familiar things, invisible.

He is going to war, she repeated to herself carefully. Ben is going to war. To suffering and hardship. Perhaps to death.

"You'll be very short of help," Ben said. "That will be the worst part, Mary. To see things go undone, and not be able to help it. Try to live with it. I'd have to live with it myself if I was here."

The ranch, the ranch. It was all Ben thought about. No, she corrected herself sharply, he was thinking about something else now, something in which she had no part, and it was only because of it that he must speak of the ranch. He was taking her into his confidence there, as he always had. But there were no words in him for this other thing. Perhaps it could not be put into words.

He was not offering reasons, or excuses, or making her a party to it. There was some part of his mind that was already far away, living a life of which she would have only scant knowledge.

"You'd better make me a list, Ben. Things you'll want done and . . . and looked after." There was something forlorn about this little phrase—her voice broke on it. Ben gazed at her thoughtfully.

"It's a good idea. I'll try. And I ought to write to my folks. Ma will want to know."

Of course. Soldiers not only had wives, they had mothers, sisters, other people with rights in them. Ben hadn't been back to Oregon since his father died. Did they hold it against him? Did they hold it against *her?*

"Have you time to go and see them? How much time, Ben?"

"About four days. Not long enough I'm afraid. But I guess I'll write right away." He lumbered over to his desk; he was tired, but intent. It was as if the letter was already forming in his mind. He sat down and opened his ledger and took a large crisp sheet from the back of it.

She could not sit still. She opened the outside door noiselessly, and stepped into the November night.

These cold blue stars that hung above her head were looking down on the battlefields too. On the glinting river among leafless woods where men lay beside their rifles. They shone on the trenches, on the ruined villages and trampled fields. How foolish she had been to think of these things as far away! They were around the corner, a man had only to say "I am going," and they rushed to meet him. They seemed immanent there, in the darkness, as close as Pine Creek Landing.

She felt like a child who has been making the most of recess, playing with all its might, till the bell rings and school begins again. Her recess was over now and the letter to Lew would never be written, the telegram never sent. No decent woman thinks of another man while her husband is away at war.

The list and Ben's writing had taken most of the night. They had not realized how late it was getting until Ben said heavily, "I could do with forty winks, Mary," and had carefully slipped his boots off and lain down on the bed, on the morning-glory-patterned quilt from the old Hollister house, and was instantly asleep. He would be a good soldier—he could sleep anywhere and anyhow when there was need.

Mary dozed fitfully, but when the children began to stir, she was quickly awake ahead of them, shushing them. "Papa is very tired," she said. She made them eat breakfast in silence, or what passed with the children for silence. They mutttered and giggled a little, made quick passes at each other and then resumed blank faces. She helped them dress, and despairing of keeping them quiet any longer, stuffed them and herself into coats and took them outdoors. Before she left she put a shovelful of coal in the stove from the precious sack outside the back door, that Ben might not be wakened by the cold.

It was a bright, still morning with arrows of sunrise pouring from the east. The ground was lightly frozen, the dust in the roadway breaking thinly under their feet. Released from their stillness, the children danced and raced around her, bringing things for her to see—a dead grasshopper, a curiously blotched leaf that looked like a face. She crossed the road with them and climbed up to Mary's Rock, where they loved to go. But there was a breeze there, a hundred feet or so above the valley floor, and their teeth began to chatter. They came down and went on along the road toward Fletch's, and Florence ran out and threw her arms around Mary.

"I know about it," she said. "Ben was up last night talking to Fletch. Oh Mary!"

"We have just four days," Mary said.

"Aren't those Lucas men awful? Always so sure they're right. . . . It could have been Fletch, you know. He told Ben he'd been thinking about it. He hadn't said a *word* to me. . . . But now, of course, he'll stay. He told Ben that, too. I have to listen," Florence said darkly. "I have to *overhear* what my own husband is going to do. Why do they only talk to each other, Mary? Aren't women important at all?"

"In a way," Mary said. "Each Lucas has some woman that's important. For what that's worth." And she knew that it was true.

"I guess it's worth a lot," Florence said less grudgingly. "Do come in and talk. I'm terribly excited. Are you scared, Mary? I don't mean for Ben. Of *course* you're scared for Ben. But of course you try not to think about it. I mean, about getting along alone, and running the place. Can you do it?"

Mary shooed the children ahead of her into the house. They tiptoed to the back room to see if they could see the baby.

"How do I know, Florence? I only know it's wartime and women must do the best they can. It's something like waking up from a dream—the dream that the War was going on somewhere and all we had to do was buy bonds and save wheat and give clothes to the refugees and it would never come any closer. Or it's like thunder and lightning going on over there and you've heard it for a long time and you know there's a storm, and all of a sudden it begins to rain where you are. I'm not explaining it very well."

"I think you're explaining it fine," Florence said. "Only Mary, we really knew, didn't we, that it wasn't that simple? At least, after Harve went."

"I had some other things on my mind," Mary said. She did not say what they were. "That reminds me, Florence—Ben writes to Harve. All the time. As if he wanted to make him feel that the place is still here. I could do it, but I don't think it would be the same, coming from me. I think it might be better if Fletch would write. The Lucas men, you know. Would Fletch start doing it, do you suppose, if I asked him?"

"Of course he would. We'll do anything, *anything*. . . . Oh

309

Mary, you must be so proud. I know it's dreadful, I know it's messing up your whole life, but how proud you must be of Ben."

"Yes, I am proud," Mary said. It was hardly more than a whisper.

Florence looked sharply at her. "Did you get much sleep last night?"

"We were talking. And writing. Ben wanted to let his folks know."

"You look terrible," Florence said with sisterly frankness. "Have you had breakfast?"

"I think so. Yes. I ate something while the children were having theirs."

"I'll keep the children here this morning," Florence said. "You just leave them. I'll bring them down after lunch. You're exhausted, and no wonder. Go home and get some rest."

Mary opened her mouth to protest, but Florence said, "I'm getting bossy, you see. Us Lucases are pretty fierce to live with sometimes. Go on now, Mary. I can handle your kids. Have you forgotten I have four little brothers?"

The sun was higher in the sky as she turned toward home. The hills around the valley marched clear and remote in an unbroken line. She had thought of them, when she first climbed off the boat with Althea, as the walls of a prison. Time after time there had been some way of escape from this prison, yet she had always stayed. And now she knew she would never leave, that the doors were closing for the last time.

She met Fletch coming up the road. He lifted a hand in greeting. "I knocked on your door," he said, "but nobody answered. So I let the chickens out, and pulled down some hay for the horses."

"Thank you, Fletch. I'll do it myself from now on."

"Ben all right?"

"Yes, he's sleeping."

"Don't blame him. They say the ground is mighty hard in France."

He gave her a rueful smile, and walked on.

The house was a temple. She entered it as a priestess might, coming to the place where she ministered.

It was getting chilly again, and she put more coal on the fire. She checked to see that she had eggs in the cooler, a jar of fruit, and a loaf of uncut bread. Ben had had nothing to eat since supper.

Then she sat down and watched him. He had sunk so deep in slumber that he had scarcely moved; the morning-glory quilt was deeply imprinted with his shape. He had finished, for the time being, all that was required of him. In the midst of his confusions, he had stumbled on a simple and right thing to do. She did not question it. She knew that being Ben, in the circumstances in which he found himself, he could do no other.

She thought of his strait and difficult boyhood. The Indian graveyard came before her, and the house in the clearing, with the pile of slashings behind it, steadily burning, since they had had to cut so many trees that there was no place left to sell the wood. It must have hurt him, that senseless waste. There were many things that had hurt Ben, that he could do nothing to change. Yet when he had incurred some penalty, he always paid it. With no fuss. He had married a frivolous woman, because he loved her. And the price had been great. He was going away now because it had turned out to be greater than he could pay. He could not be the kind of husband that Mary Hollister seemed to want.

He opened his eyes, and saw her sitting there. There were some shelves behind her head, on which the dishes of the old sprigged china were arranged. It made a pleasant picture, Mary's shapely head against the frail blue-and-white ware. He looked at it a while, and then he half turned, and put out his arm.

She left her chair and came to lie beside him, her head against his shoulder. So had she lain a thousand times, after a day's toil, or when she was heavy with child and could not rest. Seeking comfort, seeking nearness. There was no passion in it. Only the hard good feel of his flesh beneath her cheek, the solace of his long quiet body beside her.

Some small creature skittered across the roof, its little claws scratching the shingles, and then it was gone, putting an edge on the silence. . . . This was going to be all. He had not done what he had done in order to bring her back—perhaps he did not want her? She knew better. Ben always wanted her.

She could not let him go like this. She must not let the barrier between them stand. There was a way to tear it down, but a woman who has been raised a lady, who has been innocent of guile toward men, who has borne her femininity like a banner, might find it hard to do it. . . . She had torn it down once before— she had been *La Descarada*. The shameless one.

"Ben," she said, "do you love me?"

He put his other arm around her quickly. She felt his sudden weight. "Mary," he said. "Mary, Mary."

"I had to know," Mary said.

His lips were hard; they did not spare her. They bruised her throat, her breasts. . . . It was the middle of the morning; an unseasonable time, a wanton time. . . . This was the temple to which women come to give themselves as a pledge for the future. These were the rites of the temple.

You have a singular quality of dedication, Mary.

It would be as well, now, if she would stop thinking of anything that Lew had said.

19 "YES, HE LEFT yesterday." Mary set a cup of coffee before Dolly Plew and brought out a piece of cherry pie, gone a little stale in the cooler. "I'm sorry this isn't fresh. I didn't seem to have much time to bake this week."

"I never was so flabbergasted in all my life." Dolly drank the scalding coffee, and eagerly attacked the pie. "I just can't figure it out. *Ben!* Do you know why he done it, Mary?"

"Yes, I know why." Mary called her sniffling daughter to her. "Blow, darling, *blow*. That's right." Helen had a raging cold. It was impossible to keep her in bed, but she was restricted to the house, where she played grumpily with her too-familiar toys. "I don't know if I can explain it, though. It was a compulsion. The Lucases always go to a war."

"Fiddle-faddle. Looks to me like it's left you holdin' the sack. Who's goin' to do the spring work? And the summer work and the fall work, for that matter. I think the world of Ben, Mary, I've told you often enough I think you made a good pick, but right now I'm beginnin' to wonder. A man's fust duty is to his fambly."

"A man's first duty is to what he believes in. I'll do as much of the work as I can, Dolly, and let the rest go. And I've got Fletch, and Florence, and Mr. Lindsay is selling the store to a couple from the East, the man came here because he has TB or something . . . anyway the Lindsays will live at Luthermere and help me out till next fall, if I'll tutor Rose. They want to move to the coast and put her in school there. I can get the Scobie boys sometimes. And there's a fellow Charles Gillespie is trying to help, a man who is out on parole. I've found him a room at the Sawyers'."

"Old men an' children an' jailbirds. I don't hear anything about Plew and me. What's the matter—don't you like us any more?"

Mary came and kissed Dolly's withered cheek. "I didn't know

313

how much it would be right to ask of you. The work was hard on Bert this fall."

"Bert Plew ain't wore out yet, an' neither am I. Plew's a good carpenter—why don't you start him on that addition Ben was goin' to build? You git one single more kinfolk or helper in here, an' you're goin' to have ary a place to put 'em."

Mary considered this. "I don't know what Ben would think."

"Think? Jerusalem, Mary, he'd want you to *go ahead*. Ben didn't leave you here to jest set. Ain't you got no ideas how you'd like a house to be built?"

"Oh yes, I have! Put a new kitchen out on the east, where the sun would come in in the morning, and make all of this a living room. . . . I guess I could, couldn't I? Red-checked curtains in the kitchen . . . Oh Dolly, that's so *trivial*."

"Nothin's trivial," Dolly said. "You got to make a life, an' you got to make it out of what's layin' around here. You got to have it good enough fer the children—an' if *you* ain't cheered up, who's goin' to cheer up all that rag-tag and bobtail that's goin' to be workin' for you?"

David came running in, announcing that a car had stopped at the gate. He was not used to playing outside alone, and everything seemed a little spooky. Mary threw a shawl around her shoulders and went up the driveway.

The ancient-looking man at the wheel asked politely, "Kin I see the rancher, ma'am?"

"I am the rancher," Mary said.

"Oh. . . . Well . . . I got a petition here, for the power company to run a line upriver, so we can have 'lectricity."

"I will sign it." Mary let go of David's hand and opened the gate. The old man looked dubious, but he let her have the paper. She carried it in the house and put "Mary Hollister Lucas" beneath the other scrawled and familiar upriver names. Her responsibilities had begun.

Althea wrote at once, asking if Mary and the children could spend Christmas with them. Stan and Jerry were both in the Navy now, and Althea and Mr. Gillespie were alone. It would be a godsend to have the children in the house. Mary packed the suitcases and locked the door, and told Fletch, who drove them to the train, that she would be back in two weeks. She did not dare to stay longer. What could go wrong? She did not know. But if anything did, it would be her fault.

In the mail they picked up on the way to the train were the fat, colorful Christmas magazines, and a small package with a bookseller's label, though she had ordered no books. She put them into her carryall and got the children up the steps and into a seat where they watched the river and the ranches begin to race by. This would keep them quiet for a while. She disposed of the luggage around their feet, and opened her package.

Between the pages of the book lay a single hundred-dollar bill. How like Lew, not to realize that one could not spend a hundred-dollar bill in a frontier town without attracting attention! But that was all right. She had no intention of spending it. It could go back in its hiding place under the cushion of her workbasket.

I'll buy first editions, Lew had said. But this was a very ordinary little blue and gray volume, the kind that students use for English texts, the same kind as the *Virginibus Peurisque* he had carried so long in his pocket. The cover said *Marpessa,* and she did not know what it meant. She opened it at the beginning, somewhat apprehensively, and began to read.

This was no Greek myth of which she had ever heard, but it snatched her attention at once and in a moment she was back among the gods and heroes, the enchanted pages of her childhood. Apollo pleaded for the hand of a mortal girl—the long marching lines told it swiftly, accurately.

> We two in heaven dancing,—Babylon
> Shall flash and murmur and cry from under us.

And after that the shapeless appeal of Idas, poor human Idas, who could only say that he could not live without her.

Mary stopped hearing the clacking wheels, the cries of the children as they saw horses and cars on the road. Was it presumptuous of Lew to say that he had come into her world bearing godlike gifts? No, he had the right. Such gifts would not come her way again.

And like Marpessa, she had chosen the mortal, she had chosen Idas. She shut the book suddenly then, watching the blurred landscape hurry past. He understood too well, he made her plight too plain. She had not asked for pity—only to be left alone to do her best.

The white ferry came in sight, and David said, "Boat, Mama, boat." There were cookies in the carryall, and she took some out and gave them to the children. David was drowsy; she lured him away from the wonders outside and made him lie down with his head pillowed on his coat. Helen gave her mother a companionable look, and moved close, snuggling against Mary's arm. The baby had been put down for his nap; now they were two women, traveling on the train together.

When the children were both asleep, she picked up the little volume once more. She must read it all, and then she would never look at it again. She started over at the beginning. . . . These magic old words, so like the first ones she had ever learned to love, gave back an image that startled her. It was like coming upon a full-length mirror lit with some warm, remembered light. In the mirror she saw a Mary who lived simply, like the Greeks, close to her sunbaked earth; who loved it, feared it, respected it, planted it, reaped it, took water from its springs and comfort from its shade. Here in the mirror, Mary and Marpessa were one.

Yes, she could accept Lew's pity. Still better, she could try not to need it any more.

February. Should she ask Fletch to do the pruning? No. There were many things she would have to ask of Fletch, but this she could handle herself. Only the most straggly branches and the most troublesome water sprouts would have to be cut. . . . Besides, Ben had not shown Fletch how to prune. He had shown *her*.

She walked in snow up to her ankles, which were laced into Ben's old boots. Going from one leafless tree to another, she studied each one carefully, lopping off a limb here and there, leaving a trail of ragged brush which Mr. Jepley, the man the Gillespies had sent, would gather into heaps to be burned. She had asked no questions of Mr. Jepley. He was on parole after some nameless conviction, and Mary, always the optimist, took it for granted that he would "go straight" if things were not made too difficult for him. Sometimes she took the children to the orchard with her, muffled in woollens, their breath white on the air as they ran and tumbled in the snow. But mostly she left them with Florence or Dolly. And after she found Dolly flat on the floor from "a little dizzy spell," mostly with Florence. Florence met her apologies with a brisk "Shut up, Mary. You're my war work." Each night she wiped and oiled the pruning shears carefully. It seemed like a long time since Ben had reproached her for leaving them in the orchard to rust, and somehow it wasn't important now. She would make mistakes no doubt, and fail sometimes—very well, she would fail. But not from carelessness.

March. An early thaw was followed by a frost so bitter that Fletch and Mary went out to examine twig after twig with their hearts in their mouths, afraid the crop had been damaged. They found very little harm—the tiny buds were swelling and getting ready to burst from their wrappings. And Ben's letters stopped coming from Fort Riley and began to arrive from Camp Mills on the east coast.

You are never alone in the Army. I am a little bit used to it now, but it was hard at first. I remember the fine lonesome places I used to walk, along the riverbank or up the canyon. By thinking of them I can shut out the rows of bunks and the racket at mess and the gab, gab, gab. Some of the kids have a hard time settling into it. They are young and full of beans. I wish I was limber and twenty-one again, and yet, you know, I stand it pretty well. At the end of a march I feel tired clear to my . . . (Here he had inked out a word.) soles of my feet but not too used up, if you know what I mean. It's going to begin again tomorrow morning so I might as well get a good night's sleep.

The kids play a few tricks on me. They are good kids. They carry pictures of their mas and pas and of pretty girls. I guess we never thought of having pictures taken, Mary, and anyway when I shut my eyes I can see you. Just like I can see the canyons and the river.

April. She ordered spray material and box lumber, following Ben's careful notes, and Mr. Lindsay was put at the task of making up the boxes. His fumbling old fingers dropped the nails and split the cleats, but no one more expert could be spared for the job. Mary drove the spray wagon for Fletch, thankful that she had learned to do it in those first desperate days when she was Ben's only help. And often in the early morning she climbed to Mary's Rock or walked from end to end of the road through the Lucas place, watching for trouble, planning out the day. It was on one of these mornings that she saw a thin dark figure coming along the road, a pack on his back.

She waited civilly for the stranger to pass. He stopped instead and looked at her, and said, "Don't you know me, Misshollister? I'm Hans Schlogl."

Hans! She looked incredulously at him. His features were as pinched as ever under his badly cut pale hair, his wristbones still stuck out from his sleeves. She calculated swiftly that he must be close to seventeen. He was taller than she, and thin as a rail.

"Oh Hans, how wonderful to see you! I have thought about you often. I miss the school, you know. How is your mother?"

"She is good," Hans said.

Mary resisted a teacherish impulse to say "She is well, Hans, not good." Mrs. Schlogl *was* good. That tiny, sallow woman with the gnarled hands, the eyes bright with quiet joy over the fact that the law would keep Hans in school. "You did finish the eighth grade, didn't you, Hans? And graduate?"

"Yes, Misshollister."

"And where are you headed for now?"

"I do not know, Misshollister."

"You don't *know?*"

"No, Misshollister."

The bundle on Hans' back—the remote, purposeful look on his face. "Hans, you can't be . . . you aren't running away from home?"

"Yes, I am running away."

"Buts Hans . . . Oh dear, I *am* sorry. How will your mother . . . does she know?"

"My mother has packed for me a lunch."

At least, then, Mrs. Schlogl had not awaked in the morning to

318

find Hans missing. "Must you do this, Hans?" she said very gently. "Are you in trouble?"

"Do you not know, Misshollister? We are enemy aliens. Because of the War."

"But that doesn't matter!" Mary cried. "You are our neighbors, our friends. Surely no one . . . She stopped, remembering that Dolly had muttered something about the spying that was probably going on with all them Heinies underfoot. "It must be terribly hard for you, Hans. But among ourselves, we needn't think about it. It's a *dreadful* thing to leave your family and go far away. To not know who is living and who is dead, to harden your heart. Sometime you must come back, and then it hurts. Believe me. Besides," she added impulsively, "you are so young."

"I am a man," Hans said. "I do a man's work."

"But . . ."

"It is my Vater, Misshollister. My Vater says the Germans will win the War. We have no right to fight them, he says. We are only making it harder, but they deserve to win and they will win. Then our neighbors will have to eat the crow. They will come crawling to us and beg to be friends. We will be very choosy, my Vater says. All those who have worn the American uniform, who have killed Germans, will be put at hard labor. He sits and thinks about it and the veins get big on his forehead. He talks about it. Talks and talks. Sometimes his voice cracks."

Mary could not think of anything to say.

"My brothers and sisters were born here," Hans went on tonelessly. "After we came to America. They are Americans. I, only, was born in the old country. After the War it will not matter, he says, for everyone will wish to be German then. But now, when my Vater looks at me . . ." His voice was so low she could hardly hear him. "I cannot stay at home and listen any more."

"But what will you *do?* Where will you go? . . . Hansi, I need help desperately. Will you stay here and work for me?"

Hans made her a little bow. "I thank you, Misshollister. But I do not need your kindness."

"Kindness!" Mary said. "You don't understand. I'm running this place myself. My husband is gone. He is gone to the War." She paused to see what effect this might have on Hans. His pale eyes did not waver. "I'm short of help, and at harvest time I don't know what I am going to do. But you would be working for the family of an American soldier, and word is sure to get back. How would your father feel? Can you take that responsibility, Hans?"

He was silent so long that she added irresistibly, "I mustn't put pressure on you, of course. But it might comfort your mother to know that you were here."

She saw Hans' eyes follow the winding road, and she knew it was not what he had dreamed of. It would be far simpler, in Hans' view, to get far away, to take his chances. What these chances were, she shivered to think. She needed Hans' help, but no more than he needed hers.

"It makes problems for me to stay near," Hans said at last. "But it makes problems, too, for me to go away without money."

"If you work for me," Mary said simply, "you can save your wages, and by and by you can decide what to do. After the War perhaps. The War will end sometime. It *has* to."

"I do not think I am worth very much money. I have never worked for anyone but my Vater."

"You do a man's work," Mary reminded him. "I will pay you a man's wages. And you will have to cook and shift for yourself, Hans. I have no time to board anyone. Mrs. Plew is here sometimes, but I don't think . . ." She could not count on Dolly to be friendly.

The spring sun was beginning to warm up; she slipped the sweater off her shoulders. By and by Hans took his pack off too. "I will stay," he said. "I will stay until the War is over and the Americans have won it. You think that is how it will be, Misshollister?"

"That is how it will be," Mary promised him.

Ben dear,

Hans is an absolute treasure. He knows how to do everything. He is tireless. I do not think the poor child has ever done anything but work.

He borrowed a tent from Fletch, and set it on a little wooden platform which he built at the foot of the hill. I would have let

320

him sleep in the kitchen, which is nearly finished. But Hans has a strong sense of propriety.

I am so glad that you said you liked my having the kitchen built. It seemed right to go on with the house as if you were here. Sometimes I feel you *are* here. I wonder if it is because you are thinking of me. The orchard is in the most beautiful bloom, it seemed to come out all at once the way it does, and I stood in the whitemess and perfume this morning and it seemed as if you were there beside me.

Mary laid down her pen. She had been sitting with her eyes shut, willing Ben to see and smell that cloud of glory, willing her letter to carry a sense of it. As the sewing machine stopped and Elsie Yanling laid down her shears with a clatter, Mary put the letter aside. "It's been nice to see you, Elsie. And I'm glad you decided to make yourself the yellow dress. It's going to be very pretty."

"I allus favored yaller." Elsie smoothed and folded her work. "I guess maybe two, three more times now, and it'll be done. And I'll wear it come Sundays, and Sammy will be proud."

She went out stolidly with her bundle, and Mary finished the letter and stamped it and thought that though it was late in the day, she might ride down and mail it. But there was some sort of pickup supper to get, the eggs to gather and the hens to feed and the milk to strain when Hans brought it in. Among the chores she had thankfully turned over to Hans was the milking; he understood it, as he understood everything.

Supper was a kind of ceremony, no matter how meager. Part of the ritual was that no one ever sat in Papa's place; it was kept waiting for him. Mary watched the children's manners carefully as always, gave them whatever green stuff and fruit she could find, and eggs and cheese if she had no meat. They were little bottomless pits, and there was a bread pudding tonight, made with dark wartime bread and sweetened with molasses to save precious sugar, which should really fill them up. She was just getting it on the table when a horse galloped into the yard and she went to the door to see Elsie Yanling fling herself off and stumble toward the door. Elsie? She had just parted from Elsie.

The bony woman raced across the yard and flung herself at the door. "Oh Mary, they're gone they're gone, he's taken Sammy and gone. Oh God they're gone, he left me a note sayin' he's taken Sammy an' gone home. He got him outa the school. I bin away all day an' they was goin' down the road an' I never knew it." Her voice rose to a scream. "It's all your fault, you kep' me away, so he could steal Sammy. Oh if anything happens to Sammy, I'll kill you."

She fell down, scrabbling at Mary's skirt. "Do something, do something. Oh don't let them go, sweet Jesus don't let them go." She began to cry, long racking sobs, and behind Mary, Helen and David began to cry too.

"Elsie, get up," Mary said. She got the shuddering creature onto her feet and into a chair. "If he says they've gone home, what does he mean?"

"He means acrost the border," Elsie said in a strangled voice. "He only come to please me in the fust place. An' I ain't . . . we ain't . . . it ain't done no good to come. We're just as bad off as we was in Canada." Her weeping shook the chair.

"Stop it, Elsie. You can't go to pieces like this. Stop it now, we've got to talk." She was reluctant to comfort her own children in front of Elsie, but what could she do? She hugged them and wiped their eyes and said, sounding ludicrous even to herself, "We were just having supper. Will you have some supper, Elsie?" A low moan was her only answer. "Then would you mind if I give Helen and David theirs? It won't take long." Somehow she got them into their chairs and started feeding them, dishing up, giving them spoons, putting an occasional arm around each, talking to them about she had not the slightest idea what.

Over her shoulder she said, "You need a lawyer, Elsie. I'll try to get you one." How, at this hour? "And don't say your husband stole Sammy. A court might give him custody—and certainly a court would send you all back to Canada. It might be best for you to go anyway."

"I don't care what I do," Elsie said.

Forbearance came easily to Mary, and she had already lost the impulse to quiet Elsie by hitting her over the head with anything handy. But what to do with her? She could not be sent back to her empty house. The train had gone, and there was no other way into town. No white steamer now, skimming the river—no big red car with a kindly outlander behind the wheel. And no Ben to decide what to do—grimly, perhaps, but competently always.

"Have you got a drink?" Elsie raised her raddled face. "I need a drink."

There was a bottle of whiskey in the Uncles' Room; Mary had found it there after Lew's hasty departure. She had put it up in the rafters because it cost money, and perhaps someone could use it. She went out and retrieved the bottle from the high place where she had stowed it. You mix it with water, she remembered, for Dr. McClellan had prescribed it for John Muldoon when he was poorly. She brought the glass to Elsie, who took it numbly, the slow tears running down her cheeks.

Maybe I'd better have some too, Mary thought wildly. No, I'm not used to it, and I've got to keep my head. But what am I going to *do*? Now? The rest of the night?

She stood for a while in the middle of the room. Moved by a sharp and sudden hunger, she went to the long-unopened piano, and turned back the lid and sat down.

Elsie raised a languid head, and looked at her. Mary opened the Mozart at page one, and began to play.

The keys came swiftly to meet her fingers as they used to do. How stupid she had been to suppose that music had to do with Lew or with anything but her own need! The children came in, drawn by the sound. "Get ready for bed, you two," Mary said. There were times when it was better to do exactly as Mama said, without any argument. They quietly began to undress in the corner, and Helen, after another long glance at Mama's face, prudently helped David with his more troublesome buttons.

Mary finished the first sonata and began another. She stopped to tuck the children in, and to mix Elsie another whiskey and water. Then she sat down to the piano again and went on playing. This was what to do, when to do nothing was intolerable. It had been waiting here all the time, till she was ready to come back to it. Her fingers grew tired and the back of her neck began to ache, and the children subsided into sleep and at last Elsie's head drooped over. Mozart was too tiring finally and she wandered into a tender old malagueña that she had learned a long time ago, she could not remember when. It was late now, very late, and very quiet outside and the stars were shining, the big stars and the little stars, and great Capella with its rainbow glitter was rising over the shoulder of the black mountains.

"You do bring me the most interesting cases, Mary." She was sitting in the back room of Charles Gillespie's office, into which they had stepped to confer. "We'll have to ship this poor woman back, of course. I'm afraid it will cost something. How is she fixed for money?"

"I brought some with me." Mary took it out of her handbag. "Will this be enough, do you think?"

Mr. Gillespie looked curiously at the hundred-dollar bill, but he said only, "You're planning to pay her way?"

"I think I'd better. Oh Charles, I am so lucky. I have so much to be thankful for. And everything has gone wrong for Elsie."

"And you're trying to pay for your luck," Charles said. He did not sound disapproving. "Well, Mary, we all buy it, one way or another. And money is mebbe the easiest. You'll get her a ticket, then, and whatever she needs? Althea always recommends a new hat for really bad situations."

"I can't imagine Althea having any bad situations. What do you hear from the boys?"

"Damn little," Charles Gillespie grumbled. "Stan was in sick bay with something they call influenza. It swept the ship, he said. They picked it up in a port somewhere."

"I've heard of it. Jeff Porter died of it, in training camp. They have it in some of the American bases." Mary's face grew grave. "There's no cure for it, I believe."

"What's new from Ben?"

"Ben is working with mules now. He says they have a bad name that they don't deserve. They know their own minds, that's all."

She was always glad when she could make Charles smile. He came around to take her hand. "Well, goodbye, Mary. We'll see you at the house tonight?"

"I'd better stay with Elsie. Althea will understand. She knows

324

about Elsie from way back. She'll think I'm foolish, no doubt. But Charles, the amount of luck I need these days, you can't buy with just money."

"Pretty rough sledding, Mary?"

"I never knew," Mary burst out, "what it's like to be responsible for everything. To have people trust you, and do as you say, and if it doesn't work out, they'll go hungry. I never knew how close we are to trouble, day after day and month after month. We could have a bad codling-moth year and the crop would be full of worms. We could have a hailstorm and it would be badly pitted and I couldn't sell it. The spring could go dry—we didn't have as much snow as usual last winter, and the water table is low. It could stay too warm and the fruit wouldn't color up. . . . Ben faced all these things. I begin to understand why he's the way he is—hard to please, and always worrying, and . . . and hard on me sometimes. It's like walking a tightrope. And Ben did it. All the time."

"Now, Mary, don't underrate yourself. It ain't often a wife has to step into her husband's shoes. It figures they won't be a real close fit."

She gave him a grateful look. Going out to the front room, she laid the money before Elsie. "This is for your ticket, Elsie, and some toys for Sammy when you see him again. And a hotel room for tonight. And we might eat dinner in some real nice restaurant."

For the first time, Elsie showed a flicker of interest. "I allus wanted to go in one of them tony places," she said. "With a cloth on the table, an' all."

Her train was to leave ahead of Elsie's. To keep things going as well as possible, she breakfasted with Elsie on a drugstore sandwich, and window-shopped on the way to the station. At the steps of the passenger car she turned suddenly.

"Elsie, when I was your age—younger, even—I thought my life was ruined. Well, it wasn't. So long, Elsie."

She groped her way to a seat. She was dog-tired, and apprehensive about having left the children with Florence for a day and a night on no notice at all. She hoped they hadn't done anything appalling.

The train rumbled across a bridge and past the lime kiln, and picked up speed for its long journey into the interior. A shy voice asked, "May I sit with you, Mrs. Lucas?"

"Why yes." Mary drew her skirt away from the other half of the seat. The woman who sat down in it was quietly dressed; she wore white gloves, and they were clean. She had candid eyes and a spatter of freckles. Mary recognized the storekeeper's wife at Pine Creek, one of the couple who had bought out the Lindsays. It was because of them that Mr. Lindsay worked for her now, ineptly making apple boxes in the shadow of the barn.

"My name is Whitman," the woman said a little breathlessly. "Louise Whitman. We are no relation to your great Dr. Whitman, who guided so many families West. But there had already been Whitmans here before us—I often think of it. Another Mrs. Whitman, before me."

"But she . . ." Mary stopped.

"Came to a tragic end. I know. As soon as people hear our name, they tell us the story. Clyde tried to keep me from hearing it, but he soon gave up. But it is something to be proud of, is it not, Mrs. Lucas? To share a name with people like that?"

In Ben's family, who had known Marcus and Narcissa Whitman, the notion went that they had brought on the massacre by their own feckless and high-handed management, but this was no time to say so. Instead she answered, "It happened a long way from here."

"Yes. The West is very large, isn't it? I am not good about maps. Clyde shows them to me, but I have not learned to understand them. I only know that it was a long, long trip here, and I thought we would never get to the end of it."

"I felt the same way when I came. My sister and I had no idea where we were going."

"Your sister? The young woman who comes to the store with you?"

"No, that's my sister-in-law. She's Mrs. Lucas too. It must be very confusing for you."

326

"It is a little . . . strange to me still," Mrs. Whitman admitted. "But I shall learn to be at home here, I am sure. Everyone has been very kind."

From Mary's memory the phrase leaped out sharp and clear. Young Mary Hollister, scared, eager, diffident, saying *everyone has been very kind*. She abandoned the idea of catching a little nap on the train. "Does your husband like keeping the store?"

"Yes, he does. He was only a clerk where we came from. To have one's own business is nice, we think. Even if what we sell is not very distinguished. Beans and bacon, sugar and coffee. I have just been to town to put in our order."

"And chewing tobacco," Mary said. "And axle grease, and coal oil. And that little case behind the counter that has the needles and hairpins and woman-things in it. Mr. Lindsay always used to handle them as if they might explode."

"But did not Mrs. Lindsay wait upon the ladies?"

"Why no, I don't believe she ever did. This is strictly a man's country. Or it used to be. When my sister and I came into it, we were thought very queer because we planted an orchard and tended it ourselves."

"And now," Louise Whitman said, "your husband is away and you are taking care of your farm. I have heard about it."

"It's a good thing I'd had some experience."

"But how did you happen to have experience? Why did you come?"

"We inherited the place from my father, who inherited it from . . . never mind. We ran out of money, so I got the school to teach."

"And then?"

"And then my sister and I both married, and . . . and . . . the place is still there, though I don't see it often. The Lindsays are living on it now."

After a little pause, Mrs. Whitman said, "Perhaps you know why Clyde and I are here. He is consumptive." She spoke the word flatly and dispassionately.

"And he has come west to be cured."

"Very few are cured. But if it turns out that we came soon enough . . . Clyde does not complain. He only feels guilty to have brought me here. As if he could help it! And the best thing I can do for him, almost the only thing, is to make believe I really like it and that it's a great adventure."

"It *is* a great adventure. People come here on purpose, you know. To . . . to see the world. To meet the challenge of the frontier. Let's see if I can remember any of the other things Althea and I used to say to each other." She smiled and Mrs. Whitman smiled back.

"Thank you, Mrs. Lucas. . . . In the town that we came from, we had our families. Our school friends. We had never lived anywhere else. When we read the newspaper, we knew all the names. There were little parties and suppers and my Sunday-school class. And the telephone. It rang and rang. I used to tell Clyde I dreaded the sound of the telephone. Oh, Mrs. Lucas, if I could only hear it now!"

Mary nodded.

"Or hear the croquet mallets clicking against the balls, on summer evenings. And in the winter, sleigh bells. Always sleigh bells. . . . I am afraid I am being tedious. Do you care for fancywork? I brought some new crochet patterns with me from town."

"I don't crochet. But I used to make Battenberg lace. I don't suppose it's still in style."

"Oh, did you?" Louise Whitman was pleased. "My wedding dress had a bertha of white Battenberg, with a pearl in each ring. I am not fashionable. I try to wear what becomes me, and what Clyde likes. And I think the new tunics are dreadful, they seem to have no shape."

"Quite," Mary said. She had put on for this trip her old school suit, which was too tight in several places. But it was neat and businesslike, and Elsie was used to her in it.

"We must not allow Paris to dictate to us," Mrs. Whitman said, sounding very like Althea. "However, we will not criticize Paris now, will we? Is your husband near there, do you think?"

"Not very. He can't tell me where he is. The Germans have made gains, you know—ever since March. I try not to believe it will last. Something will have to happen soon."

Louise laid her gloved hand on Mary's arm. Mary could feel

the warmth of it through the leather. "God bless and keep him," Louise Whitman said.

"I visited the school, three years ago. The one I used to teach. They were playing a war game, with colored pins in a map on the wall. I didn't know then that we . . . that I . . . Some of those boys that were my pupils are in it now. Jeff Porter died in camp, from the influenza. Do you know anything about the influenza, Mrs. Whitman?"

"Not very much, except that I am afraid of it. Perhaps it will not come to us here. Clyde could not survive it, I am sure."

"They say it is hardly ever fatal to children." Mary spoke instinctively of what most concerned her.

"And you have—"

"Two."

The train lurched and roared through a little tunnel, the echoes battering at the sides of the car. When they had died away, Louise Whitman said, "I always hoped . . . I have always wished . . . but my husband's health . . . his consumption . . ."

There is a way then, Mary thought. Of course I always knew there was. Not to have children when you don't want to. When I get to know her a little better . . .

But now I don't need to know. For when Ben comes back I will have another child. I want another baby. Do I? Is that what I want?

"When we light the lamp in the evening," Mrs. Whitman said as if against her will, "there is that awful silence. We talk against it. We eat supper, and we are gay. Clyde makes little jokes so that I will laugh. He reads aloud to me sometimes, for the sound of a voice is good. But the hours go by, and now and then someone passes on the road. Between the sound of the cars on the road, it is so still. So very still. . . ."

"When you can't stand it any longer in the house," Mary said, "you go outside. It's quiet there too, and the hills are all around you, you can't see them but they are there. Your house looks unfamiliar, it is bigger somehow in the dark. The breeze blows against your face, and if it is winter, the snow crunches under your feet. The silence goes out in every direction, down to the

329

river, and up to the peaks. Everything that you ever knew, everything that belonged to you before you came here, is outside that silence."

They sat without speaking for a long while, looking out of the window. The black basalt of the lower valley dropped away and weathered granite began to take its place. At last Mrs. Whitman said, "I should like to talk with you again, when you come to the store. . . . The wild flowers have all vanished, haven't they? They were so abundant a month ago. Perhaps I could plant something in our yard. Something that thrives here."

"I'll bring you a piece of my yellow rose," Mary said.

They waved goodbye at the Pine Creek station, and Mary climbed into the hack with Fletch. A gentlewoman had come to live in Pine Creek! It was incredible. *If this is buying my luck, I must try to do it more often.*

20 EVERYONE KNEW when the last great German attack erupted in July; everyone knew when the American troops began to move forward against it and to push it back. Mary contrived to ride to the post office almost every morning at the time when last night's newspaper came in, if only to stay a few minutes. She would bend over it with Louise Whitman, who suddenly began to understand maps a great deal better as they watched the dotted line crawl across Epernay, Vaux, Soissons, Brasles. Sometimes there was a letter from Ben. Sometimes, after days of no word, a spatter of three or four of the thin, crackling envelopes. Mary read them sitting on the old brown porch steps of the store. Afterwards, at odd times during the day, she read them again.

Today's letter was unusually heavy. It had been in and out of its envelope several times by the time she sat down in late afternoon to rest, before going out to scan the irrigation ditches with Mr. Jepley.

Dear Mary,

I will write this while I have a little time as we have been very much on the move lately. We have to move nearly every night under cover of darkness. Then we sleep when we can during the day, hid in some woods, and there is plenty of work to do all the time.

There has been lots of action going on but I don't see much of it. I am with the gang that takes care of the mules. The machine guns and ammunition are hauled up as close to the front as they can go on the carts. Then the regular squads take it from there and go into the fighting. We stay with the mules back of the lines and move about until the fellows come out of the line. So we don't see any action but get some shells and a lot of noise. One soon learns to tell how close they are going to land and to duck fast. So unless there is a direct hit it isn't too bad. A lot safer than right in the line. We eat pretty regularly, which is more than the guys in action can say as we are near the kitchens and the grub can get through. I don't know much of what is going on and couldn't say anything if I did—nobody seems to know much—or care—just too damn tired. I feel sorry for all the dead horses and mules I have seen along the road—a wounded animal is put out of his misery at once. The poor beasts must have an awful time trying to figure out what we have got them into, but when it is time they can go to sleep and not start thinking about things. I try to copy them and not ask myself a lot of questions. It's best to just do your job and trust to luck.

This is a bigger world than I ever knew it was, Mary. Is that what you were always trying to tell me? I am afraid it would be a long walk from here to Greece where those old stones are, that you treasure so much, but I would like to bring you one in my hand. Like I brought you the stone from my own riverbank once. That was the day I made up my mind I had to have you, come hell or high water. You turned it around in those little fingers and you gave me that look, like it was a chunk of gold. If I hadn't been gone on you already, that look would have done it. And then we quarreled, it seemed like for no reason.

And we still do. Only you don't quarrel, Mary, you hide from me. I guess it isn't in your nature to quarrel. It has taken me a long time to find that out. My Pa and Ma flew out at each other sometimes, like most people do. I guess I thought that if you didn't like something, you would tell me. But you hardly ever did, so I figured everything was all right between us. Until I got the feeling that you were hiding from me, and finally it seemed that you were hiding from me for good.

Don't do that, Mary. When you came to me that day before I left, I was sure I hadn't lost you. Before that I wasn't sure.

As for your losing me, I'm not really in danger Mary. I would like to be up there in the front line, I'd like to take my chances with the rest. It didn't work out that way. But something could happen I suppose, and if it does, you'll still have the part of me that matters most—the children, the ranch. I'd like you to take the children down to see my folks, if it happens that I'm not there to do it myself.

The guns are blazing away up on the front again. Probably we'll have to move soon so I'd better get ready. It's hot today, and really summer. I like the feel of the sun on my back, but

I'd like it better if it was warming up the sagebrush so you could smell it clear down along the road.

I love you Mary.

Ben

She put the letter down with a nerveless hand. She had been groping her way back toward Ben along a road that seemed endless, and now it was as if she saw him coming toward her hopefully, haltingly, from the other end. . . . She had been prepared to accept the blame, to take up her duty as a wife, to pretend that everything was as it used to be.

But Ben did not want her guilt, nor her pretense. He wanted to understand.

She went out to meet Mr. Jepley, guided by the sound of his hoe, fiercely chopping at the leaky ditches. They had to be very saving, this summer, of the precious water. It was running the lowest it had in years. She walked to the foot of each short lateral trickle and cried to Mr. Jepley to let in a little more or a little less, so that it would exactly reach the end of the row. Then she went to encourage Hans, who was pulling thistles where they had crept under the fence and were breaking out in patches among the trees. The huge leather gloves on his hands made him look even thinner than usual.

"My, how *many* you've gotten," Mary said, for Hans had an anxious face that lit up astonishingly under a little praise.

"Misshollister," Hans said after a couple of preliminary swallows, "do you play the music tonight?"

"Why yes, I guess so. I usually play a little after supper."

"Would you be so kind to leave the window open on the side toward my tent? Last night you close it, and I cannot hear."

"Why Hans!" She felt a moment of embarrassment, of resentment even—she had thought herself alone and inviolable at the piano. Seeing Hans' abashed look, his air of perpetual apology for being alive, she knew that these feelings were unwarranted. She had, as a matter of fact, consigned Hans to his own private world as soon as his work was done. "Come down to the house tonight and listen if you like. The children go to bed late, because it stays light so long."

"*Danke schön*', Misshollister," Hans said, as if his English had suddenly left him. He made a great thing of heaping up the thistles, and dropped over the fence a few of the stray rocks that were always working upward in the soil. "I go now to milk the cow." He somehow diminished away among the trees, holding the leather gloves before him like a badge of office.

He had asked Mary to keep his money, except an allowance for food, saying he did not need the rest of it now; but looking at his threadbare back, she wondered if she ought to send him to town to buy some clothes and a few small comforts. She would try to think of it next payday. She went to the bank once a month, as Ben had done, and drew out enough money for Mr. Jepley and the Scobie boys, and paid any bills she had accumulated. This reminded her that she was far behind in working in Ben's ledger. If she did not tackle it soon, she would never catch up. She had better do it on Sunday, when she had thought of taking the children for a picnic along the river.

Hans presented himself at the door before the children had finished dawdling over their cocoa. His yellow hair shone wetly, the fragments of his shoes were shined. The children knew him for a familiar face, and for someone young enough to play with. They made friends quickly, bringing him their treasures of the moment—the earless cotton rabbit and the small metal fireman lost in the yard months ago and just found, minus his fire truck. He could not sit down anywhere except in the truck, for his figure fitted a slot in the seat.

"He could sit upon a spool," Hans suggested gravely. Mama was immediately importuned for a spool of thread, and the fireman sat down on it with complete success. The children were enchanted. They climbed upon Hans in the big chair, and David gave him an affectionate, cocoa-laden swipe on the ear.

But when Mama began to play the piano, they lost his attention. In vain they tugged at him and chattered, till Mama said, "Quiet, there, or else go outside." They chose to go outside, for the yard was cool in the blue shadow that fell from the hill, and like their mother, they always had unfinished work out there to do.

Mary had unearthed some of her old pieces and had been practicing them, promising herself that when she got them relearned, *really* mastered, she would buy herself some new music at last. There was the Grieg album in its pink cover, which had belonged to her teacher. There were the "Scarf Dance" and the "Minuet in G," and "Opera Gems." She had opened the Grieg at random, and begun. It was difficult, and she did not feel she was doing very well. But Hans' gaze never left her, and though he was sitting at some distance, his eyes and ears were so riveted upon her that it seemed he could not miss a single note.

She remembered what he had chosen for his recitation at the school entertainment, and thinking that this practice session was perhaps not the thing under the circumstances, she began to play (by ear, for she did not possess a copy of it) "Holy Night," and such other old German tunes as she could remember; "Die Lorelei," and "Du Liegst Mir im Herzen."

She turned at last to glance at him, to see how he liked this. Hans was sitting with his eyes closed in his white face, his hands were rigid, gripping the arms of the chair.

Oh dear, that was the wrong thing to do. "Hans," she said quickly, "would you like to see how this thing works? Come here and I'll show you."

He came to stand beside her. He was trembling, but he made his little bow. "All these keys," Mary said, "the white keys and the black keys—each one is a note, the same as a note that you would sing." She picked out, with one finger, a couple of measures of "Dixie." "When I put them together, they make a chord." She went softly through several triads, closing again on a final C.

"I understand, Misshollister. . . . I have played the concertina."

"You have? I didn't know that, Hans. Where is your concertina now?"

His silence was answer enough; it was where all his other earthly possessions were, and doubtless his heart also.

"Hans, are you . . . yes, of course you are. I am not sure I ought to ask you this, and you needn't answer if you don't want to. Is there any way you could see your family at all?"

Hans moved his head slowly from side to side. "The Vater is old, Misshollister, and I have . . ." he groped for a word in English, and did not find one. "I have him *herausgefordert*. He will not forgive."

"Then until you get your concertina back, you will play tunes with me. Play now, something that you know."

After a little hesitation, Hans put his hand on the upper keys, and fumbled for a melody. It came badly, but there was enough for her to begin to strike an occasional chord with it. The strained look began to leave his face, and when she added a flourish of bass notes, incongruous with the sentimental melody he was playing, Hans laughed aloud.

There was the sound of the rear screen opening, and Fletch came into the new kitchen and put his head through the door. He looked a little surprised, but Fletch was an understanding sort; he had, in fact, gone out of his way to give Hans a friendly word now and then. He said, "The little feller's wheezy, and Florence wants your croup kettle, just in case."

"I'll get it," Mary said. She began to rummage in the cupboard. It was getting dark, and as long as she was up, she went to call the children in. Hans took the hint and departed with Fletch. "You must come back," Mary told him belatedly, lifting the chimney off a kerosene lamp so that she could light it, and letting Helen blow out the match. Hans was in her charge; if music would help him, it was not reasonable to withhold it. From the looks of him, it would not hurt him, either, to have a glass of cocoa now and then with the children.

After she had put them to bed, she sat down to the ledger. But instead of reaching for the time sheets and statements, she took out Ben's letter, and read it again. She was alone with it now, as she had known all day she would be. Sooner or later, she would have to answer it.

The children had gone to sleep promptly; they had had a big day. To sit here alone with her thoughts was more than she could bear. She rose and went out through the kitchen and the back door into the yard, lit by an early rising moon. The smell of apples pervaded the dark, as they formed and swelled among the moon-silvered trees.

Noiselessly she walked around the house and up the driveway. In spite of what she had said to Louise Whitman, the night did not seem alien, it felt friendly and kind. *That's because I belong here. She will feel it so too, some day.* She stood, irresolute, and

336

then undid the gate on its heavy hinge and stepped out and closed it behind her. Even at night, if only for a few minutes, Mary Lucas did not leave gates open any more.

She walked slowly along the road for a little way; the dust glimmered under her feet. The shapes of the sagebrush stood like strokes of gray paint against the shadow.

I'd like it better if it was warming up the sagebrush so you could smell it clear down along the road.

She broke off a twig, and crushed it in her hands. The pungent, overwhelming smell, like no other on earth, swept through her. It was Ben, that fragrance—his stubborn toil, his abrupt speech, his eyes fixed far down the future, his rough and hungry embrace. For a moment she saw him clearly and whole, and around him the earth was torn open and flames gnawed at the sky.

She covered her face with her hands, and the night breeze came softly upriver and whipped the ends of her hair. At last she began to tear off some sprays and wrap them in her handkerchief. This was what she would send Ben—this handful of the living land, this symbol of the thing they had together. It would answer his letter, and she did not trust herself to put her questions about their future into words.

"I brought you this," Louise Whitman said, "because I wanted an excuse to ride. Don't you think I am doing rather well, Mary? Clyde is tremendously proud of me."

She sat carefully and somewhat stiffly on Rusty, who had been loaned to her for a few weeks while she took her first lessons in riding. *(If you're going to learn,* Mary had said, *you'd better learn on Rusty. He needs to be ridden, and he's the most reliable horse in the state of Washington. Then you can get one of your own.)*

Mary looked critically at her friend. "You're still not relaxed enough. Lean back. Rusty is carrying *you,* you know. You're not carrying Rusty. There, that's better. What in the world do you have there?"

"It's a parcel, and it jingles. It came in the mail today." Louise handed it over, brown paper and all. The core of it was a shoe

337

box, with the cover glued on. It had been sent first-class postage, and tied with innumerable bits of string.

"I'd better take it inside, it looks lethal. Let's see you dismount."

"I was afraid you'd say that. Do look the other way, Mary. I'm absolutely no good getting on and off."

"Nonsense. I'll give you a hand." While Louise struggled down, aided a little by Mary's outstretched arm, Rusty stood solidly and patiently with his feet apart. His manner said that he was a good and patient beast, and knew it. Mary tickled him behind the ears.

"Go on in, Louise. I'll just get Rusty a ripe apricot. He loves them."

"Now how in the world did you find that out?"

"I offered him one, to see. Horses like treats. Just like you and me. You'll learn all these things in due time."

Louise prowled through the house, while Mary fetched the scissors for the package. "Did I understand you to say you were going to add on a bedroom here?"

"Yes, I mean to. Bert Plew doesn't charge much for his time, and he needs the work. Ben would want it, I think. He spoke of it before he left. And he has a soft spot for Bert, and I have too I guess. . . . I wrote to Ben about it, but he hasn't got around to say anything one way or the other. It must be hard for him to keep track of what goes on here. Our letters are all mixed up, it takes at least three weeks for them to go or come. Anyhow, when I hear from him, I know he was all right three weeks ago."

Louise reached over and briefly brushed her hand. "Open your parcel."

Mary pried off the cover. Some miscellaneous packing fell out, among which was a jumble of five- and one-dollar bills and a few coins of various sizes. And a note.

"For heaven's sake! A legacy?" Louise said with frank curiosity.

Mary unfolded the note.

My husban says to send this. He says to say thank you. I aint sure what for but I guess you done right to have me come. Things are oll right, they coud be better and they coud be worse. Anyway I aint forgot you, you was good to me Mary. O god I suffer awful sometimes with my chest. Sammy is brite as a button and I was glad to see him and he was glad to see me. He is awful smart Mary. He is the worlds beatenest. As long as he is oll right I am oll right. I am, madam, your obedient servant.

Elsie

"One of my little projects," she said to Louise. She put the money and the message back into the box.

"I can see you aren't going to tell me. . . . You have a lot of little projects, don't you?" There was a wistful note in Louise's voice.

"I fall into them somehow. This one is finished, though." She wondered if it really was. Taking down the old workbasket from the shelf, she emptied it and began to lay the money carefully underneath the cushion. "This is money my brother gave me, a few years ago." This much, at any rate, she could tell Louise. It occurred to her that she had never shown it to anyone before. "Ben doesn't know I have it. It was supposed to be a secret between my brother and me. But Arthur wouldn't mind your knowing—you're so much his sort."

"Mary, you're extraordinary. You mean you just let it lie there? In a bank it would draw interest."

"It draws interest now," Mary said. "You should see the beautiful book someone sent me who used it. . . . You didn't happen to bring the paper, did you?"

"Of course I brought the paper. There are some more names today, Mary." The local casualty list, on the front page, was always the thing they looked at first. Mary scanned it quickly, and made a forlorn little sound. "Oh Louise . . . the Wenatchee superintendent of schools, who was so good to me when I was taking those examinations . . . his son . . ." Almost everyday now, they found familiar names.

After a little pause, Louise said, "No Lucases . . . no Whitmans, either." Her lips twisted a little. "If . . . if Clyde . . . his name won't be on any Roll of Honor. . . . Mary, you said you needed harvest help. Is there anything I can do?"

"I don't think so. Dolly Plew will cook for those who don't board themselves, and she'll take care of the overflow from the Sawyers', too, so Mrs. Sawyer can work. The Sawyers let Mr. Jepley have a room, and we're indebted to them."

"There is *something*. I can tell it from your face."

"Well, if you wanted to learn to pack apples . . ."

"I would love to. Where does one start?"

"Florence taught Fletch, and Fletch taught me, and . . . and I guess I'd better teach you, then, hadn't I? Come out to the barn, and I'll give you some idea of it."

She led the way back to the old packing bench, stored against the inside wall. In her hands were a few early apples, still green, but the first that would ripen. She pulled down a box from the stack. Paper to wrap them? She was almost out of it. You could not pack without the precious squares of paper. Ben's notes had said to order it, but somehow it had been overlooked. Everything was in short supply; was it too late? She must remedy the oversight now, at once, this afternoon.

When she had loaned Rusty to Louise, she could not find Ben's good saddle, which was kept carefully over a crosspiece at the head of the mangers. This seemed odd. It was the one she had urged him to buy as a fitting tribute to Rusty, and he would not have disposed of it without letting her know. (There was an old one available, of course—no Lucas ever threw anything away.) She searched halfheartedly in the tool shed and the Uncles' Room, but there was no time to put on a real hunt. The loss would just have to be accepted.

This morning as she took the tarpaulins off the picking ladders, stacked on a platform in the yard, the newest one was missing. She could not be mistaken. It had only been used for one season, and its bright yellow paint had still been intact.

Someone was stealing from her. She remembered a curious shortage here and there; a milking pail, a hay fork. All of it good new gear, easy to resell.

It gave her a creepy, frightened feeling. Mr. Jepley? Could she afford to ask? He was her strongest, most efficient worker. Besides, what would he be doing with such things? The answer supplied itself; it was only a short carry down toward the Sawyers', across vacant land. A passing wagon . . .

She had kept fastidiously away from such things all her life. She knew only vaguely that there were people who received stolen goods. She must find out if Fletch was missing anything. But perhaps he would have spoken of it. And would it do any good to add to his worries if he were not? The Lucases were righteous—if they had a case against someone they would press it. At the risk of losing an indispensable pair of hands? Probably. She was not ready to put it to the test. As for speaking to the Sawyers, they would throw Mr. Jepley out, on suspicion, and let it go at that. They had their own crew of Filipinos and Kanakas, for which they were disliked in Pine Creek. And she needed the room they rented to her for Mr. Jepley; she had no other place to put him.

There was nothing to do but keep her mouth shut and try to be more watchful, and to bar every window and door at night. She would ask Bert Plew to put on more locks. She already slept badly and fitfully, getting up to gaze at the children now and then. How would it be when she had to listen for sounds out in the yard and the barn?

At any rate, she had something cheerful to write to Ben today. Something besides the work reports, and the assurance that she and the children loved him and missed him, and that everything was going well (whether it was or not.)

> Ben, we have a new sign on our gate. It says "Music Lessons." I think Fletch put it up to tease me, because he heard me explaining the scale to Hans Schlogl. But a buggy stopped, and an enormously big fat lady got out, Mrs. Sedgwick from Wolf Coulee, they get their mail at Pine Creek. And they have a reed organ, and she wants me to teach their little girl to play it! Oh, Ben, I am so pleased. I give Hans a lesson too sometimes, and let him practice a little. Some day Pine Creek is going to need a music teacher, and it's going to be me. I'm not very good, but the thing is, I'm here. When I get money for giving lessons, I'll take it and study some more, make trips to Wenatchee perhaps.

She stopped dubiously. Was this the sort of thing Ben wanted to hear? But she had an urge to try to communicate with him frankly, as he had tried to communicate with her.

I'd like to start Helen soon. Not till she wants it, not till she asks. And not because she'll be very good either. There isn't any need to be a genius. I'd like her to play for the joy of it, like me.

Having said this much, she found it easy to go on.

The children ought to have the best we both can give them. We're not always going to agree about what this is maybe, but we'll both have our say. I'll try to speak out, like you want me to. It isn't easy for me to speak out, Ben. If anyone is cross with me, I can't. I guess I feel as though I must have done something truly dreadful when even someone who loves me has to scold me. Dolly laughed at me for this, but it's true.

If it made her out a weak and stupid creature, no matter, Ben had to know. She went on to say that she had ordered the apple-wrap, and been lucky enough to get some; that the flow of water from the spring was pretty meager, but would see them through. She did not mention the thefts (if that was what they were), or the spiraling price of everything she had to buy. Or anything else that Ben wouldn't know about and be worrying about already.

When the Slocums, the itinerant couple from California, drove into the yard in their covered truck fitted up for sleeping, she astonished them by hugging them both. She had been terribly afraid they would not come. Without them, she was nowhere. With them, she had barely and exactly a harvest crew. Slocum was a fast and experienced picker. He would lead Mr. Jepley and Hans in stripping the trees. Mrs. Slocum understood sorting and grading, and could teach Mrs. Lindsay to help her. Florence would be back at the packing bench, with Louise Whitman beside her. Fletch would drive the flatbed wagon, bringing in the fruit and hauling it away again, acting as orchard and shed boss, while Mary took charge of the checking and selling. Her two old men, Lindsay and Plew, she would set to nailing up and stamping, lining boxes, fetching and carrying for everyone else. Later, she managed, without compromising his dignity too much, to get Bert to spend a good deal of time with Dolly looking after the children. She told him that since she could seldom be in the house, she would feel safer if he were there. Florence and Fletch's Mickey, hardly more than a year old, became his special care, and he put the little fellow to sleep by whistling to him on a grass blade.

It was as intricate as a square dance, and one misstep was enough to throw everything off. Each night Mary went over the plans, looking for loopholes, and studied the bills of lading and the carload manifests she had made up in the past under Ben's direction, wondering if she could do it alone. She took refuge in her father's saying: *If you absolutely have to do something, God will show you how.*

There were surveyors along the right-of-way once more, up and down the roads; she saw them with a sinking heart. *Oh no, surely we don't have to go through all that again.* Buttonholing the first one who came close, Mary asked him, "Is there something wrong with the railroad?"

"No, ma'am. We're from the power company. We're fixin' to run a transmission line up the river."

"Transmission?" Mary did not know the word.

"Electricity," he said, as if to a child.

"Electricity . . . Oh!" She remembered the petition she had signed. All at once and with a leap of the heart she remembered Bob Anthony's prophecies and Ben's long-starved hope of watering the upper bench. She shaded her eyes and pointed to it. "Do you mean we could pump water up *there?*"

"Why, yes, ma'am, no doubt you can." He gave her a curious look. "Mostly when the ladies find out what's comin', they starts talkin' about electric lights and cookstoves and washin' machines."

"Well . . . well, yes, of course. But . . ." She could not contain it, she had to tell someone. "That's some of our best land up there. It's level and the soil is rich, and there's hardly any rock on it. It would plant out to ten or eleven acres we think. Ten more acres of orchard! It would make all the difference in the world."

"Guess a farmer always wants more land," the surveyor said.

343

"But when it's already there! . . . and you've had to say to yourself a hundred times, if the spring in the canyon were just a little higher. . . . Of *course* we want more land! Families do get bigger, you know, and . . ." She looked at him and saw that his eyes were twinkling.

"Yes, ma'am. This job don't pay much, but I get to bring a lot of good news to folks. Besides, I bin through it myself. I homesteaded a place on Brace Creek, never could get enough water. I proved up and sold—couldn't stick it out. You hang onto your land, ma'am."

"Why yes, I will." Mary only half heard him. *Oh, Ben, you'll never guess . . .*

It was the lump in the toe of the Christmas stocking, the plum in the pie. Hans was startled to see, when he brought in the milk, Misshollister twirling around the kitchen and blithely whistling "K-K-Katy."

The apples rustled steadily into the boxes. The wagon creaked slowly through the orchard. Every move had been planned so exactly and so often, that it seemed not quite real. These were the motions she had thought about all summer. Were they really making them now?

Going to Wenatchee every week, she conferred with buyers. She sold the first carload too soon, just missing a 9-cent-a-box price rise. Ben had always steadily refused to join a co-op or to contract the whole crop in advance—he had an instinct for timing his sales. *I will do the best I can. I will not panic.*

Whenever Fletch brought a wagonload to the railroad at Pine Creek Siding she was there on Duke, to confirm the tally and sign the papers. If it was near train time and the car was due to go out, Fletch brought Hans with him to hurry the loading. Once their car was not ready when the train pulled into the station, and they finished carrying and bulkheading at a breakneck pace while the train waited, the crew joshed, and the idling engine took long, shuddering breaths.

In Wenatchee she saw a few people with gauze masks on their

faces, to keep them from catching the "Spanish influenza." The disease had traveled at last from the Atlantic to the Pacific, taking its toll as it went. If it was coming to Pine Creek, Mary hoped that it would wait till after harvest. She could only cope with one thing at a time.

In October, the schools of Wenatchee closed suddenly, and a few days later all church services were suspended. On the first of November an emergency hospital opened its doors, to deal with the suddenly rising epidemic.

21 THE COUNTY SHERIFF came into the packing shed, followed by Mrs. Sawyer from down the road. Mary moved quickly toward them. "What can I do for you?"

The sheriff cleared his throat. "This lady wants me to bring in one o' your men. Feller that rooms at her house. Seems like they been missin' stuff from their gear."

"My husband's camera was found wadded in his raincoat, under a lumber pile up the road," Mrs. Sawyer said briskly.

"There—there can't be any mistake?" Mary knew there was no mistake, but she needed time to steady herself.

"I reckon not. Other stuff's been disappearin'. Little things here an' there."

"The man is picking, out in the orchard. You can go and get him, I guess." She did not want to see Mr. Jepley led away; she had done wrong to shelter Mr. Jepley, in order to help save her crop. She would have gone on doing wrong if she could.

"I'm sorry, Miz' Lucas." Her neighbor smiled thinly. "I can't have thievin'."

It was necessary to extend her hand to Mrs. Sawyer, and she did it. "You have no choice, I know. How are things going at your place?"

"Pretty good. We can't complain." Mrs. Sawyer beckoned soberly to her companion, and the little group in the packing shed watched as they set off down the dusty orchard track. All work had stopped; there was complete silence as Bert and Dolly, who had doubtless not missed a word, came softly out of the house and ranged themselves with the others.

At last Louise Whitman asked, "Just how bad is it, Mary?"

"If . . ." Mary tried to put her thoughts in order. "If the fruit doesn't come in steadily, you'll all lose time, and we'll get further

347

and further behind. And if we don't get it picked, of course, it will fall."

Florence's bright young voice broke in. "Mary, if we all took turns . . ."

"Oh, no," Mary cried. "Not *you*."

"I don't see why not. If you left the ladder up, and we changed every hour—we'll leave whatever we're doing, and each of us will go out and pick, till the next one is ready. I never did it before, but I can keep it up for an hour, and so can anyone else. Can't we?"

"Fletch wouldn't hear of it," Mary said.

"I'll answer for Fletch. There's not one of us that couldn't take a turn. Isn't that right?"

Mrs. Lindsay tittered. "I guess these old laigs will look kind of comical up on a ladder. Sure, I can do it."

"It's got to be *everybody*," Florence said firmly. "You understand, don't you, Mary?"

Mary saw that in this offering of their loyalty and pride, no one was to be slighted, no one left out. She listened tranced to Florence announce, "All right, it's a deal. I'll keep a list, and when it's your turn I'll call you. Mary, you ought to go first. How about it?"

She looked around at them, and there was nothing to say. She turned and left, under the shimmering sun, and walked out through the soft earth along the rutted road, and picked up the picking sack where Mr. Jepley had laid it down.

There was a lot of joking about the ladder, about Mt. Pickabit and Robbers' Roost. Hans, quietly descending now and then, helped the volunteers up and down and took out twigs and leaves they had dumped in. Mary knew that Florence had taken Fletch aside, on his first trip in, and laid down the law to him. *She's a good wife for a Lucas; better than I am.* Florence kept a schedule, and often "forgot" to call the old people; she let Fletch pick until the wagon absolutely must be driven again, and Mary until there were welts on her shoulders and purple circles under her eyes; and took many a good long turn herself, leaving Louise to keep up with the packing as best she might.

They were working a part of the orchard below the railroad

tracks, along the river. Mary had allowed the children to come out with her to play while she did her stint. It was far from the house, where they were seldom allowed to go; it had new gullies and embankments to explore. There was the sound of Uncle Fletch coming with the team and wagon, and Uncle Fletch was galloping the team, and he was whistling shrilly, calling out something. The children stopped digging and listened.

"Mary," Uncle Fletch was shouting as the wagon came careening along the road. "Mary, Mary, they've signed an armistice. I heard it at Pine Creek. They signed it yesterday, and the War is over. Mary, can you hear me? The War is over."

They did not see how Mama could help hearing him.

Mama stopped picking, and laid her arms across the top of the ladder and put her face down on them.

Uncle Fletch halted the team and jumped off the wagon and came over to the ladder. He gave her an anxious look. "You'd better come down, Mary."

After a little pause Mama said in a low voice, "I can't. My knees are weak."

"Steady now," Uncle Fletch said. "Hand me the sack." Mama reached out and gave it to him; they could hear her take a long breath. She let herself down a step at a time, and sat on the bottom rung.

Uncle Fletch said, "We didn't know it. But ever since yesterday, the guns have stopped."

"Yes," Mama said, still in that hushed voice.

"And Ben and Harve . . . if either of them . . . I would never have forgiven myself."

"But Fletch—what would we have done without you here?"

Uncle Fletch sat down cross-legged on the orchard soil. "You think it's for real, Mary? You don't think that maybe, at the last minute . . ."

"No," Mama said more strongly. "They're safe, Fletch. I feel it's true, now that I've had a minute to get used to it . . . How did you hear it? Who told you?"

"In Pine Creek," Fletch said, "they're dancing in the streets."

Mama did not speak for a while, and they sidled near, for when Mama did not talk there might be something wrong. But

Mama straightened up suddenly. "Clean your shoes off, you two," she said, "and put your sweaters back on and wipe your noses, and Helen, get those vine leaves out of your hair."

It was over. Ben was coming home. She and Ben would have another chance.

She sat in front of the stove in the new kitchen, with the oven door down for warmth. Now that the cookstove was out here, they ought to have a heating stove in the living room, where she was making do with a couple of smelly kerosene heaters. Ben would see to it. Ben would see to everything.

For the rest of her life, now, she would be plain Mrs. Ben Lucas. This was what she had wanted, and this was what she had got. There was no use trying to be more than one person at a time.

Before her slowly, in the glimmer from the firebox, passed all the Marys there would never be. She studied each one, relinquishing. The Mary who would do good, the settlement worker, the one with the gray velvet dress and the small pearls and the violets pinned to her muff. . . . *She never amounted to much. She was only my need to be needed.*

The studious Mary, the book-enchanted Mary, the one who was never going to rest until she had made her way to the old land and the magic stones. This Mary would lurk in volumes seldom opened, phrases coming less and less often to the mind. As long as she saw Althea, they would sometimes flash a line of poetry to each other, or make some silly and lovely and incomprehensible reference. But she would probably outlast Althea—and what then? *This Mary will live in my children. It is what I have to give them.*

The Mary who had wanted to follow Lew. *I wonder how she would have made out. Of course, I couldn't leave the children. Of course, I couldn't let Ben down. Is that all really? Am I glad I couldn't go?* She thought for the last time of how it would have been, to live on the Anthonys' bounty, to be fashionable and pleasure-loving and not quite respectable, to have life be all fun. *And I could have loved Lew. Any woman could love Lew. Is that why I didn't go with him? Was it too easy? Do I want the job of being Ben's wife because it is hard and costly and challenging and I won't give up?*

They finished packing out on a damp, chilly Wednesday that smelled like snow, and Fletch took off for Pine Creek with the last load. There was the house to tidy up, the accumulated washing to do. And after a few days, looking at her depleted pantry, Mary rode off on Duke, hoping to find fresh food at the store instead of the steady can-opening of harvest time. The store looked deserted, and on the screen door was a sign,

CLOSED. INFLUENZA.

Apprehensive, Mary went around to the back and knocked. A nearby window opend, and Louise's white face peered out.

"Mary, go away. . . . No . . . here." She ducked back in, and reappeared to throw out a key. "Go in and take what you need, and make out a slip. But don't come near me." A wave of fetid air welled from the open window.

"Is . . . is Clyde . . ."

"I don't know. He's alive. I had it for two days ahead of him, and I'm better, so I'm up. It's not nice, Mary."

"Tell me," Mary said.

"You don't know what to expect. With me it was vomit, I just couldn't raise my head. Clyde just fell to pieces. No, I can't tell you. They say it doesn't work on any two people the same. I'm going to be all right, I feel stronger this morning. Able to walk, that is, and do what Clyde requires. Oh, Mary, what have we done to be visited with this?"

"Nothing that the whole world hasn't done, I guess. At least it's everywhere. Do you need milk? Eggs? Bedding?"

"I need to see your face and hear your voice," Louise said. "I've done that, now, so go away. I'll manage. I didn't come halfway around the world to be widowed. I could have waited for that back East. Clyde's alive, and that's all, and that's enough. Help yourselves from the shelves." She pulled down the open window.

351

Mary did not take time to enter the store. She put the key under a porch plank, turned Duke around, and rode straight toward Indian Spring. It was a long ride, and chilly. She reached Dr. McClellan's office about noon, and by a miracle, found him in. He had waked after a nap, and was gulping black coffee. His horse had brought the buggy in, with the doctor sleeping bolt upright in it, around five that morning.

"Whitman?" Dr. McClellan said. "The Pine Creek store? I'll stop and leave some medicine, and some advice if she wants it. Sensible of her not to let people in." He was trying to care for Indian Spring and Pine Creek and the straggle of ranches up into Wolf Coulee, and he looked as if he had been hit by a rockslide. "And I'll tell you what to do, Mary, in case I'm not here when you call me. Eat lightly, but eat *something*. Make the children eat. Egg-nogs. Soup. Keep their strength up. Give them lots of liquids. If their temperatures go up, put cold compresses on their foreheads and the backs of their necks. Bathe them often in tepid water. Get a messenger to the druggist here—he knows what to send. If he runs out, write to your sister at Wenatchee to put a packet on the train."

Indian Spring had closed down for the winter. She rode along the deserted street. In the window of a general store was a resplendent jacket of blue corduroy, a little smallish, and it occurred to her to buy it for Hans. *I will stay until the War is over and the Americans have won it. You think that is how it will be, Misshollister?* That was how it had been, and now Hans must go home to his father to face whatever he had to face. He was better equipped than he had been. She went in and pointed the jacket out and paid for it, and like any Pine Creeker on a shopping trip, had it made up into a poke to fit the back of her saddle.

"I'd like Bert to come and finish off the new bedroom, Dolly. There's some work still to do on the outside, and then after it begins to snow, he can do the inside finish." Mary gave Dolly one of her butter rolls, fresh from the oven.

"Before Ben comes home, you mean. . . . I declare, Mary, I

352

think these are as good as Althea's." She looked commiseratingly at Mary's bent head, her hands letting down the hem of Helen's dress. She guessed she knew a lonesome woman when she saw one. She minded the afternoon so long ago—twenty years? thirty years?—when Bert an' her had been visitin' her folks, they was young things then an' not hardly able to keep their hands off each other, an' there was no place for 'em to git away by theirselves, an' finally they had took an' hid out in the haymow. She still remembered that afternoon in the haymow. But she only said, "You ever goin' to git that surrey fixed up, an' drive it again?"

"I don't know. I think maybe we'll get an automobile."

Dolly's jaw dropped. "Sufferin' cats, Mary! A woman can't drive one o' them things."

"We'll see. I'd like to try."

"Ben won't like it a little bit. He favors horses."

"Ben wants me to tell him when I get ideas. Maybe he'll favor it and maybe he won't. But he wants me to speak up."

"I guess you been doin' some thinkin', Mary."

"I've had time enough. . . . No, actually, Ben's been doing some. If you want to call it that. Oh, Dolly, Ben tries so hard. He has taken such good care of me always. When we had almost nothing, he gave me what he had. And when he had a little more . . ." She lifted the pearl pendant at her throat. "I began to understand Ben better when he gave me this."

"So now you want a ottymobile. Heavenly day! What next?"

"A pump to take the water to the upper bench. In fact, that comes ahead of everything. I wrote to Ben about it, and though he didn't say much, he was pleased. Guess what? He knew something would come, he always figured there would be a way."

"I never seen you so dang cheerful," Dolly grumbled. "Ain't you afraid of the sickness, an' all?"

"Of course I am. Scared silly. The Scobies have it, and the Woczceks, and the Miller Boys. How in the world would the Miller Boys catch it? They never go anywhere."

"They went to Camp Lewis to see Olly. Olly sent 'em the money. They put on their shoes an' went. It musta been a fair sight. Olly's mad as a bobcat because he never got sent over. They kep' 'im at the camp, teachin' sharpshootin'."

"Oh, poor Olly! . . . He's one of my children, you know. There's something special about the kids that went to school to me."

"Well, you still got the little Kraut. What'cha goin' to do with 'im?"

"I haven't the least idea." Mary's face was troubled. "I don't know what will become of that whole family."

"Now, Mary. You ought to be fixin' to mind your own business when Ben comes back. How is *he* goin' to feel about the Krauts?"

"I don't know. I'll have to ask him."

"How many kids did you have in that school?"

"Fourteen," Mary said fondly.

"Well, when you git fourteen o' your own, you'll quit worryin' about them others."

"Oh yes, and another thing. I'm going to have my babies in a regular hospital. They've got a lot of things to make it easier."

"Next thing you know," Dolly prophesied darkly, "you're goin' to be sendin' away for stylish clothes an hand-painted pitchers an' Turkey carpets."

"I might," Mary said.

She did not have to make up Hans' mind for him. When he came to the door that night, he was twitching with anxiety. "I must now go, Misshollister. My family is sick."

"Oh no! Not way up in there! How did they catch it?"

"I do not know. It comes. God sends it."

"Do you believe in God, Hans?"

Hans nodded. "If I did not believe in God, I would have jumped in the river. . . . Can I have my pay now, Misshollister?"

She went hastily to her desk. A check would do Hans no good. She kept some cash in the house, enough for ordinary emergencies. She counted it over hastily. Hans had worked for her the better part of a year; she had meant to lay aside money for him regularly, but there had been so many other things to think about.

There was not enough here. Going to the closet shelf, she took down her workbasket. Under the bottom pad was the spill of coins and small bills that Elsie had sent.

This would do it. The few coins that were left were scarcely enough to buy something for the children at Christmas. She was borrowing it from herself, this time, and she would probably never pay it back. It was just as well—she must try not to have secrets from Ben.

"Is your . . . are they very ill, Hans? Or do you know?"

"My Vater . . ." Hans swallowed. "My Vater does not want to live. I do not think he will. Our neighbor stopped at my tent and told me."

It was no time for soft talk or trite consolations. "When you feel as though you cannot bear it, Hans, get down your concertina. It will feel good to you again. Don't think. Don't blame yourself, or him, or anyone. Play, Hans, play. It has saved me many a time."

He asked her for waxed paper, and put the money carefully in a fold of it; he had no wallet. This reminded her of something. She went to the back room and unwrapped the blue jacket.

"I want you to wear this home, Hans. I thought of you when I saw it."

He slipped hesitantly into it, and looked down at himself. What no harrowing news could do, the gift did; Hans dissolved in tears. He slumped in the big rawhide chair, and cried uncontrollably, and Mary put her arms around his shoulders and cried too. There was no help for anything. Things were the way they were.

After a while she reached for a clean towel and wiped her eyes and handed it to him. "You did that so you could have your grief out before you go, Hans. You will be strong now. Come back to us as soon as you can. Would you like to ride one of the horses?"

"I do not know when I could return it. I will walk. I will catch rides. I go now to make my bundle at the tent."

"But it's getting dark!"

"I cannot wait. Perhaps I will sleep by the road."

She could not dissuade him, or make any useful suggestions. Before he left he stooped from his reedy height and, suddenly, gave her a quick hug; a boy's first, unpremeditated, inept embrace.

The State Department of Highways had never been so foolish as to squander any money on the road to Dutch Hill. It was an abandoned logging trace, and it zigzagged up from the place where Spicer's Mill had once been. The German settlers had worked it over themselves with pick and shovel. It led out of Wolf Coulee to the high, desolate flats where they had their wheat farms.

But it was home to Hans. The tiredness dropped from him as he climbed. The Zimmermans had a new roof on their barn; from under it protruded the old beams with the carved horses' heads that Hans loved. Around the next turn, the poplar trees that young Heinrich Knecht had planted almost hid the one-room cabin. There was no sign of life at the Knecht place; perhaps Heinrich had pulled out. Had his family been friendless, then, except for the Zimmermans? Had the two families helped and cared for each other? There was suddenly a black pit inside Hans. At its bottom, somewhere, his heart lay beating hard. *Ach Gott,* how wicked he had been to run away. . . .

He made his feet carry him around the last bend in the road. The Schlogl fields had been harvested; before the sickness came, no doubt. The scythes hung on the log wall. The pump handle was down; there must be priming in the pump.

In front of the house was a tiny rusty black figure, seated, peeling potatoes. It looked up and saw him, and the knife fell from its hands.

His mother came slowly down the path, and Hans walked forward to meet her. They halted a pace apart. His mother's face was all one hungry pair of eyes.

"*Du!*" she said.

They looked at each other for an interminable moment. Hans found his voice. "*Der Vater?*"

"*Fort, weg.*"

Gone. Gone away. His father was dead, then. He was too late. He began to tremble violently; his mother put out an arm to steady him.

He had told Misshollister that he believed in God. Where was God now? In that room with his father? He must go there. *Ach, vergib mir, vergib mir.* He must say it, at that bier; he must say it to that unseeing face. He put out his hand and his mother took it to guide him. He thought of something else as they went up the path. *"Die Kinder?"*

The *Kinder* were well enough now, his mother said in a sudden burst of flowing German; he was carried along on it wholly. He was home again, home. Anny was still weak—she had a cough. Werner had been very sick, the little Werner—he had suffered so. His mother's voice was like a wall around the world; it enclosed them, it made everything bearable. It broke off as they reached the door—she pointed silently. His father's body was in the inner room. Hans went in.

Mrs. Schlogl waited. She gave the children some supper and braided Anny's hair and sent them up the ladder to bed. Then she sat with folded hands. She had a little cinnamon on the shelf; she would make *Kuchen* tomorrow perhaps. For Hans' return. What would happen after tomorrow? It was not for her to say.

When Hans came out and dropped at her feet, sitting sprawled on the floor the way he always had, she looked down at him with wistful tenderness; his scrawny height, his thin young face, more peaceful now. In bearing this child, she had done well. And Anny, with her laughter and tears—in bearing beautiful troubled Anny, had she done well? Yes. . . . And the little folk,—Erich and Werner—who could tell? They were babies still.

"*Mutter.*"

"Yes, Hansi."

"There must be the funeral."

"Yes, Hansi."

"We must get the minister from Indian Spring."

"Will he come?"

"He will come. I will go myself and ask him."

"What will it cost?"

"I have money," Hans said. ". . . *Mutter*, did Anny go to school this fall?"

"No. Her throat is delicate. . . . I was afraid, Hansi. I was afraid to send her."

"We must not be afraid. The war is over now. She must go back to school. They must all go, when it is time. No matter how hard it is."

"Yes, Hansi."

"We must speak English," Hans said, though the flow of the warm rapid German speech was very comforting to him. "The children must speak it. In the daytime, *liebe Mutter*, we will all speak English. But in the evening, when you are tired, you and I will speak German together."

"Yes, Hansi."

The big worn rocker, empty these last few days, stood across the room; the *Ehrenplatz*, the chair of the head of the family. Was it not Hans' now, by right? She could not think of exactly how to say this, without betraying the massive and terrible figure in the next room, of which she had stood in awe for better than half her life. But she looked from Hans to the rocker, and back again at Hans.

Hans shook his head. "*Amerikanische* men do not take the best chair. In their homes, women are *verehrt*—honored. The best seat is for *die Frau des Hauses*." He rose and pushed the chair forward. "Sit, *Mutti*."

Wonderingly, she obeyed him.

She must think about Christmas, Mary told herself. She must not deprive the children. They must go to the school entertainment, and make presents for Aunt Florence and Uncle Fletch. There must be a tree, she must read them the Christ Child story. She thought it might be a good time to mention, casually as it were, that Aunt Florence was going to have another baby.

The gifts were what they could contrive out of box lumber, bits of cloth, and pictures from magazines. David made a big job of framing a wild duck for Uncle Fletch, getting as much passe-partout on himself as he did on the glass. In town she bought marbles, "sewing cards," and yarn, and for her growing daughter, a comb and brush startlingly encased in pink plush. There was a corner of the closet where these things were kept, and the children tiptoed past it with awe. No one would have thought of shattering the mystery of Christmas by peeking.

She must make a trip to Luthermere, too. The Lindsays had gone to the coast, and it stood empty again. Filling up with spider webs and rats' nests, she supposed. But she put it off. Like the orchard, she was depleted by harvest. The ever-briefer daylight travelled across frozen fields and rutted roads, and alternated with long nights of brilliant stars and stinging frost.

Olly Miller came home on temporary leave. Ezra was dead; the first death from the influenza in Pine Creek. Olly stopped by to see her and tell her about it. In his uniform he was straighter, cleaner, and if possible taller. He seemed to know what to do with his hands and feet. He asked her permission before he lit a cigarette and she watched him admiringly as he filled and rolled it.

"You look wonderful, Olly. Oh, I'm so glad to see you! How did Pine Creek valley seem to you? We took a good crop off Luthermere this fall."

"It seemed small," Olly said simply. "Misshollister, what am I goin' to do with the other old 'un, till I can git mustered out? I'll try to hurry, but everybody wants their papers to oncet. 'Lias pulled through the 'flu,' but he ain't in no shape to do for himself. Could you see your way clear to board him for a bit? He don't eat much."

Mary hesitated. "We could have the sickness any time, Olly. I don't know why we don't have it already. It's at the Deweys', and the Albrights'. It's simply everywhere. What if we get taken down?"

"I don't want to cumber you," Olly said. "Mebbe I shouldn't ask you. He ain't catching. He's been all over it now for days, an' we biled his clothes. But . . ."

Mary took a sudden resolution. "I might be glad to have him, if things got worse. He could at least answer the door, and scatter feed for the chickens."

"He could fetch for you," Olly said. " 'Lias can ride a hoss even when he ain't up to walkin' much. If you want to send word to anybody, 'Lias would take it."

Get a message to the druggist, Dr. McClellan had said.

"All right, Olly. Bring him down. I'll be glad to have him." Better not be alone in the house with the children if, as Louise had said, she could not raise her head.

So the Uncles' Room had someone in it again, and 'Lias lay meekly on his cot, or got up and pottered slowly around the yard. On Christmas Eve he sat with them while Mary read from the Bible, and afterward, as he shuffled off to bed, she was ashamed that she had even thought of turning him away. It ill became Mary Lucas to say that there was no room at the inn.

It was on the Friday after Christmas that she heard Helen give a cry of pain and fright, and saw, without surprise, a viscid nose-bleed oozing slowly down her daughter's face.

22 THE INSTRUCTIONS from Dr. McClellan were printed on her mind. She put Helen to bed, looked at David and felt him carefully and found him languid and hot. She settled him on the other pallet across from his sister. She did not feel too brisk herself, but that could wait. She found 'Lias whittling in the yard and started him on the journey to Indian Spring. He would have to take it easy, and there was no telling when he would get back. She sponged Helen's face and put cotton in her nose, and Helen was scared enough to be docile. But when the bleeding stopped and the pain stopped, it was over as far as Helen was concerned. "You mean I have to *stay in bed?*"

"You both have to stay. Dr. McClellan said so. He said I could play games with you, and sing songs, and tell stories." Mary hoped desperately that all these things would be true.

"Tell a story now," David said.

"What story?"

"About the dragons' teeths."

"No!" Helen said. "About the sleeping beauty."

"Tell a new story." David's voice was frayed, and his eyes were too bright. "Make a new story, Mama."

"Well . . ." She looked at them a little bewildered. What would keep them captive, what would bridge the endless day and the endless night? Helen looked back at her with Ben's intent and serious look; she could see the line of Ben's cleft chin in her daughter's dimpled face.

"Do you know what a covered wagon is?"

They shook their heads.

"It's a wagon you can sleep in, and put sacks and barrels and food in. To go to a new land."

"Like the Slocums' truck?"

"Yes, a little like the Slocums' truck. But it's pulled by oxen—

big, slow, patient oxen. A long team of them. An ox is friendly, you can pat him on the nose."

She had their full attention.

"When your grandpa was a little boy, he came to Oregon in a covered wagon." It was a surprisingly easy story to start. The unmarked road across the prairie, the camp at night, when the wagons were put in a circle. She kept it up thankfully for perhaps an hour, the first of the many hours that would have to pass. In the middle of a sentence David doubled up suddenly.

"I have to go to the potty. *Now*." She reached for him, but it was too late. He whispered with sudden fear, "I couldn't help it, Mama, I couldn't help it."

"It's all right, darling." She stripped the bedclothes back carefully, and began to clean him up.

The nosebleed came back and the pain came back, and Helen screamed. She screamed for minutes and then was terrifyingly still, and lay with her eyes closed and her body rigid. While she was quiet, David writhed, and tried to hold onto his bowels, and blubbered with shame. Mary left them only to bring back cups of milk and warm broth. They managed to down some, but when she forced a bit between her own lips, she went outside and quietly threw it up.

She had no idea whether 'Lias would bring the medicine, but he did. In the darkness of the first night he let himself down from his horse and put a bottle in her hands, and she read the label twice to be sure, and began to coax it down them along with the broth. She walked steadily from kitchen to bedside to the mounting pile of stinking sheets; never fast, never stopping.

Dr. McClellan came when he could. He looked around at the disordered house and the unwashed dishes and said, "I can get you some help. A girl named Joanie Varner nurses for me. She's not trained, but she's useful. I'll send her tomorrow." What day would that be? She did not know.

He left her a small bright glass clinical thermometer, fresh in its case. "Take their temperatures when they'll stand for it. Can you keep a chart, Mary?"

"I think so."

"Eat something, Mary."

"I will try."

The children were quiet for a while after he had helped her give the medicine and she had sponged their bodies. She dozed a little, and when she woke there was a note from Olly Miller in the kitchen. It showed two sets of footprints and an arrow, and she understood that he had come to take 'Lias home.

I will eat. I must eat a little. Oh God, give me the strength to keep it down.

Joanie Varner was a small dark girl with green, unsmiling eyes. She walked into the house and began at once to redd up, put the laundry to soak, and help Mary make the chart. Mary could sleep some now, though she still could not keep much on her stomach. Her arms and legs were weak, and there was a buzzing in her head, but until the children were out of danger, she could not let go.

"I'll wash the dishes," Joanie Varner said, taking them out of her hands. "You go set, Miz' Lucas."

Thankfully, Mary obeyed. The children wanted her every minute. They were in trouble, and when you are in trouble you need Mama. The story went on, though they did not always hear it. They missed important things, and had to have them repeated; they were held in the reassurance of Mama's cool, slightly unsteady voice. Joanie went back and forth from the kitchen, and on the rare occasions when she had nothing else to do, she sat down and folded her hands.

"You're very restful, Joanie," Mary said. Helen was asleep, snoring through her tortured nose, and David lay with his look fixed on distance, as though this place were alien to him. He had lost weight, and his cheeks sagged.

Joanie came over and looked at him. "The little guy is past the wust of it," she said.

"How do you know?"

"I seen plenty." Joanie brought a glass of milk. "Git this down, Miz' Lucas."

"I can't, Joanie. . . . All right." She raised it to her lips. "It'll be easier if I don't think about it. Talk to me, Joanie. Where do you live?"

"A fur piece down the river. The train don't stop there. It's a nothing sort o' place."

"Do your people have a ranch?"

"Yes, ma'am. My Pa was took with a heart complaint. My married brother runs it now."

"And you nursed your father."

"Yes. That's how I know to look after sick folks. . . . Drink your milk, Miz' Lucas."

"Then keep on talking. . . . Joanie, where did we get this milk? Has Fletch been down every day?"

"No," Joanie said rather unwillingly. "Him and his wife and the baby has got it. Her folks are over it, by now, and her Ma is there. And her brothers are in an' out."

"Is Mickey all right?"

"Why sure. Little folks generally get well from it. I guess," Joanie said soberly, "they got to live to have their share o' trouble."

"Are the Scobies doing our chores?" Mary asked.

"Yes. Now don't you fret about it." Joanie's voice seemed sometimes to come from near and sometimes far away, and Mary knew she was a little light-headed. The sweetness of the thought that her children would grow up to have their share of trouble was almost unbearable. A day ago, it had seemed too much to ask.

The medicine—was it time for the medicine? She got up to see, and clung, wavering, to her chair. Four o'clock. Yes, the chart said that at four o'clock . . . She would have to wake Helen to give it, break that troubled, heavy-breathing sleep. Helen's lashes lay in silken half-moons on her flushed cheeks, her lips moved as if to whisper something. Mary bent over and took her daughter's drowsy body in her arms and shook it gently. Helen put up a fretful arm, and slipped a little—she was almost too

364

heavy to hold. Mary braced herself and pried the child's lips open.

. . . "You'd better drink some broth, Miz' Lucas."

"Oh, Joanie! *Again?*"

"Only a few swallers," Joanie said firmly. "I'll talk if you want. What shall I talk about?"

"It doesn't matter much. . . . Joanie, have you a beau?"

"No, ma'am. Not no more. I did have a feller wunst."

"Is he . . . you mean he was in the War?"

"I don't rightly know," Joanie said. Her face was pale and composed, her slender fingers were locked in her lap. "It was before all that."

"Before the *War?*" That was a lifetime ago. "I'm sorry, Joanie, it was a silly question. All girls have beaux."

"You'd be surprised. A man's got to notice you fust, before he can take after you. An' I never did know how to git noticed much. I lived at home with my Ma an' Pa an' I hardly ever saw nobody."

"You don't have to explain, Joanie. I shouldn't have asked."

"No, I'd just as lieves tell you. You bein' a stranger, an' all. I don't think much about it any more. . . . I met him in a funny way. He scairt me, so then he had to be polite. I was gatherin' peaches out of our tree, I always get 'em for Ma an' she makes peach butter out of what we don't eat."

Mary looked at the matter-of-fact, clear oval face and capable hands. It was true that Joanie would not stand out in a crowd, but when had there ever been a crowd of eligible women in Tillicum County?

"I was tryin' to heist the box off the ground, an' it was real heavy. An' then he was standin' there. He says 'May I help you?' Like a knight-errant," said Joanie with awe. "Miz' Lucas, what *is* a knight-errant? Do they run errants for the King?"

"Something like that," Mary said. "Who was he, Joanie?"

"He was from the railroad. They was buildin' it then. After I got over my scairtness, I says yes, he could carry it fer me. An' when we got up to the house, I interduced him to Pa an' Ma, an' he stayed for supper. An' that's how it began. . . . Drink your broth, Miz' Lucas."

Mary obeyed.

"We went to the dances at the Lodge hall, and pickin' flowers on the hills. It wasn't so much what we did. We didn't do nothin', really, I guess you know what I mean. I would of—he was so wonderful. It was like you wanted to give him something. Anything you had. . . . He talked good. Like you. An' he was merry-like. Even when he was sad. His eyes had a kind of a laughing in them."

Joanie stopped to remember, but presently she went on again.

"He was a loner, too, like me. He didn't have much kin, he said, nor nobody to go home to. Only some brother he was lookin' for. So I thought surely . . . But one day he says the railroad wants him upriver, an' he has to go. An' I never heard from him again."

"Did you believe him? About having to go?"

"I did then. But I don't now. . . . Sometimes I wonder if it ever happened. . . . It was like he come up out of the ground, an' went back into it."

"Yes," Mary said absently. "They come out of the earth, or down from the hills."

"*Who* comes, Miz' Lucas?"

Helen's voice broke in. There was a clear bright note in it that had not been there an hour before. "I want my dolly. And her clothes and her trunk. And her dollbaby buggy. And her chair and her table."

"I'll get them for you." Mary struggled up.

"*I'll* get 'em, Miz' Lucas."

"Nonsense," Mary said, "I know just where they are." She was halfway across the room when she slid slowly into blackness.

A little winter wind came up, cold and sharp as a knife. Joanie knew it for what it was, the forerunner of the warm Chinook gale that would bring the spring. *That* would be a while yet. Joanie Varner was used to waiting. She managed the Lucas children the best she could, letting them play in the cupboard with the canned goods when they were tired of their toys, and finally consenting to have a covered wagon built out of a blanket across the dining table. Wisely, she did not try to keep them quiet. Their chatter would probably be more soothing to the inert figure on the bed in the corner than silence.

At intervals she roused Mary to take her medicine or sip a little warm milk. Mary's temperature had gone high, but it had subsided before the doctor came again. He was not the only one that came. Joanie opened the door to an incredibly pale thin man and an eager woman with their arms full of groceries. "How is she?" Louise Whitman asked breathlessly.

"She's so-so," Joanie said. She accepted the gifts gravely and put the perishable things outdoors in the cold. When Fletch Lucas came down, haggard and weak but already talking of getting the work started, she sent some of them home with him.

Bert Plew drove in with a load of hay, and Mrs. Sawyer sent a fresh cut of beef. Olly Miller brought nothing but himself. "I come to help," Olly said. "Like she done for me with 'Lias."

"You can get up some stove wood, I reckon. An' muck out the hen house if you want. I ain't had time."

Joanie did not really see this awkward, bashful giant—her mind was on Miz' Lucas. When he came back, after doing what work he could find outside, Joanie was looking sorrowfully at a cup of the broth she had made from the fresh beef. "She ain't takin' enough. She ain't et enough for a long while."

"Have you tried a straw?" Olly said. He had had his bout with the influenza in the Army infirmary at Camp Lewis, and this had been one of the few comforts.

"Why, no, I didn't think of it. . . . Git me one."

Olly searched a long time in the barn for clean, straight wheat straw which he trimmed up. He made several lengths of it, for they were frail and would last quick. Joanie received them with favor.

"That's a real good idea. It's goin' to take me both hands, though. How an I goin' to heist her up? . . . You know her real well? Because if you was to raise her from the pillow, I could feed her easy."

"I kin try," Olly said. It gave him a gone feeling to see that still, limp figure. She was still Misshollister, and the flu had no right to do this to her. "Is she pretty bad?"

"She's beat out. She ain't got no gumption. That's why she's gotta eat. You better stick around, an' we'll see what we kin do."

Olly had no particular need to go home, now that 'Lias was getting more peart. He sat in Ben's cowhide chair and rested in the peace of Mary's pretty living room, and stared curiously at a picture of a statue woman with both her arms broke off.

Mary moved a little, and opened her eyes. "Now," Joanie said. They moved to the bedside, and Olly mumbled,

"It's me Misshollister. I gotta help you set up. I'll go real easy-like. If I hurt you, jest holler."

The idea that she could holler brought a flicker of amusement to Mary's wan face. So light she was, Olly thought as he slipped his arm behind her, like a bony little bird. A memory crossed his mind of putting his arm around Misshollister long ago—it had not been like this. He lifted carefully and tenderly, and Joanie put the straw between Mary's lips. "This feller made you this straw so you could drink good. Now you take this whole cup, an' then I'll let the children come an' talk to their Mama for a minute." Indeed, the children had not waited; Mama was awake, and they were swarming onto the covers.

"I gotta git 'em outa here," Joanie said crossly. She noted with approval that Mary had downed a good bit. "Mister, could you take these kids outdoors fer a while? They're well enough to go a ways, but not too fur. If you just take 'em down the road, it'll work off some o' their steam."

She brought coats and boots, and Olly watched fascinated while she rassled them on. He had not been this close to little folks since school. With one of them clinging to each hand, he made his way out, his breath ballooning from him in a white cloud. Joanie closed the door behind them.

A snowball caught Olly behind the ear, and David laughed delightedly. Another one bashed him on the shoulder. "Why, you little monkeys," Olly said, "wait till I give you what-fer." He stooped to gather snow, and their cries as they ran from him cut the cold air and bounced off the frozen hills.

They were keeping something from her, Mary thought, though she could not put her finger on it. People kept coming and going. Florence was out of danger, Fletch said, though a little puny yet. They had been scared to death that the influenza would mark the new baby, but Dr. McClellan said not. Florence would have to simmer down, and not work outside any more. "There'll be plenty of help now," Fletch said wryly. He had aged, under his weather-beaten tan—he looked peaked and stern and more than ever like Ben. They were her children, Fletch and Florence; to help Florence through her pregnancy would be like cosseting her own daughter.

Slowly, her strength came back. It had been severely tried. She was content to let Joanie boss her, to depend on Olly Miller for fetching and helping out. He seemed to be there a great deal, his big frame looming in the yard or stooping to the doors. She did not want to read or sew, merely to feel the pleasure of existing, quiet in her bed. "It beats me," Joanie said, "why you don't sleep in your new bedroom. Mr. Plew's done finished with it, an' we could put a heater up there just as easy as not." How could she tell Joanie that the new bedroom was a bridal chamber, that it would be bad luck to move into it until Ben came home?

His letters had stopped, it meant that he was on his way. She did not read the paper; accounts of troop movements and demobilization meant nothing to her. Harve was in the Army of Occupation, Fletch said. He would be stationed in Germany for a while. She accepted this as she accepted everything, asking no questions. When Joanie said, "I reckon you can git up, and set in the big chair," she got up and sat in it, docilely. It felt fine.

She was sitting there when the front door opened and Althea's voice said, "Can I come in *now?*"

At one look, with a shock she felt everything jell, everything come together. Althea in black, in the black that she had worn for so many of the years of her life for so many people, that she would always wear now. Mary knew what they had been hiding, and she stood up and held out her arms and Althea ran into them. She held the tall shivering figure close, cradled the gray head on her shoulder. Althea clung to her, tearless and spent.

So we didn't go free. You never go free. There is always a

369

*price, and someone has to pay it. Charles the indispensable, whom
we cannot get along without. We will have to get along without
him now. Charles who was always so kind. "Mary, he is so kind."
Althea, my darling, it isn't fair! It isn't fair.*

She heard Han's whisper faintly in the distance somewhere:
It comes. God sends it.

Althea said in a thread of a sound, "It's just the same here,
Mary. Nothing has changed. All the way up the river, I was
watching. . . ."

She disengaged herself, and took Mary's hand. Drawing Mary
gently toward the door, she opened it and they stood looking
at the frozen landscape, the moveless, far-off, compassionate
peaks, etched with trees along their white skyline. Althea took
a deep breath. She said in a steady voice,

"I will lift up mine eyes unto the hills, from which cometh my
strength."

Joanie put her few duds into a paper sack and left it on the
front stoop. When Miz' Gillespie and Miz' Lucas had took their
time together, she quietly lured Miz' Gillespie to the room out
back and fixed her a place to wash her face and hands, and
brought her some of the broth that was always on the stove, and
Althea found herself dropping to sleep in the Uncles' Room without knowing exactly how it happened. When Joanie returned, she
said to Mary, "When the doctor comes, I'll be leavin' with him.
You ain't goin' to need me now."

"Oh Joanie, *no!* We'll need you more than ever. She's not well,
you can see that."

"You let *her* do for you," said Joanie soberly. "It'll be the best
thing. We all got to have somethin' to do, in this world. That's
why I started out to take care o' sick folks. You make her do fer
you an' the children. She needs it."

"But my husband's coming home!"

"Well, hers ain't," Joanie said. The simple fact hung in the
room with them, not leaving room for anything else. "Things'll
git fixed around, Miz' Lucas—they always do. An' Dr. McClellan'll

maybe have a new job for me. Only I wouldn't mind to go home for a while, 'cause it's goin' to be spring. The water's goin' to be comin' down the gully, an' the peepers is goin' to sing." She sighed deeply.

"I know, I know," Mary said. "I can hardly wait." She was surprised at her own vehemence. This land was hers now, and all that went with it; there was no turning back. And it was Althea's too. It would heal her, it would put itself back in her hands. Joanie was right; Althea must stay, and she must feel necessary.

Dr. McClellan seemed to take it as a matter of course. "I'm going downriver—I'll drive Joanie home. And Mary, please don't try to break any wild horses for a while, or dig any post holes. Be reasonable."

"I'm always reasonable," Mary said. "I always do what Ben thinks best, and I take everybody's advice, and try to keep out of trouble—" Dr. McClellan began to laugh, and she laughed with him. He would check up on her now and then, he said. Things were a little easier, the sickness had spent itself up among the hills. There were questions she wanted to ask, but they would keep—she would be here tomorrow, and the next day, and all year, and the years after.

Olly came just before supper. He tended the horses and milked, and chopped some wood. He came inside often, looking around the house, and while Althea was setting the table he followed Mary to the kitchen and fidgeted with his sheepskin cap. Mary poked up the fire and put on the teakettle. "You'll stay and have a bite, Olly?"

"I guess not," Olly said. "Misshollister . . . where is she?"

"Who? Oh—Joanie? Why, she's gone. We can get along all right now, she told me. Dr. McClellan thought so, too. So she . . ." Mary stopped, and looked at him. She had not known Olly this long without learning to read his impassive face.

"Whar's her home?" Olly said in his deep rumble.

"I don't know. . . . I never troubled to find out. Olly, I'm so ashamed! Some little nothing of a place she said,—a ranch way downriver—that's all I know. It's a family concern—her brother runs it. Dr. McClellan could tell you. She . . . she said she wanted to be home a while, because spring was coming. Olly, it would have been so easy for me to find out—I'm terribly, terribly sorry. What can I do to help?"

"You don't need to do nothin'," Olly said. "I'll find her. Whar is this doctor's place?"

"It's up the other way, at Indian Spring. When you get to Indian Spring, anybody can tell you. A big white house on the edge of town." She thought of the long cold road, the miles and miles of it up the river and then down. She knew they did not matter. Olly was bigger than the weather. She saw him to the door and handed him his mittens. He mounted his bony horse in the gathering dusk. Muffled to the ears, outlined against the sweep of gray sky and shadowed orchard, he seemed some dark and prehistoric figure carved from the rock and ice; but to Mary, he looked remarkably like a knight errant.

"Mary, I want Luthermere."

"You do, Althea? What for?"

"I want to come home. I want to live there. On the ground we planted ourselves."

"Alone? Oh, Althea!"

"Certainly not. My son Stan loves the land. He's always wanted a ranch. And I have a ranch for him. One of the best."

"It's not very big," Mary said doubtfully.

"I'm buying the Conway place across the road, for taxes. And if that's not enough, the Yanling ranch is vacant, and that poor girl and her husband can use the money. Stan would probably want to put up a new house. Over against the other hill perhaps. Stan is interested in a girl."

"Do you mind, Althea? Stan being interested in a girl and bringing her to Luthermere? You wouldn't feel crowded?"

"Mind?" Althea said in astonishment. "Why, Mary, I might have grandchildren! *Me!*" She took out a handkerchief; tears came rather easily to Althea these days. "Mary, it's as if Luther were coming back. He would be well pleased, I think."

She blew her nose vigorously. "I believe I *will* buy the Yanling place. It would just round us out. Do you know where Elsie is?"

"Yes, I know where she is." Mary's fingers had stopped stitching; she was gazing into space with a look that Althea knew. Althea gave her a covert glance.

"What's on your mind, Mary?"

Mary hesitated. "If you're going to buy the Yanling land, there's a piece of it that runs up and over near the school. It's too steep for planting, but it would hold a building. It seems to me . . . a library there . . . We could get books given to us, and all that. Perhaps the county would help. I've thought of it often. Pine Creek needs it. But of course, there's always the problem of who would have time to run it?"

"Why, I would," Althea said.

When the Chinook began to blow, Mary could stay indoors no longer. She walked the road, where puddles lay thinly in the hollows; she ventured into the orchard among red boughs swollen with budding wood. The river was filled with floes of ice from the melting glaciers above, and down every draw came the chanting of the wind. The children were like crazy things—they chased each other stumbling, and booed each other from behind shrubs and fences.

She took them up to Mary's Rock, where the path had crumbled in the frost. They decided at once that they would make Mama a new path, starting at the top, and they scraped and leveled a few feet with sharp rocks, bruising their little hands, and then fell to decorating it lovingly with pebbles. Mary rested beside them in the old seat formed by the rock; content to sit, and to look at the familiar contours of the valley. Across the river at the edge of the seething runoff, a lone rider with several packhorses let them stoop to drink. Around the hill at the old Piggott place the new corrugated iron roof of Fletch's front porch caught the pale sun.

Past Sawyers' and toward the Landing, the narrow white road ran crookedly and was lost among the trees. It was not heavily travelled today. A single figure on foot was walking slowly, stopping to look sometimes, straightening up as if to take a deep breath of the resin-smelling air. She watched it idly, and then the blood seemed to drain out of her body and rush back, like the river in flood.

No. No. Yes. Yes she knew that figure, she knew that walk, the walk when he was all right but very tired, the walk as if something had been accomplished, as if morning was long gone and almost forgotten, but the day was past now and the work done, and he was coming in to rest. The walk of the man who was part of this land, whose strength was renewed each time he touched it, as the strength of Antaeus was renewed when he touched the Earth, his mother.

She said to the children, "Stay here. I'm going to meet Papa." She said it so matter-of-factly that they did not look up, but went on building their pebbled path.

Down the hill. Through the crackling brush and the Oregon grape that tore at her dress, past the opening flat faces of mountain buttercups starring the ground. Down the hill, and down the road.

He saw her coming, and stopped. Everything stopped except Mary. The cliffs stood transfixed along the horizon; the pines were silent, watching. To the north the mountains folded back into the flawless sky and the arc of the great river cut the desert like a song. The hills and the sky and the river sang together, and on the crest of their song she ran toward him, and ran, and ran.